Sip.

It has always been *a peculiar fact of human existence that our capacity for the highest pleasure is necessarily limited — a restriction that even applies to Speyside's favourite malt whisky!*

The Macallan *is made only from malted barley and pure spring water. It is matured exclusively for 12 years in the luscious confines of oaken sherry casks. And when it finally emerges, smooth and mellifluous, its pleasure quotient is almost insupportable* (1).

To drink *too fast would be careless. To drink too much would be redundant. To savour slowly and moderately... why, then, just for a while, you may sip at the table of the blest.*

THE MACALLAN.
THE SINGLE MALT SCOTCH.

(1) "The malt against which ultimately all others must be judged"

THE MACALLAN Scotch Whisky. 43% alc./vol. Sole U.S. importer Rémy Amerique, Inc., New York, N.Y.
THE MACALLAN is a registered trademark of Macallan-Glenlivet P.L.C. © 1996 Macallan-Glenlivet P.L.C.

De-stress Call

Suffering from a tension-convention? Send out an S.O.S.! Visit Hammacher Schlemmer for the relaxing "Hands-Free Massager". A massager that feels so good, once you put it on, you may never take it off.

For 147 years, Hammacher Schlemmer has consistently offered the world's greatest collection of items that are innovative, unique and just plain fun. Everything we sell is of exceptional quality and, of course, unconditionally guaranteed.

Hammacher Schlemmer

ESTABLISHED 1848

New York
147 East 57th Street
212-421-9000

Chicago
445 North Michigan Avenue
312-527-9100

Beverly Hills
309 North Rodeo Drive
310-859-7255

The Paris Review

Founded in 1953.

Publisher Drue Heinz

Editors
George Plimpton, Peter Matthiessen, Donald Hall, Robert Silvers, Blair Fuller, Maxine Groffsky, Jeanne McCulloch, James Linville

Managing Editor Daniel Kunitz
Editor at Large Elizabeth Gaffney
Associate Editors Andy Bellin, Anne Fulenwider, Brigid Hughes
Assistant Editors Stephen Clark, Ben Howe
Poetry Editor Richard Howard
Art Editor Joan Krawczyk
London Editor Shusha Guppy **Paris Editor** Harry Mathews
Business Manager Lillian von Nickern **Treasurer** Marjorie Kalman
Design Consultant Chip Kidd

Editorial Assistants
Dan Glover, Molly McGrann

Readers
Neil Azevedo, Lea Carpenter, Thea Goodman, Sunny Payson, Gina Zucker

Special Consultants
Robert Phillips, Ben Sonnenberg, Remar Sutton

Advisory Editors
Nelson Aldrich, Lawrence M. Bensky, Patrick Bowles, Christopher Cerf, Jonathan Dee, Timothy Dickinson, Joan Dillon, Beth Drenning, David Evanier, Rowan Gaither, David Gimbel, Francine du Plessix Gray, Lindy Guinness, Fayette Hickox, Susannah Hunnewell, Ben Johnson, Gia Kourlas, Mary B. Lumet, Larissa MacFarquhar, Molly McKaughan, Jonathan Miller, Ron Padgett, Maggie Paley, John Phillips, Kevin Richardson, David Robbins, Philip Roth, Elissa Schappell, Frederick Seidel, Mona Simpson, Max Steele, Rose Styron, William Styron, Tim Sultan, Hallie Gay Walden, Eugene Walter, Antonio Weiss

Contributing Editors
Agha Shahid Ali, Robert Antoni, Kip Azzoni, Sara Barrett, Helen Bartlett, Robert Becker, Adam Begley, Magda Bogin, Chris Calhoun, Morgan Entrekin, Jill Fox, Walker Gaffney, Jamey Gambrell, John Glusman, Jeanine Herman, Edward Hirsch, Gerald Howard, Tom Jenks, Barbara Jones, Fran Kiernan, Joanna Laufer, Mary Maguire, Lucas Matthiessen, Dan Max, Joanie McDonnell, Christopher Merrill, David Michaelis, Dini von Mueffling, Elise Paschen, Allen Peacock, William Plummer, Charles Russell, Michael Sagalyn, David Salle, Elisabeth Sifton, Ileene Smith, Patsy Southgate, Rose Styron, William Wadsworth, Julia Myer Ward, John Zinsser

Poetry Editors
Donald Hall (1953–1961), X.J. Kennedy (1962–1964), Thomas Clark (1964–1973), Michael Benedikt (1974–1978), Jonathan Galassi (1978–1988), Patricia Storace (1988–1992)

Art Editors
William Pène du Bois (1953–1960), Paris Editors (1961–1974), Alexandra Anderson (1974–1978), Richard Marshall (1978–1993)

Founding Publisher Sadruddin Aga Khan

Former Publishers
Bernard F. Conners, Ron Dante, Deborah S. Pease

Founding Editors
Peter Matthiessen, Harold L. Humes, George Plimpton, William Pène du Bois, Thomas H. Guinzburg, John Train

The Paris Review is published quarterly by The Paris Review, Inc. Vol. 38, No. 141, Winter 1996. Business Office: 45-39 171 Place, Flushing, New York 11358 (ISSN #0031-2037). Paris Office: Harry Mathews, 67 rue de Grenelle, Paris 75007 France. London Office: Shusha Guppy, 8 Shawfield St., London, SW3. US distributors: Random House, Inc. 1(800)733-3000. Typeset and printed in USA by Capital City Press, Montpelier, VT. Price for single issue in USA: $10.00. $14.00 in Canada. Post-paid subscription for four issues $34.00, lifetime subscription $1000. Postal surcharge of $10.00 per four issues outside USA (excluding life subscriptions). Subscription card is bound within magazine. Please give six weeks notice of change of address using subscription card. While The Paris Review welcomes the submission of unsolicited manuscripts, it cannot accept responsibility for their loss or delay, or engage in related correspondence. Manuscripts will not be returned or responded to unless accompanied by self-addressed, stamped envelope. Fiction manuscripts should be submitted to George Plimpton, poetry to Richard Howard, The Paris Review, 541 East 72nd Street, New York, N.Y. 10021. Charter member of the Council of Literary Magazines and Presses. This publication is made possible, in part, with public funds from the New York State Council on the Arts and the National Endowment for the Arts. Periodicals postage paid at Flushing, New York, and at additional mailing offices. **Postmaster:** Please send address changes to 45-39 171st Place, Flushing, N.Y. 11358.

TEXAS CENTER FOR WRITERS

MFA in Writing

FICTION ★ POETRY
SCREENWRITING
PLAYWRITING

An interdisciplinary degree program offering James A. Michener Fellowships of $12,000 to all candidates accepted for study. Annual deadline for fall admission is January 15.

For an application brochure, call 512-471-1601, or write
TEXAS CENTER FOR WRITERS
J. Frank Dobie House
702 East 26th Street
Austin, Texas 78705

THE UNIVERSITY OF TEXAS AT AUSTIN

DOES YOUR READING LIST NEED DOWNSIZING?

Readers today face a dilemma — too much information and too little time. If your coffee table is covered with magazines that you won't have the luxury of reading, here's a solution: Re-engineer your reading habits. Focus on the one magazine that offers essential, superior writing every month, on every page. *Harper's Magazine.*

With a host of original features, including the legendary Harper's Index, the always surprising Readings section, and the award-winning Notebook column, *Harper's Magazine* challenges conventional thought at every turn, with wit, wisdom, and horse sense. You may well find that it offers you more than the sum total of all the other magazines you receive.

So re-engineer your reading list with a special introductory subscription to *Harper's Magazine.* Reserve your subscription now and receive 12 issues for just $12, a 75% savings off the newsstand price. Send in the coupon below and make room on your coffee table for an <u>essential</u> magazine — *Harper's.*

☐ Yes, please send one year (12 issues) for just $12.
☐ I prefer two years (24 issues) for $22.   HTP25

NAME
ADDRESS
CITY
STATE   ZIP CODE
☐ PAYMENT ENCLOSED   ☐ BILL ME LATER

**Mail to: Harper's Subscription Department,
666 Broadway, New York, NY 10012.**
For immediate service call toll free:
1-800-444-4653.

Please allow 6–8 weeks for your first issue. One-year Canadian subscriptions $23 (CDN funds), includes postage and GST. All other countries $41 (U.S. dollars only), includes special delivery.

Paris Review Bundles

The **Beat** Package $30
includes issues
#35--W. **Burroughs** interview
#37--**Ginsberg** interview and poetry
#43--**Kerouac** interview
#135--a semester with **Ginsberg**

The **Philip Roth** Package $30
includes issues:
#18--*The Conversion of the Jews*, 1958 ed.
#19--*Epstein*, 1958 ed.
#20--*Good-bye, Columbus*, 1958 ed.
#93--**Roth** interview

The **Theater & Film** Package $20
includes issues:
#38--**Arthur Miller** interview
#125--**John Guare** and **Neil Simon** interviews
#138--Screenwriting (**Billy Wilder, Richard Price**)

All Original Collector's Editions!
To order, call the Paris Review Business Office at
718-539-7085

THE CONTEST CONSULTANT
WRITE*Time* ✓ 1997
Gives you time to write!
Thousands of updates for 1997
Hundreds of New Contests

- Software designed by a writer for writers
- Lists over 2,000 contests, fellowships, scholarships, grants and awards
- Searches under categories or deadlines
- Tracks award submissions and queries
- Add or delete to create your own database

14 CATEGORIES:
Short Story
Novel
Poetry
Drama
Gay/Lesbian
Journalism
Screen/Teleplays
Residency
Nonfiction/Scholarly
Commercial
Children's Lit
Translation
Religion
Women

💾 **$80** WINDOWS/MAC

Visa/MC Accepted
1-800-891-0962

WRITE*Suite*
PURCHASE BOTH FOR ONLY
💾💾 **$100**

THE MANUSCRIPT MANAGER
WRITE*Trak*

A Writer writes,
WriteTrak does the rest!

WriteTrak tracks:
- SUBMISSIONS by Date, Manuscript Title, Publisher, Subject
- PUBLISHERS by Name, Submission Date, Manuscript Title
- MANUSCRIPTS by Title, Submission Date, Publisher
- EXPENSES by Date, Manuscript

UPDATES & PRINTS:
Expense Reports
Letters
Resumes
CV
Manuscripts
Publish & Submission History

💾 **$50** WINDOWS/MAC

Grossman Development Company
P.O. Box 85732, Seattle, WA 98145-1732
e-mail: gdc@earthlink.net http://www.writetime.com

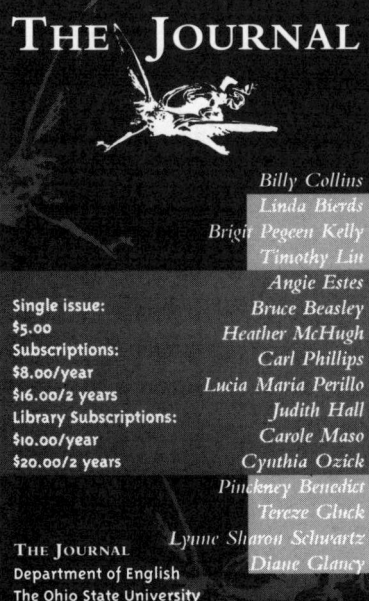

THE JOURNAL

Billy Collins
Linda Bierds
Brigit Pegeen Kelly
Timothy Liu
Angie Estes
Bruce Beasley
Heather McHugh
Carl Phillips
Lucia Maria Perillo
Judith Hall
Carole Maso
Cynthia Ozick
Pinckney Benedict
Tereze Glück
Lynne Sharon Schwartz
Diane Glancy

Single issue:
$5.00
Subscriptions:
$8.00/year
$16.00/2 years
Library Subscriptions:
$10.00/year
$20.00/2 years

THE JOURNAL
Department of English
The Ohio State University
164 West 17th Avenue
Columbus, Ohio 43210

NEW DIRECTIONS
Celebrating 60 years of independent publishing

GUY DAVENPORT
The Cardiff Team
Stories that lift out and collage into their texts a wondrous assortment of persons, events, and ideas from cultural history. "His poetic, incisive sentences flicker like pieces of a stained-glass window spread neatly on the page." —*The New York Times Book Review* $22.95 cloth

•

A Balance of Quinces: The Paintings and Drawings of Guy Davenport Text by Erik Anderson Reece. Illuminating commentary, black-and-white illustrations throughout, plus eight pages of color plates. $25.00 paperbook

Please send for free complete catalog
NEW DIRECTIONS 80 8th Ave, NYC 10011

Subscribe to the 'leading intellectual forum in the US'

—*New York* magazine

Since we began publishing in 1963, *The New York Review of Books* has provided remarkable variety and intellectual excitement. Twenty times a year, the world's best writers and scholars address themselves to 130,000 discerning readers worldwide...people who know that the widest range of subjects—literature, art, politics, science, history, music, education—will be discussed with wit, clarity, and brilliance.

In each issue subscribers of *The New York Review* enjoy articles by such celebrated writers as John Updike, Elizabeth Hardwick, Gore Vidal, Nadine Gordimer, Oliver Sacks, and countless others, as well as the literary bare-knuckle boxing of the Letters to the Editors section.

If you think you too might enjoy the penetrating insights and arguments found in each issue of *The New York Review*, subscribe now with this special introductory offer. You'll not only save over 60% ($39) from the newsstand price, but you'll also get a free copy of *Selections*. With this offer you'll receive:

➤ **20 Issues** A full year's subscription of 20 issues for just $25.97—a saving of almost 50% off the regular subscription rate of $49.50 and a saving of $39 (60%) off the newsstand price.

➤ **A Free Book** *Selections* is a collection of 19 reviews and essays published verbatim from our first two issues. In it you'll discover how certain works such as *The Naked Lunch* or *The Fire Next Time*, now regarded as modern classics, were initially perceived by critics when they were first published and reviewed.

➤ **A Risk-Free Guarantee** If you are unhappy with your subscription at any time, you may cancel. We will refund the unused portion of the subscription cost. What's more, *Selections* is yours to keep as our gift to you for trying *The New York Review*.

The New York Review of Books

Return to: Subscriber Service Dept., PO Box 420382, Palm Coast, FL 32142-0382

❏ **Yes!** Please enter my one-year subscription (20 issues) to *The New York Review* at the special introductory rate of only $25.97 (a saving of 60% off the newsstand rate). With my paid subscription, I will also receive *Selections* at no extra charge and a no-risk guarantee.

❏ $25.97 enclosed*   Charge my: ❏ Am Ex ❏ MasterCard ❏ Visa ❏ Bill me. (US Only)

Name _____

Address _____ A6LPRG

City/State/Zip _____

Credit card Number _____

Credit Card Expiration Date/Signature _____

☎ For faster service on credit card orders, fax to: (212) 586-8003.
Please include your own phone and fax in case of questions.

SELECTIONS

FREE with this offer

*Make checks or US money orders payable to *The New York Review of Books*. We accept US Dollars drawn on a US bank or Canadian Dollars drawn on a Canadian bank. If paying by CDN$ return to Mike Johnson, *The New York Review of Books*, 250 West 57 St., Rm 1321, New York, NY 10107. We cannot accept international money orders. Rates outside the US: to Canada $52.50/$69CDN , Rest of World Regular Post $56.50, Rest of World Print Flow Air Post (recommended for the Far East, New Zealand, Australia, and South America) $83.50. Credit card orders will be charged at the US Dollar rates shown. Please allow 6 to 8 weeks for delivery of your first issue.

THE BOSTON BOOK REVIEW

http://www.BostonBookReview.com/BBR

The Best of Both Worlds

The Apollonian

The Bostonian

The Dionysian

The thinking person's book review.

The aim of the *Boston Book Review* is to seek out and promote the highest achievements in contemporary writing. Readers can expect to find in the pages of the *Boston Book Review*, the smartest writers on the most important books.

Subscribe to the *Boston Book Review*. Discover the well-written.

SUBSCRIPTIONS: 1 yr. (10 issues) $24.00 paris
Canada and International add $16.00

Name _____

Address _____

City _____ State ___ Zip _____

Credit Card Payments: No. _____
or call (617) 497-0344   Exp. date:____ Signature: _____
☐ AMEX   ☐ VISA   ☐ MASTERCARD   ☐ DISCOVER

Or send check to: THE BOSTON BOOK REVIEW
30 Brattle Street, 4th floor
Cambridge, MA 02138

MFA in Writing
at Vermont College

Intensive 11-day residencies on our beautiful central Vermont campus alternate with **six-month non-resident study projects.**

Residencies include classes, readings, conferences and small workshops led by two faculty. Immersed with other developing writers in a stimulating environment, students forge working relationships with each other and with experienced practitioners of poetry and fiction.

Under the careful guidance of the faculty, students focus on their own writing for the semester study project. A low student-faculty ratio (5-1) ensures close personal attention.

On-campus housing is available and residencies are catered by the award-winning New England Culinary Institute.

We also offer **a Post-Graduate Semester** and **One-Year Intensives** for those who have completed a graduate degree in creative writing.

Scholarships, minority scholarships and financial aid available

For more information please contact:
Roger Weingarten, Director
MFA in Writing, Vermont College, Montpelier, VT 05602
Tel: (802) 828-8840 Fax: (802) 828-8649

Vermont College of Norwich University

Poetry Faculty
Robin Behn
Mark Cox
Deborah Digges
Nancy Eimers
Mark Halliday
Richard Jackson
Jack Myers
William Olsen
David Rivard
J. Allyn Rosser
Mary Ruefle
Betsy Sholl
Leslie Ullman
Roger Weingarten
David Wojahn

Fiction Faculty
Carol Anshaw
Tony Ardizzone
Phyllis Barber
Francois Camoin
Abby Frucht
Douglas Glover
Sydney Lea
Diane Lefer
Ellen Lesser
Bret Lott
Sena Jeter Naslund
Christopher Noël
Pamela Painter
Sharon Sheehe Stark
Gladys Swan
W.D. Wetherell

The Paris Review Put-on

Only $15

THE PARIS REVIEW•45-39 171 PLACE•FLUSHING, NY 11358
White with black. Quantity: _____
small ❑ medium ❑ large ❑ extra large ❑

NAME..
ADDRESS..
CITY..
STATE..........................ZIP..
MASTERCARD/VISA #_____EXP._____
PAYMENT MUST ACCOMPANY ORDER
(New York State residents please add tax.)

Come to
Kenyon
and Write,

Where

Writing

is a

Tradition.

The
Kenyon Review
SUMMER PROGRAMS
present

The Writers Workshop

June 24 – July 4, 1997

Come to Gambier, Ohio, for ten days of writing, conversation, and readings at The Writers Workshop. Enrich your own poetry or fiction, with others and in solitude, on the Kenyon College hill.

- Workshops in poetry and fiction.
- **New workshop in playwriting.**
- Time and the setting for individual writing and dialogue.
- Distinguished visiting writers in readings and discussions.
- College and non-degree graduate credit offered.

To learn more about **The Writers Workshop** and to receive application materials, call or write:
*David Lynn, editor, The Kenyon Review,
Sunset Cottage, Gambier, Ohio 43022
telephone 614-427-5208; fax 614-427-5417.*

The Paris Review

Editorial Office:
541 East 72 Street
New York, New York 10021
HTTP://www.voyagerco.com

Business & Circulation:
45-39 171 Place
Flushing, New York 11358

Distributed by Random House
201 East 50 Street
New York, N.Y. 10022
(800) 733-3000

In 1987, the Cuban Department of Revolutionary Orientation put up a billboard of Che Guevara above the heavily traveled Almendares Bridge, along with one of his slogans in neon lights: "A revolutionary has to be a tireless worker."

Arturo Cuenca, a Cuban-born conceptual artist, photographed the billboard from the back, and in the darkroom reversed the image to make the words readable—this to suggest that "in the Revolution reality never matched theory." When the work, enlarged to 1 x 1½ meters, was shown at the Salón Nacional that year, a high government official condemned it. "It is not anti-Che," Cuenca insisted, "it is against the cult of personality."

Cuenca felt so compromised that he left Cuba. He now lives in New York and keeps the photograph above the kitchen sink in his apartment.

Table of contents photograph by Arturo Cuenca.
Frontispiece by William Pène du Bois.

Number 141

Interviews

Gary Snyder	The Art of Poetry LXXIV	88
Helen Vendler	The Art of Criticism III	166

Fiction

Chris Adrian	You Can Have It	277
Peter Ho Davies	Relief	142
Elizabeth Gilbert	The Famous Torn and Restored Lit Cigarette Trick	18
Joyce Hackett	The Savant	72
John Hodgman	Ghosting	293
Michael Knight	Now You See Her	119
Rob Owen	To the Sea	213
J. David Stevens	Why I Married the Porn Star	248

Features

	The Man in the Back Row Has a Question III	257
Silvana Paternostro	Three Days with Gabo	220
Alan Ainsworth, Kevin Cantwell, Jennifer Franklin, Rick Hilles, Richard Lamb, Kate Light, Nick Norwood, Mark Scott, Brenda Shaughnessy, Marc Woodworth	A Portfolio of Ten New Poets	43

Art

Rochelle Feinstein	Double Dutch	cover
Randolfo Rocha	Word Play	135

Poetry

Anna Akhmatova	Secrets of the Trade	155
Agha Shahid Ali	After the August Wedding in Lahore, Pakistan,	163
Scott Cairns	Interval with Erato	160
James Cummins	Schindler's List	84
Edward Nobles	Architectural Digest	86
Eric Ormsby	Mutanabbi Praises the Prince	165
Baron Wormser	Shoplifting	87
Charles Wright	Black Zodiac	80

Notice	16
Notes on Contributors	306

NOTICE

It has been a policy of this magazine from its inception to publish unknown, unpublished writers. The present issue is devoted to this principle — stories by eight authors starting out. It is what we should be doing. The unsolicited manuscripts arriving daily in plain wrappers (an awesome number every year) are given as much scrutiny, if not more, than those fancied up between a literary agent's covers. The vast number of manuscripts in what is rather ingloriously referred to as "the slush" obviously poses quite a problem for the preliminary readers. It has often been said that the prototypical method (though not necessarily here) of judging a story, especially of bulk, say a two-pounder, is to read the first paragraph, then the final sentences, and if these show signs of ability, then with a sigh one starts pushing through the whole. This method is somewhat substantiated by Ford Madox Ford in a reminiscence about his editing days in 1909 for *The English Review*. A young woman named E.T. sent in a story by a shy friend of hers entitled "The Odour of Chrysanthemums," and Ford had tossed it into the Accepted basket after reading the first paragraph. Quite a show of confidence! The paragraph reads as follows: *The small locomotive engine, Number 4, came clanking, stumbling down from Selston with seven full wagons. It appeared around the corner with loud threats of speed. But the colt that it startled from among the gorse outdistanced it at a canter. The gorse still flickered indistinctly in the raw afternoon* . . .

Many years later Ford qualified his reasons in *The American Mercury* for being so sure about the writer's skills: "'*The small locomotive, Number 4*' . . . At once you know that this fellow is going to write about whatever he writes about from the inside. The 'Number 4' shows that . . . He had to give the engine the personality of a number. . . . '*With seven full wagons*' . . . The seven is good. The ordinary careless writer would say 'some small wagons.' '*It appeared around the corner with loud threats of speed . . .*' Good writing; slightly, but not *too* arresting . . . '*But the colt that it startled from among the gorse outdistanced it at a canter.*' Good again . . . Anyone knows that an engine . . . that cannot overtake a colt at a canter must be a ludicrously ineffective machine. '*The gorse still flickered indistinctly in the raw afternoon.*' . . . Good too, distinctly good . . . in a single phrase, landscape, time of day, weather, season. . . . This man knows. He knows how to open a story with a sentence of the right cadence for holding the attention. He knows how to construct a paragraph . . . You can trust him for the rest."

The author so trusted was a twenty-four-year-old schoolteacher named D.H. (David Herbert) Lawrence.

It may well be that the first paragraphs of the eight stories by unpublished writers which appear in the following pages cannot be parsed with such confidence. But in each case the preliminary readers here have enjoyed an enthusiasm surely akin to Mr. Ford's—that rather than confining a manuscript yet again to a growing heap of discards on the floor, something in it, some unexpected flow of words, the emergence of an interesting character, arrests the attention, and ultimately the exhilaration that what has caused such excitement will be passed on to subscribers and readers, and indeed to the attention of publishers. It is nice to think that what has emerged from a return-addressed envelope, probably mailed without much hope, can be off on such a journey. . . .

G.A.P.

The Famous Torn and Restored Lit Cigarette Trick

Elizabeth Gilbert

for Kate

In Hungary, Richard Hoffman's family had been the manufacturers of Hoffman's Rose Water, a product which was used at that time for both cosmetic and medicinal purposes. Hoffman's mother drank the rose water for her indigestion, and his father used it to scent and cool his groin after exercise. The servants rinsed the Hoffman's table linens in a cold bath infused with rose water, such that even the kitchen would be perfumed. The cook mixed a dash of it into her sweetbread batter. For evening events, Budapest ladies wore expensive imported colognes, but Hoffman's Rose Water was a staple product of daytime hygiene for all women, as requisite as soap. Hungarian men could be married for decades without ever realizing that the natural smell of their wives' skin was not, in fact, a refined scent of blooming roses.

Richard Hoffman's father was a perfect gentleman, but his mother slapped the servants. His paternal grandfather had been a drunk and a brawler, and his maternal grandfather had been a Bavarian boar-hunter, trampled to death at the age of ninety by his own horses. After her husband died of consumption, Hoffman's mother transferred the entirety of the family's fortune into the hands of a handsome Russian charlatan named Katanovsky, a common conjurer and a necromancer, who promised Madame Hoffman audiences with the dead. As for Richard Hoffman himself, he moved to America, where he murdered two people.

•

Hoffman immigrated to Pittsburgh during World War II and worked as a busboy for over a decade. He had a terrible, humiliating way of speaking with customers.

"I am from Hungary!" he would bark. "Are you Hungary, too? If you Hungary, you in the right place!"

For years he spoke such garbage, even after he had learned excellent English, and could be mistaken for a native-born steelworker. With this ritual degradation he was tipped generously, and saved enough money to buy a popular supper club called the Pharaoh's Palace, featuring a nightly magic act, a comic and some showgirls. It was a favorite with gamblers and the newly rich.

When Hoffman was in his late forties, he permitted a young man named Ace Douglas to audition for a role as a supporting magician. Ace had no nightclub experience, no professional photos or references, but he had a beautiful voice over the telephone, and Hoffman permitted him an audience.

On the afternoon of the audition, Ace arrived in a tuxedo. His shoes had a wealthy gleam, and he took his cigarettes from a silver case etched with his clean initials. He was a slim, attractive man with fair brown hair. When he was not smiling, he looked like a matinee idol, and when he was smiling he looked like a friendly lifeguard. Either way, he seemed altogether too affable to perform good magic (Hoffman's other magicians cultivated an intentional menace) but his act was wonderful and entertaining, and he was unsullied by the often stupid fashions of magic at the time. Ace didn't claim to be descended from a vampire, for instance, or empowered with secrets from the tomb of Ramses, or kidnapped by gypsies as a child, or raised by missionaries in the mysterious Orient. He didn't even have a female assistant, unlike Hoffman's other magicians who knew that some bounce in fishnets could save any sloppy act. What's more, Ace had the good sense and class not to call himself the Great anything, or the Magnificent anybody.

On stage, with his smooth hair and white gloves, Ace Douglas had the sexual ease of Sinatra.

An older waitress named Sandra was setting up the cocktail bar at the Pharaoh's Palace on the afternoon of Ace Douglas's audition. She watched the act for a few minutes, then approached Hoffman and whispered in his ear, "At night, when I'm all alone in my bed, I sometimes think about men."

"I bet you do, Sandra," said Hoffman.

She was always talking like this. She was a fantastic, dirty woman, and he had actually had sex with her a few times.

She whispered, "And when I get to thinking about men, Hoffman, I think about a man exactly like that."

"You like him?" Hoffman asked.

"Oh my."

"You think the ladies will like him?"

"Oh my," said Sandra, fanning herself daintily. "Heavens, yes."

Hoffman fired his other two magicians within the hour.

After that, Ace Douglas worked every night that the Pharaoh's Palace was open. He was the highest-paid performer in Pittsburgh. This was not a decade when nice young women generally came to bars unescorted, but the Pharaoh's Palace became a place where nice women — extremely attractive young single nice women — would arrive without dates, with their best girlfriends and with their best dresses to watch the

CIGARETTE TRICK

Ace Douglas magic show. And men would come to the Pharaoh's Palace to watch the nice young women and to buy them expensive cocktails.

Hoffman had his own table at the back of the restaurant, and, after the magic show was over, he and Ace Douglas would entertain young ladies there. The girls would blindfold Ace, and then Hoffman would choose an object on the table for identification.

"It's a fork," Ace would say. "It's a gold cigarette lighter."

The more suspicious girls would open their purses and seek unusual objects—family photographs, prescription medicine, a traffic ticket—all of which Ace would describe easily. The girls would laugh, and doubt his blindfold, and cover his eyes with their damp hands. They had names like Lettie and Pearl and Siggie and Donna. They all loved dancing, and they all liked to keep their nice fur wraps with them at the table, out of pride. Hoffman would introduce them to eligible or otherwise interested businessmen. Ace Douglas would escort the nice young ladies to the parking lot late at night, listening politely as they spoke up to him, resting his hand reassuringly on the smalls of their backs if they wavered.

And at the end of every evening Hoffman would say sadly, "Me and Ace, we see so many girls come and go . . ."

Ace Douglas could turn a pearl necklace into a white glove, and a cigarette lighter into a candle. He could produce a silk scarf from a lady's hairpin. But his finest trick was in 1959, when he produced his little sister from a convent school and offered her to Richard Hoffman in marriage.

Her name was Angela. She had been a volleyball champion in the convent school, and she had legs like a movie star's legs, and a very pretty laugh. She was ten days pregnant on her wedding day, although she and Hoffman had only known each other for two weeks. Shortly thereafter, Angela had a daughter, and they named her Esther. Throughout the early 1960s, they all prospered happily.

•

Esther turned eight years old, and the Hoffmans celebrated her birthday with a special party at the Pharaoh's Palace. That night, there was a thief sitting in the cocktail lounge. He didn't look like a thief. He was dressed well enough, and he was served without any trouble. The thief drank a few martinis. Then, in the middle of the magic show, he leapt over the bar, kicked the bartender away, punched the cash register open and ran out of the Pharaoh's Palace with his hands full of tens and twenties.

The customers were screaming, and Hoffman heard it from the kitchen. He chased the thief into the parking lot and caught him by the hair.

"You steal from me?" he yelled. "You fucking steal from me?"

"Back off, pal," the thief said. The thief's name was George Purcell, and he was drunk.

"You fucking steal from me?" Hoffman yelled.

He shoved George Purcell into the side of a yellow Buick. Some of the customers had come outdoors, and they were watching from the atrium of the restaurant. Ace Douglas came out, too. He walked past the customers, into the parking lot, and he lit a cigarette. Ace Douglas watched as Hoffman lifted the thief by his shirt and threw him against the hood of a Cadillac.

"Back off me!" Purcell said.

"You fucking steal from me?"

"You ripped my shirt!" Purcell cried, aghast. He was looking down at his ripped shirt when Hoffman shoved him into the side of the yellow Buick again.

Ace Douglas said, "Richard? Could you take it easy?" (The Buick was his, and it was new. Hoffman was steadily pounding George Purcell's head into the door.) "Richard? Excuse me? Excuse me, Richard. Please don't damage my car, Richard."

Hoffman dropped the thief to the ground, and sat on his chest. He caught his breath and then smiled.

"Don't ever," he explained. "Ever. Don't ever steal from me. Ever."

Still sitting on Purcell's chest, he picked up the tens and twenties that had fallen on the asphalt, and handed them to Ace Douglas. Then he slid his hand into Purcell's back pocket and pulled out a wallet, which he opened. He took nine dollars from the wallet, because that was exactly all the money he found there. Purcell was indignant.

"That's my money!" he shouted. "You can't take my money!"

"*Your* money?" Hoffman slapped Purcell's head. "*Your* money? *Your* fucking money?"

Ace Douglas tapped Hoffman's shoulder lightly and said, "Richard? Excuse me? Let's just wait for the police, okay? How about it, Richard?"

"*Your* money?" Hoffman was slapping Purcell in the face now with the wallet. "You fucking steal from me, you have no money! You fucking steal from me, I own all your money!"

"Aw Jesus," Purcell said. "Quit it, will ya? Leave me alone, will ya?"

"Let him be," Ace Douglas said.

"*Your* money? I own all your money!" Hoffman bellowed. "I own you! You fucking steal from me, I own your fucking *shoes*!"

Hoffman lifted Purcell's leg and pulled off one of his shoes. It was a nice brown leather wing tip. He hit Purcell with it once in the face, then tore off the other shoe. He beat on Purcell a few times with that shoe, until he lost his appetite for it. Then he just sat on Purcell's chest for a while, catching his breath, hugging the shoes and rocking in a very sad way.

"Aw, Jesus," Purcell groaned. His lip was bleeding.

"Let's get up now, Richard," Ace suggested.

After some time, Hoffman jumped up off Purcell and walked back into the Pharaoh's Palace, carrying the thief's shoes. His tuxedo was torn in one knee, and his shirt was hanging loose. The customers backed against the walls of the restaurant and let him pass. He went into the kitchen and threw Purcell's shoes into one of the big garbage cans next to the pot-washing sinks. Then he went into his office and shut the door.

The pot washer was a young Cuban fellow named Manuel. He picked George Purcell's brown wing tips out of the garbage can and held one of them up against the bottom of his own foot. It seemed to be a good match, so he took off his own shoes and put on Purcell's. Manuel's shoes had been plastic sandals, and these he threw away, into the big garbage can. A little later, Manuel watched with satisfaction as the chef dumped a vat of cold gravy on top of the sandals, and then he went back to washing pots. He whistled a little song to himself of good luck.

A policeman arrived. He handcuffed George Purcell and brought him into Hoffman's office. Ace Douglas followed them in.

"You want to press charges?" the cop asked.

"No," Hoffman said. "Forget about it."

"You don't press charges, I have to let him go."

"Let him go."

"This man says you took his shoes."

"He's a criminal. He came in my restaurant with no shoes."

"He took my shoes," Purcell said. His shirt collar was soaked with blood.

"He never had no shoes on. Look at him. No shoes on his feet."

"You took my money and my goddamn shoes, you animal. Twenty-dollar shoes!"

"Get this stealing man out of my restaurant, please," Hoffman said.

"Officer?" Ace Douglas said. "Excuse me, but I was here the whole time, and this man never did have any shoes on. He's a derelict, sir."

"But I'm wearing dress socks!" Purcell shouted. "Look at me! Look at me!"

Hoffman stood up and walked out of his office. The cop followed Hoffman leading George Purcell. Ace Douglas trailed behind. On his way through the restaurant, Hoffman stopped to pick up his daughter, Esther, from her birthday-party table. He carried her out to the parking lot.

"Listen to me now," he told Purcell. "You ever steal from me again, I'll kill you."

"Take it easy," the cop said.

"If I even see you on the street, I'll fucking kill you."

The cop said, "You want to press charges, pal, you press charges. Otherwise you take it easy."

"He doesn't like to be robbed," Ace Douglas explained.

"Animal," Purcell muttered.

"You see this little girl?" Hoffman asked. "My little girl is eight years old today. If I'm walking on the street with my little girl and I see you, then I will leave her on one side of the street, and I will cross the street and I will kill you in front of my little girl."

"That's enough," the cop said. He led George Purcell out of the parking lot and took off his handcuffs.

The cop and the thief walked away together. Hoffman stood on the steps of the Pharaoh's Palace, holding Esther and shouting.

"Right in front of my little girl, you make me kill you? What kind of man are you? Crazy man! You ruin a little girl's life! Terrible man!"

Esther was crying. Ace Douglas took her from Hoffman's arms.

The next week, the thief George Purcell came back to the Pharaoh's Palace. It was noon, and very quiet. The prep cook was making chicken stock, and Manuel the pot washer was cleaning out the dry-goods storage area. Hoffman was in his office ordering vegetables from his wholesaler. Purcell came straight back into the kitchen, sober.

"I want my goddamn shoes!" he yelled, pounding on the office door. "Twenty-dollar shoes!"

Then Richard Hoffman came out of his office and beat George Purcell to death with a meat mallet. Manuel the pot washer tried to hold him back, and Hoffman beat him to death with the meat mallet, too.

•

Esther Hoffman did not grow up to be a natural magician. Her hands were dull. It was no fault of her own, just an unfortunate birth flaw. Otherwise, she was a bright girl. Her uncle, Ace Douglas, had been the American National Champion Close-Up Magician for three years running. He'd won his titles using no props or tools at all, except a single silver dollar coin. During one competition, he'd vanished and produced the coin for fifteen dizzying minutes without the expert panel of judges ever noticing that the coin spent a lot of time resting openly on Ace Douglas's own knee. He would put it there, where it lay gleaming to be seen if one of the judges had only glanced away for a moment from Ace's hands. But they would never glance away, convinced that he still held a coin before them in his fingers. They were not fools, but they were dupes for his fake takes, his fake drops, his mock passes and a larger cast of impossible moves so deceptive they went entirely unnoticed. Ace Douglas had motions which he himself had never even named. He was a scholar of misdirection. He proscribed skepticism. His fingers were as loose and quick as thoughts.

But Esther Hoffman's magic was sadly pedestrian. She did the Famous Dancing Cane Trick, the Famous Vanishing Milk Trick, and the Famous Chinese Linking Rings Trick. She produced parakeets from light bulbs, and pulled a dove from a burning pan. She performed at birthday parties, and could float a child. She performed at grammar schools, and could cut and restore the neckties of principals. If the principal was a lady, Esther would borrow a ring from the principal's finger, lose it, and then find it in a child's pocket. If the lady principal wore no jewelry, Esther would simply run a sword through the woman's neck while the children in the audience screamed in spasms of rapture.

Simple, artless tricks.

"You're young," Ace told her. "You'll improve."

But she did not. Esther made more money teaching flute lessons to little girls than performing magic. She was a fine flutist, and this was maddening to her. Why all this worthless musical skill?

"Your fingers are very quick," Ace told her. "There's nothing wrong with your fingers. But it's not about quickness, Esther. You don't have to speed through coins."

"I hate coins."

"You should handle coins as if they amuse you, Esther. Not as if they frighten you."

"With coins, it's like I'm wearing oven mitts."

"Coins are not always easy."

"I never fool anybody. I can't misdirect."

"It's not about misdirection, Esther. It's about *direction*."

"I don't have hands," Esther complained. "I have paws."

It was true that Esther could only fumble coins and cards, and she would never be a deft magician. She had no gift. Also, she hadn't the poise. Esther had seen photographs of her uncle when he was young at the Pharaoh's Palace, leaning against patrician pillars of marble in his tuxedo and cuff links. No form of magic existed which was close-up enough for him. He could sit on a chair surrounded on all sides by the biggest goons of spectators—people who challenged him or grabbed his arm in midpass—and he would borrow some common object and absolutely vanish it. Some goon's car keys in Ace's hand would turn into absolutely nothing. Absolutely gone.

Ace's nightclub act at the Pharaoh's Palace had been a tribute to the most elegant vices. He used coins, cards, dice, champagne flutes, cigarettes—any item which would suggest and encourage drinking, sin, gamesmanship and money. The fluidity of fortune. He could do a whole act of cigarette effects alone, starting with a single cigarette borrowed from a lady in the audience. He would pass it through a coin, and then give the coin—intact—back to the lady. He would tear the cigarette in half and then restore it, swallow it, cough it back up along with six more, duplicate them and duplicate them again until he ended up with lit cigarettes smoking hot between all his fingers and in his mouth, behind his ears, emerging from every pocket—surprised? he was terrified!—and then, with a nod, all the lit cigarettes would vanish except the original. That one cigarette he would transform into a stately pipe, which he would smoke luxuriously during the applause.

Also, Esther had pictures of her father during the same period, when he owned the Pharaoh's Palace. He was handsome in his tuxedo, but with a heavy posture. She had inherited his thick wrists.

When Richard Hoffman got out of prison, he moved in with Ace and Esther. Ace had a tremendous home in the country by then, a tall, yellow Victorian house with a mile of woods behind it and a lawn like a baron's. He had only one neighbor, an elderly woman with a similarly huge Victorian home, just next door. Ace Douglas had made a tidy fortune from magic. He had operated the Pharaoh's Palace from the time that Hoffman was arrested, and with Hoffman's permission had eventually sold it at great profit to a gourmet restaurateur. Esther had been living with Ace since she'd finished high school, and she had a whole floor to herself. Ace's leggy little sister Angela had divorced Hoffman, also with his permission, and had moved to Florida to live with her new husband.

What Hoffman had never permitted was for Esther to visit him in prison, and so it had been fourteen years since they'd seen each other. In prison he had grown even sturdier. He seemed shorter than Ace and Esther remembered, and some weight gained had made him broader. He had also grown a thick beard with elegant red tones. He was easily moved to tears, or at least seemed to be always on the verge of being moved to tears. The first few weeks of living together again were not altogether comfortable for Esther and Hoffman. They had only the briefest conversations, such as this one:

Hoffman asked Esther, "How old are you now?"
"Twenty-two."

CIGARETTE TRICK

"I've got undershirts older than you."

Or, in another conversation, Hoffman said, "The fellows I met in prison are the nicest fellows in the world."

And Esther said, "Actually, Dad, they probably aren't."

And so on.

In December of that year, Hoffman attended a magic show of Esther's, performed at a local elementary school.

"She's really not very good," he reported later to Ace.

"I really think she's fine," Ace said. "She's fine for the kids, and she enjoys herself."

"She's pretty terrible. Too dramatic."

"Perhaps."

"She says, '*Behold!*' It's terrible, *Behold* this! *Behold* that!"

"But they're children," Ace said. "With children, you need to explain when you're about to do a trick and when you just did one, because they're so excited they don't realize what's going on. They don't even know what a magician is, Richard. They can't tell the difference between when you're doing magic and when you're just standing there."

"I think she was very nervous."

"Could be."

"She says, '*Behold* the *Parakeet!*'"

"Her parakeet tricks are not bad."

"It's not dignified," Hoffman said. "She convinces nobody."

"It's not meant to be dignified, Richard. It's for the children."

The next week, Hoffman bought Esther a large white rabbit.

"If you do the tricks for the children, you should have a rabbit," he told her.

Esther hugged him. She said, "I never had a rabbit."

Hoffman lifted the rabbit from the cage. It was an unnaturally enormous rabbit.

"Is it pregnant?" Esther asked.

"No, she is not. She is only large."

"That's an extremely large rabbit for any magic trick," Ace observed.

Esther said, "They haven't invented the hat big enough to pull that rabbit out of."

"She actually folds up to a small size," Hoffman said. He held the rabbit between his hands like it was an accordion and squeezed it into a great white ball.

"She seems to like that," Ace said, and Esther laughed.

"She doesn't mind it. Her name is Bonnie." Hoffman held the rabbit forward by the nape of her neck, as though she were a massive kitten. Dangling fully stretched like that, she was bigger than a big raccoon.

"Where'd you get her?" Esther asked.

"From the newspaper!" Hoffman announced, beaming.

Esther liked Bonnie the rabbit more than she liked her trick doves and parakeets, which were attractive enough, but were essentially only pigeons that had been lucky with their looks. Ace liked Bonnie, too. He allowed Bonnie to enjoy the entirety of his large Victorian home, with little regard for Bonnie's pellets, which were small, rocky and inoffensive. She particularly enjoyed sitting in the center of the kitchen table and from that spot would regard Ace, Esther and Hoffman gravely. Bonnie had a feline manner.

"Will she always be this judgmental?" Esther wanted to know.

Bonnie became more canine when she was allowed outdoors. She would sleep on the porch, lying on her side in a patch of sun, and if anyone approached the porch she would look up at that person lazily, in the manner of a bored and trustful dog. At night, she slept with Hoffman. He tended to sleep on his side, curled like a child, and Bonnie would sleep upon him, perched on his highest point, which was generally his hip.

As a performer, however, Bonnie was useless. She was far too large to be handled gracefully on stage, and on the one occasion that Esther did try to produce her from a hat, she hung in the air so sluggishly that the children in the back rows were sure that she was a fake. She appeared to be a huge toy, typical and store bought as their own stuffed animals.

"Bonnie will never be a star," Hoffman said.

Ace said, "You spoiled her, Richard, the way the magicians have been spoiling their lovely assistants for decades. You spoiled Bonnie by sleeping with her."

•

That spring, a young lawyer and his wife (who was also a young lawyer) moved into the large Victorian house next door to Ace Douglas's large Victorian house. It all happened very swiftly. The widow who had lived there for decades died in her sleep, and the place was sold within a few weeks. The new neighbors had great ambitions. The husband, whose name was Ronald Wilson, telephoned Ace and asked if there were any problems he should know about in the area, regarding water-drainage patterns or frost heaves. Ronald had plans for a great garden and was interested in building an arbor to extend from the back of the house. His wife, whose name was Ruth-Ann, was running for probate judge of the county. Ronald and Ruth-Ann were tall and had perfect manners. They had no children.

Three days after the Wilsons moved in next door, Bonnie the rabbit disappeared. She was on the porch, and then she was not.

Hoffman searched all afternoon for Bonnie. On Esther's recommendation, he spent that evening walking up and down the road with a flashlight, looking to see if Bonnie had been hit by a car. The next day, he walked through the woods behind the house, calling the rabbit for hours. He left a bowl of cut vegetables outside on the porch with some fresh water. Several times during the night, Hoffman got up to see if Bonnie was on the porch, eating the food. Eventually, he just wrapped himself in blankets and laid down on the porch swing, keeping a vigil beside the vegetables. He slept out there for a week, changing the food every morning and evening to keep the scent fresh.

Esther made a poster with a drawing of Bonnie (which

looked very much like a spaniel in her rendering) and a caption reading LARGE RABBIT MISSING. She stapled copies of the poster on telephone poles throughout town and placed a notice in the newspaper. Ace Douglas called the local ASPCA for daily updates. Hoffman wrote a letter to the neighbors, Ronald and Ruth-Ann Wilson, and slid it under their door. The letter described Bonnie's color and weight, gave the date and time of her disappearance and requested any information on the subject at all. The Wilsons did not call with news, so the next day Hoffman went over to their house and rang the doorbell. Ronald Wilson answered.

"Did you get my letter?" Hoffman asked.
"About the rabbit?" Ronald said. "Have you found him?"
"The rabbit is a girl. And the rabbit belongs to my daughter. She was a gift. Have you seen her?"
"She didn't get in the road, did she?"
"Is Bonnie in your house, Mr. Wilson?"
"Is Bonnie the rabbit's name?"
"Yes."
"How would Bonnie get in our house?"
"Perhaps you have some broken window in the basement?"
"You think she's in our basement?"
"Have you looked for her in your basement?"
"No."
"Can I look for her?"
"You want to look for a rabbit in our basement?"

The two men stared at each other for some time. Ronald Wilson was wearing a baseball cap, and he took it off and rubbed the top of his head, which was balding. He put the baseball cap back on.

"Your rabbit is not in our house, Mr. Hoffman," Wilson said.

"Okay," Hoffman said. "Okay. Sure."

Hoffman walked back home. He sat at the kitchen table and waited until Ace and Esther were both in the room to make his announcement.

"They took her," he said. "The Wilsons took Bonnie."

Hoffman started to build the tower in July. There was a row of oak trees between Ace Douglas's house and the Wilson's house, and the leaves from these trees blocked Hoffman's view into their home. For several months, he'd been spending his nights watching the Wilson house from the attic window with binoculars, looking for Bonnie inside, but he could not see into the lower-floor rooms for the trees and was frustrated. Ace reassured him that the leaves would be gone by autumn, but Hoffman was afraid that Bonnie would be dead by autumn. This was difficult for him to take. He was no longer allowed to go over to the Wilsons' property and look into the basement windows, since Ruth-Ann Wilson had called the police. He was no longer allowed to write threatening letters. He was no longer allowed to call the Wilsons up on the telephone. He had promised Ace and Esther all of these things.

"He's really harmless," Esther would tell Ruth-Ann Wilson, although she herself was not sure this was the case.

Ronald Wilson found out somehow that Hoffman had been in prison, and he'd contacted the parole officer, who had, in turn, contacted Hoffman, suggesting that he leave the Wilsons alone.

"If you would only let him search your home for the rabbit," Ace Douglas had suggested gently to the Wilsons, "this would be over very quickly. Just give him a half hour to look around. It's just that he's concerned that Bonnie is trapped in your basement."

"Why would we keep his rabbit? Why would we do that?"

Hoffman said to Ace, "Because of the vegetable garden. Think about this. Vegetables, Ace. Naturally, they are against the rabbit."

"If you would just let him look inside once . . ." Ace repeated.

"We did not move here to let murderers into our home," Ronald Wilson said.

"He's not a murderer," Esther protested, somewhat lamely.

"He scares my wife."

"I don't want to scare your wife," Hoffman said.

"He's really harmless," Esther insisted. "Maybe you could buy him a new rabbit."

"I don't want any new rabbit," Hoffman said.

"You scare my wife," Ronald repeated. "We don't owe you any rabbit at all."

In late spring, Hoffman cut down the smallest oak tree between the two houses. He did it on a Monday afternoon, when the Wilsons were at work, and Esther was performing magic for a Girl Scouts party, and Ace was shopping. He'd purchased a chain saw weeks earlier and had been hiding it. The tree wasn't very big, but it fell at a sharp diagonal across the Wilsons' backyard, narrowly missing their arbor and destroying a substantial corner of the garden.

The police came. After a great deal of negotiating, Ace Douglas was able to prove that the oak tree, while between the two houses, was actually on his property, and it was his right to have it cut down. He offered to pay generously for the damages to the Wilsons. Ronald Wilson came over to the house again that night, but he would not speak until Ace sent Hoffman from the room.

"Do you understand our situation?" he asked.

"I do," Ace said. "I honestly do."

The two men sat at the kitchen table across from one another for some time. Ace offered to get Ronald some coffee, which he refused.

"How can you live with him?" Ronald asked.

Ace did not answer this, but got himself some coffee. He opened the refrigerator and pulled out a carton of milk, which he smelled and then poured down the sink. After this, he smelled his cup of coffee, which he poured down the sink as well.

"Is he your boyfriend?" Ronald asked.

"Is Richard my boyfriend? No. He's my very good friend. And he's my brother-in-law."

"Really," Ronald said. He was working his wedding band around his finger as though he were screwing it on tight.

"You thought it was a dream come true to buy that nice

old house, didn't you?" Ace Douglas asked. He managed to say this in a friendly, sympathetic way.

"Yes, we did."

"But it's a nightmare, isn't it? Living next to us?"

"Yes, it is."

Ace Douglas laughed. Ronald Wilson laughed, too, and said, "It's a complete fucking nightmare, actually."

"I'm very sorry that your wife is afraid of us, Ronald."

"Well."

"I truly am."

"Thank you. It's difficult. She's a bit paranoid sometimes."

"Well," Ace said, again in a friendly and sympathetic way. "Imagine that. Paranoid! In this neighborhood?"

The two men laughed again. Meanwhile, in the other room, Esther was talking to her father.

"Why'd you do it, Dad?" she asked. "Such a pretty tree."

He had been weeping.

"Because I am so sad," he said, finally. "I wanted them to feel it."

"To feel how sad you were?" she said.

"To feel how sad I am," he told her. "How sad I am."

Anyway, in July he started to build the tower.

Ace had an old pickup truck, and Hoffman used this to drive to the municipal dump every afternoon, so that he could look for wood and scrap materials. He built the base of the tower out of pine, reinforced with parts of an old steel bed frame. By the end of July the tower was over ten feet high. He wasn't planning on building a staircase inside, so it was a solid cube.

The Wilsons called the zoning board, who fined Ace Douglas for erecting an unauthorized structure on his property and insisted that the work stop immediately.

"It's only a tree house," Esther lied to the zoning officer.

"It's a watchtower," Hoffman corrected. "So that I can see into the neighbor's house."

The zoning officer gave Hoffman a long, empty look.

"Yes," Hoffman said. "This truly is a watchtower."

"Take it down," said the zoning officer to Esther. "Take it down immediately."

•

Ace Douglas owned a significant library of antique magic books, including several volumes that Hoffman himself had brought over from Hungary during the Second World War, and that had been old and valuable even then. Hoffman had purchased these rare books from gypsies and dealers across Eastern Europe with the last of his family's money. In the 1950s, he'd given them over to Ace. Some volumes were written in German, some in Russian, some in English.

The collection revealed the secrets of Parlor Magic, or Drawing Room Magic, a popular pursuit of educated gentlemen at the turn of the century. The books spoke not of tricks, but of "diversions", which were sometimes magical maneuvers but were just as often simple scientific experiments. Often, these diversions involved hypnosis or the appearance of hypnosis. Many tricks required complicated acts of memorization and practice with a trained conspirator hidden among the otherwise susceptible guests. A gentleman might literally use smoke and a mirror to evoke a ghost within the parlor. A gentleman might read a palm or levitate a tea try. Or, a gentleman might simply demonstrate that an egg could stand on its end, or that magnets could react against one another, or that an electric current could turn a small motorized contrivance.

The books were exquisitely illustrated. Hoffman had given them to Ace Douglas back in the 1950s, because he had hoped for some time to recreate this lost conjury in Pittsburgh. He had hoped to decorate a small area within the Pharaoh's Palace in the manner of a formal upper-middle-class European drawing room, and to dress Ace in spats and kid gloves. Ace did study the books, but he found that there was no way to accurately replicate most of the diversions. The old tricks all called for common household items which were simply not common any more: a box of paraffin, a pinch of snuff, a dab of beeswax, a spittoon, a watch fob, a ball of cork, a sliver of saddle soap, et cetera. Even if such ingredients could be gathered, they would have no meaning to modern spectators. It would be museum magic, resonating to nobody. It would move nobody.

To Hoffman, this was a considerable disappointment. As a very young man he had watched the Russian charlatan and swindling necromancer Katanovsky perform such diversions in his mother's own drawing room. His mother, recently widowed, wore dark gowns dressed with china-blue silk ribbons precisely the same shade as the famous blue vials of Hoffman's Rose Water. Her face was that of a determined regent. His sisters, in childish pinafores, regarded Katanovsky in a pretty stupor of wonder.

Gathered in the drawing room as a family, they had all heard it. Hoffman himself—his eyes stinging from phosphorus smoke—had heard it: the unmistakable voice of his recently dead father, speaking through Katanovksy's own dark mouth. They heard their father's message (in perfectly accentless Hungarian!) of reassurement. A thrilling, intimate call to faith.

And so it was unfortunate for Hoffman that Ace Douglas could not replicate this very diversion. He would've liked to have seen it tried again. It must have been a very simple swindle, although an antique one. Hoffman would've liked to have witnessed the hoax voice of his dead father repeated and explained to him fully and, if necessary, repeated again.

•

On the first day of September, Hoffman woke at dawn and began preparing his truck. Months later, during the court proceedings, the Wilsons' attorney would attempt to show that Hoffman had stockpiled weapons in the bed of the truck, an allegation that Esther and Ace would contest heatedly. Certainly there were tools in the truck—a few shovels, a sledgehammer and an ax—but if these were threatening, they were not so intentionally.

Hoffman had recently purchased several dozen rolls of wide, silvery electrical duct tape, and at dawn he began winding the tape around the body of the truck. He wound long lengths of the tape, and then more tape over the existing tape, and he did this again and again, as armor.

Esther had an early morning flute class to teach, and she got up to eat her cereal. From the kitchen window, she saw her father taping his pickup. The headlights and taillights were already covered and the doors were sealed shut. She went outside.

"Dad?" she said.

And Hoffman said, almost apologetically, "I'm going over there."

"Not to the Wilsons?"

"I'm going in after Bonnie," he said.

Esther walked back to the house, feeling shaky. She woke Ace Douglas, who looked from his bedroom window down at Hoffman in the driveway, and he called the police.

"Oh, not the police." Esther said. "Not the police . . ."

Ace held her in a hug for some time.

"Are you crying?" he asked.

"No," she lied.

"You're not crying?"

"No, I'm just sad."

When the duct tape ran out, Hoffman circled the truck a few times and noticed that he had no way to enter it now. He took the sledgehammer from the flatbed and lightly tapped the passenger-side window with it, until the glass was evenly spiderwebbed. Then he gently pushed the window in. The glass crystals landed silently on the seat. He climbed inside, then noticed that he had no keys, so he climbed out of the broken window again and walked into the house where he found his keys on the kitchen table. Esther wanted to go downstairs to talk with him, but Ace Douglas would not let her go. He went down himself, and Esther slid her head under Ace's pillow and cried in a hard, down-low way.

Downstairs, Ace said, "I'm sorry, Richard. But I've called the police."

"The police?" Hoffman repeated, wounded. "Not the police, Ace."

"I'm sorry."

Hoffman was silent for a long time, staring at Ace.

"But I'm going in there after Bonnie," he said, finally.

"I wish you wouldn't do that."

"But they have her," Hoffman said, and he was now crying, as well.

"I don't believe that they do have her, Richard."

"But they *stole* her!"

Hoffman took up his keys and climbed back into his taped-up truck, still weeping. He drove over to the Wilsons' home, and circled their house several times. He drove through the corn in the garden. Forward over the corn, then backwards, then forward over the corn again. Ruth-Ann Wilson came running out, and she pulled up some bricks that were lining her footpath and chased after Hoffman, throwing the bricks at his truck and screaming.

Hoffman pulled the truck up to the metal basement doors of the Wilsons' house. He tried to drive right up on them, but his truck didn't have the power, and the wheels sunk into the wet lawn. He honked in long, forlorn foghorn blasts.

When the police arrived, Hoffman would not come out. He would, however, put his hands on the steering wheel to show that he was not armed.

"He doesn't have a gun," Esther shouted from the porch of Ace Douglas's house.

Two officers circled the truck and examined it. The younger officer tapped on Hoffman's window and asked him to roll it down, but he refused.

"Tell them to bring her outside!" he shouted. "Bring the rabbit and I will come out of the truck! Bring Bonnie! Terrible people!"

The older officer cut through the duct tape on the passenger-side door with a utility knife. He was able, finally, to open the door, and when he did that, he was able to reach in and drag Hoffman out, both of them cutting their arms over the spilled, sparkling glass of the broken window. Once outside the truck, Hoffman lay on the grass in a limp sprawl, face down. He was handcuffed and taken away in a squad car.

Ace and Esther followed the police to the station, where the officers took Hoffman's belt and his fingerprints. Hoffman was wearing only an undershirt and work pants, and his cell was small, empty and chilly.

Esther asked the older police officer, "May I go home and bring my father back a jacket? Or a blanket? May I please just do that?"

"You may," said the older police officer, and he patted her arm with a sort of authoritative sympathy. "You may, indeed."

•

Back home, Esther washed her face and took some aspirin. She called the mother of her flute student and canceled that morning's class. The mother wanted to reschedule, but Esther could only promise to call later. She noticed the milk on the kitchen counter and returned it to the refrigerator. She brushed her teeth. She changed into warmer autumn boots, and she went to the living room closet and found a light wool blanket for her father. She heard a noise.

Esther followed the noise, which was that of a running automobile engine. She went to the window of the living room and parted the curtain. In the Wilsons' driveway was a sturdy white van with grills on the windows. The side of this van was marked with the emblem of the ASPCA. Esther said aloud, "Oh my."

A man in white coveralls came out of the Wilsons' front door, carrying a large wire cage. Inside the cage was Bonnie.

•

Esther had never been inside the local ASPCA building, and she did not go inside it that day. She parked near the van, which she had followed, and watched as the man in the coveralls opened the back doors and pulled out a cage. This cage held three gray kittens, which he carried into the building, leaving the van doors open.

When the man was safely inside, Esther got out of her car and walked to the back of the van. She found the cage with Bonnie, opened it easily and pulled out the rabbit. Bonnie was much thinner than the last time Esther had seen her, and the rabbit eyed her with an absolutely expressionless gaze of nonrecognition. Esther carried Bonnie to her car and drove back to the police station.

She parked her car and got out, tucking the rabbit under her left arm. She wrapped the light wool blanket she'd brought for her father completely around herself, like a cape. Esther walked briskly into the police station. She passed the older police officer, who was talking to Ace Douglas and Ralph Wilson. She raised her right hand as she walked near the men and said solemnly, "How, palefaces."

Ace smiled at her, and the older police officer waved her by.

Hoffman's jail cell was at the end of a hallway, and it was poorly lit. Hoffman had not been sleeping well for several weeks, and he was cold and cut. One frame of his glasses had been cracked, and he had been weeping since that morning. He saw Esther approaching, wrapped in that light gray wool blanket, and he saw in her the figure of his mother, who had worn cloaks against the Budapest winters and who had also walked with a particular dignity.

Esther approached the cell, and she reached her hand between the bars toward her father, who rose with a limp to meet that hand. In a half-mad moment, he half-imagined her to be a warm apparition of his mother, and, as he reached for her, she smiled.

Her smile directed his gaze from her hand to her face, and in that instant, Esther pulled her arm back out of the cell, reached into the folds of the blanket around her and gracefully produced the rabbit. She slid Bonnie — slimmer now, of course — through the iron bars and held the rabbit aloft in the cell, exactly where her empty hand had been only a moment before. Such that Hoffman, when he glanced down from Esther's smile, saw a rabbit where before there had simply been no rabbit at all. Like a true enchantment, something appeared from the common air.

"Behold," said Esther.

Richard Hoffman beheld the silken rabbit and recognized her as Bonnie. He collected her into his square hands. And then, he did also behold his own daughter Esther.

A most gifted young woman.

Portfolio

Ten New Poets

So disparate, so distinct, even, are the new poems, the new poets who appear in all their multitudes in the office mail, so docile in their return-addressed envelopes yet so indubitable in their variety and delicacy that it would be defamatory for the poetry editor to claim more, in a generalizing way, about this particular clutch of poems than his own taste, his own delight in their particular virtues, their singular vitalities. No vogue-spotter I, nor one of those intellectual marines, as Auden used to call them, who have landed and captured a trend. Of course there are poets here who have made ekphrasis their muse, and the poets for whom history is a sort of metaphysical pathos, a refuge from happenings merely; there are the intonations of experience that move toward the experimental (not moving very far, or very fast, I must say); and there are certain homages to the great dead, the beloved masters. But it is a moment in our poetry when Anything Goes, and what is remarkable about the new poems here, is that Everything Stays, caught in the ear by that immodest twist of idiom we call style, or character, or quality. Mainly it is a matter of pleasure . . .

Richard Howard

Alan Ainsworth

Elizabeth Bishop's Novel

It was brief, she admitted, and never finished,
and what there was, she thinks, was lost, in the mistakes
of lovers. No, she stopped carrying it, (so many mistakes
in her moves!). What was it about? A black dog, a mutt,

running through a field is one image she remembers,
but she remembers it the same way one hears one end
of a telephone conversation. *Blah, blah.* She thinks the end
of the novel had a senile woman saying *sim, sim, sim.*

The funny part was that it was set in heaven,
abandoned to the wonder of this world, this Everglades,
this Elizabeth, this self, that hell. The plot,
what there was of it, was lurid (*A lurid heaven,*

how full of wonder! Marianne would have said).
It included a scene in the Keys of one fevered woman
rubbing alcohol all over (all over!) another woman.
And the graphologist, ridiculous, told the main character,

"Never get together with a man with widely separated words.
He'll never get close to anybody." That was right
in its own peculiar way, just as Elizabeth was right
in her own peculiar way, but the novel was better lost,

better not finished. She tried to imagine it in time
sitting on a closet shelf in a bungalow which disappears
a bite at a time. A drag hoe manned by a woman intent
on her work takes it down one jarring movement at a time,

and she takes no notice of the pages under the rubble,
thinks plenty about paradise but nothing of words.
That's right, Elizabeth thinks, paradise is without words
and full of a love of loss, small and never finished.

Kevin Cantwell

The Wooden Trap

The held cry of a hawk makes Thomas Hardy think
to make her believe it's a newborn's cry she hears.
Milk wets through her blouse. The other women know
at once. That's chapter one. How it starts
to grow while above his head the cumuli
accumulate. The August fields waver beyond
the privet hedge. He's given up the novel
for poetry. The women look at each other.
One counts out change on a plank counter.
That's that she says. Then exposition's drift
to flashback: How a horseshoe loosens.
How when leading the horse the master returns.
Not angry. Only to get it done right.
How she presses under the eaves of the shed
with him while the afternoon rain comes down
so hard they are nearly soaked anyway.
The editorial omniscient bites his tongue.
Innocent as it goes. The scent of windfall
rises up through the apple tree from the ground.
Some of the leaves bronze even now. There's no
turning back but that's getting ahead of ourselves.
There's Hardy. Shoes a disgrace. Canvas gaiters
undone and one foot on top of the ladder
where it narrows at the highest rung, the worn wood
twice the width of a stirrup, and one foot
in the crotch of a limb. He has it all
worked out. She's in another country where rumor's made
a place for her. Where's the little one?
they ask, but she presses past them into the lane.
It serves her right but no one says it
so that she hears. A limb tumbles through the green

cloud of foliage. And then another. He cuts it back
to make it bear, though a neighbor's stopped to tell him
it's ill-advised so late in the season.
She finds a place for herself as a domestic
until the governor says a girl's come back.
They'll have to let her go. It's dusk. The clouds
go pink to shell. He folds the little saw.
The ladder widens to its base. A trick of perspective
also that lures the gopher into the wooden box
he's set in its tunnel, the hole which looks
like an exit, the end of the tunnel, daylight,
but smaller than its head and those footsteps
on the earth above, which pause and anticipate
her every turn, and block her escape
with a garden fork plunged into the lyric dark.

Rick Hilles

The Four-Legged Man

1

I was conceived in an ordinary bed
inside the family house, my uncle Lester
listening, perhaps finding himself
beneath the new box springs. I heard

my mother's mother was a witch,
or so Father said. At any rate, she liked
to make them tea, the brew steeped
in a vat that glimmered whale-blood orange,

what settled in them uneasily stained
their mouths cornflower blue. The same tea
the doctor sipped before he had me breathe,
and found another heart that hammered

in a sunken hull of bone. I've never been
alone. I am *all* Gemini. Among the Hall
of Curiosities, we're home. The swallower
of snakes shared us lodgings for a season

and I paid him back tenfold when his constrictor
vanished in its cage. I heard the blind girl scream,
the ringmaster's only daughter, on whom
it set to strangling, undid the yard-long thigh of it,

wiped snake spit from her face, pampered
her, and still performed. That night, I found
the twin ropewalkers, red costumes pulled soundlessly
in silhouette and spilled about our lamp.

2

Word got around of our proclivities.
The dwarves, the barker's girls, the loveliest
— the fallacies of how we freaks make love
were put to bed. I have four normal daughters,

twins, with former acrobats; three sons
fathered by my brother's legs. They visit
when we're in town. At carnival, our city
blinks like fireflies, and no one eyes us twice.

Throughout, the children see things strange
or stranger than their dads: muskmelons
from Ottawa shaped like a sheriff's mistress
coupling with a squid.
                          Sights to make Jesus
weep — the pickled two-headed fetus, the aquarium
hell, where horrors wander under glass.

3

The grinder says a freak is either born
or made. But he is paid to lie. The congress
I have known is complicated: that pickled
fetus with two heads is something else,
a blown anomaly; a shrug perfected.
Life murdered by the marvel that it made.
Among the sideshow's armory, I've seen

the wonders taken from tribal villages:
Nairobi kings, their queens, and pygmies
shackled in their sleep. I've wakened to their cries:
uncomprehended squalls that weathercock
their points; nightmares of ordinary men,
made palpable, in ear-locked cells. I need
these other lives to speak about myself.

Do you know the story of the royal Yoruba
who made himself the Mudfish King? — he was
about to give a speech and could not move.
He slapped his cold, hard legs like lifeless fish,
said, "I'm of *both* worlds!" The crowd went wild.
There, cripples are put to death. I've lived the terror
of *that* life, and more, and this.
                                They say
I will awake one morning — no feeling below
my neck, feverish with the plot of my last dream:
Therein, I carry a crippled boy like matchwood
from a blackened building, undersides of tongues
and smoke wreathing our heads. Before I make it
out the door, I lose my grip. He falls,
orange-robed, a Buddhist hallowed in flame.

Three Poems by Jennifer Franklin

Role of a Lover: Albertine

Bed warming, I lie open and exact
As a needle preparing to suture.

But from above I am a fallen elm,
My hair a latticework of leaves.

The moon reveals: frost perched
On the chilled glass, my lidded eyes

Hovering towards morning. Nightly,
I enable his calculated escape from his

Fleshy cage. As he falls into my breathing
Pulse, I know his love for me is for himself.

Still I lie, as I recline, while the silk
Sheets absolve me of my wisdom.

My golden flesh arches higher than the fluted
Bedpost, weary with infinite knowledge

Of his weaknesses. Letting him believe
He is a voice of God, he worms himself

Into my niches. I lie thinking of thunder, still
And cold as a mausoleum, feigning sleep.

Daughter

I am everyone's receptacle of secrets.
Hollow as a gilded reliquary,
I hold each lie and confession

Like saints' clavicles and vertebrae.
Transparent, I display the treasures
I am trusted to safekeep.

They do not expect me to judge or offer.
To them I am as flat as a fresco,
Unremarkable face emerging

From cerulean and gold. I belong
To those who underestimate me.
The stars squint in the dormant sky.

I continue to know everything. They
Do not understand: I can undo them all;
Hypocrites, charlatans, hypochondriacs.

Each secret is the same secret.
They want me symmetrical, endorsing
Their desires. I am the unloved

Necessity. I am the quiet in a hall
When the music ceases. Someday,
I will surprise them with opacity.

I will whisper my transgressions
Into the wide mouths of poppies.
They will be my secrets. I will frighten

Them with telescope, sleeping bats,
All the unsealed letters and artless glances,
The mirrors I have gathered.

La Dame à la Licorne: Cluny Museum, Paris

It is cold but I know how to be
Even colder. I have had centuries
Of practice. Listen to me: I have
Only one desire.

Look at me trapped in sanguine,
See what it is to lie to yourself.
All day long I look and avoid looking
At my face. What I see, what others see

Of me are too different to contemplate,
Yet that is all I was made to do.
I am queen and chief spectacle, both.
Between holly and oak, the hooves

That stand in my lap are sharp.
I am not old enough, yet already creased
Like paper I fold to prepare for your eyes.
No room to move. Hung in this black

Chamber, the air tastes of dust,
But it was not always this way.
There was wine, sweat of dance, blood
From a kill. To protect us, we live here,

Carnival freaks in a cool chamber
With no windows and two doors.
Only the monkey tastes round sweets.
Pinned like this, time means nothing.

And there is nothing I enjoy. I am dressed
Darkly — crescent shaped — the moon
In a ruby sky. Only one-sixth of the time
I am permitted to sit. It is your fault.

I was not consulted about who I could become.
When I was young, I feared the penned unicorn —
The blood that ran from his speared chest
And his vulgar eyes. Now, I yearn for all

Smooth things. So much seeps into me;
I cannot tell where these petals have become
My ransacked body. Creatures hover
Above. Their breath on my neck, tugs

At my scalp. I am scraped and sampled,
Not knowing how to feel. My elbows
Are coarse, my grip tight. Just once,
I would like to kiss a cold cheek.

I have defied what you wanted for me,
My Maker. Still here, you are anonymous,
Unloved. Yet, I have long tried to unadorn
Myself for you. I would toss all the trinkets

And lavalieres into a box to escape
Worshiping. I am fabricated, no *I*,
Only your thread grouped in colors.
If I could be one, it would be that blue

For the shade of your eyes,
And the hue of your cloak,
And the sound of your voice
When you do not want to speak.

Richard Lamb

Private Parts

> *I don't know why they call them private parts.*
> *Mine aren't private.*
> —Quoted in the diaries of Evelyn Waugh

1. Me, as Seen by You as the Brothers Grimm:

A wanderer in a pair of ten-league boots,
with a faithful servant blessed by second sight,
    I cross a romantic moor
(here representing your persona),
galoomph through your more secluded self—
    (see below), reach the town of you,
insufficiently walled and defended
(you fear) by the crippled and the tetched.
    I walk into the town, stand in
the main square, boots festooned with rare bogwort,
and hand out subversive leaflets about
    how your citizenry should now
wear this, plant that, behave in such and such a way. . . .

2. You, as Viewed by Me as the Environmental Protection Agency:

A marshy delicate wetland,
sitting atop a threatened aquifer,
its population chiefly vegetable,
sometimes carnivorous,
crossed by pathways,
hidden, often treacherous. . . .

3. Me, as Designed by a French Military Architect,
   c. 1918–1939:

Turrets, flush with the ground's rise;
armored cavities of immense size;
reinforced concrete; miles and miles
of subterranean corridors.
A garrison of raw farm boys.
Cisterns for collecting rainwater
in lieu of wells. Lieutenants
drawn from among young urban swells.
Stores of ammunition. Barbed wire.
Tank traps . . .

4. You, as Seen by Me as One of the Garrison's Recruits:

"Boys, I seen her clear as day, right there, — t'were late.
It was from that cistern that she slowly rose,
a vision a loveliness, made entirely of steam,
so real the mist was flesh — each eye a single droplet's gleam.
And she was wearing not a stitch a clothes.
So she moves, and steam covers me, like.
                    Then she dissipates. . . ."

5. Us by Us as Metternich on *Realpolitik:*

From the beginning they conceived of it as a matter
of frontiers, of boundary disputes: the two suspicious
principalities, their diplomats aflutter.
A soirée: men swallowtailed, their chests clink
with enameled bronze, wives brave in watered silk.
The situation comes down to a fight:
lines crossed at dawn, early communiqués,
hussars on scout, the new sun's soft pink haze,
algebraic salvos, feints to left or right. . . .

6. The Investiture of my Fortress as Ethnic Joke:

You, elusive, marched in backwards. I
(as Poland)
had thought you were
                    leaving. . . .

Kate Light

Five Urban Love Songs

I. Can One Think

Can one think, in sunglasses, in the park; think
with the children playing and the adult banter,
and someone smoking; and experiment, in ink,
through the invading dogs, and toddler-gallivanter—?
escape the *Ice-cold-beer-and-Snapple* hawking
and the ones who target you when you're alone,
and so they stare, or come over, *talking?*
But how can I (who've been rather accident-prone)
forget it was just that dappled fate-and-chance—
and perhaps the shade of arrogance—
that brought me *you?* and though I tried to shake
you off ("Don't bother me; I'm *mean*, I'm *grieving*")
the discouragement didn't seem to *take*—
so I came to accept that you weren't leaving.
Then I'll let these clowns distract me with their dance—
there's a weird wisdom in persistence—
I'll stick to my mount of grass and moss and clover,
writing things down, and thinking things over.

II. San Francisco

Pierced tongue. Do-it-yourself lisp.
What is this? Penitence? Native wisdom?
Mutilation? or signal: *I'll do anything.*
Was it a dare? or a careful plan? Did it sting—
or ache—and does the food get caught—
and should such a person *work* in a restaurant?
Customers' stomachs can turn—or does desire
turn to *her*—to wish—to feel the fire

glide over the silver (or is it gold?) pin?
And you, my darling, with your end-
less speculation: Is *he — is she — gay?*
Does he or she want you — or me — or either way?
Why do you need to know? I am *here*.
This is my body; eat. Unwrap. Disappear.

III. Portrait of David As/Not As a Refrigerator Magnet: Universal

appeal; the most beautiful stone to pull
the image from: *David*. David of the tilted head,
the hip slung into, the arm I lived to till
the underbelly of. On my pillow, on my bed,
your body, David, undressed and dressed . . .
Now who's this in *plastic* plastered against
the refrigerator door! Not David! on whom they've pressed
pants, T-shirt, shoes; now the penis can be fenced
in skivvies; heaven-on-earth, figleaf,
in sunglasses! What they have done or think
they've done — appropriation; in short, in brief:
anyone's. Possessed, asked, *Shall we have a drink
now or later? Your place or mine?*
to toast the front — to dream the spine . . .

IV. *Souvenir de Florence* . . . David Continues on His Way

David, outside the *Academia*, makes an appearance
on T-shirts, alongside Adam touching God
's hand. Down the block the pilgrims plod,
viewers of all ages, adherents
to all faiths, come to workshop or to gape:
"He's got a big one," a schoolgirl cries
in the interior, sunlit, space;
nearby, the Slaves' unfinished eyes . . .
Outside again, David "hung" on a postcard, sunglasses on the shaft: "Hi from Florence"
(it says) — *Wish you were here, love you, hon.*

Fascination and abhorrence —
yet I cannot resist reporting. (If we ever break up,
love, I want the Stonehenge coffee cup . . .)

V. Help Me — A Flashback

I turned to you as if to say: *Push him out!*
Touch me with your brave new hands; erase
him from my ribs, from my arms, from my face . . .
Let your lips be rain falling on the drought
in my body —
                Then I was reaching
(as if I *could*) and perhaps you were fooled
into thinking me ready to be pulled
away. You wanted me, and I was beseeching
you — *Then help me* (for I could make no better
offer — it was a start — than a promise to *try* —)
push him out! — but he pushed back and I would cry
and you would kiss and as my eyes grew wetter,
you would *know*; and become angry and empty and cold.
What could I tell you — but what was already told — ?

Nick Norwood

My Work with Ludwig II
Georg von Dollmann, the King's architect

I. Linderhof

We could have finished had he kept his mind
to this, a solitary gem, its mount
near Oberammergau, the home of wood-
carvers and Passion plays, of edelweiss,
and *lederhosen*'d peasants who loved the King.
They stage Christ's suffering, his death and res-
urrection, decennially, but these same
young men — a Son of God, a dozen disciples,
thieves, Romans, whores, et cetera — keep Ludwig's
picture pinned to their peasant-bloused chests
every day as they tramp about the woods
surrounding Linderhof.
                        Their mountain idyll,
it features terraced cascades carved in hillsides,
a fountain which on the hour lifts, lifts, lifts and holds
a shaft of water a hundred feet above
the stroller's head (high enough, I suppose,
for even the walled-out peasants to see),
magnificent rooms, a Moorish kiosk and a man-
made grotto with lake illuminated green
by lights below the water. Floating above:
a tiny boat in the shape of a giant shell
and scenes from *Tannhäuser* on the lighted walls.
A recess indeed for the weary.
                              Still, some ask,
*Is this fit place for a king, a man of state,
in a shell-shaped boat on an artificial lake?*
But I've seen him there, on summer afternoons

when Munich is all heat, dust and close air,
and even in the Alps the sky reflects
the paved bustle of cities: and so I tell
them, "Yes, from here a king may truly govern,
(if only peasants trained for parts in heaven)."

        II. Neuschwanstein

Capricious castle piercing the clouds
above the valley of the swans,
beloved fortress—it was built
by men, who for the time it took,
dwelt in worlds other than their own.
Indeed, it may become the model
for men who would spin deceptive webs
for children.   Ludwig grew up just
below in the family's alpine stronghold,
Schloss Hohenschwangau, whose stone blocks
are softened, held in check, by vines
relentlessly scaling its outer walls;
its chambers spellbound by frescoes
of Lohengrin's arrival at Antwerp,
his skiff drawn by a swan, maid Elsa's
deliverance from Telramund. . . .
I think it's safe to say he never
escaped that romance.   Years later, *insane*,
he was reciting lines from Schiller—
Don Carlos—"in a very loud voice,"
when Doctor Gudden came to call.
His henchmen were with him, burghers from
the Crown Council carrying a strait-
jacket. But peasants of the valley
got wind of the plot and armed themselves
with axes, knives, and stones to guard
their unsuspecting king, locked in
drama in the Minnesinger Hall.

The villains were quickly apprehended,
Füssen's honorable magistrate summoned,
and once the doctor had time to explain,
he and his bunch were tossed in the clink—
straight off! I've always had a deep
appreciation for Schiller myself:
fast-paced action, poetic justice.

III. Herrenchiemsee

Built on the Herreninsel, a wooded island
in the middle of a lake, this yet unfinished palace attempts to reproduce Versailles:
its gardens draw and frame with leaves and flowers;
its drawing rooms are gardens of fleurs-de-lis;
and even the hall of mirrors mimic its model,
dripping and dancing with light. We only lacked
some Louis (marks and francs!) to make our court
complete. The isle itself, enchanted thing,
crisscrossed this way and that by woodland paths
exquisite for walks in summer, is a place
of shade and mystery. Arriving there,
the King directed us to light some torches
and place them on the broader trails. He dressed
his servants (including me) as the footmen of
French kings, then later, in the darkest hours,
emerged as Louis XIV!
                On an island
in a lake, the middle of night: our king was swallowed
whole by dreams, visions. Taking a carriage ride
in grand French gear, beneath the forest limbs,
through dusky smells, now faint, now blazing light
of torches, we paraded paths till dawn. . . .
The final irony, construction ended
with a watery image: having drowned the doctor,
the King tried reaching the opposite shore,
perceiving safety in its gleaming castle,
but found himself, alas, unsuited for swimming.

Two Poems by Mark Scott

Touch

Close up, much too, ivory's surface like most
surfaces is nothing smooth. To the touch
in all particulars it's what the fresh
strawberry is to the tongue, cilia
bending at the buds after lunch. Specialists
in friction will tell you what pianists

with all of Mozart's sonatas in their heads
and hands will—except the ones who never
notice—that plastic slips and ivory catches,
the catch being what you want. To the touch:
everything is what it is to the touch,
algebra included, according to experts.

Skeptics to the contrary (unregistered
voters with unlisted numbers), we grant
the other hand as soon as we see the one.
Ivory will absorb what resin can't,
the heat of playing, the hands as they travel,
heightened, across the notes, beyond the scales

they're balanced in. Streets of asphalt, crashed on,
will scrape away a subtle register
and make a subtler, sometimes called a strawberry.
You have seen it: the injured party never
lets you touch. The days pass, though, and the hands
discover in another layer old

colors of the sun, a sheen on the pink
and outermost reach that holds a slight line
between what the world calls skin, and flesh.

The Scott Boys

Slapped by saplings, hampered by roots,
our shovels went like spoons into
mouths that opened wider as we worked.
The fort when we finished
was as cool to go down in
as a thimble for a fingertip.

But even when we dug all day,
we could still make out
from where we leveled off
the greenish-gray of house
above the cheatgrass
doubling over in the sun.

The mountains must've been
too far to reach by hand,
the elms not branched enough to climb.
We never knew we were doing anything
but digging a deeper hole
than the one we dug before.

Buildings went up;
we were building down,
like the Grand Canyon,
from an overrated sky;
and we hoped we'd see by digging
if maybe we couldn't find

a better place to be than upstairs —
solider, smaller, a backup
we could back down in.

"The Paris Review remains the single most important little magazine this country has produced."

— T. Coraghessan Boyle

THE PARIS REVIEW

Enclosed is my check for:

☐ $34 for 1 year (4 issues)
(All payment must be in U.S. funds. Postal surcharge of $10 per 4 issues outside USA)

☐ Send me information on becoming a *Paris Review* Associate.
Bill this to my Visa/MasterCard:
Sender's full name and address needed for processing credit cards.

_____
Card number   Exp. date

☐ New subscription   ☐ Renewal subscription
☐ New address

Name _____
Address _____
City _____ State _____ Zip code _____

Please send gift subscription to:
Name _____
Address _____
City _____ State _____ Zip code _____
Gift announcement signature _____
call (718)539-7085

Please send me the following:

☐ The Paris Review T-Shirt ($15.00)
   Color _____ Size _____ Quantity _____
☐ The following back issues: Nos. _____
   See listing at back of book for availability.

Name _____
Address _____
City _____ State _____ Zip code _____

☐ Enclosed is my check for $ _____
☐ Bill this to my Visa/MasterCard:

_____
Card number   Exp. date

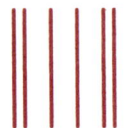

BUSINESS REPLY MAIL
FIRST CLASS   PERMIT NO. 3119   FLUSHING, N.Y.

POSTAGE WILL BE PAID BY ADDRESSEE

THE PARIS REVIEW
45-39 171 Place
FLUSHING NY   11358-9892

BUSINESS REPLY MAIL
FIRST CLASS   PERMIT NO. 3119   FLUSHING, N.Y.

POSTAGE WILL BE PAID BY ADDRESSEE

THE PARIS REVIEW
45-39 171 Place
FLUSHING NY   11358-9892

Three Poems by Brenda Shaughnessy

Afterlife, Her Empty Dress

I lie quiet among my possible suits,
feet to head, feet to head.
Blue, black, white, red.

I am grim at the waist, squandered
through the legs. Watch
with a turned-in face.

Lie with a design on my back, a spade
in clover. Been given
a flat of stone to line

my fortress, and a curtain of privacy
for your old sweet water.
Can you see me

on the other side of the jumpy garden
coiled out to you?
Blind as a wedding,

so white you're blue. Little fog queen,
without a corpse,
I take you peeled

too bright. I throw you starved of air.
I kiss you still warm,
colored with ash.

I leave you under a cloud, but I carve
you in night, that finer
edge, the old arc of your hand.

Parallax

Excluding genitalia,
What is a man?
A little boy all grown-up. A reverse neverland.

What is a woman?
Easier. She's a cipher, she hasn't been
decided yet. Also she's a queen.

If you are not here, you are not necessarily
there. Not yet.
Brown dwarfs are those sad bodies too bright

to be planets but too cool
to be stars. They lean into stars, nestled
and wary. To burn or to crust, both crisp

choices, but for this dead androgyne,
there's only Pandora's squeezebox, locked.
Come closer, toward the light.

Kitten, sixpack, magnolia,
a goose behind a desk. Please let us
find ourselves a suckhole forever.

I could never stop. I would never start again.
Bacon, bucket, queerbaby,
I am so big I will not smell you.

We all know Gaea and Apollo
never made it with each other. Territorial.
Brushfire. I have already expelled you,

and now have the luxury of knowing you
differently: perversely leonine
with a hex on your light-haired belly,

and swinging,
first dangerous, then fragile, then repulsive,
then repulsed.

Interior with Sudden Joy

after a painting by Dorothea Tanning

To come into my room is to strike strange.
My plum velvet pillow & my hussy spot
the only furniture.

Red stripes around my ankles, tight
as sisters. We are maybe fourteen, priceless
with gooseflesh.

Our melon bellies, our mouths of tar. Us four:
my mud legged sister, my bunched up self,
the dog & the whirligig just a prick on the eye.

We are all sewn in together, but the door is open.
The book is open too. You must write in red
like Jesus and his friends.

Be my other sister, we'll share a mouth.
We'll split the dress
down the middle, our home, our Caesarian.

When the Bishop comes he comes
diagonal, from the outside, & is a lie.
He comes to bless us all with cramps,

mole on the chin that he is,
to bring us the red something,
a glow, a pumping.

Not softly a rub with loincloth
& linseed. More of a beating,
with heart up the sleeve.

He says, *The air in here is tight & sore
but punctured, sudden, by a string quartet.*
We are! In these light years we've wrung a star.

I am small for my age.
Child of vixenwood, lover of the color olive
and its stain.

I live to leave, but I never either.
One leg is so long we can all walk it.
Outside is a thousand bitten skins

and civilization its own murder of crows.
I am ever stunned,
seduced whistle-thin

& hot with home. Breathless with
mercury, columbine. Come, let us miss
another wintertime.

Two Poems by Marc Woodworth

The City from a Field

He is looking at the city from a field,
    the flowers at his back elaborate symbols
        of some spurned reality:
    pinwheel semaphores, all petal and pistil,
the ghosts of spiked streetlights now sealed

and invisible in the urban tantric
    and this misremembered daylight.
        Only from this vantage —
    call it *the past* — does the streets'
multiform argument yield its false logic,

can the dialogue of smokestack and steeple sound audibly.
    Do you hear the singing of the distant revenants,
        see their somnambulant circuits,
    their routes buried like the tunnels of ants?
Their only meted fate is irreality.

As seen from here, the men of reason pass unseeing
    the men of spirit in the boulevards,
        a warmth moving through a coolness.
    Even in the bustling streets and railway yards
these walkers disappear in a spell of edges

and the rapt geometries of the perfect planes
    of sun-gilt facades, the unbroken phalanx
        of tall windows adamantine,
    beautiful as this field's thwarted blue phlox,
even the architecture's run of miles wanes

in the distance as perspective collapses
    on its way to the unalterable, unreachable apex
       and the biggest building on the block
    turns vaporous, a proof against its marble fact:
at this remove, the city as it is and will remain disappears.

The City from the Center

The workers labor in the emptied lot,
    the sweat of summer's aluminum noon
       tempering the dry glint of pick and shovel
    in the half-dug dirt of the new foundation,
the pressed layers where the past slept in oil and slate.

They turn and work in the crucible of the city
    straining their ropes of muscle to complete
       the undreamed equation of renewal and decline
    unsolved by the architect purged of shale and soot
at his clean table far from this brute whorl of activity.

No one looks up, the towering cranes of crossed iron,
    the crucifix and curtains in the empty windows
       unreal above the protest of the steel and stone,
    the city's receding fan of standing buildings slowed
and emptied by the hungers of this yawing pit of generation

    from which the new city rises and every made thing's context
       changes, new relations, unthought of, unseen
          by the faceless walkers behind the bulwarks,
       who pass incurious this world of levels and lumber, the
                                    clean
fill, the spun rays that turn beneath the mason's cart.

It is the dead who will soon inhabit the well-meant stories
                                                  still unbuilt,
        their offices now on floors of air, their desks at rest
            in ether, porous drawers of ink filled with nothing.
    The workers never see their buildings finished
or walk the polished marble, thralls instead to the economies
                                                        of silt.

They are stalled in the making of your city,
        shuttled to the next excavation with their shovels
            but unavailable as Romantic ciphers
        for your fantasy of a righted world or as devils
in the nightmares you claim have made your children dirty.

Try to see them more abstractly, not just sweat in the cotton
        of their thin shirts and their burnt whiskers of ash,
            but as backs and arms that turn to wings,
        beating toward no promised end, annihilating a specific
                                                            past
once dense with meaning, the invention of generations now
                                                    forgotten.

The Savant

Joyce Hackett

Signor Perso was the last person who knew who I'd been, and when I found him — naked but for his dressing gown, his white mustache perfectly groomed, his hands folded over the little volume on his chest as if he'd laid himself out for the occasion — my stomach fluttered in a moment of giddy, untethered possibility. Without thinking much I set my passport in the hotel ashtray and lit it on fire; before its flames withered, I had thrown on my clothes. But when I opened the door a flurry of ashes swirled up into the restive air, and instead of leaving, I rushed back to try and catch them before they could drift down onto his body. His utter stillness ridiculed my frantic, stupid groping until I quietly stood over him amidst the black snow. After a while, though I knew I shouldn't, I touched his face. My finger scudded against his dead cheek, and there I was, sitting on the bed in our pensione suite, stuck behind a wall he had sailed over effortlessly, without me, in his sleep.

I turned off the light and sat down. I unbuttoned my coat. There was no point, really, in fleeing. With my history it would only be quixotic not to expect this sort of thing, wherever I went. Even at the Milan airport, as Signor Perso had breezed through the checkpoint for Italian nationals, I'd gotten stuck standing in a line of Americans so long and stagnant it curled back onto itself like a tangled flystrip, and when I suddenly couldn't see him I was sure he'd died. Now, a fortnight later, I was not terribly surprised. I confirmed the pronunciations of *cadavere* and *coffina* in my handy plastic-coated dictionary and compiled a short list of new words I might now need. And while the Italian police put me on hold, I practiced his signature, over and over, until my scrawl matched the top of his traveler's checks.

There was one minor problem. I found Signor Perso in the middle of the night, and towards dawn, after hours of wrestling him into a suit and tie, I got horribly hungry. There were two eggs left in the tiny kitchenette refrigerator. I thought I should probably eat them. But I had never actually cooked breakfast, or any other meal. I had lived in hotels with my father, Yuri, since I was seven; when I wasn't touring, my mother cooked; and later on Signor Perso had insisted on making me breakfast in bed, every morning, because he had stroke-induced aphasia, kept losing the words for things, and the ritual of breakfast was a firth flowing surely towards memory. Still, I got out a spoon, determined to scramble the eggs. But something was wrong, stubborn gobs floated up to the surface no matter how hard I stirred. I thought I remembered from TV that you put milk in scrambled eggs, but there wasn't any milk, and now the eggs were gooey and ruined and I couldn't even boil them. For a minute everything started closing in. But then I held my breath to slow down my heart, the way I used to do just before I went on stage, and I calculated the number of minutes Signor Perso had now been dead. Once I had a number, I could breathe again. It was proof that time was passing, was not one moment stretched out in an infinite retard but a current, towing the moment away. I placed the ashtray of ashes and the bowl of egg goo on the shower floor, turned on the spigot and stepped under the water. After about an hour, when all evidence of the substances was gone, I took off my clothes and washed. When I had dressed again I sponged all trace of my ashen fingerprint from

Signor Perso's cheek. Then, as a flat slate light diffused the dark, I played to him.

No one heard me. For a number of years now I have muted my cello by wrapping a thick silk sash between the strings and around the bridge, and wedging its ends firmly into the *f*-holes. To save my ear from being dulled by too much sound. That was how it started, anyway. I used it on tour, to warm up for performances. The silence forced me inside, forced the music back up into my nervous system, until all the notes of a perfect performance played on my flesh, all at once. Then, in concert, the sound burst from my bow's slice like the flesh of an overripe plum.

In any case, I was not arrested. At dusk, after over sixteen hours — luckily my teacher had just bathed, and hardly smelled at all — a *commedia buffa* traipsed in. The bumbling carabinieri in their tricornered hats were surprisingly manageable; they seemed to feel that Signor Perso's Italian passport simplified his death. When they finally arrived, their flimsy interrogation was of limited duration. Once they ascertained that I was neither the wife nor the granddaughter they let the matter drop and took a protective, tactful stance. The only question directed towards me was the captain's greasy, expectant *Looks like my size?* as he fingered the hem of Signor Perso's pants, and even that was only provoked by the detective's astute observation that pleats that looked that good on a dead guy had to be Italian tailoring. I managed to avoid a confrontation that might have led to further questioning by declining to speak when, after several unsuccessful attempts to upend Signor Perso's body into the pensione's tiny elevator, they dropped him on the carpet, from waist height, and lit up: after a suitable caesura I simply walked out into the hall, picked up the cuff link that had rolled from Signor Perso's wrist, and set it atop the ashtray's tiny, pristine dune, thus forcing them to extinguish their cigarettes between their fingertips, and carry him down eight flights of stairs.

At the funeral, though, something happened. Something I never expected, even playing a cello as staggering as the

Savant. As I rocked the bow in a balance exercise, I tried to remember the last time I had played aloud, unmuted, in the company of a live being. I could not. Worse, my world-famous cello was nothing like I expected. Its voice was trapped within its body, it sounded wooden and unresponsive, like a cello wrapped in a cocoon. Its ancient bridge was parched and shrunken, the action way too low. The strings buzzed every time I shifted; they were unwrapped steel and they cut into the pads of my fingers. The sonority was hideous. It sounded like the bass board was coming unglued.

Together we spun out a weakish, introspective, almost mousy sound. The muscles in my bowing arm were somewhat, well, completely gone from playing muted for so long; the precision of movement needed to bring out a decent tone was wildly beyond their atrophy. I cramped my hand trying to bow hard enough to fill the Romanesque basilica; but I couldn't get the heroic attack of a Strad or a Montagnana. What a joke, I thought, the old saw about instruments picking up the sound of their former owners—if the Savant had absorbed any patterning from its years of being played by Vrashkansova, its wood had long since ceased to resonate at her frequency. I was having so much trouble manipulating it that I was practically leg-wrestling the thing. But then I somehow pulled off a phrase a bit like the way Vrashkansova did it on that old Victor 78 of her last public recital, in Prague, in 1937. It slid out without my doing, as if she had suddenly reached up from the dead to grasp my bowing hand. Everything became different then, the way someone's looks change completely when you fall in love with them. I stopped trying to play well, and I stopped trying to play loud. I gave in. Suddenly the Savant's laryngitis took on texture and mystery. I was playing the Fauré *Élégie*, and for a second, for literally just an instant, I heard a sound so round and deep, so full of air and space, that I shut my eyes and forgot the death.

Vrashkansova was Signor Perso's idol; in Paris, just before the war, he had taken a master class with her that he said had changed his life. In photos she wore dark mourning dresses; she was tiny, always slightly hunched; you had the feeling she carried the weight of the world on the small hump that peeked out from between her shoulders. On the recordings her low voice hovers behind the Savant like a mourner at a wake, quietly chanting the ritual lament. Music resonated through her body, and took physical control. What I heard was beyond even her, a voice so sacred and whole that I began to wonder whether an inanimate object could possess the spirit of God. A long still spell opened where each note came in slow motion. Phrases fell like ribbons.

Signor Perso's leftover confidence, his huge memory of hearing me as a child, had been crushing me for years. The longer he held fast to his faith in me, the more ashamed I was to make a sound, until finally I'd just stopped making them. Now, after eleven years, I poured out effortlessly into every corner of the octagonal dome and in its side chapels. All at once, sound saturated the air. When I drew back my bow I felt the tension on it, felt it pulling the breath out of the audience. A frisson of old excitement jolted through me. I wondered what he'd say.

It had not really occurred to me, until that moment, how enormously *dead* Signor Perso actually was. My gut sucked down—like a plane door opening, midair—and when I came back the piece was nearly over, I was outside the cello and outside my playing, the breath seeped out of the music, the sound straight and hard and too correct. What followed was the usual disaster: half of me rushed towards the end, dying to get it over, while the other half was seized by a terrible urge to go back and start from the beginning. But the music was gone, shriveled back onto its score, to flat staves and clusters of spots as tiny and anonymous as the dark-veiled widows dotting the wooden pews.

Performance is final, final the way things are that burn up time. A great performance is precious for just that reason, that it can never be repeated: but because *I* was performing—the wilted wünderkind heard herself—this chewed-over epiphany freighted each note with a heavy-handed finality, a wheedling undertone of romanticism at its cheapest, until it was all I could do to clench onto the sounding of the notes.

The eleven days Signor Perso and I had been in Milan had been the coldest anyone could remember. The morning of the service, as I was dressing for my interview at the Petywards', the owner of the pensione near the Brera where Signor Perso and I had been staying had banged on the door and demanded money; so I had put on my best black dress, not my warmest outfit, because I knew that no matter what happened at the interview, I couldn't come back before the memorial, or indeed, ever again. Now, standing in the little piazza in front of the church, I was freezing. I had thought that after I performed, someone at the memorial would offer me a ride; as I was leaving I had carried the cello awkwardly, with the bulge facing in, like a TV actor playing a cellist: I've been lugging a cello continuously since I was four and have to do this to seem at all helpless. But what had happened on the platform was the kind of private transcendence that is embarrassing to watch. And only six people had shown up; I didn't know any of them, and none of them knew me; in Italy familiarity and introductions count for a lot. Also, as the church-mouse organist drooled out the end of the *Élégie* on his abysmal spinet piano, I had stopped playing midphrase and walked off the platform. Which may have been a factor.

There were no taxis. It was a Saturday evening, but other than the triumphal statue of Augustus presiding over an absurdly grandiose Roman colonnade, the streets were empty. Fog curdled above the gray heaps of snow. Another snowstorm was forecast for later that night, but the air was still too wet for snow, wet with that cold that enters and takes root. I stood in the deserted piazza deciding what to do, while not deciding anything. In a lovely post-performance coda, the theme from Schubert's *Unfinished* came on in my head and cloyed there. Suddenly, in front of the long colonnade, a rusty tram squealed up like a cattle car. I realized I had been standing outside the basilica for a half hour. I was freezing. It was headed through a huge arch in the ancient city wall. This seemed like the wrong direction. As the tram hurtled into the dark a spark ignited a vast overhead web of wires which I hadn't noticed. It occurred to me that I had never *been* on a tram. It would cost money. I hoisted up the cello and headed in the other direction. It did occur to me, as I started to walk, that someone might try to steal the instrument. Several doughy, touristic librarians in the States had helpfully cautioned that in Italy, everybody steals everything. But one strategy for managing disaster involves walking towards it, daring it to happen. If I carried the Savant on foot, I thought, I would look like a student. I looked scruffy, a bit unkempt; no one would speculate very long about what I had inside my scuffed, brown, hard-shell case. From the looks I'd gotten on the street, I'd understood that the notion that a young woman with puffy eyes and tacky American clothes could be carrying a rare, sixteenth-century cello, let alone one of the thirty-eight instruments that Charles IX ordered from Andrea Amati in the early 1560s, was not within their realm of stylistic possibility. That I would have *the* Amati, the *freak* Amati, sized wrong and completed in error, the only one he made that both swelled with the warmth and complexity of the best cognac in France—Amati's signature tone—but also had the burn of it, the acoustics for a modern hall, the caterwaul of a Strad—this notion was pretty much outside the range of possibility to a bunch of people who seemed so inundated with style and beauty, with *class*, that they seemed to have inbred out the gene for depth perception.

Besides, at the memorial, just before I began playing, I had calculated that I had passed the three-day anniversary, in minutes, of Signor Perso's death. This I took as a sign I was surviving. To make matters worse, I was under the spell of the kind of absurd yet practical thinking that subtly undermines everything during a crisis: in spite of the bitter cold, in spite of the instrument I was carrying, though I was wearing stockings, though everything was icy, it seemed an ingenious plan to save the taxi money, which was the last of Signor Perso's money, and try to walk.

For as long as I can remember, exposure to cold has pitched

me close to hysteria. That pain's petty tyranny, the tiny focus it exacts, exceeds my interest in the quotidian. But I didn't panic immediately. The blocky neoclassical facades all looked familiar, and though that morning Mr. Petyward had sent his limo to pick me up, and I had barely seen anything through the tinted glass windows, I wandered through Milan's twisting streets expecting his apartment to somehow turn up. I was even congratulating myself for hiking over the heaps of plowed snow when I looked up through the undulating, arrow-topped gate guarding the archways of a tiny courtyard and recognized the square, fat, rough-hewn tower of the old Roman circus that Signor Perso had pointed out. I realized I was nowhere near the Petywards'. I did not, in fact, have their address. I had left it at the pensione. It suddenly got much colder. I sprinted out into the big cross-street, to get as far as I could before my knowledge expired.

But my heel caught in some tram tracks. And I tripped, on my own cello. And once I knew I was falling I let go and fell like a dead body falls.

Charles Wright

Black Zodiac

Darkened by time, the masters, like our memories, mix
And mismatch,
               and settle about our lawn furniture, like air
Without a meaning, like air in its clear nothingness.
What can we say to either of them?
How can they be so dark and so clear at the same time?
They ruffle our hair,
               they ruffle the leaves of the August trees.
Then stop, abruptly as wind.
The flies come back, and the heat —
               what can we say to them?
Nothing is endless but the sky.
The flies come back, and the afternoon
Teeters a bit on its green edges,
               then settles like dead weight
Next to our memories, and the pale hems of the masters'
   gowns.

•

Those who look for the Lord will cry out in praise of him.
Perhaps. And perhaps not —
               dust and ashes though we are,
Some will go wordlessly, some
Will listen their way in with their mouths
Where pain puts them, an inch-and-a-half above the floor.
And some will revile him out of love
               and deep disdain.
The gates of mercy, like an eclipse, darken our undersides.
Rows of gravestones stay our steps,
               August humidity

Bright as auras around our bodies.
And some will utter the words,
                    speaking in fear and tongues,
Hating their garments splotched by the flesh.
These are the lucky ones, the shelved ones, the twice-erased.

                              •

Dante and John Chrysostom
Might find this afternoon a sidereal roadmap,
A pilgrim's way . . .
                    You might too
Under the pre-jaundiced outline of the quarter moon,
Clouds sculling downsky like a narrative for *whatever comes*,
What *hasn't happened to happen yet*
Still lurking behind the stars,
                         31 August 1995 . . .
The afterlife of insects, space graffiti, white holes
In the landscape,
                such things, such avenues, lead to dust
And handle our hurt with ease.
Sky blue, blue of infinity, blue
                         waters above the earth:
Why do the great stories always exist in the past?

                              •

The unexamined life's no different from
                              the examined life —
Unanswerable questions, small talk,
Unprovable theorems, long-abandoned arguments —
You've got to write it all down.
Landscape or waterscape, light-length on evergreen, dark sidebar
Of evening,
           you've got to write it down.
Memory's handkerchief, death's dream and automobile,
God's sleep,
           you've still got to write it down,

Moon half-empty, moon half-full,
Night starless and egoless, night blood-black and prayer-black,
Spider at work between the hedges,
Last bird call,
            toad in a damp place, tree frog in a dry . . .

        •

We go to our graves with secondary affections,
Second-hand satisfaction, half-souled,
            star charts demagnetized.
We go in our best suits. The birds are flying. Clouds pass.
Sure we're cold and untouchable,
            but we harbor no ill will.
No tooth tuned to resentment's fork,
            we're out of here, and sweet meat.
Calligraphers of the disembodied, God's word-wards,
What letters will we illuminate?
Above us, the atmosphere,
The nothing that's nowhere, signs on, and waits for our
  beck and call.
Above us, the great constellations sidle and wince,
The letters undarken and come forth,
Your X and my X.
            The letters undarken and they come forth.

        •

Eluders of memory, nocturnal sleep of the greenhouse,
Spirit of slides and silences,
            Invisible Hand,
Witness and walk on.
Lords of the discontinuous, lords of the little gestures,
Succor my shift and save me . . .
All afternoon the rain has rained down in the mind,
And in the gardens and dwarf orchard.
            All afternoon

The lexicon of late summer has turned its pages
Under the rain,
                abstracting the necessary word.
Autumn's upon us.
The rain fills our narrow beds.
Description's an element, like air or water.
                                  That's the word.

James Cummins

Schindler's List

A man makes a film.
He is a Jew, a midwestern
Jew, from Cincinnati.
He knows as much as I do
about the Holocaust,

learned the same way:
newsreels, mostly, film—
the power of the image
on celluloid eclipsing
the power of the word.

Already, we are brothers,
brothers in the facile.
Yet he did not forget, or
not hear the word spoken
in his grandmother's kitchen,

the parlor where Grandpa
rocked and smoked. He
remembered, and when time
came for him to turn his
face to God for forgiveness—

if only for his films—
like so many of us he
faltered first, then turned.
He did not stand free,
speaking only to the sky,

his tears falling back
to earth—anyway, hadn't
DeMille done all that?—
but wherever he stood or sat,
or bent and moaned,

wherever he prayed to be
allowed to speak, to show
the beautiful dead eyes
that he, too, remembers,
that he, too, loves:

wherever this goes on
in him, it goes on in me,
too. Always, we are
brothers in the facile
humiliations, not

history's. Afterwards,
he will take a girl
to a party on a yacht—
who knows what a man
so rich can do? And I

will go my way, not
rich, in love with failure.
Yet he is humiliated,
too, no one is spared
in this century, and I

should love myself,
what gods I know tell
me: I know it's true.
But the world that made
him, made me, too.

Edward Nobles

Architectural Digest

   Whose woods these are I think I know . . .

I take her, painless, through the glass.
Her dress tears off. I covet that.
The glass is beautiful, sharp and steep—
the way the cracks just stop. At the table's feet.

Each wooden leg curls into a lion's paw.
Escorted by toes, in the center, a claw
that rips into the carpet, but will not tear.
I love the dress; I hold it near.

The neighbor's house, through glass, is gray.
No windows this side; they face that way.
In a magazine on the window's ledge,
where in the binding glass shards wedge,

I see a church in construction—no steeple.
Its glass, stained, looks lethal.
I want the dress to touch upon the glass.
I'm lost inside design, the magazine and Mass.

Baron Wormser

Shoplifting

The store dick lays a hand on your shoulder
Three steps from the exit. He asks what's
In your pockets but it's more like a statement
Than a question. Two candy bars and a roll of film.

Your stomach melts and your heart starts to beat
Like when you used to race on the playground.
He tells you to sit down on the bench by the doors.
Usually there are some old people sitting there

Gabbling about bargains but no one's around
This late in the evening. You expect the manager
To show up and give you a lecture about kids
Nowadays but he doesn't

And when the cop appears he doesn't say
Anything special beyond you'll have to go to court.
When he gives you the paper he's almost smiling
Or he's not there at all, he's not seeing you.

Thoughts, thoughts . . . your head's raw dough
One moment, light as a balloon the next.
They're always playing a song in the background
In these stores that you can't quite identify.

Your foot's tapping to the vacant beat
And after the cop leaves and you
Can leave you don't for some minutes.
You don't even own a camera.

Initial draft
Conception 8:IV:1956
            occured during a long talk
            with HASEGAWA Saburo on Sesshu.

8:V:1956
"Essay on Landscape Painting" will be:
The human eye, the thing perceived, the
art of brush and again the thing, the
naked eye; the seawater bubble in the
skull that sees; a bead in the chain
that is! Man is Nature looking at itself —
evolved to have an eye to see.
                                    → another
                                    nebulous string image

"Must a man see all mountains and seas
to love them?" Isonokami a yakatsugu   how'd he get
                                         into a
                              Keene I p 163   one dim.
                                         ; rep hu image —

Sokei-an's Commentary on Rinzai:
    "It has been said by one of the ancients:
    'Mountains, rivers, and the great earth
    are our home whither we finally
    return'"

×1±y for Floods it shd be: COLUMBIA MĀ

A manuscript page from Mountains and Rivers Without End *by Gary Snyder.*

Gary Snyder
The Art of Poetry LXXIV

Gary Snyder is a rarity in the United States: an immensely popular poet whose work is taken seriously by other poets. He is America's primary poet-celebrant of the wilderness, poet-exponent of environmentalism and Zen Buddhism, and poet-citizen of the Pacific Rim — the first American poet to gaze almost exclusively west toward the East, rather than east toward Western civilization. A Snyder poem is instantly recognizable, and often imitated badly: an idiosyncratic combination of the plain speech of Williams, the free-floating, intensely visual images of Pound and the documentary information of both; the West Coast landscape first brought to poetry by Robinson Jeffers and Kenneth Rexroth; the precise and unallegorized observation of everyday life of the classical Chinese poets; and the orality of Snyder's fellow Beats.

He may well be the first American poet since Thoreau to devote a great deal of thought to the way one ought to live, and to make his own life one of the possible models. In person, he is full of humor and surprisingly undogmatic, with the charisma of one who seems to have already considered long and hard whatever one asks him. Snyder is an encyclopedia of things, both natural and artificial: what they are, how they were made, what they are used for, how they work. Then he quickly places that thing into a system that is ecological in its largest sense. Now in his mid-sixties, he would be a likely choice for a personal sage: sharp, wise, enthusiastic and an unexpectedly good listener.

Gary Snyder was born in San Francisco in 1930 and moved shortly after to the Pacific Northwest. Growing up in Washington state, he worked on his parents' farm and seasonally in the woods. He graduated in 1951 from Reed College with a degree in literature and anthropology. After a semester of linguistics study at Indiana University, he transferred to the University of California at Berkeley as a graduate student of Oriental languages, and became actively involved in the burgeoning West Coast poetry scene.

In the summer of 1955, Snyder worked on a trail crew in Yosemite National Park and began to write the first poems that he felt were truly his. That fall, he participated in the famous Six Gallery reading — featuring the first performance of Ginsberg's "Howl" — which launched the Beat movement. (Snyder appears as the character Japhy Ryder in Kerouac's The Dharma Bums.*)*

In 1956, he left the U.S. for what was to become a twelve-year residence abroad, largely in Japan. In Kyoto he pursued an intensive Zen Buddhist practice. During this period he also worked in the engine room of a tanker traveling along the Pacific Rim, and spent six months in India with Ginsberg and several others, where they had a notable discussion of hallucinogens with the Dalai Lama. In 1958, his translation of Han Shan's work, Cold Mountain Poems, *appeared. His first book of poetry,* Riprap, *was published in Japan in 1959. This was followed by* Myths & Texts *(1960) and the two pamphlets published by the Four Seasons Foundation in 1965 that gained him a wide readership:* Riprap and Cold Mountain

Poems *and* Six Sections from Mountains and Rivers Without End. *The first trade edition of his poetry,* The Back Country, *appeared in 1968.*

Snyder returned to the United States in 1969 to build a house in the foothills of the northern Sierra Nevada, where he still lives today in a family household that balances modern and archaic technologies. He continues to travel widely, reading poetry and lecturing on Buddhism, the environment and bioregional issues. He works with the local Yuba Watershed Institute, and since 1985 has been teaching at the University of California at Davis, where he helped to form a nature and culture discipline.

His essays have been collected in Earth House Hold *(1969);* The Practice of the Wild *(1990) and* A Place in Space *(1995). The poetry he has written since his return to the U.S. has been collected in* The Back Country *(1968);* Regarding Wave *(1970);* Turtle Island, *which won the Pulitzer Prize in 1975;* Axe Handles *(1983);* Left Out in the Rain *(1986); and a selected poems,* No Nature *(1992). In 1996, he published the completed version of* Mountains and Rivers Without End, *the long poem he had begun forty years before.*

The interview took place before an audience at the Unterberg Poetry Center of the 92nd Street Y in New York City on October 26, 1992 and was later updated. What the transcript doesn't show is how often the conversation was punctuated by laughter. We began with some talk about the imminent presidential election and then turned to the question of poets and political power. Questions were then invited from the audience.

INTERVIEWER

When Jerry Brown of California was running for president, people were kidding you that if he were elected, you would be named Secretary of the Interior. Now, the thing that interests me about this is that you are the only poet in America for whom there is any scenario, no matter how far-fetched, of actually entering into real political power. Is this something you think poets ought to do? Would you do it?

GARY SNYDER
I've never thought seriously about that question. Probably not, although I am foolish enough to think that if I did do it, I'd do it fairly well, because I'm pretty single-minded. But you don't want to be victimized by your lesser talents. One of my lesser talents is that I am a good administrator, so I really have to resist being drawn into straightening things out. The work I see for myself remains on the mythopoetic level of understanding the interface of society, ecology and language, and I think it is valuable to keep doing that.

INTERVIEWER
But it is abnormal for poets not to be involved in the state. The United States remains an exception to most of the rest of the world, where poets commonly have served as diplomats or as bureaucrats in some ministry.

SNYDER
Oh true. The whole history of Chinese poetry is full of great poets who played a role in their society. Indeed, I do too. I am on committees in my county. I have always taken on some roles that were there for me to take in local politics, and I believe deeply in civic life. But I don't think that as a writer I could move on to a state or national scale of politics and remain a writer. My choice is to remain a writer.

INTERVIEWER
Let's get on to the writing and go back forty years or so. One of the amazing things about your work is that you seemed to burst on the scene fully formed with *Riprap* and *Cold Mountain Poems*, which were published in 1959 and 1958 but written earlier in the fifties when you were in your twenties. The poems in both books are unmistakably Snyder poems, and apparently, unlike the rest of us, you are not embarrassed by the work of your youth, for you picked eighteen of the twenty-three poems in *Riprap* for your *Selected Poems*.

SNYDER

Actually the poems in *Riprap* are not the poems of my youth. Those are the poems that I've kept because those were the ones I felt were the beginning of my life as a poet. I started writing poems when I was fifteen. I wrote ten years of poetry before *Riprap*. Phase one: romantic teenage poetry about girls and mountains.

INTERVIEWER

You're still writing that!

SNYDER

I realized I shouldn't have said that as soon as the words were out of my mouth. I would like to think that they are not romantic poems but classical poems about girls and mountains. The first poet that touched me really deeply, as a poet, was D.H. Lawrence, when I was fifteen. I had read *Lady Chatterley's Lover* and I thought that was a nifty book, so I went to the library to see what else he had written, and there was something called *Birds, Beasts and Flowers*. I checked that out. I was disappointed to find out that it wasn't a sexy novel, but read the poems anyway, and it deeply shaped me for that moment in my life.

And then phase two, college. Poems that echoed Yeats, Eliot, Pound, Williams and Stevens. A whole five years of doing finger exercises in the modes of the various twentieth-century masters. All of that I scrapped, only a few traces of that even survive. I threw most of them in a burning barrel when I was about twenty-five.

So when I wrote the first poems in *Riprap* it was after I had given up poetry. I went to work in the mountains in the summer of 1955 for the U.S. Park Service as a trail crew laborer, and had already started classical Chinese study. I thought I had renounced poetry. Then I got out there and started writing these poems about the rocks and blue jays. I looked at them. They didn't look like any poems that I had ever written before. So I said, these must be my own poems. I date my work as a poet from the poems in *Riprap*.

INTERVIEWER

What got you back to poetry at that moment? Was it primarily the landscape?

SNYDER

No, it just happened. What got me back to poetry was that I found myself writing poems that I hadn't even intended to write.

INTERVIEWER

And what poets were important to you then? Who were the masters at this point?

SNYDER

When I was twenty-two or twenty-three, I began working with Chinese and found myself being shaped by what I was learning from Chinese poetry, both in translation and in the original. And I had been reading Native American texts and studying linguistics.

INTERVIEWER

What were you finding in Chinese poetry at that time?

SNYDER

The secular quality, the engagement with history, the avoidance of theology or of elaborate symbolism or metaphor, the spirit of friendship, the openness to work and, of course, the sensibility for nature. For me it was a very useful balancing force to set beside Sidney, *The Faerie Queene*, Renaissance literature, Dante. The occidental tradition is symbolic, theological and mythological, and the Chinese is paradoxically more, shall we say, modern, in that it is secular in its focus on history or nature. That gave me a push.

INTERVIEWER

Were you getting the ideogramic method from Pound or from the Chinese poetry directly?

SNYDER

From the Chinese poetry directly. I could never make sense of that essay by Pound. I already knew enough about Chinese characters to realize that in some ways he was off, and so I never paid much attention to it. What I found in Pound were three or four dozen lines in the *Cantos* that are stunning—unlike anything else in English poetry—which touched me deeply and to which I am still indebted.

INTERVIEWER

Pound as a landscape poet?

SNYDER

No, as an ear. As a way of moving the line.

INTERVIEWER

Since we are talking about Chinese poetry I wanted to ask you about the Han Shan translations, *Cold Mountain Poems*. It is curious because Chinese poetry is so canonical, and Han Shan is not in the canon. I think at the time there were people who thought that you made him up. I wondered how you discovered him?

SNYDER

Well, he is only non-canonical for Europeans and Americans. The Chinese and the Japanese are very fond of Han Shan, and he is widely known in the Far East as an eccentric and as possibly the only Buddhist poet that serious Far Eastern *littérateurs* would take seriously. They don't like the rest of Buddhist poetry—and for good reason, for the most part.

To give you an example: in 1983 I was in China with a party of American writers—Toni Morrison, Allen Ginsberg, Harrison Salisbury, William Gass, Francine du Plessix Grey and others—and we were introduced to some members of the Politburo upstairs in some huge building. The woman who was our simultaneous interpreter introduced me to these bureau members—I am embarrassed to say I don't remember who these impressive Chinese persons were—by saying, "He is the one who translated Han Shan." They instantly started loosening up, smiling and quoting lines from Han Shan in Chinese to me. He is well known. So whose canon are we talking about?

INTERVIEWER

You haven't continued to translate much. Was this just something you felt you should do at the moment but that later there was too much other work to do?

SNYDER

There is a line somewhere—is it Williams who says it?— "You do the translations. I can sing." Rightly or wrongly, I took that somehow, when I ran into it, as a kind of an instruction to myself, not to be drawn too much into doing translation. I love doing Chinese translations, and I have done more that I haven't published, including the longest *shih* in Chinese, the *Ch'ang-hen ko*, "The Long Bitter Song" of Po Chü-i. So I am not just translating these tiny things. I am working right now on finishing up the *P'i-p'a hsing*, the other long Po Chü-i poem about the woman who plays the lute. And I've done a few T'ang poems. Maybe someday I'll get to doing more Chinese translations.

INTERVIEWER

Getting back to the early poems: it's interesting that the American West is essentially invented in literary American poetry by two of your immediate predecessors, Robinson Jeffers and Kenneth Rexroth. Did you feel that they opened it up for you somehow, made it acceptable to write about?

SNYDER

Definitely. Jeffers and Rexroth both, as you say, were the only two poets of any strength who had written about the landscapes of the American West, and it certainly helped give me the courage to start doing the same myself.

INTERVIEWER

What about the community of poets at the time? Philip Whalen, Lew Welch, Allen Ginsberg, Michael McClure, Robert Duncan, among others. One gets the sense that this was the only community of poets in which you were an active participant, that since that time you've been involved in other things. How important is a community of poets to you or to any poet? And what has happened since?

SNYDER

I think that rather than the term *community* it would be more accurate to speak of a *network* of poets. *Community* is more properly applied to diverse people who live in the same place and who are tied together by their inevitable association with each other, and their willingness to engage in that over a long period of time. But that is just a quibble.

When you are in your twenties, in particular, and you are a working, dissenting intellectual and artist, you need nourishment. Up in Portland, where I went to college, there were only a couple of other people you could talk to about poetry—Philip Whalen and Lew Welch and William Dickey. We started hearing little echoes of things in California and ended up there, all of us—for the comradeship, for the exchange of ideas. That was before the Beat generation broke onto the scene. I met Jack Spicer, Robin Blaser, Robert Duncan, Madeline Gleason, Tom Parkinson, Josephine Miles, William Everson, Kenneth Rexroth—that whole wonderful circle of San Francisco Renaissance people, such brilliant minds, such dedication to the art and such unashamed radical politics. Most of them were conscientious objectors in World War II, had rejected Stalinism early on, and with Kenneth Rexroth had formulated an antistatist, neoanarchist political philosophy, anarcho-pacifism, which at that time in American history made great sense. I was proud to be part of that circle at that time.

That group was enlarged when Allen Ginsberg and Jack Kerouac came onto the scene and the phenomenon that we are more commonly aware of as the San Francisco Beat generation poetry emerged. But it came out of that group of Duncan, Spicer, Rexroth and Blaser that was already eight or ten years old — it wasn't just created by Allen and his friends. Through Allen I began to meet people from the East Coast. I met Kenneth Koch, Ed Sanders, Anne Waldman, Jerome Rothenberg, Don Hall, James Laughlin, Robert Creeley, Ed Dorn and many others. I still keep in touch with many of them. A wonderful circle.

INTERVIEWER

Has the Beat thing been a burden for the rest of your life? Are you tired of hearing about the Beats?

SNYDER

I was for a while, but nobody has been beating me on the head with it lately.

INTERVIEWER

I am surprised that very young people now are so fascinated by the Beats, compared to the hippie movement. As an old hippie I think we're much more interesting. What do you think they see in the Beats?

SNYDER

Gee, I don't know if I should say this to you. When I look at the differences, one that emerges is that the political stance of the West Coast Beats was clear. They were openly political and, in terms of the Cold War, it was a kind of a pox-on-both-your-houses position. Clearly our politics were set against the totalitarianism of the Soviet Union and China, and at the same time would have no truck with corporate capitalism. Today you might say, "Okay what else is new? Do you have any solutions to suggest?" I understand that, of course, but at that time the quality of our dissent alone was enough to push things in a slightly new direction. What it led to in the poetry was a populist spirit, a willingness to reach out for an audience and an engagement with the public of the United

States. This swell of poetry readings, going to all of the college towns and the big cities, which started around 1956, transformed American poetry. It was a return to orality and the building of something closer to a mass audience.

I do feel that there was a visionary political and intellectual component in the hippie phenomenon, but it is harder to track out what it is. It wasn't so clearly spoken and it was outrageously utopian, whereas the Beat generation's political stance was in retrospect more pragmatic, more hardheaded, easier to communicate, and it didn't rely on so much spiritual rhetoric. So that might be one reason, just as the punks rejected hippie spiritual rhetoric and went for a harder-edged politics, well, the Beat generation had a harder-edged politics.

INTERVIEWER

As long as we're talking about hippies, what about drugs? Obviously in the fifties and sixties you experimented with hallucinogens. Did it help or hurt the writing? Tear down obstacles or erect new ones? Or was it ultimately irrelevant?

SNYDER

That's a whole topic in itself, that deserves its own time. I'll just say that I am grateful that I came to meet with peyote, psilocybin, LSD and other hallucinogens in a respectful and modest frame of mind. I was suitably impressed by their powers, I was scared a few times, I learned a whole lot and I quit when I was ahead.

INTERVIEWER

Going back—you basically left the scene in 1956 to go to Japan.

SNYDER

In May of 1956 I sailed away in an old ship, headed across the Pacific for Japan.

INTERVIEWER

Why did you go? It seems like it was an exciting moment in America when you left.

SNYDER

Well, exciting as the scene was looking in 1956, I was totally ready to go to Japan. I had laid plans to go to the Far East, oh, three years prior to that, and had had several setbacks. The State Department denied me a passport for some of my early political connections.

INTERVIEWER

Would you have gone to China if the political situation had been different at the time?

SNYDER

I certainly would have.

INTERVIEWER

It would have completely changed the course of the rest of your life.

SNYDER

I'm sure it would have changed my life, although I don't know just how much, because my focus in going to the Far East was the study of Buddhism, not to find out if socialism would work, and the only Buddhists I would have found in China would have been in hiding at that time and probably covered with bruises. So it wouldn't have been a good move.

INTERVIEWER

I get the sense that you are much more attracted to Chinese poetry than Japanese poetry.

SNYDER

To some extent that's true. It is a karmic empathy that is inexplicable. I love Japanese literature and Japanese poetry too, but I feel a deep resonance with Chinese poetry.

INTERVIEWER
You stayed in Japan for ten years?

SNYDER
I was resident in Japan for about ten years, and I maintained residence there for twelve. I was away part of the time working on oil tankers and teaching at the University of California-Berkeley for a year.

INTERVIEWER
And how many years were you in the monastery there?

SNYDER
I was in and out of the monastery. That was where my teacher lived, and I was resident in it for *sesshin*—for meditation weeks—and then out, then in again. I had a little house that I rented just five minutes walk from the Daitoku-ji monastery.

INTERVIEWER
Are you still a practicing Buddhist? Do you sit every day?

SNYDER
Almost every day. *Zazen* becomes a part of your life, a very useful and beautiful part of your life—a wonderful way to start the day by sitting for at least twenty, twenty-five minutes every morning with a little bit of devotional spirit. My wife and I are raising a thirteen-year-old adopted daughter. When you have children you become a better Buddhist too, because you have to show them how to put the incense on the altar and how to make bows and how to bow to their food and so forth. That is all part of our culture, so we keep a Buddhist culture going. My grown sons say, when they are asked what they are, because they were raised that way, "Well, we are ethnic Buddhists. We don't know if we really believe it or not, but that is our culture."

INTERVIEWER

What does *zazen* do for the poetry? Do you feel that there is a relation there that helps somehow in the writing?

SNYDER

I was very hesitant to even think about that for many years, out of a kind of gambler's superstition not to want to talk too much or think too much about the things that might work for you or might give you luck. I'm not so superstitious anymore, and to demystify *zazen* Buddhist meditation, it can be said that it is a perfectly simple, ordinary activity to be silent, to pay attention to your own consciousness and your breath, and to temporarily stop listening or looking at things that are coming in from the outside. To let them just pass through you as they happen. There's no question that spending time with your own consciousness is instructive. You learn a lot. You can just watch what goes on in your own mind, and some of the beneficial effects are you get bored with some of your own tapes and quit playing them back to yourself. You also realize—I think anyone who does this comes to realize—that we have a very powerful visual imagination and that it is very easy to go totally into visual realms where you are walking around in a landscape or where any number of things can be happening with great vividness. This taught me something about the nature of thought and it led me to the conclusion—in spite of some linguists and literary theorists of the French ilk—that language is not where we start thinking. We think before language, and thought-images come into language at a certain point. We have fundamental thought processes that are pre-linguistic. Some of my poetry reaches back to that.

INTERVIEWER

You've written that language is wild, and it's interesting that, in your essays and in some of the poems, you track down words as though you're hunting or gathering. But do you believe that language is more a part of nature than a part of culture?

SNYDER

Well, to put it quite simply, I think language is, to a great extent, biological. And this is not a radical point of view. In fact, it is in many ways an angle of thought that has come back into serious consideration in the world of scientific linguistics right now. So, if it's biological, if it's part of our biological nature to be able to learn language, to master complex syntax effortlessly by the age of four, then it's part of nature, just as our digestion is part of nature, our limbs are part of nature. So, yes, in that sense it is. Now of course, language takes an enormous amount of cultural shaping, too, at some point. But the structures of it have the quality of wild systems. Wild systems are highly complex, cannot be intellectually mastered — that is to say they're too complex to master simply in intellectual or mathematical terms — and they are self-managing and self-organizing. Language is a self-organizing phenomenon. Descriptive linguistics come after the fact, an effort to describe what has already happened. So if you define the wild as self-managing, self-organizing and self-propagating, all natural human languages are wild systems. The imagination, we can say, for similar reasons, is wild. But I would also make the argument that there is a pre-linguistic level of thought. Not always, but a lot of the time. And for some people more than other people. I think there are people who think more linguistically, and some who think more visually, or perhaps kinesthetically, in some cases.

INTERVIEWER

Getting back to Buddhism for a second. For many poets, poetry is the religion of the twentieth century. And I'm curious what you get, in that sense, from Buddhism that you don't get from poetry?

SNYDER

I had a funny conversation with Clayton Eshleman, the editor and poet, many years ago while he was still in Kyoto. Clayton was talking, at length and with passion, about poetry.

And I said to him, "But Clayton, I already have a religion. I'm a Buddhist." It's like the Pope telling Clare Boothe Luce, "I already am a Catholic." I don't think art makes a religion. I don't think it helps you teach your children how to say thank you to the food, how to view questions of truth and falsehood, or how not to cause pain or harm to others. Art can certainly help you explore your own consciousness and your own mind and your own motives, but it does not have a program to do that, and I don't think it should have a program to do that. I think that art is very close to Buddhism and can be part of Buddhist practice, but there are territories that Buddhist psychology and Buddhist philosophy must explore, and that art would be foolish to try to do.

INTERVIEWER
So you mainly draw that line on ethical grounds?

SNYDER
Well, there's ethics, there is philosophy, there is the spirit of devotion, and there is simply its capacity to become a cultural soil, a territory within which you transmit a way of being, which religion has a very strong role in. And then there is the other end of religious practice and Buddhist practice, which is to leave art behind. Which is to be able to move into the territory of the completeness and beauty of *all* phenomena. You really enter the world, you don't need art because everything is remarkable, fresh and amazing.

INTERVIEWER
So how do you keep writing?

SNYDER
Because you don't want to live in that realm very much of the time. We live in the realm of forms, we should act in the realm of forms. Jim Dodge and I once went to a Morris Graves exhibit in Oakland, where he was arguing with me about this Buddhist position in regard to art. I was saying, "You don't

need art in a certain sense, Jim." So he went to the Morris Graves exhibit looking at the Morris Graves paintings, and I went through it looking at the spaces between the paintings with as much attention, and pointing out wonderful little hairline cracks in the plaster, the texture of the light and so forth. There is a point you can make that anything looked at with love and attention becomes very interesting.

INTERVIEWER
So you think people should read the margins of your books?

SNYDER
This is an oral art. They should listen to the unsaid words that resonate around the edge of the poem.

INTERVIEWER
Just as Chinese poetry is full of empty words, deliberately empty words for the *ch'i*, the sort of breath, to circulate through. In 1970 you moved back to the Sierra Nevadas, and you've been there ever since. I think from that moment on, when you finally settle down, you're talking much more about a poetry rooted in place.

SNYDER
Certainly a number of the poems written since 1970 reflect the position of being in a place, a spot in the world to which I always return. A lot of poems, however, do come out of my hunting and gathering trips to other territories. The idea of being a person of place never excludes the possibility of travel. To the contrary, it reminds people of place — everybody else in the world except Canadians, Australians and Americans — that they know where they come from. They have a place to go back to. They have no difficulty answering the question, "Where are you from?" But Americans often can't answer that question. They say, "Well, do you mean where I was born or where I went to high school, or where my parents live now, or where I went to college, or where my job is, or where I'm

going to move next year?" That's an American dilemma. So having a place means that you know what a place means. And if somebody asks you, "What folk songs do you sing where you come from?" you have a song you can sing to them. Like in Japan, say, where you're always being asked to sing a song from your native place.

INTERVIEWER
Yes. Ours is "I Love New York in June." Do you think that sense of place is primary for the poetry?

SNYDER
Not in any simple or literal way. More properly I would say it's a sense of what *grounding* means. But place has an infinite scale of expansion or contraction. In fact, if somebody asks me now, "What do you consider to be your place?" my larger scale answer is, "My place on earth is where I know most of the birds and the trees and where I know what the climate will be right now, roughly, what should be going on there on that spot on earth right now, and where I have spent enough time to know it intimately and personally." So that place for me goes from around Big Sur on the California coast all the way up the Pacific coast through British Columbia, through southeast Alaska, out through southwest Alaska, out onto the Aleutian chain, and then comes down into Hokkaido and the Japanese islands, and goes down through Taiwan. Now that's the territory I have moved and lived in and that I sort of know. So that's my place.

INTERVIEWER
Since we're talking about your map of the world, people have wondered about the general absence of European civilization—or at least Europe after the Paleolithic—in your work. To me it's no more shocking than the absence of Asia—not to mention Africa—from everyone else's work. But still the question comes up. Is this a deliberate criticism of Eurocentrism or merely just the track your interest followed?

SNYDER

It's true that I haven't visited Europe much, but it isn't totally absent from my poetry, and there are some key points in my work that connect with occidental cultural insights that are classical, if not Paleolithic. The scholar Robert Torrance even wrote a little paper on the occidental aspect of my work. Much of the value I find in the West is in the pre-Christian, the pagan and the matrifocal aspects, however. And I track things like connections I fancy that I can see from Greek poetics to the Arabic poetry of Spain, in turn to Lorca, in turn to Jack Spicer. And the Bogomils, Waldenses, Albigenses, shepherds of Montaillou, Anabaptists, Quakers, Luddites, Amish and Wobblies have my gratitude, of course. And now that I'm getting old enough to enjoy hotels as well as camping I think I'll start visiting Europe. I loved Spain—I went there recently.

INTERVIEWER

I want to change gears and talk about the word *work*, which is central to all of your writing. You've written, to take one of many examples, "Changing the filter, wiping noses, going to meetings, picking up around the house, washing dishes, checking the dip stick, don't let yourself think these are distracting you from your more serious pursuits." What does this mean for a writer who would feel that her or his "real work" is the writing, and that all these other things are overwhelming?

SNYDER

If one's real work is the writing and if one is a fiction writer, I guess one's work as a writer really holds one to the literally physical act of writing and visualizing and imagining and researching and following out the threads of one's project. However, if one is a nonfiction prose writer or a poet, one is apt to be much more closely engaged with daily life as part of one's real work, and one's real work actually becomes life. And life comes down to daily life. This is also a very powerful Buddhist point: that what we learn and even hopefully become enlightened by is a thorough acceptance of exactly who we are and exactly what it is we must do, with no evasion, no hiding from any of it, physically or psychologically. And so finding the ceremonial, the almost sacramental quality of the moves of daily life is taught in Buddhism. That's what the Japanese tea ceremony is all about. The Japanese tea ceremony is a model of sacramental tea drinking. Tea drinking is taken as a metaphor for the kitchen and for the dining room. You learn how to drink tea, and if you learn how to drink tea well, you know how to take care of the kitchen and dining room every day. If you learn how to take care of the kitchen and the dining room, you've learned about the household. If you know about the household, you know about the watershed. *Ecology* means house, *oikos*, you know, from the Greek. *Oikos* also gives us economics. *Oikos nomos* means "managing the household." So that's one way of looking at it. I understand that there are other lines and other directions that poets take and I honor them. I certainly don't believe there's only one kind of poetry.

INTERVIEWER

I have a line from Auden here that "the goal of everyone is to live without working." And basically what he's saying in the rest of the passage is that work is something that other people impose on us.

SNYDER

I would agree with Auden. The goal of living is not to consider work work, but to consider it your life and your play. That's another way of looking at it.

INTERVIEWER

But how is that different from Calvinism, in the sense of extolling the virtues of work?

SNYDER

Well, work per se does not bring about salvation, nor is it automatically virtuous. It has more the quality of acknowledgment and recognition and making necessity charming. And it's not always charming, and nothing I've said should lead us to think that an oppressed worker should swallow and accept the conditions of his life without fighting back. It's none of that really. Your question catches me a little bit by surprise because I am so far removed from being a puritan in any way, and so is Buddhism, incidentally. There is a very funny quality in Buddhism, which is enjoying and acknowledging badness. So you can be bad and still be a good Buddhist. So everything I say has its reverse. "I hate work," you know, let it all go. Or as W.C. Fields once said, "If a thing is worth doing at all, it's worth doing poorly."

INTERVIEWER

Speaking of the doing of things, let me ask you about your mechanics of writing. I gather you have some complicated system of file cards, even for the poems. Can you describe that?

SNYDER

Most writers I know, and certainly prose writers, have a well-organized shop. There are moves in longer poetic projects that are very like the work of researchers. I tell young would-be poets not to fear organization, that it won't stultify their scope. I use some systems I learned from anthropologists and linguists. Now I use a computer too. A friend who's a professional hydrologist gives a good caution, "Write up your field notes at the end of each day!" And then get them into your hard disk fairly soon and always back that up. The main thing though is to give full range to the mind and learn to walk around in memory and imagination smelling and hearing things.

INTERVIEWER

Your poems are notable both for their extreme condensation and their musicality. Do the lines come out in such compact form? Are the poems initially much longer and then chipped away? Do you consciously count syllables or stresses, or do you mainly write by ear?

SNYDER

There is one sort of poem I write that is highly compressed and has a lot of ear in it. As a poem comes to me, in the process of saying and writing it, the lines themselves establish a basic measure, even a sort of musical or rhythmic phrase for the whole poem. I let it settle down for quite a while and do a lot of fine-tuning as part of the revision. Doing new poems at readings brings out subtle flaws in the movement or music to be immediately noted. I don't count syllables or stresses, but I discover after the fact what form the poem has given itself, and then I further that. Of course I write other sorts of poems as well—longer, less lyrical, formal, borrowings or parodies, and so forth. I am experimenting with switching back and forth between a prose voice and a lyric voice in some of the work I'm doing now.

INTERVIEWER

I gather that, unlike many writers, you publish very slowly— allowing things to sit for years before they're brought out in the world. Why is that? And what works are currently hanging up to dry?

SNYDER

Well, I have found that if you let a poem sit around long enough, you come to see and hear it better. Not that a poem in progress doesn't reach a point of being pretty much finished. So I don't rush it—it's a matter of allowing intuition and taste to come into play; you choose to hold onto a piece, waiting for some little turn of insight. This is true of prose writing, too. But letting it wait might be a kind of luxury sometimes because there are often urgent reasons to get things into the world, especially essays dealing with current issues. I recently finished a project I called *Mountains and Rivers Without End*—a series of longish poems that I have been working at for decades. And I'm glad I let it wait that long, it is more tasty.

INTERVIEWER

Why do you think it took so long?

SNYDER

Well of course when I launched myself into this in 1956, having just finished the book-length poem *Myths and Texts*—which only took three years—I thought it would be wrapped up in five or six years. I started studying *The Lotus Sutra* and some geomorphology and ecology texts as a bit of beginning research, and also I set sail for Japan. It all got more complicated than I had predicted, and the poems were evasive. So I relaxed, and thought, However long it takes. I kept my eye on it, walking, reflecting and researching, but didn't make any big demands on the mountain-goddess muse. So it worked out to about one section a year for forty years.

INTERVIEWER

How does it feel, having completed a forty-year-long project like *Mountains and Rivers Without End*?

SNYDER

How does it feel to finish it? I'm truly grateful. Now I have further work with it though—I'm learning how to read it aloud, and I'm still learning more about its workings.

INTERVIEWER

As with Pound and the *Cantos*, did you find it impossible to tear yourself away from *Mountains and Rivers* to work on other things?

SNYDER

As I say, I was pretty relaxed about results for a long time. But I did keep a really sharp focus going, never neglected it. Through those years I also wrote and published fifteen or sixteen books. Then, between 1992 and 1996, seeing the shape of the whole forming up, I put *Mountains and Rivers* ahead of everything else—stopped all other sorts of writing, neglected the garden, let the pine needles pile up on the road, quit giving poetry readings, didn't answer mail, quit going to parties, my old truck quit running—til it was done.

INTERVIEWER
Working on a book for forty years, do you carry the germ of your next project? What *are* you going to do next?

SNYDER
What I want to do next is restart the garden and the truck, go out with the young people to some deserts and rivers and maybe cities, and reengage with a bunch of old friends. And then back to prose and the thorny problems of our time.

INTERVIEWER
You're one of the few poets whose work is accessible to a non-poetry-reading public. Yet somewhere you say—you're talking about Robert Duncan—that it's the poetry you never fully comprehend that most engages you. I was wondering whether you consciously strike out obscurities, thinking of the general reader, to make the poetry accessible?

SNYDER
Semiconsciously. I've written a number of different sorts of poems and there's a percentage of my poetry—maybe twenty-five percent, maybe forty—that is accessible. I think partly that has been a function of my regard for the audience, my desire to have some poems that I knew that I could share with people I lived and worked with. Certainly a number of the work poems, and poems of travel and poems of place, are works that I could and did share with neighbors or with fellow workers on the job. I've always enjoyed that enormously. At the same time there are territories of mind and challenges that are not easily accessible. I've written a number of rather

difficult poems. I just don't read them at poetry readings as a rule.

INTERVIEWER

Let me quickly ask you about your book of selected poems. *No Nature*, as a title, obviously takes many aback. It seems apocalyptic until you realize that it's a kind of Buddhist joke: the true nature is no nature, the nature of one's self is no nature. Is that correct?

SNYDER

Yes, and it's also a critical-theory joke.

INTERVIEWER

In what sense?

SNYDER

In that some folks hold that everything is a social construction, and I add that society is a natural construction, including the industrial and the toxic.

INTERVIEWER

It's interesting that, for someone involved as much as you are in the environmental movement, your work is surprisingly without disasters. There's very little bad news in the poetry — no Bhopals, no Chernobyls. Are you setting positive examples? Or are you just cheerful?

SNYDER

There are several poems that have some very bad news in them. Going all the way back to a poem written in 1956 called "This Tokyo." And the poem that I wrote as an op-ed piece for *The New York Times* in 1972 called "Mother Earth: Her Whales." However, I feel that the condition of our social and ecological life is so serious that we'd better have a sense of humor. That it's too serious just to be angry and despairing. Also, frankly, the environmental movement in the last twenty years has never done well when it threw out excessive doom scenarios. Doom scenarios, even though they might be true, are not politically or psychologically effective. The first step, I think, and that's why it's in my poetry, is to make us love the world rather than to make us fear for the end of the world. Make us love the world, which means the nonhuman as well as the human, and then begin to take better care of it.

INTERVIEWER

Many are surprised to discover that you're not a vegetarian and not a Luddite, but rather a carnivore with a Macintosh. This sets you apart from, on the one hand, many Buddhists, and, on the other, from a certain branch of the environmental movement. Any comments?

SNYDER

Come, come, I'm not a carnivore, I'm an omnivore. Carnivores have ridiculously short intestines! I am a very low-key omnivore at that, as are most of the Third World people who eat very little fish or meat, but who certainly wouldn't spurn it. I did a whole discussion of this question — for Buddhists — in a recent issue of *Ten Directions*, from the Zen Center of Los Angeles. The key is still the first precept: "Cause least harm." We have to consider the baleful effects of agribusiness on the global environment, as well as have concern for the poor domestic critters. Ethical behavior is not a matter of following a rule, but examining how a precept might guide one, case by case.

Now, as for environmentalists, my Earth First! and Wild Earth friends are pretty diverse, but one thing they all share is that they are not prigs or puritans. They do ecological politics as a kind of contact sport. I'm all for that.

As for computers: the word processor is not the agent of transformation, it's language that is the agent. The word processor is just a facilitating device. Keep your eye on the ball!

AUDIENCE MEMBER

I was on the phone this afternoon with my teacher, who is a Lakota. I mentioned that I was going to see Gary Snyder.

And she said, "Oh, Gary Snyder. He's an Indian. Ask him if he knows it." Do you know that you are an Indian? A Native American.

SNYDER

That was very kind of her to say that. I don't know if I know I'm an Indian or not. However, I do know that I'm a Native American. Here again is a Turtle Island bioregional point. Anyone is, metaphorically speaking, a Native American who is "born again on Turtle Island." Anyone is a Native American who chooses, consciously and deliberately, to live on this continent, this North American continent, with a full spirit for the future, and for how to live on it right, with the consciousness that says, "Yeah, my great-great-grandchildren and all will be here for thousands of years to come. We're not going on to some new frontier, we're here now." In that spirit, African-Americans, Euro-Americans, Asian-Americans, come together as Native Americans. And then you know that those continents that your ancestors came from are great places to visit, but they're not home. Home is here.

INTERVIEWER

But do you think that the myths that come out of here belong to everyone?

SNYDER

They belong to the place, and they will come to belong to those who make themselves members of this place. It's not that easy, however. It takes real practice.

INTERVIEWER

I'm just playing devil's advocate for a moment. I know in the seventies there were Native Americans who were criticizing you—I don't think rightly—essentially saying, "Hey, white boy, keep your hands off our coyote."

SNYDER

You know, coyote—the trickster image—is found all over the globe. In myth and world folklore, it blankets the planet from forty thousand years ago on. It is totally cosmopolitan, and we know this. So, in that sense, mythology and folklore are archaic international world heritages. The question is to understand what to do with them and how to respond to them. The stories about Coyote Old Man are in fact genuinely something that came out of Native American experience, broke through the civilization-history time barrier and are now fully rooted in twentieth-century literature. That's something that has come across. It's quite amazing. And I'm sure that other things will prove in time to have come across like that. You can't be against it. It makes both worlds, the old and new, richer, and it testifies to the openness of the imagination.

AUDIENCE MEMBER

There are a lot of things that are splitting the country apart nowadays. Does this scare you?

SNYDER

Well, along with everyone else, I have very troubled moments about the future of the United States and our society. And it would be foolish to say that I've got any easy answers. For those who can do it, one of the things to do is not to move. To stay put. Now staying put doesn't mean don't travel. But it means have a place and get involved in what can be done in that place. Because without that we're not going to have a representative democracy that works in America. We're in an oligarchy right now, not a democracy. Part of the reason that it slid into oligarchy is that nobody stays anywhere long enough to take responsibility for a local community and for a place.

AUDIENCE MEMBER

In a radio interview several years ago, you were asked about your politics and you responded that you were an anarchist. Can you explain that, and how that really works?

SNYDER
You know I really regretted saying that on the radio. That was on "Fresh Air." I try not to say that on the radio. In fact, I try not to even use the word *anarchist* because it immediately raises the question that you just raised which is, "Can you explain that?" The term shouldn't be used, it has too many confusing associations. Anarchism should refer to the creation of non-statist, natural societies as contrasted with legalistically organized societies, as alternative models for human organization. Not to be taken totally literally, but to be taken poetically as a direction toward the formation of better and more viable communities. Anarchism, in political history, does not mean chaos, it means self-government. So a truly anarchist society is a self-governing society. We all need to learn better how to govern ourselves. And we can do that by practice, and practice means you have to go to meetings, and going to meetings means you'll be bored, and so you better learn how to meditate.

INTERVIEWER
The tao of bureaucracy.

SNYDER
That's right. The tao of bureaucracy. Anybody who meditates knows how to handle boredom so then you can go to meetings. That's how I got into politics.

AUDIENCE MEMBER
You've had to submit to a very rigorous discipline in your religious practice, learning of languages and study of poetry. Do you find your students now willing to submit to that kind of discipline?

SNYDER
You know, I never felt like I was submitting to discipline. Since I was about sixteen or seventeen, I've never done anything I didn't want to do. It was always my own choice. When

I was studying Chinese, it was what I wanted to do. I could have left at any time, nobody was paying me to do it, and I didn't have any parents insisting that I do it. So, I don't know how to answer that. I've always operated from my own free choice. However, I certainly would say that a highly motivated person, willing to engage intensely with something, is not easy to find among the students I've run into. But there are always a few that have some sort of fire under them.

AUDIENCE MEMBER
What would you tell sixteen-year-olds with the world before them, what should they do?

SNYDER
This is one of the occupational hazards of being a poet. You're asked questions that you really don't know an answer for. I'd say the same thing that I say to my eighteen-year-old stepdaughter: you're going to have to get a lot of formal education. And don't think that a four-year education is the end of it. Nowadays you have to go on a little bit farther or it isn't going to mean a whole lot. But even while doing education, don't think it makes you superior to uneducated people or illiterate people, because there's a tremendous amount of cultural wisdom and skill out in the Third World, out in the pre-literate world that is intrinsically every bit as viable as anything that Euro-American society has created. And then the fundamental ethical precept: whatever you do, try not to cause too much harm.

—Eliot Weinberger

Now You See Her

Michael Knight

Xavier tells me he is upstairs doing his homework, but I know that he is watching our new neighbor. Grace Poole lives in the townhouse just across a narrow alley from our own. I was taking trash to the alley on Monday, when I noticed my son at our second-story window, his face close enough to the glass to breathe mist onto it. I followed his eyes across the way, and there was Grace Poole, standing naked in her kitchen, sipping from a coffee mug. She gave no indication that she saw me or that she saw my son, perfectly still, entranced, huffing brief ghosts of longing against the pane. Today is Friday, and I've been watching her myself ever since. I have the benefit of binoculars.

I believe that I should be angry at him, should sneak up the stairs, right now, kick his door open and demand to know what he thinks he's doing. But I'm not angry. X—he has started calling himself X—is thirteen. I remember thirteen and being full of that strange water, drawn and released by the sight of a woman, tides and moon. X was in such a hurry to get to his window after school that he didn't even stop to wonder why his old man is home this early in the day. How can I be mad at him? Grace is, at this moment, swimming closer to me through the binocular lenses.

I have often thought about having the talk with my son, about what I would tell him. The birds and the bees, the facts of life. For a man who spent his days talking, my own father, a professor of literature, was surprisingly inarticulate. He was maroon-faced and shifty and read me a poem about love. He tried to establish a connection.

"Do you know what I mean, Byron?" he said. "You know already, right?"

"Sure. I've got it covered," I said. I was twelve and only four years from discovering that I had nothing at all covered.

X has never seemed the right age for that sort of talk. Nine and ten, still too much a boy. Eleven, the year his mother died. My wife, Sarah. I couldn't get my head around anything that year, except the fact that she was gone. Her absence was everywhere. Dust on the piano keys. Dirty dishes in the sink. A coolness beneath my covers, in place of her body heat. Twelve, our move to the city, to Alexandria, at the beginning of the school year. That seemed weight enough for both our shoulders. I sold the piano. X had a short-lived fling with smoking cigarettes. Now, thirteen and suddenly he is too old for all that.

It could be that I am avoiding the issue. Nine months ago, I went to the library and xeroxed copies of the male and female anatomy, those full-body biology-textbook shots, intending to make my presentation to him. I wanted to keep it clinical, the way I would have shown a customer at my veterinary clinic that their dog was having pregnancy complications. My intention was to leave love out of it. On my way home, I saw a terrifying vision of what I would do when the conversation turned to actual procedure. I pictured myself placing the male copy on top of the female copy, between my hands, and rubbing my palms together. I broke out in a humiliated sweat. I jerked the car over to the curb and slipped the pages into a gutter. X probably knows the basics already. What he doesn't know, the smooth way morning light looks on a woman's skin, the way her hair can play between bare shoulder blades, Grace across the way, with her potted daisies on the windowsill, will surely teach him.

To the uninitiated, it would appear that Grace Poole has renounced clothing altogether. She has dark curly hair, all of it, and wild eyebrows and is so pale as to be distracting. It's true that she walks from room to room naked. Sleeps and feeds her dog, watches television and eats breakfast without clothes. Grace spends almost all of her time at home, clothesless. These things I have learned in the four days since I discovered my son's little secret. And his homework fetish began almost two weeks ago, just about the time our new neighbor arrived.

When she does go out, Grace makes the act of getting dressed almost unbearably alluring. The slow taking away of my guilty pleasure. She makes her body a secret again, dressing slowly, as if she regretted having to do it at all. A reverse striptease; I imagine balloons inflating around her as she pulls pins out of them. The sight of her rolling panty hose over lightly muscled calves and dimpled knees, tugging them over the crescent folds where her supple thighs meet her bottom, shifting her hips side to side, or standing in the middle of the room, slipping her arms into the sleeves of a clean shirt, buttoning it over her breasts, breaks my heart. I have not seen a naked woman since my wife was alive.

Now, Grace is talking on the telephone. She has six phones, each one a different color, lined up on a card table against her downstairs window. My first thought was phone sex, but that would be too perfect. She is standing behind the table, arms crossed beneath her breasts, lifting her brown nipples, pinning the phone against her shoulder with her cheek. I can just make out the blue earpiece in all that hair. Her eyes are almost the same color. The wall behind her is lined with cardboard boxes, stacked three high, each one imprinted with the same logo — a rust-colored rooster — and writing in Spanish. I hear my son trotting down the stairwell and just have time to drop the shade in my study and stash the binoculars between the chair and my lower back before he opens the door. I can't get my hands on any documents to look busy, so I stare at the ceiling and pretend that I was daydreaming. Watching Grace seems like daydreaming sometimes, languorous as jasmine.

"Shouldn't you be working, Dad?" X says. "Somebody's got to put food on the table around here." He is standing just inside the room, still in his school uniform, gray slacks and blue shirt, now untucked. X is blond and tan and brown-eyed. He looks exactly like his mother. I try to find traces of myself in him when he doesn't know I'm watching. While he sleeps, his cheeks flush with dreaming. At dinner, sitting in front of the television, holding his plate near his chin, his eyes half closing when he lifts a mouthful. Usually, I don't find anything, and when I do, those things are fleeting, an expression, a gesture, gone almost as soon as I've seen them. The sight of him, of his mother in him, makes me feel guilty about watching Grace. He is smiling strangely, and I can't tell if he is onto me.

"I thought maybe we could do something together after school," I lie. "I didn't know you'd have so much *homework*."

I say homework in italics, hoping to catch him off guard, to put him on the defensive for a change. He leans into the door frame, shoves a hand into his pocket. I can hear the muffled thump of a tennis ball on the public courts across the street.

"Yeah, well." He shrugs and looks in the direction of the tennis sounds.

"Besides, I'm on emergency call tonight. I thought an afternoon off would do me some good." This is the truth. I have become part of an arrangement of the three local vets, where one of us stays on call twenty-four hours on alternating nights. The other offices transfer their emergency patients after business hours. "So, what do you say? Should we go down to the mall and look at that CD player you want?"

He brightens visibly.

"Cool," he says. "Let me change clothes and we're gone."

He pivots on a heel and goes stomping back upstairs.

After my wife died, I moved my son from our farm in Loudon County to this place, a brick townhouse in Alexandria, anonymous among rows of similar buildings. Ours wasn't a working farm, just some land, the old farmhouse and the sagging barns behind it and a grain silo, which Sarah called the Leaning Tower of Loudon. My practice has boomed since our move to the city. My clientele, though, has changed from horses and hearty dogs to mostly cats and those dogs which need constant grooming. Poodles and such, city dogs. I never would have thought that grooming would become a vital part of my practice, but I've recently hired an assistant, Sissy, for just that purpose. Sissy is young and attractive and people like her, and the owners of my new patients seem to find something charming, something quaint, in having a country doctor for their pets. I make my manner brusque and forceful and have lately found myself speaking in colloquialisms to fit the part that has been given me. They often ask why a veterinarian, a natural lover of animals, does not have a pet of his own. I mention lack of space and the inclemency of keeping animals confined to the city. A happy dog is a running dog, I say. I made that up. And they nod and look at the floor, guilty in their minds of animal cruelty. They like my subtle scolding.

What I don't tell them is that I once saw a Siberian husky called Bear run over by a lumber truck, flatbed strapped with skinned trees. This was before X was born, and Sarah and I loved that dog as if he were our child. She would put a plate for him under the dinner table so he could have his meals with us. On cold nights, he slept in the bed between us, his head on a polyester pillow that Sarah bought because it turned out he was allergic to down. All of us slept on polyester pillows. I still do. To console her on the evening of the accident, I had to promise that we would never have another pet. I'm not certain how serious she was about the promise, whether it was just one of those things people do at a time of tragedy, self-denial as punishment for some implicit fault in the affair, but our farm was without animals until her death.

X found a cat curled up in the grain silo the month after Sarah's funeral, and I gave in to his pleading and let us keep it. The cat was never fond of me, ignored my attempts at affection, hissing at my touch and rushing to X for protection. The cat wouldn't eat until the kitchen lights were off, and I had gone up to bed. Late one night, I went down to the kitchen for a snack and flipped the light switch and surprised him at his bowl. He skittered across the linoleum, out of the little pet door and our lives. We never saw him again. I tried fish, after the cat, for X's sake but could never remember to feed them or change their water and, when I did remember, I thought of Sarah and the promise that I had made.

Grace Poole and her shar-pei, Candle, are new patients of mine. I have never found any truth in the idea that people and their pets come to look alike over time. Candle is all wrinkles and short, wiry hair and full of high-strung motion. They have only been in once, for a flea dip and groom, but Sissy noticed something about Grace immediately. Sissy is nineteen and always teasing me about not dating. While Grace was filling out her paperwork, she pulled me aside and said, "Bingo. That's the one. Ask her out, Dr. Shaw. We'll double. You can set me up with that pretty son of yours."

She also teases X, when he sometimes comes in to earn his allowance after school. Both of us, X and I, clearly enjoy it.

"Can't. She's my new neighbor," I said. "If it didn't work out, I would always be running into her at the mailbox."

"If you don't get a date soon, the customers are going to think you're gay. Think about what that would do to business," she said.

After X left for school today, I called the office, told Sissy and my other assistant, Roy, to take the day off and spent the morning watching Grace. From the window in my study, I can see into her kitchen and living room, but when she went to the second floor, I had to dash up to X's room and crouch on his bed, where I imagine he must watch her. Our separation on the stairwell was torturous. The dog followed her everywhere. I wondered what my son thinks when he does his spying. I crossed my arms on the sill, the way he does, and pressed my forehead to the cool glass. I pulled his blanket over my shoulders. She must seem to him unreal, a gift so lucky, so fantastic, he can hardly believe in her. I pictured him saying honest prayers that she wouldn't go away. The image so perfect and fragile that to touch her, even to imagine touching her, might make her come apart in wisps of smoke. X's return from school confined me to the study, and now I have lied my way into having to leave the house altogether, but I don't mind really.

One thing has impressed me about X since my discovery. He hasn't brought anyone over to watch with him. When I was his age, the first thing I would have done was have a dozen friends lined up at the window eating popcorn or something. Having a secret to share made me feel important. But not X. He doesn't want to share her. He doesn't want to spoil whatever it is he's feeling up there. I hope he doesn't know that he's splitting time with his father.

It is almost five o'clock by the time we leave. X is very careful when dressing for the mall. He has selected a plain white T-shirt from The Gap, Levi's jeans and brand-new Nike hightops. Close to two hundred dollars for the whole outfit. I had no idea. His mother did all his shopping. I have suits that cost less and, except for the shoes, he looks like a fifties hoodlum. I half expect him to roll a pack of cigarettes in his shirtsleeve.

We drive a while, all interstate and highway on the way to the mall, and X is quiet, maybe thinking about his CD player, maybe thinking about Grace. The breeze from the open window whips his hair. I let myself think about Grace, too. I'm not sure how I will react when I see her again in person. In the flesh, so to speak. Our meeting, as neighbors, as doctor and patient, is inevitable. I wonder sometimes if she knows that she is being watched, if the absence of curtains on her windows is deliberate and not, as I tell myself, just because she's new in town. I don't think she knows that her vet lives next door—the last four days, I've been getting my mail under cover of darkness—but I wonder if she can feel our eyes on her, if the two of us are giving off some kind of lonely vibe. X is staring, blank-eyed, in front of us. Our thoughts of Grace fill the car as palpably as the quick air.

"How about you roll that window up and let's get some AC going," I say.

He rolls his eyes at me but does as I ask. He turns on the radio, and I turn it down a little. X does a sigh, one that is full of implications.

"Dad, I need to ask a favor," he says. "There's this girl I

want to ask out, and I was wondering if you'd drive us to the movies. Her parents could drive, but they're real old, and they want to drive too much, you know. They're happy-assed about stuff like that. They get off on participating."

At first, I'm panicked. He's going to ask Grace to the movies. But that's absurd and besides, Grace has her driver's license. At the same time, I'm unreasonably happy that he's asked me to be their chauffeur. I struggle to withhold a barrage of questions. I turn the radio back up.

"Sounds like fun," I say.

He nods and grows remote again. A woman in an antique convertible, a De Soto or something, passes us on X's side. It has fins and everything, makes her look like a movie star. Both of us turn to look.

I say, "How would you feel about your old man getting a date soon?"

"Cool," he says.

"That wouldn't bother you?" I'm surprised.

"No way," he says.

"Understand that I loved your mother. I will always love your mother," I say.

"Mom's dead," he says. "She'd understand."

X is a man of few words, the strong silent type. Add a scuffed leather motorcycle jacket to his outfit, and he could double for Marlon Brando in *The Wild Ones*. X's mother died of an infection resulting from her tubal ligation. Almost an unheard-of cause of death, the doctors said, but this I already knew. Even vets know a thing or two about people medicine. Sarah was alive in the hospital less than a week. I had always wanted a big family, wanted the constant clamor of children in our house, but there were medical reasons for the operation, and Sarah softened things by saying how much the idea of raising an only child appealed to her. We could spoil him rotten, give him whatever he wanted. She wouldn't have to divide her love, she said. Two ways was enough.

I have never actually admitted the possibility of dating again, though I have begun to entertain it more and more recently. Particularly with Sissy's insistence and the arrival of Grace Poole.

The reawakening of those boyhood desires. Naked is after all, still naked, even to a thirty-six-year-old widower.

The mall is massive and intimidating, but X moves through it easily, as if it were his natural habitat. He wanted me to give him the credit card and wait in the car. He told me he was a smart shopper. I told him that was quite possibly the most hysterical thing I had ever heard. He grabs my arm and jerks me along when I stop at the map to look for the stereo store. He knows where he is going and remains, always, about three paces ahead of me. In front of a store called Southern Culture, he freezes and raises his hand to me, fist clenched, like a soldier walking point. He is so definite in his motion that I go still as well. I think he must have seen that in a Vietnam movie.

"Wait here," he says.

I do as I am told. X weaves through the steady flow of shoppers, across the wide aisle, to three girls who look about his age. They are standing in front of a pet store, one of those places where the animals are caged behind a glass wall. The girls look happy to see X. He gives them all a smile and pushes his fingers through his hair, his mother's hair, weightless and golden. They laugh at something he says and one of the girls, the prettiest, lays a hand on his shoulder. X doesn't acknowledge the hand, lets her leave it there, waits for them to finish laughing. He's doing an eyebrow raise, as if surprised that they could find him so funny, so charming. My son is a natural. He would probably do better with Grace Poole than I would. X looks over his shoulder at me, casually, sees me watching and gives me a dirty look. I spin around to face the shop window. Southern Culture specializes in reproduction antebellum antiques. Polymers where there should be pine. Porch Jockeys with machine-induced paint chips.

In the window directly in front of me is an awkward looking fake antique telephone, black with brass cradle and receivers, the works. I don't think there were telegraphs before the Civil War, much less telephones, but seeing it there makes me wonder what Grace Poole could be up to with all those phones. Her conversations only last a minute or two and she takes notes while she is talking. I never heard of a phone-sex girl taking notes, except maybe to get credit-card numbers, and she does too much writing for that to be the explanation.

X returns and leads me to the stereo store. He has a short discussion with the salesgirl, who is very attractive and all business. She is wearing a tan, ankle-length skirt, slit open to the knee. She is impressed with my son's knowledge of electronics and shows me the model that he wants. It holds ten CDs and is apparently the only type made on earth that can continue playing while the carriage is ejected and still rotating. On sale for $1,300.00, speakers and receiver not included. I ask if that's a feature he absolutely must have.

"It's the best, Dad," he says. "Think of it as a long-term investment."

X has one arm crossed at his stomach, cupping the elbow of the other arm in his palm. He is stroking his chin, one foot forward, weight back, as if regarding a masterpiece of art.

"Tell me again," I say. "Whose child are you?"

The salesgirl looks from X to the CD player and back to X.

"He'll definitely be getting his money's worth, Dad," she says.

"It is, unfortunately, and I'm sure much to both of your disappointments, not his money," I say.

We settle on something more reasonable.

In the car, X is again silent. I have embarrassed him both in front of his friends by staring and in front of the salesperson by being cheap. Six hundred dollars isn't cheap in my estimation, but clearly X is disappointed. I resent his sullenness and try to get him talking again.

"What about Grace Poole?" I say. "Our new neighbor."

He tenses a little but doesn't look at me.

"What about her?" he says.

"You know, for my date," I say. "We could double. Miss Poole and I could go to the movies with you and your girlfriend."

X turns his head slowly to look at me. He is angry. Before the last words are out of my mouth, I understand that it was the wrong thing to say, that I said it to provoke him. He gives me a mean, shallow laugh.

"She's so out of your league," he says.

Three months after Sarah died, I broke X's wrist. We were

on the lawn playing football and he was running wildly by me, at the point in our game when I would let him go past me, through the pair of apple trees we used as a goal line. Let him do his touchdown dance, spike the ball, spread his arms like wings and prance in a circle. I ran after him and caught him from behind, wrapping him up, jarring the ball loose, driving him down. His arm went out to brace himself and the wrist snapped audibly—he asked me later if I had heard it—a sound like it too was surprised to find me on his back, the ground coming up so fast. X carried his cast, proudly, like a club.

X won't let me help him assemble his new stereo. He doesn't even allow me to help him carry it from the car. I return to the study, lock the door behind me, and take up my binoculars. Grace is on the phone, a pink one this time, and she is wearing a cream-colored bra, but that is all, like she was just getting ready to dress when the phone rang. She scratches a pencil across a pad, tears the sheet loose and jams it down on a thin spike attached to a metal base. I can't see the dog. Grace never does get up to dress, which I am glad of, just keeps on answering phones, first one, then another, putting one on hold and coming back to it. She is a popular lady. I can't figure out the phones.

It isn't long before my house is full of music. I go out of the study and stand at the bottom of the stairwell to let the sound come down to me more clearly. There are long windows on either side of the front door leaking weak light into the foyer. The song that X is playing sounds familiar, something from the seventies, heavy with feedback guitars, but I can't put my finger on its name. Probably I heard it on the office radio. Sissy likes that sort of music, calls it classic. And suddenly, I'm remembering Sarah and me, trying to manhandle a piano through the front door of our farmhouse. X was maybe seven, too small to help, so he supervised. The piano was on a dolly, but even so we kept banging it into walls and furniture, filling the house with resonant discord, and the air was full of the smell of hay grass—someone was always cutting hay out there, if not on our land then on the next farm down the road. Just follow the white wooden fence — a sweet smell, like the cakes Sarah would try to bake, and botch more often than not, leaving them in the oven too long or screwing up the recipe. Dessert was the most hilarious time of day in our house, cakes looking like deflated footballs, pies blackened like bituminous coal. It made me hungry, that smell. I was always hungry in Loudon County.

X was trying to talk his mother into letting him have a horse just before she died. He had nearly convinced her to break her promise. X guaranteed that he would let us choose the horse, if he was allowed to give it a name. For X, this was a major concession. I never said anything directly to him, but after he was asleep and Sarah and I were alone in bed, I would argue against this idea — not the horse itself but X choosing the name. A horse is too noble an animal. I see horses everyday with ridiculous, childish names, I said. Black Beauty, Sox, Paint. I had a patient called Fanny. It's degrading to them, Sarah. She told me that if there was going to be a horse, which there probably wasn't, it would be X's and X should name it. She would prop her back against the headboard and smoke cigarettes, tipping ashes into a ceramic bowl in her lap. Smoking was her secret vice; she didn't want X to know that his mother sanctioned such a nasty habit. What are you talking about, Byron? she'd say. You're the one that's being juvenile. I wonder now what name he would have chosen. The boy who has nicknamed himself after a letter in the alphabet.

When I take up my binoculars again, Grace is nowhere to be found. Almost a half hour passes, the light fading between our homes, without a trace of her. She must have gone up for the night. She is X's until dawn. I would like to creep upstairs and stand in his doorway, the door just slightly open, and watch him watching her. Not to catch him red-handed but just to look at him, see if he is the same sort of voyeur as his father.

Grace comes running down the stairs into my line of sight. She stops in the middle of the room, breathless, harried, and stands there one hand pushed up into that mass of brown hair, holding it back away from her forehead. Her lips are moving, but I can't see who she's talking to. She walks over to the black phone, picks it up and starts to dial, then stops and drops the receiver on the table and runs back upstairs. When she returns, the dog is in her arms, her back arched under its weight. Candle is not moving in a way that is frightening. Not loose and recently dead but stiff, body wracked with sporadic trembling. My first thought is Lyme disease, but that's unlikely. The disease is carried by ticks that don't exist in the city. I saw it dozens of times in the country.

Grace lays Candle on the table, using her elbow to move the phones. She finds a phonebook and begins rifling through it, back then forward again, as if she were having trouble concentrating. I realize, suddenly, that she is looking for my number. I retrieve my own phonebook from the desk drawer and look for her name, but it isn't there. That makes sense, she's new to town. Besides, I couldn't call her. She would know that I had been spying on her.

I watch her stop turning pages, watch her dial and speak into the receiver but my phone never rings. I think, at first, that she has called another vet, that she didn't like me when I met Candle the first time. I'm crushed. But, finally, my phone rings. It is Sissy. She's manning the office line tonight.

"Get your act together," she says. "We've got an emergency call. Grace Poole. Her dog is sick. Maybe tonight's your big chance, Dr. Shaw. A woman with a sick dog. She'll be super vulnerable." She waits a moment for me to laugh and, when I don't, becomes professional again. "The dog is paralyzed except for muscle spasms. She's coming in."

"I know," I say.

"What?"

"Nothing," I say. "I'll be right there."

I am holding the binoculars in one hand, the phone in the other. Grace has disappeared upstairs, momentarily, and returns carrying a bundle of clothes. I watch her dress. She pulls on walking shorts, cut high and flattering, and a T-shirt. She is barefoot and doesn't bother with underwear. Candle, she gathers in her arms and, burdened with the dog, she can't open the door. It is all I can do not to go outside, cross the little alley between us and help her.

I wait until I hear Grace's car door close, hear the engine

start. Wait until her headlights pass my window, casting shadows, before I get up to leave. I find X in the foyer, sitting at the bottom of the stairs. It is almost dark and he is brushed with the last delicate light from the street.

"I want to go," he says.

We look at each other for a long moment, neither of us speaking. X is still wearing his mall clothes. He looks worried but never takes his eyes away from mine. For an instant, I think I see something familiar in his face, something that I recognize. It is at those moments, when the veneer of his confidence has cracked just a little, when he shows, like light creeping under a doorway, in his eyes, in the set of his mouth, traces of being a boy, that I imagine a little of myself in him. It is at those moments when I love him most.

"Okay," I say.

My clinic is only a few blocks away, but the drive is intolerable. I force myself to go slowly, to brake at every stop sign, to signal at every corner. X won't look at me, keeps his eyes on other people's houses, the occasional warmth of their lighted windows. Grace is crying by the time we reach the office, sitting Indian-style in one of the plastic waiting-room chairs. There are circles of dirt on the balls of her feet, and I can see a shadow on her thigh made by the leg of her shorts. I remember that she isn't wearing underwear. When we come in, she wipes her eyes and tries to fix her hair, which is wild and spiraling. She is very beautiful like that. X is wide-eyed. I think he is amazed to be seeing her in person, amazed that she exists beyond those windows.

I can't think of a suitable colloquialism, so I say, "It's going to be all right, Miss Poole."

Sissy and the dog are in the examination room waiting for me. Candle is still trembling, her ID tag clinking against the examination table's metal surface.

"Her temperature is high," Sissy says. "That's all I knew to do until you got here."

"Lyme disease," I say.

I look around the door to the waiting room. X is sitting

about four chairs over from Grace, looking petrified, eyes glued to the floor.

"Miss Poole, has this dog been out of the city recently? Camping or something?" I say.

"Yes," she says. "About a week ago."

"Any ticks on her?"

"A few," she says. She is calming some.

"Good," I say. "I'll get her fixed up."

I wish I could stop talking like a country doctor, just for a minute. I push my fingers through Candle's fur until I find what I'm looking for, the bull's eye reddening of a tick bite at her shoulder. I give the dog a muscle relaxant to stop the spasms and a shot of tetracycline for the Lyme's, because it won't hurt her either way. I have Sissy take a blood sample. These are the things I understand. This is the place where I know what I am doing. I stroke the dog, pulling all that loose skin out straight, then letting it wrinkle up again, until she quiets. I whisper nonsense in her ear. "Pretty dog, pretty dog. Tell your mother good things about Dr. Shaw."

"That dog was messed up," Sissy says. "It's a good thing you were home and not out painting the town like you usually are."

"Hoot with the owls at midnight, and you can't fly with the eagles at dawn," I say. I smile at her.

"C'mon, Dr. Shaw," she says, rolling her eyes in the direction of the waiting room.

X and Grace are talking when I go back into the other room. They don't hear me come in. X is smiling but differently from the mall, nervous and grateful for her attention. He is tapping his feet, wringing his hands. Grace seems relaxed, settled some. It hasn't occurred to me until now to wonder how old she is. Maybe twenty-eight, twenty-nine, not too young. Somewhere between X and me but closer to me. There are alot of things I hadn't thought to wonder about her.

"Candle is going to be good as new," I say.

They look up at me, lips parted slightly, surprised to find me there.

"That's great," X says. His enthusiasm is genuine.

"Thank you so much, Dr. Shaw," she says, standing, taking

a few steps in my direction. "Sorry I got so emotional there. That isn't like me. It's Candle. Do you have pets?"

"I have X," I say. "He's sort of like a pet."

She smiles and looks back at my son who, to my surprise, is also smiling. X is watching me, not angry, but definitely watching, waiting to see what I will do.

"A very cute and charming pet he is," she says. "Does he do any tricks? Sit, X. Roll over, boy."

"Grace is in the mail-order business, Dad," he says, too eagerly. "She does clothes for this Venezuelan company. Environmentally correct sweaters and stuff."

X and Grace. They are on a first name basis. She waves his comment away and says, "I just got the job. They're a penny-ante operation. Won't even give me a computer or an office phone. I have to do everything by hand."

"Really?" I say.

My heart starts kicking, my tongue goes gummy in my mouth. At least that explains the phones. Now, I know something else about her. What I don't know is what to talk to her about. I can't very well talk about the fact that I've been spying on her. I can't tell her that I see her in my sleep. I launch headlong into my spiel about Lyme disease—it's an inflammatory disease, I say, caused by tick borne *spirochete*. The symptoms include joint pains, fatigue and sometimes neurological disturbances. I hear my voice, droning on like a nightmare biology teacher, but I can't shut up. Did you know that this disease was named for Lyme, Connecticut, where a particularly deadly outbreak was studied? She nods along with my words, trying to seem interested. I force myself to stop talking. I remember X and how at ease he was with those girls at the mall. I run my fingers through my hair, smile the smile and cock my hip like some kid. It doesn't feel right, feels foolish. The proper words for this moment—Grace in the washed-out light from the fluorescent bulbs, X with his hands in his pockets, his eyes full of sympathy—do not exist. I am aware that nothing can happen between us, not after what X and I have been doing the last few days, but I don't want it to be over just yet. Any moment now, I think, and she will disappear.

Portfolio

Word Play

Randolfo Rocha

HATE

HOPE

LIES

AGE

LIFE

FAITH

Relief

Peter Ho Davies

Sometime between the cheese and the fruit, while the port was still being passed, Lieutenant Wilby allowed a sweet, but rather too boisterous fart to slip between his buttocks. The company around the mess table was talking quietly, listening to the sound of the liquor filling the glasses, holding it up in the lamplight to relish its color against the white canvas of the tent. It was, Lieutenant Bromhead had just explained, a bottle from General Chelmsford's own stock, and not the regulation port issued to officers. A hush of appreciation had fallen over the table.

Of course, Wilby had known the fart was coming, but it was much louder and more prolonged than he had anticipated and the look of surprise on his face would have given him away even if Major Black to his left, the port already extended, had not said, "Wilby!" in a sharp, shocked bellow.

"Sorry, sir," Wilby said. His face burned as if he'd been sitting in front of the hearth at home, reading by the firelight. He risked one quick glance up and around the table. "Sorry, sirs." Chaplain Pierce was looking down into his lap, exactly as he did when saying grace, and Captain Ferguson's mustache was jumping slightly at the corners, like the whiskers of a cat that had just scented a bowl of cream. Lieutenant Chard, however, sat just as he appeared in his photographs, his huge pale face tipped back like a great slab, rising above his thick dark beard.

As for Bromhead, he looked only slightly puzzled.

"What?" he said. "What is it?"

Wilby, staring down at the crumbs of Stilton on his plate, groaned inwardly. Bromhead's famed deafness was going to be the end of him.

He looked up under his brow as Bromhead's batman, who had just placed the fruit on the table, leaned forward and whispered all too audibly in his ear, "The lieutenant farted, sir."

"Chard?" Bromhead asked. Behind his beard the older lieutenant turned the color of claret. Bromhead, himself, wore only a thin mustache and sideburns, and Wilby thought he saw a flicker of a smile cross his face.

The batman leaned in to him again.

"Wilby," he whispered.

"Ah," Bromhead said sadly. He stared at his glass. An uncomfortable silence fell over the mess table. Wilby's mortification was complete. And, perhaps because he wished himself dead, a small portion of his recent life flashed before his eyes.

•

The lieutenant had been suffering from terrible flatulence all the way from Helpmakaar. At first, he had thought it was something to do with his last meal (a deer shot, several times, by Major Black, which he could hardly have refused in any case) but as the column approached Rourke's Drift his bowels seemed in as great an uproar as ever. Fortunately the ride had been made at a canter, and he'd been able to clench his mount between his legs and smother the worst farts against his saddle — although the horse had tossed her head at some of the more drawn out ones — but as they came in sight of the mission station the major spurred them into a trot and then a run so that their pennant snapped overhead like a whip. Legs braced in the stirrups, knees bent, his body canted forward over his mount's neck, the lieutenant had had no choice but to release a crackling stream of utterance.

At first, there was some undeniable relief in this, but as each dip and rise and tussock jarred loose further bursts, he was obliged to cry, "Ya," and "Ho," as if encouraging his horse, to mask the worst outbreaks. He was grateful that over the drumming of hooves and the bugler who had hastily run out to welcome them to camp no one seemed to notice, but the severity of the attack made him doubt that he had not soiled his breeches and at the first opportunity he sought out the latrine to reassure himself.

Having put his mind at rest, seen to his tentage and placed his horse in the care of the groom he shared with the other junior officers, Wilby had taken himself off to the perimeter of the camp. Despite the newly built walls and the freshly dug graves—they were overgrown already, but their silhouettes were clearly visible in the long pale grass—it was all familiar to him from the articles in the *Army Gazette*, and in his mind he traced the events of the famous defense that had been fought there not three months before.

Fewer than a hundred able-bodied men, a single company plus those left behind at the mission hospital, had fought off a force of some five thousand Zulus—part of the same *impi* that had wiped out fifteen hundred men at Isandhlwana the previous day—holding out for upwards of ten hours of continuous close fighting and inflicting almost five hundred casualties on the enemy. It was a glorious tale and Wilby didn't need to look at the page from the *Gazette* that he kept in his tunic pocket to recall all the details. He had read and reread it so often on the ride out from Durban that it felt as fragile as an illuminated manuscript. "You'd think it was a love letter," the major had scoffed.

He should be rejoicing to be here, standing on the ground of the most famous battle in the world, and yet he only felt the churning of his wretched stomach. Tomorrow they would ride out, the first patrol to visit the site of Isandhlwana since the massacre.

He stared out in the direction they would take in the morning. The ferry across the drift was moored about two hundred yards away and on the far bank the track ran beside the river for a half mile or so and then cut away over a low rise and out of sight. Wilby found himself thinking of the Derbyshire countryside near his home . . . and fishing — up to his thighs in the dark cool water, feeling the pull of the current but dry inside his thick leather waders. He supposed the sight of the river must have brought it to mind.

It was Ferguson who found him out there. He saw the captain running towards him, his red tunic among the waving grass, shouting his news.

"Wills, we are invited to dine with Bromhead and Chard. You, myself, the major and Pierce."

"Truly?" Wilby caught his friend's arm, and Ferguson stooped for a moment to catch his breath. Then he shook himself free and took a step back, squared his shoulders and held up his hand as if reading from a card.

"Lieutenants Bromhead and Chard request the pleasure of Major Black and his staff's company for dinner in their mess at eight o'clock."

Of course, it was a little unusual for two lieutenants to invite a major to dinner, but by then Bromhead and Chard were expected to be made majors themselves — not to mention the Victoria Crosses everyone was predicting — and the breach of etiquette seemed altogether forgivable to Wilby. A dinner with Gonville Bromhead and Merriot Chard was simply the most sought after invitation in the whole of Natal in the spring of 1889.

"Good Lord, Fergie," he said. "Why, I must change."

He had spent the next hour in his suspenders and undershirt polishing the buttons of his tunic, slipping a small brass plate behind them to protect the fabric and then working the polish into the raised regimental crests and burnishing them to a glow. Next he worked on his boots, smearing long streaks of bootblack up and down, working them into the hide with a swift circular motion, and then bringing the leather to a shine with a stiff brush. He thought hard about the thin beard and mustache he had begun to grow three weeks before and with a sigh pulled out his razor. Ferguson, waxing his own mustache, paused and watched him in silence, but Wilby refused to meet his eye. His mustache would never be as good as the captain's anyway. Fergie's mustache was justly famous in the regiment, said to be wide enough for troopers riding behind him to see both ends. Wilby knew that wasn't quite true. The captain had made him check. He stood behind him trying to make out both waxed tips. In the end, they had had to call in the chaplain and standing shoulder to shoulder, about five feet behind Ferguson, Wilby and Pierce had each been able to see a tip of mustache on either side.

Wilby lathered the soap in his shaving mug and applied it with the badgerhair brush his father had given him before he'd come out on campaign. The razor was dull and he had to pause to strop it, but he managed to shave without drawing blood.

Finally, he extracted his second set of epaulets and his best collar from the tissue paper he kept them in and had Ferguson fix them in place. The fragrant smell of hair oil filled their tent as they each in turn vigorously applied a brush to each other's tunics. Without a decent mirror, they paused and scrutinized each other carefully, then bowed deeply—Wilby from the waist, Ferguson taking a step back and dropping his arm in a flourish.

The meal had gone well at first. The major had introduced him to first Chard and then Bromhead and he'd looked them both in the eyes (Chard's gray, Bromhead's brown) and shaken hands firmly. In between, he had made to clasp his hands behind his back and been sure to rub them on his tunic to ensure they were dry. "How do you do, sir?" he had said to each in turn.

"Very well," Chard had said in his gruff way.

"Splendid," Bromhead had told him a little too loudly.

The story of his deafness, that he would almost certainly have been pensioned off if his older brother had not been on Chelmsford's staff, was well known among the junior officers. It was said that he had only been given B company of the 2nd/24th because it was composed almost entirely of Welshmen and it was thought that his deafness wouldn't be so noticeable or important to men who spoke English with such an impenetrable accent. There was even a joke that Bromhead's company had only received its posting at Rourke's Drift because the lieutenant thought the general had been offering him more pork rib at the mess table. "Rather," he was reputed to have said. "Sounds tasty."

Some of the officers still made fun of Bromhead, but Wilby put it down to simple jealousy. For his own part, he thought it more not less heroic that Bromhead had overcome his disability. He had a theory that amid all the noise of battle a deaf man might have an advantage, might come to win the respect of men hoarse from shouting and deafened by the report of their arms.

At dinner, Wilby had waited until the major and Ferguson had each made some remark or other, nodded at each response and echoed the chaplain's compliments on the food. Only then, as the batman passed the gravy boat among them did he ask a question of his own.

"How does it feel?" he said. "I mean, how does it feel to be heroes?"

Bromhead looked at him closely for a moment, but it was Chard who answered.

"Well," he began. He stroked his beard and it made an audible rasping sound. "I would have to say, principally, the sensation is one of relief. Relief to be alive after all — not like the poor devils you'll see tomorrow — but also relief to have learned some truth about myself. To have found I am possessed of — for want of a better word — courage."

"Rather," Ferguson said. He grinned at Wilby.

What a blowhard, Bromhead thought. It pained him that Chard's name and his own should be so inextricably linked.

Bromhead and Chard. Chard and Bromhead. He felt like a blasted vaudevillian.

"It's an ambition fulfilled," Chard went on, ignoring the interruption. "Since I was a little chap I remember wondering—as who has not?—if I were a brave fellow. Cowardice, funk—more than any imagined beast or goblin, that was my great terror. And now, I have my answer." He paused and looked around the table slowly and this time it was harder for Wilby to hold his gaze. "If the chaplain would be so good as to forgive me, I rather fancy it is as if I have stood before St. Peter, himself, not knowing if I were a bally sinner or no, and dashed me if he hasn't found my name there among the elect."

The chaplain smiled and bobbed his head complacently. Wilby and Ferguson glanced at each other again, their eyes bright, but not quite meeting in their excitement.

"Heavens!" said Bromhead, clearing his throat. "For my part, being a hero is nothing so like how I fancy a beautiful young debutante must feel." There was a puzzled round of laughter, but Wilby saw Chard press his lips together—a white line behind his dark beard—and kept his own features still. "You've seen them at balls, gentlemen, there are one or two each season, those girls who aren't quite sure, but then discover all of a sudden quite how delightful they are. Oh, I don't know. Perhaps their mamas had told them so, but they'd not believed them. After all, that's what mamas are for. They'd not known whether to listen to their doting fathers and all those old loyal servants, surely too ugly to know what was beautiful or not anymore. And then, suddenly, in one evening, confound it, they know. And all around them, instantly, why who but our own good selves, gentlemen—suitors all."

Wilby could see Ferguson smile and he knew he was thinking of Ethel, his betrothed. He had seen such women as Bromhead described himself, but his own smile was more rueful. (He remembered one long conversation with a certain Miss Fanshaw who had cheerfully told him that she had sent no less than five white feathers to men she knew at the time of the Crimea—"And you know," she had told him earnestly, "not one of them returned home alive.") The major he knew would be thinking of his wife, home in Bath, and the chaplain, he supposed, of God. He saw Chard, bored, study his reflection in the silverware.

"Anyway," the major said. "Put us out of our misery. Let's hear all the details of this famous defense of yours, eh? Give us the story from the horse's mouth, so to speak."

"Oh, well," Bromhead opened his hands. "It was fairly fierce, I suppose. The outcome was in doubt for some hours." He faltered and Wilby who had been leaning forward eagerly, sat back and saw the others look disappointed. This was after all what they had come for.

Chard, however, stepped in. He was an officer of engineers and he believed in telling a tale correctly.

He told them about the hours of hand-to-hand combat, of the bayonets that the men called "lungers" and of the *assegais* of the Zulus. How the men's guns had become so hot from firing that they cooked off rounds as soon as they were loaded causing the men to miss, so hot that the soft brass shell casings melted in the breeches and had to be dug out with a knife before the whole futile process could begin again. He told them about men climbing up on the wall they'd built of biscuit boxes and mealie bags and lunging down into the darkness; of the black hands reaching up to grab the barrels and the shrieks of pain when they touched the hot glowing metal. Shrieks that were oddly louder than the soft grunts men gave as a bayonet or assegai found its mark. He told them about the sound of bullets clattering into the biscuit boxes at the base of the wall, and rustling in the mealie bags nearer the top, so that you knew the Zulus were getting their range. He described men overpowered, dragged over the walls, surrounded by warriors. How the Zulus knocked them down and ripped open their tunics, and the popping sound of buttons flying loose. "That would be the last sound a lot of our chaps heard," he said. With their tunics open the Zulus would disembowel them, opening men from balls to breastbone with one swift strike.

"I swear I'll never be able to see another button pop loose

from a shirt without thinking of it," Chard said. He took a sip of wine. "Of course, you'll see a good deal of that handiwork tomorrow, I'll warrant."

That was when Wilby began to feel his flatulence return, and his discomfort grew even when Bromhead broke in and explained that the Zulus believed that opening a man's chest was the only way to set his spirit free from his dead body.

"Really, it's an act of mercy as they see it," he said. "I hope so, at least. There was one poor chap of mine, a Private Williams. Bit of a no-account, but a decent sort. I saw him get fairly dragged over the wall before I caught hold his leg. This was quite in the thick of it. There were so many Zulus trying to rush us from all sides they were like water swirling round a rock in a stream. Quite a ghastly tug of war I had for him with them. Every time they had him to their side he'd give one of those little grunts Chard was talking about, but then I'd pull like mad and when I had him more to me he'd look up and say in a cheery way, 'Much obliged, sir.' In the end, they began to swarm over the walls all about us and I had to let him go to draw my pistol. I told him I was sorry — I fancied he'd be in a bad panic, you know — but he just said, 'Not at all, sir,' and 'Thank you kindly, sir.'"

Bromhead paused.

"I was going to write to his people. Say how sorry I was I couldn't save him. But dashed if he didn't join up under a false name. A lot of the Welshmen do it seems. For a long time I thought they were all just called Evans and Williams and Jones and what-have-you, but it turns out that those are just the most obvious false names for them to choose. His blamed leg — you know I can't get it out of my mind — how remarkably warm it was."

He sat back and the batman took the opportunity to step forward with the port. Bromhead watched in silence as the glasses filled with redness.

Wilby had managed a few quiet expulsions, but then came the surprising and ruinous fart.

The silence around the table seemed to go on for hours—Wilby could hear the pickets calling out their challenge to the final patrols of the evening. Finally, Bromhead looked over and said genially, "Preserved potatoes." He shook his head. "Make you fart like a confounded horse."

He waved his man forward with the cigars and as they passed around he leaned in towards the table and looked around at them all.

"Reminds me of a story," he said, cutting the end of his cigar. "I haven't thought of it in years, mind you—about a bally Latin class, of all things." He ran the end of the cigar around his tongue and raised his chin for the batman to light him. "Hardly the story you expected to hear, but I'll beg your indulgence." He took a mighty puff and began.

"Well, we had this old tyrant of a teacher, Marlow, his name was, of the habit of making us work at our books in silence every other afternoon. Any noise and he would beat you with a steel ruler that he carried from his days in the navy. Now that was fear. I swear it was rumored among us—a rumor spread no doubt by older boys to put a fright on us and, who knows, still attached to some teacher down to this day—that boys had lost fingers, chopped clean off at the knuckle by that ruler.

"I must have been upwards of twelve or so. I can't recall quite the circumstances, but I'd bent over from my desk to retrieve a pen I'd dropped—or more likely some blighter had thrown—on the floor. We were always trying to get some other poor bugger to make a sound and bring down the tyrant's wrath upon their heads, but anyhow, as I say, I'd bent over to pick up my pen—I was in the middle of translating 'Horatio on the Bridge' or some such rot—and, what do you know but I farted. Quite surprised myself. Quite taken aback, I was. Not that it was an especially, you know, loud one. More of a pop really. Or a squeak. Hang me if that's not it either. Let's just say somewhere between a pop and a squeak. Hardly a decent fart at all, if the truth be told, it's rather astonishing

I can remember it so well. No matter. Whatever the precise sound of the expulsion, in that room with everyone trying to be still it was like a bally pistol shot, like the crack of a whip.

"Well the fellows behind me, of course, went off into absolute fits and gales. Up jumps the tyrant brandishing his ruler and I fancy I'm for the high jump now. The whole room falls silent as the grave and the old man stalks up the aisle between our desks looking hard all about him.

"'John Beddows,' he says to one of the chaps behind me, and his voice is veritable steel. 'Would you mind telling me what is the source of this hilarity?'

"'Nothing, sir,' says John — a decent enough sort, loafer that he was — and I begin to think I might be spared, but dash me if the old man doesn't persist.

"'Nothing,' he says. 'You had to be laughing at something, boy. Only idiots laugh at nothing. Are you an idiot, Mister Beddows?' And he bent that ruler in his hands.

"'No, sir,' says John pulling a long face. 'Please, sir. Gonville Bromhead farted, sir.'"

Wilby risked a glance around the faces at the table and saw that Ferguson was grinning broadly, his teeth showing around his cigar. The chaplain, too, was struggling to keep a straight face and even Major Black had a curious look in his eye. Only Chard showed no glimmer of humor. He had stubbed out his cigar and taken an apple which he was chewing steadily.

"Of course," Bromhead went on. "You can imagine the pandemonium. You'd have thought there was a murder in progress and to be honest I could have cheerfully strangled Beddows. I let out a swear or two under my breath, but the tyrant himself was at a loss for a moment. All I could do was snatch my hands up from where they'd been lying on the desk and press them into my pockets.

"'Silence!' the tyrant finally bellowed, and then with me cringing, 'That's quite enough drollery, gentlemen. Back to work. All of you.'

"Of course, it was only a reprieve of sorts. The worst was still to come. By-and-by, we came out for our break and the other chaps started up a game of tag. I was too angry or ashamed to join them. I took myself off to a corner of the yard and watched. One person would be on, his tie would be undone, and he'd tag another who'd also pull his tie open and they'd keep tagging until everyone had their ties hanging loose. Only when some of them ran closer to me did I catch the name of the game. 'Funky Farters.'" Bromhead looked around him, his face a mask of tragedy.

"That dashed game became the craze at school for months, although I can tell you I never played it. I had dreams, nightmares really, of boys going home at the holidays and teaching it to their friends and in this way the detestable game—and my disgrace—spreading to every durned school in England. Can you imagine? I couldn't shake the notion. I thought with certitude that affair would be the only thing I'd be known for in my whole life. I thought, I'll die and my only lasting contribution to this life will be a fart in a confounded Latin class."

The table was roaring with laughter by now, the chaplain dabbing at his eyes with his napkin, Ferguson clutching his sides, and the major positively braying. Ash from the almost extinguished cigar in his hand peppered the table as he shook. Wilby found himself laughing, too, uncontrollably relieved. He caught Bromhead's eye and the older lieutenant nodded.

•

The meal broke up shortly after—the major's patrol would have to leave camp at first light—and the men went out into the night to find their own tents. Bromhead leaned back in his chair and watched the major sidle up to Wilby and Ferguson and say, "I remember once letting loose a mighty one on parade in India," and the two young officers staggered with laughter. The chaplain was the last to leave. He smiled at Bromhead and shook his head. "An edifying tale." Then he hurried after the other three and Bromhead saw him put an arm around Wilby's shoulder.

Only Chard stalked off alone, his back straight and his chin held high. "Now that man," Bromhead said to his batman, "mark my words—has never farted in his life. It'd break his back to let rip now." He lit another cigar and smoked it thoughtfully, while the batman cleared the plates from the table.

"It's a terrible thing being afraid, Watkins, do you not think?"

The batman said he thought it was.

"Join me," he said and he poured two glasses of the celebrated port and they sat and drank in silence for a moment.

"Bloody rum thing. Zulus thinking to find a fellow's soul in his entrails, eh?"

The batman nodded. The port tasted like syrup to him and later he would need a swig of his Squareface—the army-issue gin in its square bottle—to take the taste away.

It was late and the light breeze through the tent felt cold to Bromhead. He always took more of a chill when he'd been drinking. He pulled a blanket off the cot behind him and draped it around his shoulders. "Like an old woman," he said. He wrapped his arms around himself under the blanket, clutching his shoulders, and thought again how really remarkably *warm* Private Williams's leg had felt.

"Wake me," he said to the batman, "before the major's patrol leaves in the morning. I think I should like to see them off."

Anna Akhmatova

Secrets of the Trade

1. Inspiration

It happens like this: a kind of lethargy,
In my ears the sound of a clock chiming,
Thunder fading in the distance.
Trapped, unrecognizable voices
Wail and cry out to me: the closing in
Of some mysterious circle.
But from this abyss of whispers and bells
Rises a single all-conquering sound,
Despite the forest's surrounding
Silence — hear grass growing,
Hear the wood troll walking with his sack.
And listen! The sound of words,
Rhymes signaling their arrival,
And I begin to understand:
Lines simply taken down
Appear on pages white as snow.

2.

I have no use for battlefield odes,
And the charms of an intricate elegy.
For me a poem must be impromptu —
Not a matter of tradition.

If you only knew what kind of trash
Poems shamelessly grow in:
Like weeds under the fence,
Like crabgrass, dandelions.

An angry shout, the smell of fresh tar,
Mysterious mildew on the wall—
And a poem begins sounding fervent, tender,
Making us all joyful.

3. The Muse

How can I live with this burden—
And yet she's called The Muse.
"She's with you in a meadow . . . ," they say.

They say, "Divine muttering!"
She'll seize you worse than a fever
And then, for an entire year, nothing at all.

4. The Poet

You call this *work*, this breezy life:
Overhearing something
In music, then passing it off
Half-seriously as your own.

Casting someone's merry scherzo
Into lines of some sort,
Swearing it's your own poor heart
That aches in a bright meadow.

Then eavesdropping on the woods,
On the seemingly mute pine,
While everywhere fog stands
Like a smoke screen.

I take right and left
Without the least pang of guilt:
A little from mischievous life,
All from night's silence.

5. The Reader

The poet can't be too sad
Or, worse still, too sly.
For general understanding,
The poet must be open wide.

The footlights in front of him,
Bare and bright, deathly;
The cold blaze of limelight
Branding his face.

But every reader is a secret,
A buried treasure, of sorts—
Even the last to come,
And remaining a lifelong mute.

There's the one nature keeps from us
Whenever she feels like it;
There's the one who weeps helplessly
At the prearranged hour.

And *there* (darkness,
shadows, chilly air)—
And *there*—the unknown eyes
That speak to me till dawn.

About some things they rebuke me,
About others they agree.
And so it goes, like a silent confession,
The flow of our warm exchange.

Life on earth is short,
Our given sphere constricted,
But the poet's unknown friend
Is constant and eternal.

6. The Last Poem

Bursting into the house like startled thunder
The first one comes, breathless, laughing,
Fluttering at my throat and spinning
To the sound of its own applause.

Another is born in the silence of midnight,
Stealing upon me from who knows where.
It peers at me from an empty mirror,
Mumbling something pitiless.

Then from nowhere come others
Which seem not to notice I'm here.
They trickle down the white page
Like spring water in a ravine.

And there's one that roams secretly—
No sound no color, no color no sound—
It plays with light like a faceted stone.
It grows, thrives, and won't be taken alive.

One, drop by drop, sucked all my blood
As young love did, that nasty girl.
Then, without a word,
Turned wholly speechless again.

And then came the worst fate of all.
It left. In its wake it left the signs
To circumscribed infinity.
And without it, I'm here with death.

7. An Epigram

Did Beatrice have Dantesque visions?
Did Laura write Petrarchan sonnets:
I've taught women to speak, O God—
But how can I teach them silence?

8. Poems

Wrung-out insomnias,
Pooled wax at the base
Of a guttering candle,
The morning's first sound
Of a hundred white bells.
Warm sills under Chernigov moons.
Bees and clover, darkness and dust,
Suffocating heat.

9.

Many things want my voice to praise them,
Many things rumble, seemingly speechless;
Or they gnaw at rocks underground in the dark,
Or they show up in a circle of smoke.
But because I've not settled my score
With wind, water, and fire,
Sleepless nights can suddenly take me
To the very gates that lead
To the morning star.

*—translated from the Russian
by Jo Ann Clark, with Zhenya Zafrin*

Scott Cairns

Interval with Erato

That's what I like best about you, Erato sighed in bed, *that's why*
you've become one of my favorites and why you will always be so.
I grazed her ear with my tongue, held the salty lobe between my lips.

I feel like singing when you do that, she said with more than a hint
of music already in her voice. *So sing*, I said, and moved down
to the tenderness at the edge of her jaw. *Hmmm*, she said, *that's nice.*

Is there anything you don't *like?* I asked, genuinely meaning
to please. *I don't like poets in a hurry*, she said, shifting
so my lips would achieve the more dangerous divot of her throat.

Ohhhh, she said, as I pressed a little harder there. She held my face
in both hands. *And I hate when they get careless, especially*
when employing second-person address. She sat up, and my mouth

fell to the tip of one breast. *Yes*, she said, *you know how it can be—*
they're writing "you did this" and "you did that" and I always assume,
at first, that they mean me! She slid one finger into my mouth to tease

the nipple there. *I mean it's disappointing enough to observe
the lyric is addressed to someone else, and* then, *the poet
spends
half the poem spouting information that the* you — *if she or
he*

*were listening — would have known already, ostensibly as well
as,
or better than, the speaker.* I stopped to meet her eyes. *I know
just
what you mean*, I said. She leaned down to take a turn, working my chest

with her mouth and hands, then sat back in open invitation.
Darling, she said as I returned to the underside of her breast,
have you noticed how many poets talk to themselves, about
themselves?

I drew one finger down the middle of her back. *Maybe they
fear
no one else will hear or care.* I sucked her belly, cupped her
sopping
vulva with my hand. *My that's delicious*, she said, lifting into
me.

Are all poets these days so lonely? She wove her fingers with
mine
so we could caress her there together. *Not me*, I said, and ran
my slick hands back up to her breasts. I tongued her thighs.
I said, *I'm not

lonely now.* She rubbed my neck, *No, dear, and you shouldn't
be.* She clenched, *Oh!
a little early bonus*, she said; *I like surprises.* Then, *so
few poets appreciate surprises, so many prefer to speak*

*only what they, clearly, already know, or think they know. If I
were a poet . . . well, I wouldn't be one at all if I hadn't
found a way to get a little something for myself—something
new*

from every outing, no? Me neither, I said, if somewhat indistinctly.
Oh! she said. *Yes!* she said, and tightened so I felt her pulse against
my lips. She lay quiet for a moment, obviously thinking.

Sweetie, she said, *that's what I like best about you—you pay attention,
and you know how to listen when a girl feels like a little song.
Let's see if we can't find a little something now, especially for you.*

Agha Shahid Ali

After the August Wedding in Lahore, Pakistan,
for Shafaq Husain

we all—Save the couple!—returned to pain,
some in Massachusetts, some in Kashmir
where, wet by turns, Order's dry campaign
had glued petals with bullets to each pane—
Sarajevo Roses! A gift to glass,
that city's name. What else breaks? A lover's pain!
But happiness? Must it, too, bring pain?
Question I may ask because of a night—
by ice sculptures, all my words sylvanite
under one gaze that filled my glass with pain.
That thirst haunts as does the fevered dancing,
flames dying among orchids flown in from Sing-

apore! Sing then, not of the promising
but the Promised End. Of what final pain,
what image of that horror can I sing?
To be forgotten the most menacing!
Those "Houseboat Days in the Vale of Kashmir,"
for instance, in '29: Did they sing
just of love then, or was love witnessing
its departure for other thirsts—the glass
of Dal Lake ruffled half by "Satin Glass,"
that chandeliered boat barely focusing
on emptiness—last half of any night?
In Lahore the chanteuse crooned "Stop the Night"—

the groom's request—after the banquet. *Night,*
that Empress, is here, your bride. She will sing!
Her limbs break like chrysanthemums. O Night,
what hints have been passed in the sky tonight?
The stars so quiet, what galaxies of pain

leave them unable to prophesy this night?
With a rending encore, she closed the night.
There was, like this, long ago in Kashmir,
a moment—after a concert—outside Kashmir
Book Shop that left me stranded, by midnight,
in a hotel mirror. Would someone glass
me in—from what? Filled, I emptied my glass,

lured by a stranger's eyes into their glass.
There, nothing melted, as in Lahore's night:
Heat had brought sweat to the lip of my glass
but sculptures kept iced their aberrant glass.
To be forgotten my most menacing
image of the End—expelled from the glass
of someone's eyes as if no full-length glass
had held us, safe, from political storms? Pain,
then, becomes love's thirst—the ultimate pain
to lose a stranger! O, to have said, glass
in hand, "Where Thou art—that—is Home— / Cashmere—
or Calvary—the same"! In the Cašmir

and Poison and Brüt air, my rare Cashmere
thrown off, the stranger knew my arms are glass,
that banished from Eden (on earth: Kashmir)
into the care of storms (it rains in Kashmir,
in Lahore, and here in Amherst tonight),
in each new body I would drown Kashmir.
A brigadier says, *The boys of Kashmir*
break so quickly, we make their bodies sing,
on the rack, till no song is left to sing.
"Butterflies pause / On their passage Cashmere—"
And happiness: must it only bring pain?
The century is ending. It is pain

from which love departs into all new pain:
Freedom's terrible thirst, flooding Kashmir,
is bringing love to its tormented glass.
Stranger, who will inherit the last night
of the past? Of what shall I not sing, and sing?

Eric Ormsby

Mutanabbi Praises the Prince

Abū al-Tayyib al-Mutanabbī, the greatest of all classical Arabic poets, moved from court to court in Syria, Egypt and Iraq, earning his living as a panegyrist. He was murdered by robbers in 965.

The luscious reddening gold of the emir's coin
Buys my encomia. I haggle in magnificence,
Or then I elbow-dust his aureole.
But such praise costs. The syllables are pearl
Nipped from the darkness of Bahraini seas
By clever divers, or rubies of Kashmir
Pried from reluctant mines.

Let others gown the Prince in obsequious fabrics
Or snuggle bracelets and rings of hammered gold
Over his wrists and fingers, or incense his hair
With myrrh or labdanum, or dunk his feet
In subtle unguents brought from Hadramaut.
I garment him in the golden fragrance of praise
That gives men life forever, that will ring
In the shadowy mouths of the unborn,
His great-grandchildren's unimagined progeny,
In chains of consequence effected by the will
Of the Compassionate across ungenerated time.

A manuscript page from an essay by Helen Vendler.

Helen Vendler
The Art of Criticism III

Helen Hennessy Vendler was born in Boston in 1933. She studied chemistry at Emmanuel College, a Roman Catholic school for women in Boston, and went to the University of Louvain after graduation on a Fulbright fellowship. She took her Ph.D. at Harvard in 1960 with a dissertation on Yeats, and the following year began teaching at Cornell. She later held regular appointments at Swarthmore, Haverford, Smith and Boston University, as well as a Fulbright professorship at the University of Bordeaux. In 1981 she joined the faculty of Harvard. In 1990 she was given the title of Porter University Professor.

Vendler's academic successes have been complemented by numerous appointments in non-university settings. She has been consultant poetry editor to The New York Times, *presi-*

dent of the Modern Language Association, and, since 1978, poetry critic for The New Yorker.

Vendler's books include Yeats's Vision and the Later Plays *(1963),* On Extended Wings: Wallace Stevens's Longer Poems, *which was awarded the James Russell Lowell Prize in 1969,* The Poetry of George Herbert *(1975),* The Odes of John Keats *(1983),* Wallace Stevens: Words Chosen Out of Desire *(1984),* The Music of What Happens *(1988),* Soul Says *(1995),* The Given and the Made *(1995),* The Breaking of Style *(1995) and* Poems, Poets, Poetry *(1995). She received the National Book Critics Circle Award for Criticism in 1981 for* Part of Nature, Part of Us: Modern American Poets. *She has edited two books: the* Harvard Book of Contemporary American Poetry *in 1985 and* Voices and Visions: The Poet in America *in 1987.*

The following interview with Helen Vendler took place in the second-floor living room of her townhouse in Cambridge, a few blocks away from the Harvard English department. Mrs. Vendler wore a loose maroon sweater and black slacks. Around us were the mementos of a life devoted to poets and poetry. "Everything in this room was given to me," she admitted. As we began our interview, Mrs. Vendler looked weary, but seemed to get a second wind as we continued. She'd awoken early that morning, worried about a meeting with her tax accountant. It was one of many appointments necessary before leaving for England, where she would be in residence at Magdalene College in Cambridge for the spring. After the interview we lingered on her stairwell, where many framed holographs and broadsides of poems—from A.R. Ammons, Frank Bidart, Seamus Heaney, Howard Nemerov and Stephen Spender—were hung. There was also an occasional poem, a quatrain accompanying a stamped print of a peacock, received from James Merrill. And there was a poem, sent along with a doll-sized gavel, from Elizabeth Bishop, when Mrs. Vendler was elected the second vice-president of the Modern Language Association. An expression of anxiousness came over Mrs. Vendler's face as we looked over this large wall of mementos, until she asked, like a concerned parent, if she had forgotten to mention anyone in her interview.

INTERVIEWER

Under the burden of manuscripts to read, letters of recommendation and endorsements of tenure to write, and student papers to grade, when do you find time to write?

HELEN VENDLER

I always write after I think for quite a long time, so the actual writing time is rather short. I think a lot of the work gets done when you have something on your mind while you're doing many other things. Your unconscious mind is turning this over and over underneath, and then one morning you wake up with a whole lot of things formulated that you haven't been consciously working on. At that point you can sit down and write. So, it's not that it takes very long when I actually do it, but it takes quite a long time to work up to it.

INTERVIEWER

Do you think that your teaching has helped your criticism?

VENDLER

Oh, it would have to, if only because you learn more poems by heart every year from teaching them. They work on you then in a different way from the way they work on you when you're reading them off the page. They live in you in different rhythms and come to mean more when you know them by heart.

INTERVIEWER

Do you write for a particular audience?

VENDLER

No, I write to explain things to myself.

INTERVIEWER
So your audience is yourself.

VENDLER
Well, I think of my audience in part as being the poet. What I would hope would be that if Keats read what I had written about the ode "To Autumn," he would say, "Yes, that is the way I wanted it to be thought of." And "Yes, you have unfolded what I had implied," or something like that. It would not strike the poet, I hope, that there was a discrepancy between my description of the work and the poet's own conception of the work. I wouldn't be very happy if a poet read what I had written and said, "What a peculiar thing to say about this work of mine."

INTERVIEWER
No poet has ever done that?

VENDLER
No, not yet. I should add that they may have been too polite to say that.

INTERVIEWER
Do you think your criticism is hard to read?

VENDLER
I think that a lot of things are hard to read if you're not in the vocabulary flow of that particular discourse. I sometimes forget that even though the words I'm using are fairly ordinary words, the concepts around which they cluster, which are the long concepts of literary tradition, may not be familiar to an audience. People who write about science for the general public also have to think a little about making certain concepts clear that would be second nature to anyone in their labs.

INTERVIEWER
Do you think of yourself as the heir to a particular critic? You worked on your Ph.D. with I.A. Richards, didn't you?

VENDLER

No, I audited two classes of his when I was in graduate school at Harvard. The chairman would not permit me to take Richards's class because Richards was based in the School of Education, not in the Department of English (Richards came to Harvard on a Carnegie Grant developing Basic English). His course was scratched off my program card by the chairman, and Chaucer was sternly substituted for it. Nothing daunted, I simply audited a course and a seminar from Richards. He certainly was the most important influence on me, except for John Kelleher. They were the two most indelible teachers that I had at Harvard — I.A. Richards because he gave full weight to every word in a poem and might track the history of a word back to Plato, taking it back through various philosophical and literary associations until the whole historical and cultural richness of the word was exposed. And John Kelleher, because he saw the human situation from which a given poem would arise; since he was an historian, he noted the political situation, or the social situation. In each case, in his class in Irish poetry, the poem was seen to spring out of the trial, struggle, relation of events in the history of Ireland. So in those two ways — both contextualizing ways, historically contextualizing in the case of Kelleher, and philosophically and literarily contextualizing in the case of Richards — they influenced me. They were both magnificent readers of poetry aloud.

INTERVIEWER

How would you describe the hybridization of those two influences in yourself?

VENDLER

Oh, I'm far less contextual than John Kelleher. You of course learn what you need to read a particular poet, as I learned something about Rosicrucianism and the history of Ireland and occultism and Japanese Nō drama, say, to write about Yeats. You couldn't not get up those contexts, but for me they are only the groundwork, not central. I'm far closer to Richards, though I am much less philosophical than he was. I think I see words in their literary connotations, but not so much in their philosophical history as Richards did.

INTERVIEWER

As you age do you find yourself valuing different kinds of poems or different traits of poems?

VENDLER

I don't believe that poems are written to be heard or, as Mill said, to be overheard; nor are poems addressed to their reader. I believe that poems are a score for performance by the reader, and that you become the speaking voice. You don't read or overhear the voice in the poem, you *are* the voice in the poem. You stand behind the words and speak them as your own—so that it is a very different form of reading from what you might do in a novel where a character is telling the story, where the speaking voice is usurped by a fictional person to whom you listen as the novel unfolds.

In terms of reading different poets as one gets older . . . I've been reading old-age poetry for so long, I feel as though I had the poems before I needed them in terms of life, but I certainly needed them in terms of art. I needed "The Auroras of Autumn" when I was twenty-three; and you always need art that is good no matter what its theme, at all ages. So I wouldn't say that I'm now looking for old-age poetry. The only time in my life that I remember looking for poetry, because I didn't already have some in my head, was when I became a mother and I was looking around for poems about motherhood. I looked, but I didn't find any except Sylvia Plath's. Hers were the only ones I knew, and they meant a lot to me then, especially those beautiful ones about her child waking up in the morning, or herself getting up at night and hearing the vowels the child utters, rising like balloons.

INTERVIEWER

Do you feel confined in any way as a critic?

VENDLER

Well, Barbara Smith once said to me, "But, Helen, you're so narrow." And I said to her, "What do you mean, Barbara? All of lyric from Shakespeare till now?" And she said, "Oh, you know what I mean." And what she meant at the time was that I wasn't doing theory. From one perspective, so-and-so's book may seem narrow, while it may seem very deep and rich to someone else.

INTERVIEWER

Do you feel confined as a woman critic in any way?

VENDLER

No, I don't think the mind is gendered. I know that's not a popular position these days, but I never felt the mind to be gendered and perhaps that may be because I always read poetry. When I was a young girl reading and the page said, "My heart aches, and a drowsy numbness pains my sense," or "So are you to my thoughts as food to life," it never occurred to me that these thoughts were not available to me because they had been uttered by an author who was male. I didn't care who had uttered them. They seemed good things to say at a given moment. Now, I know women who've had very different experiences when they were young; I've heard many people say, "I never found myself responding until I came to . . . " And it might be *Jane Eyre*, or it might be *Wuthering Heights*, or it might be *Emma*. I finally realized that those women were novel readers, and what they were looking for was a story like their own story, or a story in which they could imagine themselves playing a role. Of course, if you are a girl reading *Oedipus Rex*, there is no role for you to play as hero. So if you have a naturally fictional imagination, you might say, "That's not a story into which I can walk." But I didn't have a fictional imagination, so I didn't run into that particular difficulty.

INTERVIEWER

Is there anything you fear as a critic?

VENDLER

I fear giving short shrift to something that is really very good, which I don't recognize at the time. We all know critics who have done that: the critics of Keats who told him to go back to his apothecary pots; the critics of Stevens who thought he was a dandy; the critics of *The Waste Land* who thought it was a hoax; and, perhaps, myself as a critic, say, of Pound, about whom I've never written, whom I think of as a minor poet of the fin de siècle and the early century. I don't admire the *Cantos*; perhaps that's a big blind spot in me since there are certainly many exquisitely gifted readers and writers who have admired the *Cantos*. But I can't. I've tried over and over. As Pound himself said later on, "I cannot make it cohere," and they don't cohere for me. Perhaps I'm missing a great body of work because of some defect in me. That's not how I see it, but it is how others see it.

INTERVIEWER

What about as a woman, is there something you fear?

VENDLER

I have always feared the criticism that the world offers you when you're a woman who is not conventional. In many ways, I am conventional: I have a conventional-looking house, I wear conventional clothes, I don't do terribly unconventional things in public — so that I might to some appear conventional. On the other hand, given my upbringing and the expectations of my society, my behavior was not conventional. And I felt isolated and alienated. I still experience that feeling of being alone in a room, when no one in the room is like you.

INTERVIEWER

Do you think the content of your reviews ever grows as a result of your own language instead of a poet's?

VENDLER

Oh, no. My language is so much the inferior of the poets'. Even a minor poet has far greater gifts of language than I have.

INTERVIEWER

Do you think you have ever either overpraised or damned something?

VENDLER

Well, I know there are people who think I've overpraised things. I'm sure Randall Jarrell would have thought that I overpraised Stevens's long poems, since he found them humorless and elephantine. And I'm sure people have thought there are contemporary poets I've overpraised.

INTERVIEWER

But none that you have changed your mind about.

VENDLER

No, I think people I have admired have worn remarkably well over the years, whether they are uneven poets, as some of them are, where I like some works better than others, or whether they maintain a consistently high standard as, say, I think Seamus Heaney has done, volume after volume.

INTERVIEWER

And an example of an uneven poet would be?

VENDLER

Ginsberg, for instance, where I think there are always wonderful poems in every volume but the volumes are very uneven in poetic quality. Nonetheless, the people I have written about the most seem to have had good staying power for me over the years. I think of the earliest people I wrote about—probably Lowell, Rich, Ginsberg, Merrill, Ammons, Bishop—all of them have the power to maintain a critic's interest over many, many years.

Usually, I think there's nothing to be said about mediocre poetry. It's like being a talent scout for an opera company, when all you can say about the voice you hear is, "No, it has no carrying power, it hasn't any capacity to stay on pitch, it hasn't any sense of innate rhythm, it hasn't any expressive color, it hasn't interpretive power . . . it's just no, no, no." If you're a talent scout, what you like is to have a voice come along that not only has interpretive color, carrying power and musical intelligence, but is also distinctive in timbre. Then you can say a lot about the voice. When qualities are *not* there, it is very hard to describe, since you're describing absences. When the qualities *are* there you delight in showing how they're deployed.

INTERVIEWER

When you read a poem, do you see meaning or hear language first? Or, to put the question another way, are you aware of subject and theme first or does style, voice . . . the way words rub against one another engage you first?

VENDLER

I think what hits you on the page is different with different poets. I remember the first thing striking me about Stevens was hearing his voice on a record. Suddenly, this voice was unspooling. I didn't even know what the poem was about. All I knew was that there were these wonderful lines that I would never have willingly walked away from. I went out and read all of Stevens. So it can be a voice that grips you, that is doing something with language long before you know the theme. In the case of Jorie Graham, it was reading some poems in *The American Poetry Review* and hearing a new rhythm. I am convinced her rhythms come from Italian, or maybe from French; it's some foreign rhythm that she has brought into English. I hadn't ever heard that rhythm before. I don't even remember now what the poems in *APR* were about; I only remember the new rhythm that was not known to me before.

INTERVIEWER

Does a poet come to mind whose theme first riveted you?

VENDLER

Yes, but I think it was because it was very well done formally. *A Change of World*, Adrienne Rich's first book, was given to me as a present by the woman I worked for, the registrar of Radcliffe College (I was working as temporary office help). She gave Rich's book to me when I left her office after the year I had worked for her. When I sat down and read it, it was just astonishing (as I wrote later) that someone my age was writing down my life. That was an immediate thematic connection with an American woman of my own generation who was writing down love poems, family poems, that were gripping to me. The one that struck me the most was a poem called "The Middle-Aged," which was about living in the house of your parents and not thinking of it as your own house. That was the way I had felt about my parent's house; I couldn't believe someone had written that down.

INTERVIEWER

Yet, I've read that you think of yourself as among what Roland Barthes calls "explorers of the bliss of writing," as opposed to those who look for meaning, import, philosophy, social truth. Is this true?

VENDLER

On a spectrum of A to Z, yes, I think so. It's not that I'm indifferent to meaning. Reading the Rich poem about parents and children was transfixing to me at that time when I so badly needed explanations of relationships. But I think you come to need explanations of the world somewhat less intensely after adolescence, when you make up a world picture of your own. Though with each crisis that you come to, when the world has to be reinterpreted . . . for instance, the first real death you encounter . . . you go back with that same hunger looking for someone to interpret the event for you. I still feel that with poets older than I, that they're interpreting the next stage of life for me. Certain ones I've come to depend on for that—Ammons, Ginsberg, Merrill. When Merrill died, I suddenly felt a terrible depression as I realized that he wouldn't be there to tell me what life was like between seventy and eighty, so I wouldn't know before I got there. Each one tells you something slightly different. It's not that younger people can't tell you things, too. They can and do, but they can't tell you what it's like to live between sixty and seventy if they're living between twenty and thirty.

INTERVIEWER

What about irony? Is it something you prize in a poet?

VENDLER

I don't think there is any conscious writing without irony, because there is always the irony that you're writing in the present about something that happened in the past. There's always a spectatorial irony in a poet of any developed self-consciousness. There is an irony implicit in writing itself. Then, there is the spectrum of the ironic from, say Elizabeth Bishop, who is a wonderfully ironic poet—"awful but cheerful"—about herself and about her life, all the way down to a rather unironic poet, like Hopkins, of whom one of his school fellows said, "Hopkins gushes, but he means it." I like both ends of the spectrum. There are hardly any good poets I don't like. I think Pound and Browning are the only two poets whom I don't feel close to.

INTERVIEWER

Do you have a low tolerance for humor? I think of a poet like May Swenson who has a real lightness of touch but not so much astringency. Does that explain why you find her less appealing?

VENDLER

Well, I think it's more that she's a very visual poet engaging in observation of the natural world, but without as much philosophical or emotional ballast as I would like. I'm not visual enough to be satisfied with a poem of almost pure visualization and registering. I love humorous poems. His humor is one of the things that attracts me to Ginsberg.

INTERVIEWER
Who are the other poetry critics that you admire? I wonder particularly about younger critics like Dana Gioia and William Logan.

VENDLER
To tell you the truth, the people who have been most interesting to me over time have been poets writing criticism; and I wish poets wrote more criticism. Pieces about the state of poetry in the United States, like Dana Gioia's, don't interest me. I want someone to take me inside the heart of a piece of writing, and I don't think of Dana Gioia as writing that sort of criticism. He may have done such work, but I haven't seen it. Seamus Heaney writes wonderful essays on poetry. I admire the kind of poetry critic that Randall Jarrell was in his pieces for *The Nation*, and I think of the prose about poetry that Auden wrote, which is so distinguished. I haven't followed William Logan's criticism.

INTERVIEWER
Is there an American poet whose criticism you admire?

VENDLER
Louise Glück has written extremely well on poetry. She has just brought out a book of exceptionally intelligent, acute and beautifully written, trenchant essays. Sometimes I like what Mary Kinzie writes. She's more moral than I like; she often gives more weight to the morality of the poetry than to its vividness. I admire Dave Smith's passion in his essays on poetry.

INTERVIEWER
What about Rich's prose?

VENDLER
That has been mostly political rather than critical. I like Richard Howard's descriptions of some poets, though he does

less criticism now than he did earlier. I'm sure there are many others that I'm forgetting to mention. I've always admired Calvin Bedient's work very much. I've admired Stephen Yenser's work on Merrill and Lowell; Stephen Yenser writes as a poet. Calvin Bedient is writing poetry, too. I think it's the criticism of a person who is a poet, or at least has the sensibility of the poet, that I like.

INTERVIEWER
The critic Bonnie Costello was a student of yours, wasn't she?

VENDLER
No, she was never my student; she was my colleague at Boston University. Someone like Bonnie has a more philosophical and analytic mind than I do, and often brings a more speculative mind to, say, a descriptive poem than I would. I might tend to stay with the level that the poem sets itself and enter the poem at that level, and Bonnie might enter it at a level of the philosophical question that the descriptive poem raises about seeing, and then describe it in that way. She taught me how to read Marianne Moore, and I will be eternally grateful to her for that.

INTERVIEWER
What were your parents like? Did they read poetry?

VENDLER
My mother was a schoolteacher who taught the first grade for fourteen years before she married in 1930. Since in those Depression years married women were not allowed to teach because it would take the money from a breadwinner, my mother lost her job and never had a job again, which was, I think, a great loss to her. She was a great reader of poetry from Shakespeare to Tennyson, and always had very many books of poetry around the house; she quoted poems naturally in conversation. She took us to Mass every morning; I was

introduced early to liturgy, hymns, Gregorian chant. The schools that my parents sent me to from the sixth grade onward were Catholic schools where we sang the liturgy in Latin, and that was extremely interesting to me. I began to learn Latin by myself in the seventh and eighth grades and then studied it in high school.

My father was a teacher of Romance languages who was bilingual in Spanish and English. My mother was a graduate of Boston Normal School, as it was then called, which was to become Boston State Teacher's College. My father had graduated from Boston College in 1915, and then had taken a master's degree in education at the Boston Normal School in 1916, where he met my mother and proposed to her; she didn't marry him until 1930. Meanwhile, he went off to Puerto Rico and Cuba and worked and taught English there. He first worked for the United Fruit Company but then became a teacher of English in Luquillo, Puerto Rico. He had kept up with my mother during those thirteen years; eventually he returned when she agreed to marry him. He got a job in the Boston school system and taught Spanish, French and Italian; he also taught these languages to my sister and me. He began a Ph.D. at Boston University but dropped out after having passed his orals; by that time he had three children. Later, he became head of the Romance languages department at Boston English High School. He took early retirement, as school conditions declined, but he was unhappy not working, and so became a messenger for a law firm for the last fifteen years of his life, and enjoyed that very much.

INTERVIEWER

Did you write poetry as a schoolgirl?

VENDLER

Yes, I wrote my first poem when I was six, and I went on writing until I was twenty-six, and then I stopped. I had found my real vocation as a critic by then, through writing my Ph.D. dissertation.

INTERVIEWER

What was your home life like as a girl? Is it true there was no gift-giving in the house?

VENDLER

We got gifts for Christmas, but they were books, especially books in foreign languages. I didn't ever have a doll, that I recall, until an aunt gave me one when I was twelve. Another aunt gave me a brocade jewel-box when I was twelve, and I kept it all my life because it meant so much to me to have a present; it was stolen in a break-in when I was lecturing at Berkeley a few years ago, along with the jewelry that was in it. I minded the loss of the jewel-box more than the loss of the jewelry. But normally we didn't have birthday presents. We sometimes had homemade presents. My father and grandfather made me some little furniture. My paternal grandfather was a carpenter. He lived with us from the time I was twelve till the time I was about twenty or twenty-one, and he and my father used to make little things of wood for us. I don't think there were other presents that I can recall.

INTERVIEWER

Was there a TV and radio in the house?

VENDLER

No, we never had a TV and we weren't permitted to listen to the radio. We weren't permitted to go to the movies, either, because my parents thought of those as unimproving ways to spend time, though my mother used to let us listen to the radio the nights my father was out teaching night school. We regularly listened to "I Love a Mystery," and I liked that very much. I never saw many movies growing up. I read a great deal.

INTERVIEWER

You were a chemistry major in college. Do you think your scientific training shaped your voice as a critic, or shaped the manner in which you read poems? I've heard you say that you're quite literal-minded; is that because of the scientist in you?

VENDLER

No, I think that's what made me able to enjoy science, because it is so grounded in material reality. What science did for me was to train me to look for evidence. You have to write up evidence for your hypothesis in a very clear way; your equations have to come out even; the left side has to be balanced by the right side. One thing has to lead to the next, things have to add up to a total picture. I think that's a natural thing to do with literature, too. I feel very strongly that anything you say should be backed by evidence from the text, so that you follow a constant loop between generalizations and evidence. I don't like criticism that is simply rhetorically assertive at a very high level without much reference to evidence in the text.

INTERVIEWER

Do you consider yourself a feminist?

VENDLER

In action, yes. I don't think of feminism as a scheme of thought, I think of it as a way of life. That is, I believe that I want the good of women in my own profession and in other professions.

INTERVIEWER

You mean in a legal sense?

VENDLER

Yes, I believe women should have equal rights. They did not when I was starting out in the profession. Many schools didn't hire women. Many schools wouldn't hire women except to teach freshman and sophomore English. They didn't allow women to be on the tenure track but kept them as permanent lecturers, even if the women had greater ambition than that. I would like an equal floor of opportunity for women, and that seems to me a feminist conviction. No, it doesn't seem to me a feminist conviction, it seems to me a conviction of justice. I don't think you should have to be a feminist to think that women should have equal rights. There were men who thought that women should have equal rights, not because they were feminists, but because they were interested in justice. That women should have justice before the law, should have justice in academic treatment, should have equality in marriage — those are all things I believe.

INTERVIEWER

But in the case of Adrienne Rich, it would appear that you no longer feel that she is "writing your life," as you once did.

VENDLER

Oh, she is in some ways . . . the sadness she feels about loss that is part of getting older, the appreciation she feels for certain things that she didn't have time to appreciate earlier. I think in *An Atlas of the Difficult World* there is a great appreciation of the American landscape, which in a sense she almost didn't have time for earlier. Now she can actually look in a way that you can when you're older and you're not taking care of small children, or you're not so hell-bent on trying to get something accomplished. I still see many parallels in our lives, and I'm very much interested to watch her decade by decade, too, as I always have been.

INTERVIEWER

You have written in an essay on Rita Dove that "no black has blackness as sole identity," and further "no black artist can avoid, as subject matter, the question of skin color, and what it entails; and probably the same is still true, if to a lesser extent, of the woman artist and the subject of gender."

How do you feel about identity-markers in the teaching of literature today: black studies, gay studies, women's studies, and the criticism built up around them?

VENDLER
I was never solely drawn to writing about women authors, chiefly because there weren't that many vivid writers of poetry who were women. And there are many men I am not drawn to write about. I don't think I'll ever write about Alexander Pope, and I don't think I'll ever write about Emily Dickinson, but not because Dickinson is a woman or Pope is a man. They are not on my wavelength as much as some other authors, and life is short. I've never wanted to write about Irish-American authors, though I was born and raised in an Irish-American community. I've never wanted to write about Catholic authors as such, though I was born and raised a Catholic. Those aspects don't seem to define me. I'm much more drawn to authors that I feel close to by temperament. I feel close to Stevens by temperament, I feel close to Keats and to Herbert by temperament. They are indolent and meditative writers. I don't mean indolent in personal character, but they like to roam freely in their thinking about a topic, so that Herbert will come back and back to affliction and Keats will come back and back to the sensuous life. Emily Dickinson cuts things off very short, and that always seems to me rather shocking. She ends poems too soon for me. When I think about the poets that attract me, it's much more because of a deep congeniality than from something which seems to me so superficial as either religion of origin, gender or ethnicity of origin. Temperament seems to me more deeply fundamental than any of those things.

Now if I were black, I might not feel temperament to be more fundamental than being black, or (had I been Jewish in Nazi Germany) being Jewish, because when your whole life is conditioned by a single fact dictating whom you can marry, where you can live, whether you will have to go to prison, what you can buy and sell, whether you can go to a university or not, that fact colors everything. I think in America today, every single aspect of your life, if you're black, is affected by that identity-marker. I don't feel that any of my early identity markers so confined or coerced my life that I had to see my life in terms of *it*. So many gay people have been repudiated by their families, or discriminated against in jobs, that it too might seem to be an overwhelming identity-marker at the moment in America.

INTERVIEWER

In the introduction to your latest collection of reviews, *Soul Says*, you speak of the soul and the self in the lyric as different from one another. Could you say a little bit about that?

VENDLER

Well, with the rise of identity defined almost solely through race, ethnicity or gender, I think we've forgotten the identity that speaks when one is speaking to oneself. That is to say, one is more conscious of those things — class, race, age, sex — when one is in the presence of others. It's the difference principle that makes you consciously say, "I am black and you are white, I am old and you are young, I am a woman and you are a man." But when you're by yourself you don't need so powerfully to assert any one of those identities; when you speak to yourself, you rarely say, "I, as a woman, am saying this to myself," or "I, as a sixty-year-old, am saying this to myself." You tend merely to say, "I am saying this to myself," because in the absence of others you can be yourself without external reference. Lyric comes out of that self that is less socially marked than the self that we normally refer to as our social identity. That's why I took the title *Soul Says* from the title of a poem by Jorie Graham, because I think the word *soul* sums up the speaker of lyric.

INTERVIEWER

Do you think there are any huge movements in American poetry today?

VENDLER

I think of the poetry after World War II as suffused by Freud. Some people call it confessional poetry, but it seems to me to be Freudian poetry. All of those poets—Plath, Berryman, Lowell—spending an hour a week in a therapist's office made a powerful turn towards the family romance. I don't think Eliot or Pound would have thought of sitting down and writing about what life was like with Mummy and Daddy at home. I don't know that the poets I've named thought they were living in an era of the Freudian poem. Other poets escape that. You wouldn't say that Ammons's poems (though he is of that generation) are Freudian poems; they are not.

INTERVIEWER

Didn't you once say that in Heaney, and maybe Jorie Graham, and one or two others, you felt there was a trend to go back to some preliterate aspect of life? In Heaney's case for instance, now that he'd done the family, done the political situation, et cetera, what was there left in terms of subject? There was this desire to go back to . . .

VENDLER

I think I said to the perceptual: that is, who are we when we are living in the sensorium of the world? I think of that question as very strongly present in somebody like Charles Wright, whether he is registering evening over Laguna Beach or a moment in Venice. It's the influx of many things—the stars, the flowers on the trees, the night wind, the grass at his feet—the total perceptual field that's being registered. Any slight shift in the field will cause an entire shift in vocabulary to accommodate it; the source of the vocabulary is not what you want to get said in a philosophical sense or propositional way, but rather what the world is feeling like at this moment. That is also present in Mark Strand's *The Continuous Life*, where he is doing a very abstract version of the sensorium. It certainly is powerfully there in Jorie Graham.

INTERVIEWER

Is there a place in poems for issues, real-life opinions and political platforms?

VENDLER

There is a place in poetry for everything. But as Wilde said, something is well-written or ill-written, that is all. To be more serious, it seems to me that all poetry has social value. It isn't only "protest poetry" that has value for society, though sometimes protest poets think that their protest poems are directly socially useful. Somebody writing more abstract poetry, like John Ashbery or Charles Wright, might not be thinking, Is this poetry socially useful? In my view, it doesn't matter what the topic of a genuine poem is; it is socially valuable because it is an integration of experience and language.

INTERVIEWER

Are you interested in politics? Do you read the newspaper?

VENDLER

I read the newspaper every day. And I am interested in politics to the extent that I grieve over the imperfection of it. If you grew up as I did in a corrupt state . . . Massachusetts had a machine-politics for a long time, dominated, first, by the white Anglo-Saxon Protestants, next by the Irish. The whole thing was already predetermined and predecided. The machine was very strong, and politics was a self-oiling mechanism. It didn't have much to do with the will of the people, it had to do with subtle interlocking arrangements between politics and business. In that sort of city, you become very cynical about politics, very young. As long as senators are millionaires, politics will not be just.

INTERVIEWER

Do you have an agenda for American poetry?

VENDLER

I don't think of myself as being *in* American poetry. I mean, I'm concerned with poetry, but I'm as likely to be reading Czeslaw Milosz as to be reading Mark Ford, or Dave Smith, or Charles Simic or you. Sometimes it's an American poet, sometimes an Eastern European, sometimes a Spaniard. It might be Octavio Paz . . . I don't much care. I am devoted to English because it's my mother tongue. I'll never feel that way about any other language except Spanish, which I have also known since birth. Both of them have resonances of the mother tongue for me, and both of them are immensely moving to me. But I don't feel a particular nationalistic attachment to American poetry over or against any other poetry written in the world.

INTERVIEWER

Do you see yourself as anachronistic in the manner you write about poetry as a close reader?

VENDLER

Well, I've never liked the term *close reading*. I'd like to know who thought it up.

INTERVIEWER

What do you call it?

VENDLER

Reading from the point of view of a writer. The people who in the United States pioneered what is now known as close reading were poets like John Crowe Ransom and Randall Jarrell. But close reading has existed forever. There have been commentators on Homer since the dawn of time; those were the close readers of Homer. I think of close readers as people who want to read from the point of view of someone who composes with words. It's a view from the inside, not from the outside. The phrase *close reading* sounds as if you're looking at the text with a microscope from outside, but I would rather think of a close reader as someone who goes inside a room and describes the architecture. You speak from inside the poem as someone looking to see how the roof articulates with the walls and how the wall articulates with the floor. And where are the crossbeams that hold it up, and where are the windows that let light through?

INTERVIEWER

Recently, in *The New York Times*, you said, "the canon is not made by anyone except other poets. Long after the tumult and the shouting die, who remembers a single review of Shelley or Byron or Wallace Stevens?" This strikes me as astonishing coming from someone who has spent much of her life writing reviews. What has been your motivation?

VENDLER

I think of the reviews I've written as a continuing self-seminar in contemporary poetry. A new poet would appear, and I would want to track the progress of that person, see what happened next. I'm always curious about what poets will do next. That's why I wrote the Ellmann lectures on the breaking of style. It did interest me very much when, say, Charles Wright after writing *Bloodlines* would suddenly write something like *China Trace*. Why was he doing this? What was behind it? Things like that make me sit down and think. A familiar poet doesn't set the same problem as your first encounter with a brand new writer. It's the hardest thing to do, to see a book that no one has ever seen before except its author, to say something about it, to investigate it and solve its poetics to your own satisfaction. Reviewing was a way of earning money, but it was a way I really delighted in.

INTERVIEWER

What is your perception of your own power?

VENDLER

I can see that it seems a great deal of power to a young writer to be reviewed or not reviewed in *The New York Times*

... as though it could make or break the book. Reviewing may seem like power, but it's very ephemeral power. Yes, if I review a book in *The New York Times* or *The New Yorker* more libraries will buy it, but that doesn't mean it will be looked on favorably in fifty years. There are millions of books that have been bought by libraries that nobody will ever read again after the year in which they're published.

INTERVIEWER

I wondered how you felt being depicted in *The New York Times* recently by a caricaturist as a head on a tank.

VENDLER

I thought it was very funny. My son, much amused, said, "My mother is a tank." The odd thing for me in seeing it is that I write mostly appreciative reviews, so a tank armed with a phallic howitzer, or whatever my fountain pen was supposed to be, seemed to me not quite the right representation for the kind of admiring reviews that I normally write. However, since a female who expresses herself decisively seems to this world someone armed with ammunition, it's probably fair enough.

INTERVIEWER

Do you think people are afraid of you?

VENDLER

"I must be proud to see / Men not afraid of God, afraid of me," said Pope, satirizing the opposition. One should not fear the exposure of truth, since the truth makes us free. If it is truth, what I've written, then it shouldn't make anyone afraid. If it's not truth, it has no power, so no one need be afraid of it.

INTERVIEWER

What is your response to the criticism that you reject the Romantic tradition and all those American poets that are its literary descendants, like Galway Kinnell, Donald Hall, Theodore Roethke and Philip Levine, that you prefer instead the poets who are stylists, technicians, poets who are "cool" instead of "warm"?

VENDLER

The poets that I like are unsentimental; the poets that I don't like are sentimental, very frequently. The poets I think of as sentimental, someone else might think of as descended from the Romantic tradition. But there are many other poets who descend from the Romantic tradition whom I admire very much. Ammons is a direct descendant of the Romantics, as a nature poet, and yet I don't see Ammons as sentimental at all, far from it. Practically everybody in America descends from the Romantic tradition. What I think sentimental is what others think feelingful, and that's a line that people draw in different places. What is "warm" for one is sentimental for another. And I may have had a more unhappy life than someone else. Someone else may see amplitude and joy where I see self-delusion and sentimentality.

INTERVIEWER

What about the criticism that you favor a poetry of the terribly well-educated?

VENDLER

All good poets are terribly well-educated, otherwise they wouldn't be good poets. They have to have enormous linguistic command to write poetry well. Someone like Blake who never went to a university, someone like Whitman who never went to a university, who could say they were uneducated? Melville said the whaling ship was his Yale College and his Harvard; for Blake and Whitman, the printing press was a university.

INTERVIEWER

How do poems enter into your life on a daily basis?

VENDLER

They help me to know what I'm feeling. Out of the depths of my heart will come a quotation completely unbidden. And then I will think, Oh, so that's what I am feeling today. On any occasion when a response is called for, what usually comes to my lips is a line from some poem or other. My son laughs about this and says, "A quotation for every occasion, Mom." He doesn't understand how my first response can always be a line from someone else, but it is. I've absorbed so much poetry over the years, that there are just hundreds and hundreds of lines in my mind. And when one of them floats up out of the mass, I know it's telling me something.

INTERVIEWER

I noticed you used the word *body* to describe the style of a poem in your new book, *The Breaking of Style*. Why is that?

VENDLER

Well, there has been so much emphasis on the body lately in critical language. I was trying to think of the way the physical body manifests itself to me — other than in ordinary daily-life ways — I mean, how it manifests itself to me in my consciousness. And I realized that when I know a poet's writing well, I know it in the way I would know a physical body by sight. It has a contour that changes over time; you feel that the very spare contours of some late Stevens poems are very different, say, from the more baroque contours of some of his earlier poems. And it's almost as though . . . well, he says it himself in "The Dwarf":

> Now it is September and the web is woven.
> The web is woven and you have to wear it.
>   . . .
> It is all that you are, the final dwarf of you,
> That is woven and woven and waiting to be worn. . . .

The new body of style, "the final dwarf of you," is a moral body as well. The body presents itself to me as something that can be given a shape in words. The many bodies in the physical universe are matched for me, and symbolized for me, by the many bodies of the verbal universe.

INTERVIEWER
Then you believe that all poems, in a sense, have bodies and souls?

VENDLER
Yes, the body is the sinew of the language, as when Hopkins said, praising Dryden, that in him you find "the naked thew and sinew of the language." You feel that the richly opulent Keatsian temperament is different from the briskly social Browning temperament. The body of the verse gives you a sense of an alert, greyhound body in one, and a fluid sensuous body in another.

INTERVIEWER
Does criticism have a body? Do you feel that your body is represented in your criticism?

VENDLER
I don't think it's a direct representation of the person's body. If you gave visual representation to the body of Hopkins's style, it would probably be more like Felix Randal the farrier, whereas Hopkins himself was frail and thin. So it's not the physical body that's represented but something in the way of being in the world that's represented. I think my way of being in the world is in part an intellectual way and the criticism represents that. Access to the world for me is through both mind and feelings. I am not satisfied with having a feeling unless my mind is also thinking about the feeling, interpreting the feeling. Uninterpreted feeling is for me a painful state.

But I would say that criticism doesn't have so pronounced a stylistic body as poetry. Even Seamus Heaney's criticism doesn't have so pronounced a style as his poetry. Even Randall Jarrell's criticism, vivid and brilliant though it is, doesn't have that Jarrellian nostalgic sweetness and infantile yearning that is in the poetry. You can summon up Jarrell from his poetry better than you can from his prose.

INTERVIEWER

In your introduction to that same book, *The Breaking of Style*, you write, "The forgettable writers of verse do not experiment with style in any coherent or strenuous way. They adopt the generic style of their era and repeat themselves in it." Yet aren't there extraordinary examples of poets, like George Herbert, as you point out, who do not break their styles, or change their bodies, to borrow your trope, as in the case of Emily Dickinson?

VENDLER

Well, each case is special. In Herbert's case we have an extraordinarily short writing life. Most of the poems are written in the last three years of his life, when he was between thirty-seven and forty. I don't know what he would have done if he had lived longer, had he done more writing. I can't think of any long-lived poet who stayed the same all his life. Even Emily Dickinson, who decided to take a prosodic form and keep it invariant, has very powerful changes of style. She goes back and forth between a sort of girlish style, which she uses even very late, and a powerful metaphysical style. I wouldn't say that there's no change of style in Emily Dickinson.

Ginsberg seems to me the person who best fits the description of somebody who finds one way of writing and continues to write in that way. But Ginsberg is saved by his really zany, wildly irregular imagination. When you open a new book by Ginsberg, you don't know what topics will appear in it.

INTERVIEWER
How did you first meet Robert Lowell?

VENDLER
I think I had met him on a few occasions, but I really talked to him for the first time after a reading of James Merrill's. We

sat down and began to talk, and from then on we were friends. We were talking about Stevens, and about Lowell's own work, and we were laughing a lot; he was a wonderful conversationalist. He said to me, "You don't like 'Esthétique du Mal' as much as I do." And I said, "No, I like it the way I like all of Stevens, but it's not my favorite Stevens poem." "Oh, it's *my* favorite Stevens poem," he said. And when I said, "Why?" he replied, "Because it's the *most like me!*" It was charming and it made me see "Esthétique du Mal" in a new light; I could see how he and Stevens came out of Baudelaire, and that was the way they were alike.

INTERVIEWER

Cambridge can seem like a very little village sometimes. Do you ever grow weary of the poetry scene here?

VENDLER

I'm not in "the poetry scene" here. That is to say, I'm a native Bostonian, I've lived in this area since I was born, my parents and my grandparents both lived here, and my sister and brother, cousins, aunts and uncles, and friends live here. I never felt that the scene that I was in was either necessarily the intellectual scene or the poetry scene. I'm very happy that I will die where I was born; it is a great gift to have continuity in your life. I was out of Cambridge for many years teaching at Cornell and Swarthmore and Haverford and Smith and so on. But I'm glad to be back. I go to some poetry readings, it's true, but I also go to family weddings and funerals and I also see old friends from Boston University and Smith.

INTERVIEWER

Is there no poet for whom you would like to write a biography?

VENDLER

Oh, no. I couldn't keep the index cards straight. I'd get all the dates wrong. I'm not an historian, and I don't have a head for history. Biographies, histories, novels, essays, autobiographies all seem to me less riveting by a million miles than a good poem, and almost none of them are as well written as a good poem.

INTERVIEWER
Do you have a favorite among your own books?

VENDLER
My favorite is my Keats book, because it's the one in which I felt I could give the poems their due. It's hard when you're writing about, say, Stevens's long poems to do justice to a poem that may be eight hundred lines long. When I finished writing on the ode "To Autumn," which has thirty-three lines, I saw that I had written fifty pages. And I thought, That ratio probably seems excessive, more than a page per line. But it struck me as just about right for "To Autumn." Maybe it should have even more pages. If I had had to write about "To Autumn" in ten pages, I would have felt pained with frustration.

INTERVIEWER
Do you cook or sew?

VENDLER
I used to sew all the time when I was young. I made my own clothes, made clothes for others. I used to do alterations for everybody in the family. I used to cut hair, do home permanents. I never liked to cook. I was very clumsy in chemistry and used to knock over with an inadvertent move of the elbow solutions that had taken three weeks to make. I can make a dinner, but it's not something I enjoy, and it's something that makes me anxious.

INTERVIEWER
Do you collect anything?

VENDLER

Broadsides. I love poems by themselves on a piece of paper. I think all poems should appear by themselves; you should see them one at a time, with only one on a page. When a broadside is printed up, and you have only one poem, it's thrilling.

INTERVIEWER

Do you like to sing, or do you like opera?

VENDLER

I love vocal music of all kinds. I didn't have records when I was young, but I used to take opera scores out of the library to transcribe. I didn't know you could buy paper with staves on it so I used to draw my own staves. Then I'd borrow the score from the Boston Public Library music room (a wonderful resource) and copy down the arias I wanted on my homemade staves and write out the words underneath them. We did have a piano, so I could pick out arias on the piano, and I learned a lot of operas that way. *The Ring* does seem to me the best and the most comprehensive operatic picture of the universe, yet I'm deeply attached to lieder as the corresponding art form to lyric.

INTERVIEWER

Do you have a pet at home?

VENDLER

I've always had cats, my family always had cats, my son has a cat. We are not dog people. Right now, my cat is a large, terrified Himalayan named Shiva, who was an abused cat. Because she's a Himalayan it seemed to me she should have some kind of Indian name, and because Shiva represents creation and destruction at once, it was a name I responded to and liked.

INTERVIEWER

Do you have a motto?

VENDLER

A motto. What an interesting idea! "God and the imagination are one," from Wallace Stevens? "How high that highest candle lights the dark"?

INTERVIEWER

Do you like to travel to certain places?

VENDLER

I like to have seen the world. D.H. Lawrence once said one wants the experience of having been married, and travel is like that. Travel is often agonizing in the process, but in retrospect it's so revelatory not to have a blank place on the map. Before I went there, Hungary was just a large blank spot with nothing in it, and now when I see it on the map, I remember the Danube bend and Esztergom and Lake Balaton and beautiful fields, and the river and the chain bridge.

And the same with China, China was nothing to me until I went to China, and I'm forever grateful . . .

INTERVIEWER

You went to China because your daughter-in-law is Chinese?

VENDLER

No. I took my son to China with me when he was a college senior. He enjoyed it so much that he wanted to go back; so he went back and taught English, and met his wife there.

INTERVIEWER

Is there a living person you most admire?

VENDLER

It's more a plethora than a dearth. I mean, I admire so many writers. I feel extraordinary grief when I lose one: I still mind terribly having lost Lowell; I still am feeling acutely the impact of having lost Merrill. And the impact of having lost Sylvia Plath, though I never knew her. Then there are moral heroines and heroes that I admire.

INTERVIEWER

You mean that are not poets.

VENDLER

Yes, totally inconspicuous people who have led exemplary lives.

INTERVIEWER

Friends of yours, or public figures?

VENDLER

Some of them are teachers, some relatives, some friends. I don't know personally any public figures; I don't think of them so much. I think of the uncomplaining, of the remarkably generous, of the witty. What would we all do without the witty?

INTERVIEWER

Is it hard to be friends with poets whom you do not admire?

VENDLER

I don't think I've ever been friends, exactly, with somebody whose work I don't admire. My closest friends have not, on the whole, been poets. They have often been other women bringing up children . . . relatives, friends, literary women, colleagues.

INTERVIEWER

Do you think that knowing a poet could interfere with your assessment of him or her?

VENDLER

I don't think so, because I have been assessing poets since I was about fifteen. When I was a girl, I used to go to poetry readings at Harvard, and I would sit in the audience listening to Dylan Thomas, e.e. cummings, T.S. Eliot, Robert Frost, whoever happened to be coming through. I think that the assessing of poets is a quite impersonal act that usually occurs spontaneously as the poem rises off the page to meet you. And you are either repelled by it or attracted by it, or are indifferent to it. The poem is something quite other than the person who writes it.

INTERVIEWER

Have you ever had a confrontation with a poet you reviewed?

VENDLER

Yes, it was a poet whose criticism I had criticized. I had said that he had a tin ear, which is something a poet doesn't want to hear. And I'll never forget his response. At the time I reviewed him, we had never met; later, we were both at a party. When we were introduced, he laughed with gaiety and said, "Ah, a hostile reviewer!" I was so taken by the generosity of his response that, of course, we became friends. I still think that was a remarkable response.

INTERVIEWER

Are there writers you'd like to have known?

VENDLER

Keats, of course. Everybody would have liked to have known Keats. Shakespeare.

INTERVIEWER

What about recent writers?

VENDLER

I wish I had set eyes on Stevens once. It grieves me that we were alive at the same time but that he was dead before I read him. I would have liked to have seen his face and heard his voice, just to have had an immediate sense of his character.

INTERVIEWER

Why do you think it is that prosody, lineation and grammar are not much talked about by critics?

VENDLER

Well, we don't have rhetorical training any longer in the schools—the extraordinary rhetorical training of the study of Latin, translation from Latin. We're missing all of that fantastic elaboration that even the grammar school student in Shakespeare's time went through. The sense of etymology that came from Latin is missing; the sense of English grammar that came from diagramming sentences has gone. What you have not been trained to recognize, you don't see. We don't see certain figures of speech that were once commonly known, because we're not trained to recognize them. It's a matter of bringing poetic means to consciousness. Knowing another language helps to bring them to consciousness, translation does; but these are not common features of schooling now.

INTERVIEWER

What about creative-writing workshops, do you have an opinion about them?

VENDLER

I've only sat in on two single workshops in my life, so I certainly couldn't have an opinion. One truth that is rather neglected in creative-writing workshops is that all good poets of the past, almost without exception, were at least bilingual if not trilingual.

INTERVIEWER

Do you think there's a subject that is taboo in poetry?

VENDLER

Subjects are rarely taboo in poetry these days, but certain forms of expression are denigrated. It was hard for someone like Amy Clampitt to be accepted because she used very ornate vocabulary, and it was considered elitist (by some commentators) to write in the way that Amy Clampitt wrote. It was a diction perfectly natural to her since she was, among other things, a reference librarian, a bird-watcher and a much-traveled person.

INTERVIEWER
Yet her subjects were very contemporary, weren't they, using as just one example, violence towards women?

VENDLER
Yes, but even so there was a great deal of irritation expressed against her style. Certain styles are taboo, especially in the kind of democratic ethos where poetry is supposed to be accessible and inviting. A lot of people found the ornateness of her surface repellent. I didn't, but other people did. So I would say that certain styles may be more taboo than certain subject matters.

INTERVIEWER
Are you more interested in the lyric poem than in, say, narratives or dramatic poetry?

VENDLER
Yes, because I think in good narrative poetry or good dramatic poetry the poetry has to play a subordinate role to the principal structure that animates that genre. That is, the principal structure of narrative is some ongoing linearity; it may, like Spenser, never get to an end, but it has to appear to be heading towards an end. And the same in drama: the principle of conflict on which drama lives has to be the generating principle, and the poetry is subordinate to that generating principle. So that in the dramatic poem or the narrative poem poetry is chiefly an expressive not a structural means whereas in the lyric poem, it is a structural end.

INTERVIEWER
What, in your view, is the function of the lyric? Can it be ideological or philosophical?

VENDLER
Any statement not only can be but probably must be ideological, that is to say coming from some viewpoint or other.

And there's a long and noble history of philosophical poetry, from Lucretius on, that finds itself at home in a discourse it shares with some forms of philosophy—discourse about the soul or the self or about the realm of ideas. A poetry exhibiting strong ideological content—a strong religious content, a strong political content, a strong feminist content—can be just as good as any other sort of poetry. English has a lot of good religious poetry that has very strong ideological content. There is nothing in itself about a strong ideological position (think of Milton) that prohibits writing good poetry; it's all in how it's done.

INTERVIEWER

Do you think there's much cross-fertilization between American poetry and that of Ireland and Eastern Europe or South America?

VENDLER

Yes, it's one of the best things that has happened, I think, to American poetry, which originally looked almost exclusively towards English poetry. Then, with the rise of international modernism, there's a sense of immense energy coming into Eliot from Laforgue and Mallarmé; coming into Yeats from the Nō drama; and coming into Pound from China and also from Italy. This kind of cross-fertilization seems to me not only very useful—think of the influence of Trakl or Neruda or Milosz on contemporary poets—but indispensable to poetry.

INTERVIEWER

You have spoken about how you wanted a mirror of your feelings in poetry. Is it fair to assume that poets who do not embody your feelings are poets you cannot write about?

VENDLER

There are certainly feelings that I may not have experienced and can't respond to well. They might be the feelings of going out on a hunt with your grandfather, something I've never done. They might be feelings of a son to his father, which I believe are probably different from those that a daughter feels towards a father. There aren't perfect overlaps in feeling among people. The poetry of war is something I find hard to respond to adequately.

INTERVIEWER

What's the first poem you remember reading?

VENDLER

I suppose they were hymns. We sang hymns in church, and my grandfather, who had a very resonant baritone voice, was the head usher in the church. I remember him striding down the middle of the church collecting money in the offertory basket while singing whatever the offertory hymn might be. That was before I read poems. I suppose *A Child's Garden of Verses* was the first poetry I remember being read to me.

INTERVIEWER

In your introduction to *Soul Says* you comment that "the poets about whom I have written in the essays in this book are poets whom I admire." Yet there are rather harsh pieces on Adrienne Rich and Robinson Jeffers included. Do you not perceive them as negative reviews, or is your inclusion of these pieces an effort at endorsement in spite of the review's negative contents?

VENDLER

What I endorse in anybody (if one can speak of such a thing as endorsement) is a style that has become recognizable among the styles of its century. I think you do pick up Adrienne Rich and think, That's Adrienne Rich; and I think you do pick up Robinson Jeffers and think, That's Robinson Jeffers. In my mind, that is a very high and rare and unusual achievement by any writer. Yet I also think that there are people who use their idiosyncratic style to better or to worse advantage. So if I point out something that seems to me strained or forced or incomplete about a poet, it is nonetheless said about a poet I admire.

INTERVIEWER

What do you think James Merrill's contribution was to the last half-century of poetry?

VENDLER

Writing the best sonnets . . . he certainly did wonderful things with sonnets. A sequence like "Matinees" seems to me such an inventive poem; or his most recent one, the fifteen-line sonnets of "The *Ring* Cycle" in the new book, *A Scattering of Salts*, where he does "Matinees" over. It's a form that he came back to all his life and seemed to find increasing amusement and pleasure within. That kind of inventiveness and fertility seems to me characteristic of what Merrill could do with all the forms in English. He never ceased to experiment with form in the most exhilarating and unexpected ways. In the last book, there's a poem called "Self-Portrait in Tyvek (TM) Windbreaker" where he says "Sing our final air," and then there's a stanza of quasi-ottava rima full of asterisks and crossouts and mistakes. To think that your final air is something radically, formally and even semantically incomplete, is something that only Merrill would have done.

INTERVIEWER

I think I heard that was the first poem he wrote on the computer . . . it might be that there was something about the machinery that permitted him that freedom. And what about Amy Clampitt? I mention these two, of course, because they are recently deceased.

VENDLER

I liked Amy Clampitt's whole project. It was a project aimed at having a complete voice in a way that a lot of women poets have not aspired to. It was a voice that was interested in society and in the private life, in love and in nature, in travel and in intellectual things, in science and in family matters, in the past as well as the present. Given the restricted experience of most women in the past, it was exhilarating to see someone with as various a voice as Amy Clampitt, rather than a woman's poetry that consisted solely of the domestic voice. And a poetry that didn't consist solely of the protest voice, though the protest voice is very evident in Clampitt: protests against the domestic life of women; protests against government policy. But it was a voice that also loved high intellectuality and all that that implied, which the usual protest poetry doesn't often embody.

INTERVIEWER

A handful of poets have chosen suicide. Do you have a view about suicide?

VENDLER

Well, a handful of other people have chosen suicide, too. Doctors, accountants, dentists, what have you. The highest rate of suicide is among physicians, partly because they have access to drugs that make it easier to commit suicide. I don't think that the poets' suicides are necessarily consequent upon their having had the disposition or the talent to write poetry. On the contrary, as many people have said, it was probably their poetry that kept them alive and kept them from committing suicide earlier. Creative effort is such a passionate process in itself, it's a way out of depression rather than into it.

INTERVIEWER

I know you're not a practicing Catholic; does that mean that you don't believe in an afterlife?

VENDLER

I don't believe in anything of that sort.

INTERVIEWER

Meaning you're an atheist?

VENDLER
Yes.

INTERVIEWER
But don't you believe in the existence of souls?

VENDLER
Only so long as they have bodies. I do believe we are something other than our corpses, but what we are is a functioning biological mechanism. And when the biological conjunctions stop, then the mechanism can't work anymore. We have a very highly organized nervous system, which when it works well is something that we refer to as the soul.

INTERVIEWER
Do you think that your soul is happy in your body?

VENDLER
Well, no. Is anybody's soul happy in his body? Think of Marvell's witty poem, taking off on St. Paul's protest by the soul, "Who shall deliver me from the body of this death?" Marvell's body replies, "O who shall me deliver whole / From bonds of this Tyrannic Soul?" Body and soul have rarely got on well.

INTERVIEWER
I remember your once saying that you had an Irish peasant body. Do you still feel that way?

VENDLER
Yes, I do. I see it in myself and in my father, whose body I've inherited: a stocky body with stamina and a certain peasant drive, maybe.

INTERVIEWER
Have you ever not been able to write?

VENDLER

Yes, when I was ill and had entered a period of great exhaustion where I simply didn't have the mental energy to write.

INTERVIEWER

Do you work daily? What is your routine?

VENDLER

No, I have no routine. I hate routines. I have no fixed hours for sleeping, eating, waking, working.

INTERVIEWER

Do you write at a desk or in bed or on a sofa?

VENDLER

I write in various places . . . sometimes on the sofa, sometimes in bed, sometimes sitting at the computer. I hate routine more than anything else. I'm a night person, so I tend to write later in the day rather than earlier, but I have no fixed hours and no fixed days.

INTERVIEWER

How did you begin to review for *The New Yorker*?

VENDLER

Well, I had done reviewing for *The New York Times* for some years, then Mr. Shawn phoned me up and asked if I'd like to write about poetry for *The New Yorker*, and I said yes. That was in 1978.

INTERVIEWER

Had he read a particular piece?

VENDLER

He didn't say. I suspect it was Howard Moss who probably had been following my writing in the *Times* and who suggested me to Mr. Shawn.

INTERVIEWER
At sixty-three you show no sign of slowing down. Do you feel that you have slowed down?

VENDLER
What I mind more than slowing down, which everyone has done by sixty-three, is that in a day you no longer have a third wind and sometimes you don't even have a second wind. I always had a third wind for many years, and then I always had a second wind. Now, if I've had a hard day, I don't feel disposed to write at night. What I miss more is the inevitable sense of distance from younger poets. You always know the poets of the generation ahead of you, and also of your own generation, the companions of your journey through life. You also tend to know, I think, the poets of one generation down, that is to say fifteen to twenty years younger than yourself. They're pretty close to you too. But then you lose touch. I would be surprised if there were a critic who was in touch at the age of sixty-three with what was going on with the twenty-four year olds.

INTERVIEWER
Have you been happy with your vocation?

VENDLER
Well, since I can't imagine any other . . . well, no, I can imagine one other. I do have a fantasy life in medicine. There are some versions of medicine that I could have practiced with some enjoyment, especially the ones that require complicated diagnoses. If you're a doctor, you certainly don't have time to write, and that's what turned me away from medicine. I realized that I was spending my time in the library stacks of poetry, not of science.

INTERVIEWER
I understand you're just completing a book about Shakespeare's sonnets. Might one say that you've come to Shake-

speare by way of Stevens and Keats? If so, where will you go next?

VENDLER
Shakespeare has always been there. I memorized so many of Shakespeare's sonnets when I was fifteen that when I later came to Keats and Stevens it was Shakespeare that I saw in them. They all interpenetrate by the time you know them all. Where I'll go next, I don't know. I have a deep wish to write on Milton, but that would take a long time because I'd have to make myself into a Miltonist first. I'd also like to write a book on Yeats's lyric styles, because most of the work on Yeats has been animated by biography more than by poetry.

INTERVIEWER
How is your study of the Shakespeare sonnets different from others? I gather you do not read with the usual social or cultural or moral agenda.

VENDLER
During the nineteenth century, the study of Shakespeare's sonnets was governed by a biographical agenda. Later, it was also governed by the "universal wisdom" agenda: the sonnets have been mined for the wisdom of friendship, the wisdom of the acquiescence to time, the wisdom of love. But I'm more interested in them as poems that work. They seem to me to work awfully well (though not everyone thinks so). And each one seems to work differently. Shakespeare was the most easily bored writer that ever lived, and once he had made a sonnet prove out in one way, he began to do something even more ingenious with the next sonnet. It was a kind of task that he set himself: within an invariant form, to do something different—structurally, lexically, rhythmically—in each poem. I thought each one deserved a little commentary of its own, so I've written a mini-essay on each one of the 154.

INTERVIEWER
How does American poetry look to you at the end of the twentieth century? Are you hopeful for the next?

VENDLER

I don't think poetry is killable. At one point, Ezra Pound wrote sardonically of "the filthy . . . unkillable infants of the very poor." And I think of poetry as one of those. It will keep cropping up no matter what is done with it, because human beings feel such a perennial impulse to play with language. It's like any other kind of play . . . play with notes, play with colors, play with line, play with rhythm. The human impulse to play with a given medium seems to be ineradicable.

INTERVIEWER

"Is criticism a true thing?" Keats asked. What would be your reply?

VENDLER

It can never be true for the poet because what the poet has said, he has already said, and therefore criticism seems either deflective or odious. But for the critic, criticism is a form of natural self-expression, as poetry is to the poet. So, for a critic, criticism is a true thing. Criticism isn't written for poets, it's written for other readers. One hopes it is true for other readers if it's true for oneself.

—Henri Cole

To the Sea

Rob Owen

I stepped over two weeks of May Anderson's mail and around Charles's vomit and into the living room and the foul air, second crack at this, rolled her onto her back and found two thousand dollars. Jesus, I thought, and on *Freshly Picked Coconut* day, too.

I stepped over the grass that was three weeks high, across a creaky wooden porch, through a screen door, then past a wooden one with a couple of letters still stuck in the slot, over a pile of mail—bills, expired circulars from the grocery store, catalogues—through a heavy stench, over a puddle of hour-old vomit, down the hall into the living room, into a stench even heavier, over to the rug, where a stain the shape of May Anderson outlined her body.

I stepped with mud-stained work boots, across grass that I mowed years ago for a quarter when five bucks was the going rate, but Crazy May was as old as Methuselah and how would she know the going rate, and maybe she was stuck in that time when she was being generous by paying a fourteen-year-old kid a quarter for pushing an antiquated mower over an acre and a half of grass and weeds, and maybe a quarter was just all she could afford, I thought, but here, across the yard, over the porch, through the door, the hall, the stench, and under Crazy May, between her and the stained rug, was a roll of hundreds, twenty of them.

Oh my.

I woke up this morning in a good mood, because *Freshly Picked Coconut* day is the first day of March, *South Pacific* on my three hundred and sixty-five sailboats and ports of call calendar. This is a day I've been looking forward to. February was *The Far East*. Bleak. President's Day was the nineteenth, *Sea Gypsy Village, Thailand* day — not a particularly happy scene, a market scene, a mad scramble for money and goods. *Drying Squid* day fell on the twenty-first, Ash Wednesday — you could smell it. Sandwiched between the two was *Eye of the Wind*, a timid ship struggling against a stormy sea, the background a gray black sky. February had been full of grim days. On one of these, in the middle of the month, May Anderson rolled up all her money and died right on top of it.

March, however, is a bright, happy month, full of sunsets and spinnakers and blue water. I knew things would look up once March arrived. I've looked ahead to April, *California and Points South*, and it looks just as cheery.

Does May have any people, Helen said.

Of course, I said, May is *The Continent*. May is full of people. There's a fat, bald sea captain on Memorial Day, *A Falmouth Salt*. And there are others, I said, sea people, adventurers, all over May.

Good God, she said, I'm not talking about your calendar, I'm talking about May Anderson, does she have any people.

I said, No, I don't think so.

Surely she must, Helen said, she's old enough to be a great, great grandmother.

Maybe she outlived all her people, I said.
Helen doubted it, said it's not supposed to be like that. The older you live, the more people you should have.

I stepped in, looked down, and ran out of the living room, jumped over the vomit, kicked through the mail, sending a *People* magazine out onto the porch ahead of me. Bent over the magazine, hands on knees, drawing deep breaths and trying to keep my stomach, I studied a suddenly fascinating ad on the back cover.

A middle-aged lady stands in front of her car in front of two teenagers with white polo shirts and towels shoulder draped, all in front of the Super Brite Auto Wash, all staring at her shiny red car, her Buick Skylark. She looks pleased, not only that the car is so clean, but that it's her car and the two guys who washed it, dried it and buffed on a fresh coat of wax are still staring at it, at her. She thinks these boys are pleased to have had the opportunity to wash such a fine car, her car. She thinks she has made their day. She thinks they're staring at her thinking only a woman like that could drive such a car. She thinks they're standing there thinking that maybe one day they will have a woman like that who has a car like that. She thinks they may, too. That's why she grins so. They agree. That's why they grin so. These aren't your career car washers. This is a summer gig for these boys. Come September they're packed for the Ivy League, ready to get back to econ and pre-law. That's why this scene is so sweet, she thinks. These boys are attracted to Buick Quality.

I stepped from a freshly filled grave that had been dug for the first time, what, seventy-five years ago, before metal coffins, before cement boxes housed the caskets, when this small town was even smaller—good Lord—and there was one funeral home and you got a pine box, and a hundred years later the box would finally collapse and the earth would sink a couple of feet. One of my jobs is filling in the old graves. Peaceful job: I like this one more than some of the others. I came out of the graveyard and Mr. Loflin told me to go over to May Anderson's house.

Who was it, Helen said.
May Anderson.
Dear God, she said, I didn't think May would ever die.
Wasn't May the one Frampton used to torment.
Frampton was a funny dog, I said.
Helen said, Frampton used to terrorize that lady, I remember now.
Frampton has been dead for years, I said.
Helen said, That dog loved everyone but May Anderson, and she was always walking by your house, walked everywhere, and I remember how she used to scream when she saw him, and that only got him riled up, and you and your brother couldn't catch him, and he'd run circles around May, and you'd chase him, and the neighbors would come out because she could really scream, I mean for such an old lady, old even then.
He never bit her, I said.

I stepped out of the hearse and onto the curb in front of the firehouse where Charles was hosing down the fire truck, and next to the fire-engine red he seemed a little green, which was disturbing because Charles is always first on the scene and he's usually not affected. Charles said that May Anderson was an old, old lady.

Helen, a young, young lady, hasn't moved for three hours. Is she dead, I wonder. She's not dead, and I don't really wonder if she is. This isn't a boy in bed with a dead girl story, certainly—she snores lightly anyway. The story as we approach 5 A.M. is about two thousand dollars of stinky, hundred dollar bills.

May Anderson could have very well died on Valentine's Day, *Long Tails at Low Tide*, two rotting, abandoned boats on a desolate beach, one with a broken mast, one without a mast altogether, another grayish February sky. She was there in an empty house, feeling alone, which is no good in a town as small as this one. She decided to rake out all her money and count it and roll it. Two thousand dollars was comforting, raised her spirits. She danced around the room with it, around and around, I bet, spinning, money clutched against her heart, whirling about the room until, finally, she dropped.

Charles had said that he'd given the place the once over after the mailman phoned all frantic—mailman smelled her through mail slot—that he called off EMS because there was no emergency here, and why bother calling the ambulance all the way down from Greensboro, when this sort of call just pisses them off, he said, and when they get pissed off they tend to take forever to get down here when there's a real emergency, which is what we would surely have as soon as the one ambulance that services this town was off on a call as trifling as this one. He said if I could just swing by and get her and run her on up to Greensboro everyone would surely breathe easier—he said that. He said I should watch my step, it looked like the mailman had thrown up by the front door.

I get all the shitty jobs.

I wrapped a towel that I'd dampened at the spigot on the side of the house around my face and I went back in and found Crazy May's dead hands tucked under her and clutching a roll of bills, hundred dollar bills. May was lying belly down, rump up, right half of her face pooled on the floor, left ear up, eyes wide, mouth open, surprised to see me, sorry she was dead like this, more than a little embarrassed by the smell.

I drove from the morgue to the diner, Kidd's. I must have had that smell on me, but I couldn't smell it. I sat at the counter beside Clifton, a plumber, and one of his lackeys. They looked at me funny I noticed, but nobody said anything. Buster Kidd stood behind the counter stirring sugar into a jug of tea with his fist, arm elbow deep in it.

Buster, I said, let me paint a picture for you. May Anderson has been dead in her house for two weeks, maybe longer, I said.

Cliff got up, put five bucks on the counter, and he and his lackey walked out the door.

That's hard work you smell, I called through the screen door. I had intended to buy everyone's lunch, but thought better of it.

She looked strange lying like that with her rump in the air, awkward, so I rolled her on her side. That's when I saw the money. Who knew May Anderson had money. Who knew May Anderson. She died and no one noticed. Were it not for the mailman, she'd still be alone in her living room. Any people she had didn't deserve this money. Dammit, she said, I've been waiting here for two weeks and no one comes. No one even stops by. No one calls. Charles runs in, throws up and runs out. Big fireman. Here, you take this money. No one else wants it. You take it.

Dear Father, Helen said, burn those clothes.

Helen ushered me directly to the shower. I showered with the money. I'm worried that the smell didn't come off, that it's there and I can't notice it because I've been around it, that whenever I spend it there will be a scene.

It's 4:42 A.M. I find myself wide awake. I'm lying on my side, as there is no room for me to lie flat. I am balanced on the edge of the bed, and I feel like I will fall off it if I move even slightly. Helen's ass is in the small of my back. She's been in this exact position since she fell asleep. I've had the urge to shift my weight every fifteen, twenty minutes. My left arm is tucked under me. It has passed through the pins and needles stage of falling asleep and is now dead to the touch. My left leg aches.

I left the diner and went back to May Anderson's house and sprayed down the rug and stacked the mail up neatly by the door and cleaned up Charles's vomit, which was probably the worst job of the day. Then I went around back and pulled the old mower out of the shed, and, after a brief struggle to get it going, I pushed it around the yard. As I pushed, I thought, Some fresh coconut this day is turning out to be. I thought about a vacation. I thought about driving down to the coast, to Cape Hatteras, chartering a solid ship and sailing up the intercoastal waterway. Two grand would cover that. I could breathe the salty air, swim and fish and sun myself in the waters where Blackbeard sailed and stood tall on deck, twisting fuses into his curls. Head all ablaze, he'd board a ship like the devil himself. I could go there.

Three Days with Gabo

Silvana Paternostro

Distressed by what he saw happening to Latin American journalism, Gabriel García Márquez, the Nobel laureate author of *One Hundred Years of Solitude* and a former newspaper reporter himself, started in March 1995 what he describes as "a school without walls" — the Foundation for a New Ibero-American Journalism. Its purpose is to rejuvenate, through traveling workshops, journalism in the region. He insists that what is being taught and practiced needs urgent renovation and complains that today's journalists are more interested in chasing after breaking news and in the perks and privileges of a press pass than they are in creativity and ethics. They pride themselves on being able to read a secret document upside down, he says, but their work is full of grammatical and spelling mistakes and it lacks depth. "They are not moved by the basis that the best story is not the one that is filed first but the one that is told best," he wrote in his inaugural remarks.

García Márquez is critical of the way universities and newspaper publishers in Latin America are treating the profession — which he considers the best job in the world. Disagreeing with the professional schools' stance that journalists are not artists,

García Márquez considers that print journalism is "a literary form." He would also like to convince newspapers to invest less in technology and more in training personnel.

With the support of UNESCO, García Márquez's foundation, based in Barranquilla, Colombia, has organized, in less than two years, twenty-eight workshops attended by three-hundred-and-twenty journalists from eleven countries. The themes of the workshops have ranged from teaching the narrative techniques of reportage in print, radio and television, to discussions of ethics, freedom of the press, reporting under dangerous circumstances and the challenges of new technology for the profession. The workshops are taught by established professionals and are intended for the younger generation of journalists, preferably under thirty, who have at least three years of experience. Although based in Colombia, the workshops have also been conducted in Ecuador, Venezuela, Mexico and Spain. The centerpiece of the foundation's curriculum is the three-day workshop taught by García Márquez on reportage.

As a freelance journalist who has been writing about Latin America in English, I applied and was accepted for his fifth workshop. I was so excited to meet him that I, who am late for everything, was the first to arrive at the Spanish Cultural Center in Cartagena, a beautifully renovated two-story house with red begonias and a fountain in the courtyard, owned by the Spanish government. The setting could not be more appropriate. Cartagena is home to García Márquez, and many of the characters from his fiction walked the narrow cobblestones of the city's colonial center. A few blocks away from the Cultural Center, at the Cathedral's Square, Florentino Ariza noticed Fermina Daza's walk was no longer that of a schoolgirl. Sierva María de Todos los Angeles, the twelve-year-old girl whose hair continued to grow long after she died, lived in the Convent of Santa Clara nearby. Adjacent to the walls that kept Cartagena safe from English pirates, García Márquez's house here is so close to the convent — now a five-star hotel — that guests have an unimpeded view right into the author's home. "It was embarrassing," one guest at the hotel told me. "I could see him having breakfast every morning. Finally, I closed the curtains."

THREE DAYS WITH GABO

Monday, April 8, 1996
9:00 A.M.

I am one of twelve journalists sitting around a large wooden oval table. We are very quiet, like disciplined students in a Jesuit school waiting for class to begin. Gabriel García Márquez opens the door and comes in, looking at us mischievously, as if he knows how nervous we are. García Márquez—Gabo as everyone knows him—is dressed in white. Here on the Caribbean coast of Colombia, men often wear white, white all the way down to their shoes. He says good morning and, just for a second, it feels as if we might stand, bow or curtsy and answer in unison: *"Buenos días, profesor."*

The two empty seats in the room face the windows with their backs to the door. Gabo picks out César Romero, the Mexican journalist sitting next to me—we are facing the door—and asks him for his seat.

"I've seen too many cowboy movies," he says, "I never sit with my back to the door. Plus, I'm sure I have more enemies than you do."

"Don Gabriel," says César Romero, "of course."

As Gabo walks over, I remember my conversation with a Cuban friend who recently graduated from the film school that García Márquez founded outside of Havana and where he sometimes teaches. "You'll have a great time," Juan Carlos said. "He always pays more attention to the women than the men in the class. He says women bring him luck." I look around the table. Out of the twelve participants, Andrea Varela and I are the only women.

Gabo sits down to my left, and I am nervous. My hands start to sweat. I dry them against my pants. I cross my arms. He crosses his legs. I look down at the floor. His pointy, well-polished shoes are white. I look up. His watchband is also white. I focus on his *guayabera*, those shirts favored by Latin men, worn outside the pants, that rest on the hips, have four pockets, and sometimes embroidery and ruffles. I have always identified them with grandfathers, cabinet members and landowners—men who usually smell of cologne and sometimes of scotch. His shirt is simple, no ruffles, no smell, and made of such fine linen it is almost see-through. His seersucker pants make a funny, unexpected contrast.

He places on the table a black leather purse, the kind men started carrying around in the seventies. With his glasses on, he takes out the list of class participants from a black folder—where he also has the articles we had been asked to submit, a piece of reportage for Gabo to criticize and edit during the three days he will work with us. The only sound is the rumbling of the air conditioner. No one really looks at him, yet all of us, bona fide reporters, have been in situations much harder to handle than this one. Rubén Valencia, from Cali, traveled by himself to Urabá, Colombia's most violent zone, where drug traffickers, guerrilla and paramilitary groups massacre each other. Wilson Daza spent twenty days roaming downtown Medellín with drug pushers, prostitutes and gang members. César Romero covered the Zapatista insurrection in Chiapas. Edgar Téllez investigated President Samper's alleged link with drug cartels.

But ever since Gabo won the Nobel Prize in 1982, he has gone from being the writer of *One Hundred Years of Solitude* to being a celebrity and an important political actor. In Latin America, especially in Colombia and in Mexico where he spends most of his time, not even presidents have his stature. Here his stardom compares only to that of soccer stars and beauty queens. People stop him on the street for autographs, even those who have not read his books. Presidents, ministers, politicians, newspaper publishers, guerrilla leaders consult him, write him letters, want him around. Whatever he says, on whatever subject, makes the headlines. Last year a guerrilla group in Colombia kidnapped the brother of a former president. Their demand was that García Márquez accept the presidency. In their request they wrote: "Nobel, please save the Fatherland."

For us Colombians, to refer to García Márquez by his nickname *Gabo* is to bring his success closer to us, and like a proud family make his greatness our own. In a region consumed by violence, poverty, drug-trafficking and corruption, he is the son the family shows off—even those who disapprove of his friendship with Fidel Castro. In Barranquilla, my hometown, where he worked as a reporter in 1950 and where he met his wife Mercedes, *su mujer de siempre*, he has been completely embraced. He is not even Gabo but Gabito—the affectionate diminutive by which parents, spouses and friends call their dear ones.

His name comes up in our beauty pageants as often as the Pope's. The contestants' answers have become repetitive: Who is your favorite author? García Márquez. Whom do you admire the most? My father, the Pope and García Márquez. Whom would you like to meet? García Márquez and the Pope. If the same questions were posed to a Latin American journalist, the answers would probably be the same—perhaps leaving out the Pope. For us, Latin American journalists in the early stages of our careers, he is a role model. We like to say that before he was a novelist he was a reporter. He says he has never stopped being one.

Gabo reads our names off the list and adds a comment—always curious, always warm—to each. Rubén Valencia and a few others call him *maestro*, which to me sounds a little too respectful. I've called him Gabo many times when talking about him, but once in his presence that feels a little too forward. He is friendliest with Andrea, who has already been in a workshop with him. "You spend more time here at the workshops than at work," he jokes, calling her Andreita. "We're going to call your boss and ask her to send your bed over." Andrea is shy, and Gabo's warmth makes her blush.

The door opens in a rush and a young man—out of breath, a light blue shirt glued to his chest and a newspaper tucked under his arm—brings in the heat and the chaos of downtown Cartagena.

"*Permiso*," he apologizes, and sits quickly next to César Romero.

"And who are you?"

"Tadeo Martínez."

Tadeo is nervous, and Gabo knows it.

"Tadeo Martínez. *El Periódico de Cartagena*," he says, reading from his list. "Your colleagues are here from, let's see, Caracas, Bogotá, Cali, Medellín, San José, Mexico, New York and Miami but you, coming from around the corner, are the last one to arrive."
We all feel bad for him, but then Gabo shakes his head and smiles.

10:00 A.M.

Gabo starts by talking about his book on Simón Bolívar — our George Washington, Thomas Jefferson, Benjamin Franklin, all of the Founding Fathers wrapped up in one — who liberated five countries from Spanish rule and envisioned a unified Latin America, an empire running from California all the way down to Tierra del Fuego. *El Libertador*, as depicted in portraits on every public office wall, is always dressed in a starched military uniform, ready for battle or riding his white horse.

"But no one ever said in Bolívar's biographies that he sang or that he was constipated," says Gabo. He adds that he believes the world is divided into two groups: "Those who shit well and those who don't; it makes for very different characters. But historians don't say these things because they think they are not important." His dissatisfaction with the cardboard image that official historians have given to his hero explains why he decided to write *The General in His Labyrinth*, whose pages contain the complete story of the figure who has been such an important influence on his political thought. He tells us he wrote it in the form of a *reportaje*, reportage.

"Reportage is the complete story, the complete reconstruction of an event. Every little detail counts. This is the basis of the credibility and the strength of a story. In *The General in His Labyrinth* each verifiable fact, no matter how simple, can strengthen the whole work. For example, I placed a full moon — that full moon which is so easy to insert — on the night that Simón Bolívar slept in Guaduas on May 10, 1830. I wanted to find out if there was a full moon that night, so I called the Academy of Science in Mexico and they found out that there actually was one. If there wasn't, well, I would just cross out the full moon and that's that. The moon is a detail that no one notices. But if there is one false fact in a reporting piece, then everything else is false. In fiction, if there is a fact that can be verified—that there was a full moon that night in Guaduas—then the readers are going to believe everything else."

Someone asks about fiction techniques in reportage. Gabo replies that he admires the work of Gay Talese, Norman Mailer and Truman Capote, all of whom have practiced New Journalism. "The only literary aspect of New Journalism is its narrative style. Literary license is allowed as long as it is believable and stays true to all the verifiable facts."

As he says this, I recall the piece Gabo wrote about Caracas in a terrible drought and about a man who had taken to shaving with peach juice—a fact that is definitely credible, and verifiable, but one that reeks of literary license. It has been said that Gabo is too creative to be a good journalist. After all, he is the same writer who in his novels, with a straight face, had Remedios the Beauty levitating to the skies and the smell of Santiago Nasar after his well-announced death penetrating the entire town.

As if reading my mind he says, "The strange episodes in my novels are all real, or they have a starting point, a basis in reality. Real life is always much more interesting than what we can invent." He says that the ascension of Remedios the Beauty was inspired by a woman he saw spreading clean white sheets with her arms stretched out to the sun. He has also said that "to move between the magical and the incredible, one has to become a journalist."

He tells us about *Tale of a Shipwreck*, which was originally written as a series of stories when he was working as a staff reporter for *El Espectador* in Bogotá. He had been assigned to write the adventures of a sailor lost at sea but the story was of no interest to him. "Every newspaper had written about it." But then he relented. In those days, the fifties—as in the days when Charles Dickens's novels appeared in the London broadsheets—serialization was a common marketing tool. Gabo's job was to interview the sailor and write his story in segments. After the first two parts were published, Don Guillermo Cano, the paper's editor (assassinated by drug cartels in 1986), walked up to his desk. "'*Oiga* Gabrielito, those things you are writing—are they fiction or are they true?' I told him, 'It is a novel and it is true.' Then he asked me, 'And how many more parts are you thinking of submitting?'

"'Two more,' I said.

"'No way, sales are up threefold. Give me a hundred.'

"I wrote fourteen.

"I knew the sailor had spent fourteen days lost at sea," Gabo tells us, "so I decided to write fourteen chapters, one for each day at sea. I sat down with the guy again and started slicing his days thinner. I began by asking him what he did every day, then what he did every hour, and then every minute. I asked him what time the sharks arrived; what time he ate."

Noon

It is almost lunchtime. Gabo began talking at nine sharp and he has not stopped. More than teaching, Gabo chats, tells stories. For more than three hours, the twelve of us have sat, saying little. I have not had breakfast but I am not feeling hungry. He doesn't drink coffee but many of us do. It is the perfect accompaniment to his stories.

Storytellers, he says, are born, not made: "Like singers, to be a storyteller is something life gives you. It cannot be learned. Technique, yes, that can be learned, but to be able to tell a story is something with which you are born. It is easy to tell a good storyteller from a bad one: ask someone to tell you about the last movie they've seen."

Then he emphasizes, "The difficult thing is to realize that you are not a storyteller and then have the courage to move on and do something else." César Romero later tells me that of all Gabo's statements this is the one that struck him the most.

He gives an example. Soon after he received the Nobel Prize, a young journalist in Madrid approached Gabo as he was leaving his hotel and asked for an interview. Gabo, who dislikes being asked for interviews, refused to give one, but invited her to accompany him and his wife throughout the day. "She spent the whole day with us. We shopped, my wife bargained, we went to lunch, we walked, we talked; she came with us everywhere." When they returned to the hotel and Gabo was ready to say good-bye, she asked him for an interview. "I told her she should change jobs," says Gabo. "She had the complete story, she had the reportage."

He went on to talk about the difference between an interview and reportage—a confusion, he says, journalists are constantly making. "An interview in print journalism is always a dialogue between the journalist and someone who has something to say or think *about* an event. Reportage is the meticulous and truthful reconstruction *of* an event.

"Tape recorders are nefarious because one falls into the trap of believing that the tape recorder thinks, and so we disconnect our brains the moment we plug in the cord. A tape recorder is a digital parrot, it has ears but it doesn't have a heart. It does not pick up details so our job is to listen beyond the words, pick up on what is not said and then write the complete story." He looks down at the pile of papers in front of him — our articles! "Writing is a hypnotic act," he says. "If successful the writer has hypnotized the reader. Wherever there is a stumble the reader wakes up, comes out of the hypnosis and stops reading. If the prose limps, the reader abandons you. One must keep the reader hypnotized by tending to every detail, every word. It is a continuous act where you poison the reader with credibility and with rhythm." He pauses, then taps on the papers. "Now I must tell you that I read the articles you've all sent and I was *fully awake* the whole time."

I gasp, some giggle, and others move around uncomfortably in their chairs.

1:00 P.M.

"Let's see what's in the paper today." He reaches across the table for Tadeo Martínez's newspaper. "Is there a story we could go out and cover?" he asks. He studies the front page and shakes his head in disapproval. "Incredible," he says. "This is a local paper and not one story about Cartagena on the front page. Tell your boss, Tadeo, that a local paper should have local front-page news.

"Nothing here," he mumbles as he turns the pages. "Let's see, something here. *Stove for sale, unused, unassembled stove. Must sell. Call Gloria Bedoya, 660-1127, extension 113.* This could be a story. Should we call? I bet there's something here. Why is this woman selling a stove, why is the stove unassembled? What do we know from this about this woman? Could be interesting." He pauses, waiting for us to get excited. But no one seems to be interested in finding out why a woman is selling an unassembled stove, especially when we can keep listening to him.

Gabo sees stories everywhere. During the next three days he says *"eso es un reportaje"* (that's a story) constantly. I realize that Gabo is full of nostalgia. He misses being a reporter. "Journalism is not a job, it's a gland," he says.

It is not a coincidence that his new book, *News of a Kidnapping*, is a work of nonfiction. It allowed him—during the three years it took him to write it—to be a reporter once again. It is the story of nine kidnappings engineered between 1989 and 1991 by Pablo Escobar, the head of the violent Medellín drug cartel, who wanted to avoid at any cost Colombia signing an extradition treaty with the United States. In keeping with his motto ("Better a grave in Colombia than a cell in the United States"), Escobar pressured the government by bombing buildings, killing presidential candidates, ministers, judges, police officers and ultimately kidnapping nine people, eight of whom were journalists.

Vividly and eerily, Gabo reconstructs the six months of captivity—recording the impatience and anxiety not only of the kidnapped and their families but also that of the kidnappers, members of Escobar's cartel, and of the government officials involved in the negotiating process. Of course, as García Márquez, he had the kind of access any journalist would desire. He was able to meet with the families, with government officials, including three former presidents. He talked with the teenagers who kept guard, who listened to Guns 'n Roses and watched *Lethal Weapon* on video repeatedly, high on crack with their machine guns cocked next to them — kids who kill for the cartels in order to buy refrigerators for their mothers. When Gabo started writing the book, Pablo Escobar was already dead — shot by police forces in 1993. But he had access to the drug lord's principal partners, the Ochoa brothers, who received him in jail. Escobar's lawyers showed him handwritten letters. "Every single detail in this book is real; as much as it was humanly possible to verify the facts, they were verified. If Pablo Escobar himself could not revise the text, it was because he was dead. I know he would have agreed to meet with me."

The fact he can meet anyone he chooses makes Gabo miss the days when he was a faceless journalist, one who could pick up a pad and go find out why the stove is unassembled. "It is difficult for me now to write a reporting piece. I wanted to write about that village whose bread supply had been poisoned but I knew that if I went there the news would be distorted; *I* would become the news." He is referring to an incident which occurred outside of Bogotá a few years ago — a whole town poisoned.

Apart from allowing him to go back to journalism, *News of a Kidnapping* served another purpose. "I wanted to see if I was still able to write like a journalist," he tells us. "It has been the most difficult book I've written. It is much easier to write fiction, where I am the master, I control it all. But this was written as if for the newspapers. I wrote this book without using a literary adjective or a metaphor. It was a useful exercise because it is important for me not to repeat myself. The challenge of writing *Autumn of the Patriarch* after writing *One Hundred Years of Solitude* was self-imposed. I could have written three hundred *One Hundred*s. I knew how to do that, so I decided I would write *Autumn* in a very different style. *Autumn* was not successful when it came out. If I had written another *One Hundred* it would have been better received." He smiles and tells us that one of his most satisfying moments was seeing in the United States an edition of *One Hundred Years* with a gray stripe down one side which read: From the author of *Love in the Time of Cholera*. "This was the victory over *One Hundred Years*," he says.

"As writers we also have to defend ourselves from those authors we like. It is easy to fall into a trap and start imitating them. For example, people like to say I imitated Faulkner, but during my trip to the American South, when I went with Mercedes, a son still in arms and twenty dollars to our name, I realized I was identifying not so much with his writing but with a reality, which is that the American South is like Aracataca."

Aracataca is the small town in the Caribbean region of Colombia where he was born, about two hundred miles from where my grandfather grew up. Something has felt familiar ever since Gabo walked into the room, sat next to me and started talking. He has said many times that he retells the stories his grandmother told him. Listening to Gabo makes me feel as if I am listening to my grandfather — if only my grandfather could write!

Gabo leans back in his chair, touches his white mustache and warns us, "You are not writing well if you feel happy when the phone rings and you answer it; or if there is a power blackout and that makes you happy. But if you are on track and the phone rings, you won't answer it; you will damn the lights if they shut off." His example about the electricity must seem farfetched to some, but to us Latin American journalists, blackouts and the loss of the text on our computers are always in the backs of our minds. Gabo, who once lost a whole text, now has his own emergency generator.

He begins to read paragraphs out loud from some of our articles; he offers light copyediting. Some of the sentences are too long and Gabo pretends to be choking as he reads along. "We have to use breathing commas," he says. "If not, the hypnotic act does not work. Remember, wherever there is a stumble, the reader wakes up and escapes. And one of the things that will make the reader wake up from hypnosis is to feel out of breath."

We have spent almost the entire morning listening to Gabo teach by telling stories. Our job, I've realized, is to kick back and enjoy him — as if we are on an extended coffee break or drinking at the nearest bar. "I know journalism cannot be taught, it must be lived, but I can transmit to you some of my experience. There are no theories. Reality has no theories, reality narrates. From it we have to learn."

After Lunch

> The light in the room was so dim that it took a moment for their eyes to adjust. It was a space no longer than two by three meters, with one boarded-up window. Two men were sitting on a single mattress that had been placed on the floor: they wore hoods, like the men in the first house, and were absorbed in watching television. Everything was dismal and oppressive. In the corner to the left of the door, on a narrow bed with iron posts, sat a spectral woman with limp white hair, dazed eyes and skin that adhered to her bones. She gave no sign of having heard them come in; not a glance, not a breath. Nothing, a corpse could not have seemed so dead. Maruja had to restrain her shock when she realized who it was.

Gabo is reading a chapter from *News of a Kidnapping*. I am willing to surrender to his words, except his white shoes are impossible to ignore. I close my eyes to give myself entirely to his "poison."

> At night the silence was total and the solitude immense, interrupted only by a demented rooster with no sense of time who crowed whenever he felt like it. Barking dogs could be heard on the horizon, and there was one very close by that sounded to them like a trained guard

dog. Maruja got off to a bad start. She curled up in the mattress, closed her eyes, and for several days did not open them again except when she had to, trying to attain the privacy she needed to think with more clarity. Not that she slept for eight hours at a time: she would doze off for half an hour and wake again to the same reality, the same agony waiting to ambush her. It was a permanent dread: the constant physical sensation in her stomach of something hard, coiled and ready to explode into panic. Maruja ran the complete film of her life in an effort to hold onto good memories, but disagreeable ones always intervened . . .

He reads the entire chapter. I feel Marina Montoya's panic as she dressed in the pink sweat suit and men's brown socks and said good-bye to her two roommates. I am transported to the cramped room where the guards are telling Marina she is going to be freed. But everyone knows that the high heels she wears with the sweats are taking her to her execution.

"Any comments? Anything I should change?"

No one says a word.

"It is an investigation of three years," he says with pride. "The research was crucial. Every fact that could be verified was verified. I give credit in the book to my research assistant."

Gabo is talking, but my head is still heavy. I haven't come out of my hypnosis. I feel groggy and can still see Marina's body, dressed in pink, lying dead on the grass that divides the only road to Bogotá's airport, the same one I take every time I visit my parents.

"A good piece of advice is first to write the beginning and the ending. Begin with an anecdote and close with a resonant ending. Then fill in the in-between. You have to fence in your story, almost as if with cattle. If not, you keep researching, and that could take you anywhere. You have to enclose the story, you have to learn how to end the circle of information. Details are the key. You must hold on to a thread in the narrative. If not you get swamped. Even Cervantes lost a donkey, and we must avoid losing as many donkeys as possible," he says.

"One of the big problems about writing is worrying too much. If you could just write it as you speak it, that is the dream of a writer, to be able to write as one speaks. It's not done, because when one tries, one realizes how difficult it is to do. In Mexico I used to write with my windows open, so I would hear the birds or the rain, and I would include them in the text I was working on. Not anymore. That thing about only being able to write in a particular space, in a particular way, is a novelist's mania. Now I can write anywhere just as I used to do when I was a reporter. I just plug in my PowerBook in any hotel room. But I am used to writing on the long screen. I save as I write and transfer to a floppy disk right away. Each chapter is a file."

He tells us he is hooked on writing on screens shaped like pages. But they aren't manufactured anymore. "I buy all the ones I can find. I have eleven," he says. "I believe one needs to buy anything that makes our job easier. Computers are extraordinary. I can prove it. I started writing on a computer with *Love in the Time of Cholera*. I went from writing one page to writing ten a day, from writing a book every seven years to writing a book every three. Still, writing never stops being difficult. Staring at a blank page, one gets the same anxiety as with sex, always anticipating if it's going to work or not. There's always the anguish. As Borges used to say: what God is the God behind the God who moves the pieces of chess?"

He tells us he knows that the worst moment for a writer, or for a journalist, is facing the blank page and shares what for him has been one of the most useful tips, what Ernest Hemingway told *The Paris Review* in 1958: "You read what you have written and, as you always stop when you know what is going to happen next, you go on from there. You write until you come to a place where you still have your juice and know what will happen next and you stop and try to live through until the next day when you hit it again."

"I write from eight-thirty in the morning to about two or three in the afternoon," Gabo says. "From those long years at the chair I've developed a bad back; that's why I play tennis every day. Sometimes after I finish, my back pain is such that I just have to throw myself to the floor." It is a little before seven when he looks at his white watch. "You guys are not going to make me miss my tennis," he says. He gets up and walks out.

Tuesday, April 9
9:00 A.M.

Almost fifty years ago today Gabo lost his first typewriter — the one he used to write "The Third Resignation," his first published short story. He was an unhappy law student living in an inexpensive hostel in downtown Bogotá. He missed the heat of the Caribbean coast. He rarely went to classes: law, which his family expected him to study, had never interested him. At lunchtime on April 9, 1948, Gabo was about to sit down to eat when he overheard that Jorge Eliecer Gaitán, a popular young presidential candidate who was shaking Colombia's traditional political structure, had been shot.

Gabo tells us that he got to the square only to find "people were already soaking their handkerchiefs in Gaitán's blood." The streets of Bogotá burned and Gabo's typewriter went up in the conflagration. Colombia was paralyzed. Universities shut down. It was a few months later, here in Cartagena, that Gabo, at the age of nineteen, started his life as a journalist by writing editorials.

"I was walking around one day and Zavala, the editor of *El Universal*, was sitting at his typewriter outside on the square. He tells me, 'I know you.' He says, 'You are the guy with the short stories in *El Espectador*. Why don't you sit down and help me with this editorial I'm finishing?' I wrote something. Zavala took out his pencil and crossed some things out. The next time I wrote an editorial, he scratched out only a few things. By the third day I was writing without editing. I had become a journalist."

He is not sitting next to me today. He is not wearing a white guayabera but a turquoise short-sleeved silk shirt. The shoes are still white. My connection with him feels distant but I'm still drawn to his tales. "I started making money from writing when I was forty-three years old," he tells us. "I bought my first house, the one in Cuernavaca, in 1970, twenty-five years after my first story was published. I calculated that to take my sons to the movies back then I had to write twelve pages, and to take them to the movies and buy them ice cream I had to write twenty. When I lived in Paris, I didn't keep constant hours and wrote mostly at night. During the day, I had to worry about feeding myself. Now I know it is better to write during the day, on a computer, with a full stomach and with air-conditioning."

Coffee Break

Jaime Abello, the foundation's director, has hired a photographer and calls us together for a group picture. The foundation issues no certificates: "Life, in its due course, will decide who is capable and who is not," Gabo has said. "At least, you can all go back with a souvenir," Jaime says. "Come and sit on the stairs."

Gabo is complacent and sits in the middle. The photographer from *El Universal* orders us to smile at the camera.

"Wait," shouts the woman who runs the Center. "I want a picture with Gabo." She climbs over us and sits next to him.

1:00 P.M.

It was inevitable. Fidel Castro had to come up. We were, or I should say I was, waiting for the right moment. Gabo wants to talk about ethics: should a reporter read a document left unattended, one that has the potential for a scoop?

His question gives me a chance. "I had an experience like that," I say. In 1991 I attended the opening ceremony of the first Ibero-American presidential summit, held in Guadalajara. Castro was told that all the dignitaries had to limit their speeches to seven minutes. Everyone waited apprehensively for Castro's turn since he is known for his long speeches. We all wondered if Castro, who the day after the triumph of the revolution in 1959 ad-libbed for seven hours, would keep to his instructions. He spoke for exactly seven minutes. President Balaguer of the Dominican Republic spoke for forty-five.

During the break, the pool of journalists, including myself, surrounded Fidel. In person he looms larger than life, even if his military uniform seemed a little faded and the collar of his shirt too frayed. As he walked outside, the crowd followed him. He seemed to love it.

"*Comandante*, I cut cane in the Venceremos Brigade," a journalist yelled.

He stopped and looked for the voice. "Where?"

A woman extended a black-and-white photograph over the crowd — a picture of the two of them together when his beard was dark. "Can you sign it, *Comandante?*"

"Was it hard to speak for seven minutes?" someone else called out.

"I was tricked," said Fidel. "They told me that if I spoke for longer than seven minutes all of the bells in Guadalajara would toll."

I had noticed a small, crumpled piece of paper next to a yellow pad where he had been sitting. As the crowd moved out with him, I returned to his seat and picked up the ball of paper. I opened it and read his small and cramped handwriting: *"Por cuánto tiempo habré hablado?"* (How long have I spoken?) On the bigger pad, Fidel had made a list of the presidents and the amount of time, to the exact second, that each had spoken. I walked away leaving the note behind. I've regretted it ever since.

"I would definitely have grabbed it," says Gabo. "Believe me, if he thought it was so important, he would have never left it there. Yes, I would have kept it as a souvenir."

As I had hoped, Gabo begins to speak about Fidel Castro. He talks about Cuba openly, with concern and passion, like a university student who keeps a poster of Che Guevara on the wall. But about Fidel, he speaks without really saying anything negative, compromising or even revelatory. "I speak about Fidel more from sentiment than from a place of judgement. He is one of the people I love most in the world."

"A dictator," someone says.

"To have elections is not the only way to be democratic."

The American journalist in the group keeps after him. Gabo starts to answer, but sees we are taking notes. His voice turns stern: "This is not an interview. If I want to express my opinion on Fidel, I'll write it myself and believe me, I'll do a better job."

Perhaps feeling somewhat guilty for snapping at us, he describes a profile he wrote about Fidel. "I gave it to him to read. In it, I was critical. I spoke about the situation of the free press. But he said nothing about that. What really irked him about my article was that I mentioned he had eaten eighteen scoops of ice cream after lunch one day. 'Did I really eat eighteen scoops?' he asked me repeatedly."

After Lunch

"Tell us about your trip to Chigorodó." Gabo is calling on Rubén Valencia.

Chigorodó is a village in Urabá, Colombia's most dangerous region — which is saying a lot coming from a country that has been described as the most violent in the world. The Gulf of Urabá, on the western coast of Colombia, is a geographical Molotov cocktail. It has the country's most fertile land; it is a point of entry for arms and a port of exit for drugs; it has poor peasants and rich landowners; it has guerrilla groups, military forces and death squads. Last year, one thousand people were killed, victims of political violence. According to a newspaper report, a twenty-year-old hitman has already killed eighty-three people. In August of 1995, eighteen people were killed inside a dance hall. Massacres like this are frequent.

Rubén is the last person I would have expected to visit Chigorodó. He is a scrawny young man with square glasses too big for his face, with so much prescription in his lenses that his eyes seem tiny. "I went there," he says, "to write about the effect that violence was having on the lives of the people in the area, to find the human face of the story."

The piece he published is the one he submitted to the workshop. Gabo is holding it in his hand. "Tell us what happened from the moment you arrived? Who was the first person you talked to?" he asks.

"The town was desolate, maestro. I found a twelve-year-old kid, I asked him if he knew where the dance hall was and he took me there. After the massacre, there was an exodus; all the peasants left in fear." Valencia tells us that he walked around looking for someone to talk to, but fear and silence were all he found. A woman stopped on a motorcycle and offered him a ride to Apartadó, about a half-hour ride in the rain, where he could get more information. He checked into the Hotel Las Molas. On his third day there, a visitor was waiting for him in the lobby.

"Are you the person who is investigating the massacres?" the stranger asked him. "Let's go out and have a drink. I think you want to talk to me."

"Sorry," replied Valencia. "It's too late. I don't go out after dark. Do you want to come up to my room?"

THREE DAYS WITH GABO

Once in the room, the man asked, "What have you found out? What do you want to know?"

"I'm a journalist, I'm trying to find the human face to this conflict."

"Ah, ya."

"Who are you?" Valencia finally asked him.

"I am an angel," said the man.

"What kind of an angel?"

"An angel with a white wing and a black wing."

"And with what wing will you be talking to me?"

"That depends."

"On what?"

As Valencia speaks, we are all silent, immersed in his story. I am feeling somewhat envious, what a story!

"But that is not what I read here," says Gabo, raising the article. "Why didn't you write that story? Why didn't you write that just the way you just told it to us. That's the story I would have written.

"Describe that man," says Gabo looking at him.

Rubén remains silent.

"Can you remember his face?"

"Yes."

"What animal did he remind you of?"

"An iguana."

"That's it, you need nothing more." says Gabo. "You lost the trip, my boy. We are not sociologists, we are tale-tellers, we tell the stories of people. Reporting with a human voice is what makes journalists big. Where is that story?"

Rubén, who insists on calling García Márquez *maestro*, responds: "It's not easy. When I propose to write that story, my editor tells me, 'Valencia you are not García Márquez. Stick to the facts!' "

3:00 P.M.

"Daza, why don't you read us one of your pieces?" Gabo asks. I am feeling impatient. The day is almost over. The workshop is almost over, and Gabo has not said a word about my piece. Because I had written about Cuba I thought he would show a particular interest. But he has not even acknowledged reading it.

Daza has written about one of Medellín's underground characters—a profile of a man who prefers the company of animals to humans. He shares his daily *buñuelo*, a fried dough, his only meal, with a pet rat. He carries a chicken on a leash and keeps fleas in his room. Daza reads it to us. The piece is touching, the writing lyrical, maybe even too lyrical. It is not traditional reportage.

"I will not touch Daza's writing," says Gabo. "He might be inventing a new form here, one I know nothing about."

If he thought it was good or bad, we do not know.

Daza is not only daring in his writing style. He is the only one who has shown some disdain: "Gabo is a little full of himself."

Daza had been sent to cover the Ibero-American presidential summit, which in 1994 was held in Cartagena. Reporters were furious because dignitaries were impossible to interview. Gabo, being an important political actor, was there as a guest in a delegation. He was reported as saying that, instead of complaining, journalists need to go out on the street looking for stories, and not expect news to be handed to them on silver platters. If the presidents were unavailable, a good journalist would find a story nonetheless.

Refuting him, Daza says, "It was easy for you to say that. I wrote a story about how unfair I thought that comment was, especially coming from you. I mean you were there, behind doors, with all of the presidents."

"I was not there as a working journalist."

Daza admits that Gabo's reprimand was useful. He gives an illustration: when he then was sent to cover the summit of the Group of the Non-Aligned Countries held in Cartagena last year, he didn't go to the convention center where the leaders were meeting. To write about Yassir Arafat, who was attending, and about the Israel-Palestine conflict, he went to one of Cartagena's many poor slums instead—to one that is actually called Palestina. He wrote a story comparing Arafat's

situation with that of a girl living in Palestina, marginalized in the outskirts of a rich, tourist-filled city.
"You learned the lesson," says Gabo.
"You were also at that meeting." Daza is unrelenting. "You were there with the Cuban delegation."
"I was there," Gabo says impatiently. "I was there because there were rumors that there was going to be an assassination attempt on Fidel. And the Cuban security wasn't going to let Fidel be part of the procession so I proposed to go on the horse-drawn carriage with him. I told them that here in Colombia if I'm on board, no one will shoot. So five of us squeezed into the carriage, tight, joking. While I was telling Fidel that I was sure nothing was going to happen, the horse actually tripped."

Dinner

He is having dinner with us at La Vitrola, Cartagena's most cosmopolitan restaurant. The decor is more British colonial than Spanish, but the group of Cuban musicians dressed in white sings traditional *sones*. It is where Colombia's upper class eats when they are vacationing, where the president stops by for a drink. Soap-opera stars, small but flashy drug dealers, young rich kids on their first date, the few local yuppies all come too. The menu resembles that of a New York restaurant. The vinaigrette is made with balsamic vinegar, the mozzarella is fresh and the wine, for Colombia, is good.

We sit and wait in a small room sipping fruit punches. Gabo arrives wearing a dark blue jumpsuit, zipped from his navel to his chest. Caribbean man by day, by night he seems as though he has just jumped off the cover of a record—funk or disco. His shoes are exactly the same model as this morning's but this time they are gray. He asks the waiter for a whisky. We go to the private room next to the entrance. He sits between Andrea and me.

The menu is fixed: fried zucchini followed by a choice of shrimp in coconut sauce or red snapper in cream.

"That's too heavy for me to eat at night," Gabo complains.

The host comes over. "I can give you the snapper, grilled with no sauce? Or a pasta?"
"What kind?"
"How would *you* want it?"
"Simple."
"How about *pasta in brodo*."
"Perfect. Bring me that."
I ask if I can have the same; I have felt feverish all day.
"Two of those," Gabo tells him.
When the wine is served, he declines and keeps drinking his whisky.
The restaurant is filling up. Our table is in plain view. Everyone notices Gabo. He requests that the doors be closed, and I ask the waiter to do so. A reporter from *Newsweek* who has come from Buenos Aires to interview Gabo is sitting at my left. I speak to him for a while but I really only want to talk to Gabo, whisper to him, not share him with the rest of my colleagues.
I turn to him. We converse about many things. He wants to know why and where I live in New York. I tell him I live in the Village and I ask him if he likes New York. He does very much, but not when it's too cold because he likes doing nothing better than walking through the streets. I tell him I will take him around the Village, and he promises to call. We talk about Cuba, about Barranquilla, about Bill Clinton, *The New Yorker* and Sunday magazines. He tells me in intricate detail about a short story he wants to write and about a yellow silk shirt he has, one he wears when he feels in love. His glass is empty so he sips from mine. "I like being around women. I know them better than I know men. I feel more comfortable around them; I grew up with women around me."
The waiter walks over and hands Gabo a white napkin, folded. He opens it and reads what's on it. He tells the waiter to say nothing. It must be difficult to have everyone want something from him all the time. He has told us about a friend running for the assembly who called him up: "Gabo, can you write something about me, say something about me, even if it's just to insult me."

THREE DAYS WITH GABO

The door opens and a man peeks in. Gabo looks up, stands up and, with his arms extended, walks over, *"Ah, mon ami, quelle coincidence."* I suppose it is the man who had sent him the note on the napkin. As he sits back again he whispers in my ear, "I just want to escape out that window."

Row One (top): Tadeo Martínez, Oscar Becerra, Wilson Daza, Alejandro Manrique, Elias García; Row Two: Manuel Bermudez, Jaime Abello, director of the Spanish Cultural Center, García Márquez, Tim Johnson, Andrea Varela; Row Three: Juan Manuel Buelvas (Abello's assistant), César Romero, Rubén Valencia, Silvana Paternostro, Edgar Téllez.

Wednesday, April 10
9:30 A.M.

Gabo is sitting at the head of the table again, reading from what appears to be a manuscript, waiting for everyone to arrive. He knows the class went out after dinner last night. He looks amused at the last ones arriving late, perhaps with a hint of nostalgia. Everyone looks sleepy, unshowered and irritable with pounding headaches from too much anisette. He looks sparkling clean in his white outfit.

I sit at the other end of the table and I wonder if he has not mentioned my piece to keep me on tenterhooks. Time is ticking, an hour left, and Tadeo's story about a convicted Spanish woman in Cartagena who was not allowed to serve her prison sentence because she was HIV-positive is still being discussed. "You have the best story here," says Gabo, "but you got lost telling it; this makes no sense."

He finally looks at me. I am less nervous than when he first sat next to me but nonetheless my heart races.

"Silvana has good taste in music," Gabo says. "Like me, she likes Van Morrison."

My piece is about the difficulties young rock musicians have in Cuba, where the state does not support them and private initiatives are impossible. I wrote about a struggling troubador with a stringless guitar whose voice I described as like Van Morrison's.

"Silvana has written a good piece, well-structured. I wouldn't change anything," Gabo says. But he disagrees with some of my descriptions: "Is it necessary to say that a television is broken, that it is black-and-white and that there is no money to fix it? There are many homes right here in Cartagena where money is short and TVs are not in color. Would you write that if it weren't about Cuba?"

We go back and forth on the subject of culture control in the Cuban government. "I've talked to them many times," he says as if frustrated that they haven't listened to him. Then he gets up, walks over to me and hands me my piece. He has not done that with anyone else.

He walks back to his seat. My feet are not touching the ground. I feel like Remedios the Beauty—I'm levitating.

Gabo has a last comment to make: "I see you all—and in your fears, in your clumsiness, in your questioning, I am reminded of the way I felt when I was your age. Telling you about my experiences has also allowed me to look at myself. After all, it will be fifty years since I started writing—every day of my life. If you don't like your job, resign. The only thing you die from is from doing something you don't like. If you like your work, you have longevity and happiness assured."

Everyone makes a queue toward him. Copies of *One Hundred Years of Solitude*, *Chronicle of a Death Foretold*, *No One Writes to the Colonel* all need to be signed. He inscribes all, and shakes everyone's hand. Rubén Valencia hands him a copy of *Autumn of the Patriarch*. Curious to know what Gabo would write to someone who has been so respectful and so adoring, I ask Valencia to show me the inscription. It reads: "From the patriarch of the workshop." César Romero wants his book signed for his newborn son. Gabo writes: "For Rodrigo when you were beginning."

I have not brought a book for him to sign. I wait next to the door. As he sees me, he smiles the same smile of mischief he had when he entered the room the first time. "And you Silvana, aren't you sad it's over? Aren't you going to cry?"

Why I Married the Porn Star

J. David Stevens

She can quote Milton Friedman from memory. She can lock her ankles behind her head.

When my mother asks why I married her: I mean, why her and not one of the trillion other girls in the world, why not Lucy Hoffmeiller next door who's the picture of respectability in the neighborhood but would probably get kinky in private, if that's what you're looking for, I reply, I don't know, because I love her. Love, repeats my mother. What do you know about love?

Our first meeting: in the exotic foods section of the local market, reaching for the same kumquats. She was the All-American Girl almost—calves a bit too big, cheekbones too low, hips a touch wide. Later, she would look into my eyes and say that she wanted to take care of me.

She wears only business suits. Her closet overflows with them. She owns no bustiers, no leather bodysuits, no whips, no sexy G-strings, no crotchless panties or fishnet. She is a nineties woman, my wife. She means business.

We don't have a problem with it, her sister Evelyn claimed when I went to her family's house for our first Christmas together. Sure, maybe at first, but it's only natural then, until you get used to it. Besides, it's nice to have a celebrity around, at least that's what the neighbors say. I'm sure you saw the children waving as you came in. They don't know any details, mind you. We're all Christians here—we just say "movie star" and watch their eyes light up. I mean, even Alice Shockley—the Mrs. *Reverend* Shockley—will tell you in private that the whole thing has really brought the community together. But why do you ask? Do you have a problem with it? Silly me, of course you don't. What could shock a poet? Oh, you better not stand too close to that mistletoe, naughty boy. We're not all as uninhibited as my sister, but none of us balks at tradition.

Her hair is blond, and her eyes are blue. Her breasts are real.

We don't have close friends, by and large. Sometimes we hang out with the other porn stars, but I have no idea what to talk about. When they learn I am a poet, they are always intrigued. They say I am in the same business as them, just working a different side of the street. Once a brunette with breasts the size of two challah loaves and breath reeking of Jim Beam plopped down in my lap and told me to write a poem for her. She forced my hand down her blouse and squeezed her fingers around mine. For inspiration, she said. Between her breasts, I could just make out the low-pitched wailing of her heart.

Sometimes when I want to have sex, my wife says that she has a headache. I ask, Did you have a headache all day? Yes, she replies, but that was business—do you stop working because you have a headache? Somehow I think she misses the point.

Our city is not one where you would expect pornographers to live. Not to imply anything about the insidious nature of pornographers—this is no conspiracy. It's just odd for a city as conventional as ours. For instance, our street alone boasts four Baptist churches, and just one block over, the entire avenue is devoted to statues of Civil War heroes, dark and imposing in the sense of tradition they inspire. The city loves the war. People here identify themselves by the battles in which their ancestors fought and died. On the Fourth of July, more people stand when the band plays "Dixie" than when it plays "America the Beautiful." The pornographers have ties to the war, as well. One pornographer, who also owns a dry-cleaning business, paid to have the remains of his great-great-great-great uncle moved from South Carolina to the city cemetery so that the old soldier could be buried with his regiment. The pornographer says he loves the South as much as he loves America. His wife is big in the DAR. They have been to our house for drinks, but because of my reluctance to talk politics, we are not close. The pornographer and his wife are not flashy people. When they bow their heads in church, you would not be able to pick them out from the rest of the congregation. My wife is correct, though, when she says that they cannot be upheld as true representatives of the porn industry. They are only representatives of what I choose to see. The other pornographers are nothing like them.

She has a small tattoo just above her left elbow, a dove with an olive branch in its mouth. She explains, I didn't know it meant anything when I picked it out. I was just a kid. I thought it looked cool.

From the window by my writing desk, I can see Robert T., the doorman, ushering women from cars at the curb. Robert calls me Mr. Albright and pretends to fuss each year when the Pulitzers are announced and my name does not appear on the list. How is Mrs. Albright? he asks conscientiously when I return from my daily jog. Once, when he thought I could not hear, he looked at my wife and said, Gotta get me some of that. And all I could think was, You can, Robert. Just $19.95. Shipping and handling not included.

You don't have to worry about my having an affair, my wife says. What do I want with sex? Every woman should be as faithful as me.

Occasionally she brings home videos to review. She sits before the TV, taking notes on a yellow legal pad in bright red pen. She wears lavender bifocals only at home. The company she works for may let her direct next year, and she asks what I think of this scene or that. Since we have been married, I have seen her in every position imaginable, with a man, a woman, men, women, both. The images no longer excite me. But I can't get over watching her watching herself, sliding her bifocals up the bridge of her nose like a scientist hovering over some new discovery. The voyeur observed. The cerebral irony makes me both horny and ashamed, so much that I have stopped questioning whether the two impulses are truly different at their base. I should take her now, like a beast, bifocals and all. I should write a poem. I am a genius of the perverse, a perverted genius. If only my wife could curve to me like verse — if only verse could hump like a dog.

But love, she continues. Love is a different story.

Don't get me wrong, her brother Edmund admitted after several swigs of eggnog, no woman of mine would ever do what she does. But to be honest, I've watched a tape or two. It's like peeking through the bathroom door at them when you're a kid. You got sisters? No? Well, you know what I mean. And hey, if you don't have a problem with it, I say

what the hell. It's not like you're married to her or anything.
Oh, really? In your pocket? I bet a rock like that set you back
a bundle. Oh, no, I won't say anything until you make your
move. But listen now, you treat her right. She's my sister. I
love her.

Each year we go to the porn-star awards ceremony, and each
time I wonder how they determine who wins. Who is acting
and how? My wife has won many times. Sometimes while she
sleeps, I hold my hand very close to her cheek and wonder if
she must act with me. If she acts better than other women.

So what is love? I insist. Love, she says, is the words around
a roll in the sheets—love is the silence between the gasps.
Face down, I feel her thighs on either side of me, her fists
kneading a pain into the small of my back. Leaning close to
my ear, she whispers, this is good stuff, are you taking it down?
I buck my hips to roll her off. She licks her teeth in serpent
ecstasy, and her eyes are shattering mirrors in which I am lost.
You should be a poet, I say.

But love has to be something more. Something deeper.

I go to the private screenings of her movies. She comes to
the private readings of my poems. Being honest, I am a mediocre poet, and the people who come to hear me are mediocre
artists in their own right. But we are passionate in our fallibility
and cling tightly to ideals that have inspired the truly mediocre
for centuries. Mediocre sculptors surreptitiously inspect my
wife from across the room. Mediocre photographers cup her
jaw in their hands and promise impossible miracles. Mediocre
actresses say, If only I had a body like yours.

I have tried to write her love poems but inevitably fail.
Words cannot hold her like fingers. She struggles too much.
As to poetry—well, poetry is too imperfect a form for either
of our imperfections.

She has a Psychic Friend—her one vice, she claims—and runs up our VISA bill with 900-number calls. My friend says I have a problem with intimacy, she declares after hanging up—can you believe it, me, intimacy? Intimacy isn't necessarily sex, I reply, it's more like love. If you're suggesting I have a problem with love, she replies, I want to know what accusations like that say about you. Me, I stammer, I don't have a problem with love—with love or anything else. Well, says my wife as she slides another tape into the VCR, neither do I.

There once was a man from Nantucket. Would you call that a poem?

But love, she admits, must be more than an exchange of fluids. I know the difference between business and pleasure.

Once I told her that I could not understand how the men watching her fantasized about her so. It's kind of pathetic, I said, don't you think? To which she replied, I'm not the woman you see. The woman you see is something you've made up, the same way I make myself up when I put on mascara, or a costume, or take any of them off. That's the way reality is. You of all people should know that. I'm no more than a part I have to play, a few words or less, and reality can go to hell.

Sometimes when we screw, the slats of the bed come loose and the whole frame collapses onto the floor. But by then we are too anxious to stop. We bounce around the mattress like stones loosened from a hillside. She bites my shoulder. The wet sheet flails my skin and sticks to her long, blond hair. I love you, I scream. Deeper, deeper, my wife replies.

She has a vaguely heart-shaped mole on the back of her neck where her hairline ends. Right at my brain stem, she likes to say. It's a sign, you see—I had no control over what I chose to do with my life. It was preordained.

Last night on TV, there was the story of a Norfolk man who caught his wife in bed with her lover, so he killed them both, cut them into a hundred pieces and piled their remains on a quilt, which the women of his wife's family had made as a wedding gift. When questioned, he told police that he only wanted to make her happy, and now the three of them—wife, lover and quilt—could be together forever. That's a guy who has a problem with love, one cop remarked to the camera.

Now and then I ask, Am I good in bed? To be honest, she says, I've never really thought about it.

And then there's Crazy Ethel, the homeless woman who makes her home on the sidewalk opposite our building. She says that she was put under a spell by a man whose love she refused, and it made her teeth fall out. She keeps her teeth in a *Ziploc* bag in her shopping cart and will show them to passersby for a quarter. For a dollar, she'll pull out a clump of her own gray hair and promise to bless you over it when the moon is full. She says that God will punish the wicked. I give her a quarter. She eyes me sternly and says, You know who you are. I give her a dollar for good measure. Not that I think I am wicked. But sometimes I wonder if I can be condemned for someone else's sins, if my wife's sins are my own, passed to me through the sweat and saliva of our love. Of course, none of this should matter since God is all-merciful. The young men in starched white collars who stand on the street corner with salvation on their tongues know this. God is love, they declare. But is He a lover? The distinction is essential, inescapable. Or is it? Is God a businessman? What kind of clothes does He wear?

Shall I compare thee to a summer's day? What does this guy know about love? There is more love in a chipped press-on fingernail scratched down your back than in any stanza this guy could utter.

She has a small scar on her left foot where the doctors cut away an extra toe after her birth. Sometimes I can still feel it, she says, or maybe I just think I can. It's not like I remember it. Still it would have made me special, and now it's gone. So I miss that toe. Sometimes I think that's what love is, an extra toe. Sometimes I think it wasn't a toe at all, but my heart, and it's out there in a jar of formaldehyde on some doctor's mantle, waiting for me.

Mediocre poets are a curse, a blinding light switched on only halfway. Lazy mediocre poets are even worse. I should do something definite. Leap from the window beside my desk. Make love to my wife with the camcorder running. Get baptized. Give Crazy Ethel so much money that she plucks herself bald and blesses me for it until the day she dies. Punch Robert T. in the nose. Punch another mediocre poet in the nose. If I had courage to do any of these things, I might figure out what love is, beyond broken mattresses, beyond poetry, beyond bright young men on street corners who drool cleansing fire, beyond a woman whose breasts grow larger as her heart ticks away, beyond my wife, beyond corrective bifocal lenses. Man, woman, men, women. Beyond seeing, almost beyond sense. Together, beyond.

But when she asks if I have a problem with what she does, I simply wonder whether or not my problems make a difference to her. Only sometimes, she admits, turning away, only sometimes.

And I am not a hero. Several blocks over, the marquee of the adult video arcade advertises a movie starring my wife. In one of the small booths, I slide my quarter into the slot, and the screen buzzes to life. The volume on the machine is broken, so I imagine that my wife speaks poetry as she does what she does, but not one of my poems. I want to see her on the couch with her pad and pen. The light here burns my eyes. From the booth adjoining mine comes a low moan and the sound of a shoe knocking against the wood in steady rhythm. My wife turns and gyrates, ebbs and flows. She is a picture on the screen, a collection of color, a few electric needles, no more. As the camera closes in on her face, her mouth hangs open in expectant silence. I can count her teeth, and my shoulder tingles for the anticipated bite. The man in the next booth screams, I LOVE YOU, and I reach out to touch the screen. Love, I think before my quarter runs out, what do you know about love?

The Man in the Back Row Has A Question III

For this feature we have selected answers to a questionnaire sent out to a number of distinguished editors. We are grateful for their cooperation.

Morgan Entrekin, Publisher, Grove/Atlantic
Gary Fisketjon, Senior Editor, Alfred A. Knopf
Jonathan Galassi, Editor-in-Chief, Farrar, Straus & Giroux
Reginald Gibbons, Editor, *TriQuarterly*
John A. Glusman, Executive Editor, Farrar, Straus & Giroux
Daniel Pinchbeck, Editor, *Open City*
Lois Rosenthal, Editor, *Story*
Richard Seaver, Editor-in-Chief, Arcade Publishing
Max Steele, Editorial Board Member, *Story*
Karl Wenclas, Editor, *New Philistine* (a literary newsletter)

Is there a dominant trend in contemporary fiction?

Giving labels to groups of writers is at best a harmless parlor game and at worst a gross generalization of the work of very individual talents, but here goes: there are four general trends in fiction that I see. One, the "traditional" novelists, these are the masterful writers working at the top of their form writing "conventional" novels with beautiful prose and complexly rendered characters in imaginatively crafted narratives. Among my favorites: E. Annie Proulx, Richard Ford, Jane Smiley, Jim Harrison, Cormac McCarthy, Robert Stone. Two, multicultural fiction—self-explanatory, voices from the edges of mainstream white European culture—Toni Morrison, Salman Rushdie, Francisco Goldman, Ben Okri, Junot Díaz. Three, transgressive or edge fiction—writers that shock with portrayals of extreme behavior, usually sex—Bret Easton Ellis, Will Self, A.M. Homes, William Vollmann (the short books), Darcey Steinke, Dennis Cooper. Four, hyper-intellectual or "smart" fiction, descended from the high postmodernists Robert Coover, Thomas Pynchon, John Barth. Current practitioners: David Foster Wallace, Lawrence Norfolk, William Vollmann (the long books). I am sure that some of the writers I publish would be offended at being thrown into such simplistic categories (for instance, Will Self is as much a descendant of Nabokov as of William Burroughs), but for parlor game's sake, there it is.

Oh, I guess there is a fifth category—creative writing grad school fiction, people who write beautiful sentences and paragraphs, but have nothing to say. One of my friends used to call this the "divorce and cancer in Connecticut" school of fiction.

—Morgan Entrekin

Ethnicity, perhaps, sometimes as a matter of happenstance, occasionally in the manner of outsider art. In general, of course, trends exist only at the bottom of the barrel.

—Gary Fisketjon

It seems to me there are several competing trends—solipsist, totalist, tribalist—which reflect other forces in society. Sometimes more than one of these tendencies is active in a writer's work.

—Jonathan Galassi

Whatever the trends may be in contemporary fiction, some of them are working on us — as writers and readers — without our full awareness, much less our consent. These unwanted trends would have to do with what is happening to print culture, not only because of electronic text itself but also because of what electronic text itself technologically derives from and cannot counter — the mass media's speed, oversimplification, cacophony, falseness to reality and jump-cutting of thought. The unceasing saturation of our minds by the images and techniques of mass media have unavoidably conditioned our habits of thought and feeling. Nothing can reverse this trend. In fiction, one sees this in the artistic decisions that are made by writers whose sense of pace, dialogue and scene are closer to that of TV and movies than of fiction at its most interior, and whose way with language is impatient (sometimes even when quite clear) rather than exploratory.

Another of these imposed trends in contemporary fiction would have to do with the changes in bookselling (and thus of the availability of books) that have already been wrought by the hand-in-hand dance of commercial publishing and chain stores, a dance that looks like life here and there but has a lot of death in it. It threatens small independent publishers with death, as they are tremendously disadvantaged by the financial structures, procedures and conditions that favor the huge publishing and bookselling corporations and which the corporations have imposed on everyone. It threatens independent bookstores with death for the same reasons. And has killed and is killing most of them. Thus certain kinds of writing, although not the writers, live under mortal threat — the writing usually called *serious* that must go under the yoke of marketing, along with Cocoa Puffs, Old Spice, *People* magazine and Diet Coke. For a few wonderful books, this is wonderful (and for many awful books, or book products). For the rest of all our good books, new and old, it is not wonderful. If it's an idea-in-an-image that's being sold when Diet Coke is sold — the idea of sugar, disguised by the idea of being beautiful by being slender — then what is the idea or image, our culture asks me to ask myself, that I am selling with my novel? Does it matter if I protest that this is the wrong question? Not to the wholesale book buyer, the marketing director of the bookstore chain or the publisher, the book-review editor (!) of *USA Today* or *Vogue*, the radio talk-show host.

So these trends in contemporary fiction are not pushed ahead by artistic inquiry and discovery, by the writer's desire to find a way to describe what our lives are like and to explore what our language is doing and can do; instead, they are marketing and merchandising trends driven by the pressures for shareholder profit on one side, and the consumer appetite for novelty on the other. But in the bookstores ideas and styles, narratives and structures of feeling now have a shelf life like that of perishables in the supermarket, or new products in a trial promotion. On the other hand, thanks to the chance to make money by *marketing* fiction to new audiences outside the white middle-class mainstream, commercial publishers provide a few more opportunities to writers who represent (in both senses) what has not before been seen in literature — the realities of experience, culture and language different from that middle-class mainstream.

The ferment of the mass media even welcomes the small disturbances of difference, truth-telling, opposition, counter-examples. These create otherwise unrealized opportunities to invent yet more new salable products (including attitudes and feelings) and to market with new images and catchphrases. And while mass marketing does a few good things, carrying into bastions of prejudice and received opinion the iconoclastic levity of certain forbidden images ("Cross the Border with Taco Bell"), it rapidly consolidates all its immensely bad accomplishments and drives serious writing out to the far margin of its false, cheerful, acquisitive consciousness. If I asked myself, as writer and editor, which trends in fiction are really and truly trends *in fiction*, how can I know that my answer is not false, if I think that such trends can exist apart from the opinions, beliefs and habits that we share within the economic structure of our way of life? If trends of resistance can be so happily ingested by that which they resist, I need to keep in mind — as a writer and reader — that even if the effect or presence of serious writing became nil, it would still be important for it to exist.

And it doesn't have to become nil. The outskirts of mass marketing, although they feed the rapacious center, willy-nilly, are where all the interesting things happen, and at least they are happening. The twentieth century has been the century of fiction. And the second half of the century has seen an extraordinarily widespread and brilliant flowering. While one might not know it from looking at either mass-market fiction or the continuous present-day American flood of naturalistic, claustrophobic first-person serious American novels of private experience, whether low-life or suburban, we have been living for fifty years in the age of Patrick White, Ralph Ellison, Nadine Gordimer, García Márquez, Clarice Lispector, Frank O'Connor, Eudora Welty, Italo Calvino, Danilo Kiš, J.M. Coetzee, Alice Munro, Juan Rulfo, Jorge Luis Borges, Grace Paley, Milan Kundera, Günter Grass, Marguerite Duras, Wilson Harris, Hélène Cixous, many more of their stature, and hundreds of younger writers also of extraordinary inventiveness, seriousness and worth. If only more contemporary American writers took their inspiration from writers like these instead of from superficial models.
— Reginald Gibbons

Yes, it's not selling as well as it used to.
— John A. Glusman

The dominant trend in contemporary fiction is probably a product of the writing programs. The writing programs help to codify the techniques of fiction writing. Yet they don't encourage fiction writers to see their work as belonging to larger continuums of history and philosophy. Young writers tend to exit the academy with a refined craft but a lack of original content and vision. Perhaps because of the increased specialization encouraged by the M.F.A. programs, the scope and subject of much fiction seems to be growing smaller.
— Daniel Pinchbeck

I see more stories these days that deal with brutality and dysfunction. The shock quotient seems to be de rigueur in many stories. Sometimes I find it disheartening.

—Lois Rosenthal

One seems to be: taking classic (or commercial) genres—detective, romance, even historical fiction—and infusing them with literary quality.

—Richard Seaver

A dominant trend in anything at the particular moment it is dominant is already dead, to be replaced in twenty years—or two—by something already present, something stronger, something better. A dominant trend is like light we see now in the sky of a star burned-out a generation ago.

—Karl Wenclas

What are the hallmarks of a good story? How do you know when it's good?

I work more with novels than short stories but I would say the criteria for "how I know it's good" hold true for both forms. I look for a distinctive voice, an original vision and sharp, startling prose.

—Morgan Entrekin

Engaging language and characters. When I read it.

—Gary Fisketjon

A good story represents the successful completion of an arc, which can be achieved in numberless ways. Stories often have too much or too little in them. The elegant attainment of a limited objective produces a powerful effect that is deeply striking and satisfying.

—Jonathan Galassi

I don't know how to characterize a good story in general. Aren't the most memorable stories not like anything one has seen before? And, in turn, they affect everything one reads afterward. How could one have predicted them even on the basis of the best stories one has read so far? William Goyen said, "Style is the transformation of material." It's that transformation that most interests me as a reader (and thus as an editor), especially if the material is already familiar. Of course, absent this drive to create something genuinely new, then sometimes honesty and truth-telling may do, whether the writing is elegant, precise, subtle, clear or, conversely, raw and intuitive, a rush or immersion—whether the artistic model is Isak Dinesen or Nelson Algren. . . . But, honesty and truth-telling not only with regard to the material but also with regard to language—the only other aspect in common that might be seen in most admirable fiction is a certain attitude toward language itself: a spirit of exploration, an awareness of the slipperiness and instability of language used unthinkingly, and the redoubled slipperiness and instability of language used thinkingly.

—Reginald Gibbons

A distinct voice, economy of language, clarity of thought, emotional resonance.

—John A. Glusman

The hallmark of a good story is that you have to read it to the end. You know it is good if you then want to read it again. As Cyril Connolly wrote, "Literature is the art of writing something that they will read twice; journalism what will be grasped at once, and they require separate techniques."

—Daniel Pinchbeck

I know a story is great when I can't forget it, when it changes my mind, introduces me to new people, transports me to another world. I look for stunning phrases that make my heart leap, and I don't mean look-at-me-I'm-tap-dancing-on-the-page kind of writing.

—Lois Rosenthal

Language, style: talent and craftsmanship. Old cliché about "not being able to put something down" is still the best test. Another test: does it envelop, make you forget or become oblivious of the outside world. Really good stories are rare; the best stories have pace: they immerse the reader right from the start and keep him immersed all the way through.
—Richard Seaver

A good story becomes an instant memory. One is satisfied. A need has been met. Something unknown before has been known and completed. You know it's good when a sincerely felt emotion or action has been given a surprising and totally appropriate form.
—Max Steele

A good story has conflict and narrative drive. It portrays sharp contrasts of good and evil, and harsh depictions of depression, resolution, energy and life. It contains great speeches voiced by dynamic characters eager to love, fight, challenge and die; to change the world. A good story is colorful and relevant; passionate, polemical and melodramatic. No one today writes such stories.
—Karl Wenclas

To what extent can editing improve a story?

To the same extent that it can improve a novel; that is, not much. A careful reading can point out certain infelicities of style or dialogue, lapses in characterization of story-telling tactics, or other instances where the writer momentarily loses sight of otherwise high and compelling standards.
—Gary Fisketjon

Editing can call attention to diversionary material, or to tonal problems. And many stories have difficulty ending, which an editor can make suggestions about. But I don't believe in heavy tailoring.
—Jonathan Galassi

There is probably no fiction that could not be altered, yet again, if only in small ways, to improve some effect, to catch hold more tightly of an idea or a theme, to push a little farther what the language can do. To that extent, there's almost nothing that couldn't be improved by editing. But there are few editors whose understanding, energy and time can match the demands of that editing, and there are plenty of writers who for whatever reason do not welcome such suggestions. (For good reasons as well as bad.) The question for me as an editor has been not "How often do you come across writers who don't need editing?" but how often I find the time, and muster the tact, to embark on the process of working in detail with a writer. It can be fascinating, triumphant and mutually beneficial work. But do I adequately understand what the writing is all about? What the writer is after? I want and don't want to reshape a story into the kind of thing that I, for my own reasons, most admire and most want to publish. Anyway, strong work often already contains within itself the answers to the editing questions that it raises—if a writer or editor can see them.

—Reginald Gibbons

Vastly.

—John A. Glusman

Editing can streamline a piece and boil it down to its essence. The greatest example of this I can think of is Pound's reworking of Eliot's *The Waste Land*. Through massive cuts a form miraculously emerged.

—Daniel Pinchbeck

Editors can help writers look at a story from a different point of view, point out strengths and weaknesses writers may not see because they are so close to the work. Ultimately writers must not make changes that do not seem true to them. But editorial polishing can make a story the best it can be.

—Lois Rosenthal

Little if we're talking about short stories exclusively—some valuable tightening is probably an editor's only significant contribution. In novels, editing (especially pruning) can do much more to make a story read better.
—Richard Seaver

Tactful editing, in which an editor or teacher sees what the writer is attempting, can improve almost any story.
—Max Steele

Stories should not be edited.
—Karl Wenclas

How often do you come across writers who don't need editing?

Not often enough.
—Morgan Entrekin

Never.
—Gary Fisketjon

The more experienced a writer is, the less he or she is going to require in the way of editorial intervention. At the same time, I think it's true that eminent writers don't always get real attention paid to their texts; generally, they appreciate it.
—Jonathan Galassi

Rarely—which is a good thing, because otherwise I'd be out of work.
—John A. Glusman

We are slowly taking a more proactive stance toward editing as the magazine continues. At first, we left a lot of stories completely alone because part of what we wanted was an impression of idiosyncratic voices bouncing off of each other, even in some cases down to odd spelling or syntactical choices. We wanted a feeling of lunacy hiding within cogency, and vice versa. In some cases, however, it is just so clear that a few changes or cuts will make a story come alive, and then we work on it.

—Daniel Pinchbeck

Seldom.

—Lois Rosenthal

In fiction, fairly frequently, though apparent structural flaws are usually fatal. In nonfiction, *lots* of editing.

—Richard Seaver

I've never seen a manuscript that could not be improved by editing.

—Max Steele

Who is your greatest literary discovery, and who got away?

Among my "discoveries," (although usually I didn't discover them, someone—an agent, a magazine editor, another writer—sent them my way) Bret Easton Ellis, Francisco Goldman, Will Self, Sherman Alexie, Dagoberto Gilb, Rian Malan. Among those that got away—fifteen years ago I had an opportunity to publish Paul Auster and stupidly didn't.

—Morgan Entrekin

Lord only knows—though *discovery* seems rather too grand a word to describe what essentially is the act of recognizing goodness or excellence, and that, after all, isn't terribly difficult.

—Gary Fisketjon

You can't ask an editor that question!

—Jonathan Galassi

1) Rosario Ferré, Dale Peck, Denise Chávez, Lois-Ann Yamanaka, Pablo Medina, Kathleen Cambor, Michael Grant Jaffe and E. Annie Proulx, whose first book, *Heartsongs*, I published, though Tom Jenks deserves the credit for having discovered her.
2) E. Annie Proulx.
—John A. Glusman

We have "discovered" writers only in the same dishonest sense that Columbus "discovered" America. Truly, writers discover themselves. My favorite discoveries so far have actually been uncoveries—*Open City* has published otherwise lost works by Richard Yates, Cyril Connolly and Terry Southern.
—Daniel Pinchbeck

Samuel Beckett.
—Richard Seaver

I can not claim to have taught them but the following have been in my seminars: Russell Banks, Lawrence Naumoff, Alane Mason, Will Blythe, Jill McCorkle, Tim Mizelle, Melanie Sumner, Randall Keenan, and as many more equally as good. Who got away? Max Steele. A careful writer who became a reader. A teacher and editor. An old man.
—Max Steele

I have announced the future greatness of underground writers Stephen Durst, Ammi Keller and Jen Gogglebox.
—Karl Wenclas

Can you recognize the influence of a workshop?

No.
—Morgan Entrekin

Not for no reason is it a truism that writers with workshop experience tend to produce cleaner, more competent work.

But the implied corollary—that this work necessarily lacks heart and soul, somehow—gives the noble savage too much credit and amounts to another form of Chicken Little-ism.

—Gary Fisketjon

Some writing "teachers" tend to have a very strong magnetic effect on students; but real writers will eventually find a way to slough this off. Stories written under the influence—which are probably most stories—are easily recognizable, and usually don't need to be published.

—Jonathan Galassi

A workshop story is one which by the conventionality of its artistic choices—narrative formulas and devices, subject matter, point of view, verb tenses—implies that the writer preferred to study with someone like me, and sit around in a group, rather than study at great sources, living or dead. Why work to earn the approval of a group of ordinary writers when you can study in the greatest detail with the writers I have mentioned above? True, it is harder and lonelier to do that kind of studying—harder to go inside the way another writer writes and make some of it your own, lonelier and even frightening to embark on that conversation with an absent presence who will answer only by example. But it can also be exhilarating as well as instructive. And that's what jazz musicians do, exuberantly, and, however they feel when they are inside it, (some) painters, and choreographers, and composers.

—Reginald Gibbons

Sometimes.

—John A. Glusman

Great writers shine no matter where they come from. I can't say I see a "workshop influence" on writers.

—Lois Rosenthal

I see well-told, competent stories that can only be called workshop stories. They did not demand to be told. It's as if the writer went out of his way to write a story about characters he does not like or hate in situations that are either mundane or borderline unbelievable. On the happy side, many students are looking for models to Ionesco, Ghandolfi, Beckett, Borges, Cortázar and Calvino and are getting away from the plain styles of Hemingway and Raymond Carver. It frees them to write magic realism which indeed is sometimes magic.

—Max Steele

Workshops and their constipated, homogenized products are a putrid disease inflicted upon contemporary readers raised on the violent noise of rock n' roll and the violence and inequities of life who are looking in vain for fiction that can arouse their emotions and intelligence and sustain their interest.

—Karl Wenclas

Do you have a bête noir among current varieties of fiction?

Creative writing, grad school fiction.

—Morgan Entrekin

Foot-stamping, would-be reinventions of "the novel," which already has seen it all, been there, done that, and can be anything it likes anyway.

—Gary Fisketjon

Solipsism, totalism, tribalism—any school or program that inspires inauthentic gestures in writers.

—Jonathan Galassi

Anything that's been done more than once.

—John A. Glusman

Perhaps because *Open City* seems vaguely downtownish and has published some experimental fiction, we receive a lot of submissions from people writing about nightlife experiences in New York involving massive amounts of drugs, sex, frequent vomiting and other bodily expulsions. For a while, many of these pieces seemed to bear a return address somewhere along Ludlow Street, so I dubbed them the Ludlow Street School. Someday, we hope to publish them all on a web site, *Open Sewer*.

—Daniel Pinchbeck

Market-driven fiction: trying to calculate the market and then writing to capture it, i.e. *Bridges of Madison County*, *The Horse Whisperer* or *A Year in Provence*.

—Richard Seaver

Southern stories written in the first person, where the folksy narrative voice tends to take the place of characterization, plot and intelligence. Henry James says tell the story from the point of view of the person who comprehends the most. The new school of southern caricature has a dictum that says tell it endlessly from the point of view of the person who talks the most. And stories that begin with the narrator waking up. Nothing is going to happen for the next five pages at which point the narrator may be awake enough to find his story.

—Max Steele

Fictions that use pretentious French expressions as an indication of breeding and class.

—Karl Wenclas

Is the use of word processors an influence on contemporary writing?

Yes, it makes writers sloppier, and makes books less coherent as a whole, generally because they are written in parts.

—Morgan Entrekin

Probably so. Books seem to be getting longer all the time — which is ironic, given the short attention spans of so many readers.

—Jonathan Galassi

Yes, on the one hand, they make it much easier for editors to read manuscripts. On the other hand, they make it that much easier for writers to overwrite.

—John A. Glusman

It is possible that word processors encourage a lot of bad literary habits. On the other hand, they don't make writing any easier. I fear the next wave of speech-to-text technology that is going to allow anyone to speak their memoir or novel into a computer, leading to some kind of nefarious deluge of unconstructed text.

—Daniel Pinchbeck

Well, you would think they would cause worse logorrhea than a southern accent, but good writers seem to be aware of that danger. In fact there are more good short-shorts and instant and sudden fictions being written now than ever. Writers who have word processors usually have E-mail too and that strange terse E-mail style is counteractive to processor prose.

—Max Steele

Can you think of a writer whose influence on young writers is destructive?

No.

—Morgan Entrekin

Any writer whose influence is direct and exclusive, as opposed to osmotic and inclusive.

—Gary Fisketjon

I can think of several, but I don't think you can blame the writers—the fault lies with their imitators.

—Jonathan Galassi

Newt Gingrich.

—John A. Glusman

I don't think any particular writer's influence can be so destructive. The most destructive influence on style may be "Joe Journalism," the flat, affectless, staccato approach to prose many writers pick up from working on newspapers and magazines, or writing ad copy or press releases.

—Daniel Pinchbeck

Grisham or anyone who gets a million-dollar advance and plants bad seeds (go commercial!) in younger writers' heads. Perhaps any dominant writer of any period who fosters imitation—in recent years, John Irving and Raymond Carver, writers whose skill makes the success of their prose look easy.

—Richard Seaver

For fifty years now I have loved everything about Eudora Welty but most of all her early short stories. It grieves me to say that "Why I Live at the P.O." has ruined more young writers than any story and has helped turn southern writing into stand-up comedy.

—Max Steele

John Updike. Thomas Pynchon. Henry James. Chekhov.

—Karl Wenclas

What is the state of contemporary fiction?

Very healthy.

—Morgan Entrekin

Still ticking.

—Gary Fisketjon

There's tremendous vitality in the field, an awful lot being done and much of it noteworthy, but have we really seen the emergence of the voices who are going to dominate and define the generation of writers in their thirties and forties? I think this has to do with the rather parlous status of writing in contemporary culture. It's not that it doesn't matter, but it has more competition; writers can't take being paid attention for granted anymore. The arena is too noisy. In the end, though, it may be the quiet work that will matter the most.
—Jonathan Galassi

As the poet Muriel Rukeyser wrote, "The universe is made of stories, not of atoms." How will we ever represent and explore fully what it is like to feel and think, to live in language, to shape a story, in our bizarre, heartrending, contradictory time of the juggernaut dollar and the peace activist, TV and the chanted wedding-feast praise-poem, massive corporations and the neighborhood no, starving refugee camps and cornucopian supermarkets, the drug trade and alternative medicine? We need to hear from every sort of writer in every corner of this infinitely cornered planet. Even if our gloomier thoughts are true about the future of all the mechanics of publishing and disseminating writing, of educating children to read, and of preserving the institutions—like literary magazines and public libraries—that most protect fiction (and poetry), it is still important that serious writing exist and continue to keep coming into existence. The loss of fiction and poetry, as resources available to anyone who wants them—and, what is worse, the loss of wanting them—would be devastating. Fiction and poetry are irreplaceable ways of thinking our way into and through our own existence. There are no adequate substitutes. Certainly not reading mass-media newspapers and magazines, much less passively watching films and TV. And in fact, no matter what good purposes that fiction and poetry have served in the past (and even evil purposes, when they are used to manipulate feeling), in our time, as never before, serious writing must actively contend against the pervasive mass-media, formulaic, product-oriented pressures on thinking and feeling that are inherently destructive and false. I don't concede to either sardonic or cheerful postmodernists that the shimmering of images is modern identity. I am certain that in most of the world, from Chicago neighborhoods to those refugee camps, identity is still a complex contest between interiority and encounter, between spirit and matter, out of which comes not an end but a deepening of the process of living. If in the next decades those who still live in premarketing cultures are driven by global consumerism straight into a life with mass media, without recapitulating the transition from oral culture to a mature print culture that has produced all of what we call literature, then the fate of fiction and poetry seems bleak, the fate of interiority itself seems in danger, and the material hardship and destitution that rule the planet as a whole, unlike the prosperous stretches of our republic, will also become the spiritual impoverishment of all of us.

—Reginald Gibbons

My response to your first question notwithstanding, I think it's healthier than ever. I can't recall a time when the climate was more receptive to hearing a diversity of new voices—Chicana/o, Asian-American, Native American, Cuban-American, Puerto Rican, Haitian, Dominican, to name just a few.

Paradoxically—and unfortunately—there are fewer and fewer mainstream venues, among book and magazine publishers, for enabling those voices to be heard by the largest possible audience.

—John A. Glusman

While contemporary popular fiction rages on the best-seller list, contemporary literary fiction becomes increasingly marginalized with each decade. Younger writers lack the authority from which to step forward and combatively embrace and criticize the culture, as Norman Mailer or Allen Ginsberg did in decades past. Fiction seems to be going the way of poetry, created for an increasingly specialized audience and ignored outside of that framework. I hope this situation can be reversed.

—Daniel Pinchbeck

That's a solemn question. I think fiction today, as it has always been, is an essential part of life. I hope it continues to change, surprise, anger and enthrall.

—Lois Rosenthal

For serious, young fiction: commercially disastrous, almost inviable. Yet the urge to write seems untouched; compare the quality of American fiction today with a) other periods and b) other cultures, and in both quantity and quality, now is impressive.

—Richard Seaver

Does one dare even to try to answer such a question? All I can say is that I have read short stories professionally now for more than forty-five years and I think they are more exciting, and daring, than anytime in this century. Young writers no longer listen to the old academic saying: Write what you know about. Today, with the World Wide Web, a person knows everything or nothing. Maybe we should teach: Write about what you love.

—Max Steele

You Can Have It

Chris Adrian

In fact there were two boys born that night. Jesus was first, long awaited, expected. His twin brother was a surprise. The angels ignored him. His mother was disconcerted by this squalling, irascible, utterly normal newborn who cried out for her breast while his brother lay, the sum of all peace, in the makeshift crib. There was no aureole of light about the second child's face; no star shining down specifically on his soft pink head. The animals gave him a first look, but not a second. It was his brother to whom they bowed down, the sheep and the lambs and the donkeys and the cows.

In fact, no one at all paid him much attention that night, even his mother nursed him only distractedly, gazing down on the shining face of her eldest. It is understandable — remember who his brother was! — that he should get the lesser, far lesser, package of attention. It's fine that the wise men, when they came, had no frankincense, gold or myrrh, had not even some cheap wooden toy for this child. Fine too that the angels, when they finally acknowledged his birth, did so with gossipy whispers, saying, "Where'd *he* come from?" Because his father, though distracted at first by the miraculous, heavenly presence of his foster child, noticed the younger son before anyone else but Mary, and said to her, "Look darling, this one has *my* eyes."

It was true. The younger's eyes were brown, not blue like Jesus's, like Mary's and like God's. They were dark brown like the earth in the manger, and straw brown like the hay in the manger, striated like the grain in wood. They were the only miraculous thing about him.

Joseph said, "This one is *my* son, my very own." And he picked up his son and spun with him around the room, while his older son smiled at them with his heavenly mouth and his wise blue eyes, while his wife laughed for the joy of her husband, and while the angels whispered, louder, more fiercely, like bitter, winged old women. While the world greeted its savior this father danced with this other, lesser son. Did you know this? Had you already heard?

You know now. And I can tell you, it is within the limits of my authority to reveal this because I was that boy. I am that mundane twin.

•

Sadie, Peter's wife, is leaving, so this is our last meal together, all thirteen of us, me and the eleven others who were once the wives of my brother's disciples. Mai-Lin has made us a big feast, the sort of thing they eat in her homeland, far from here, up and to the east of our house by the sea. We live in the house my brother and I built with our father.

I've kept building, since Papa went away, and Jesus went away, adding room after room. Now there are thirteen — that's all we need — but I'm still building. We've got a big piece of land, lots of room to grow, and I'm interested in continued expansion, in continued experimentation with form and style. When I'm not busy in the clinic — and often I'm not, the wives can do everything but the actual laying-on-of-hands — then I'm out building. My favorite part of the house has always been whichever portion was not finished. My favorite part now is the fourteenth bedroom, which I only started a few weeks ago. Through the bones of the room one gets a terrific view of the sea. I sit there often, watching, taking a break from hammering or sawing or whatever, and sometimes I think I see my brother, out on the waves, walking towards me, walking home. So I run down to the beach to get a closer look, but always it's just a boat.

•

My brother died many years ago. I say died, but of course he didn't really die—some have seen him since. However, I haven't seen him since that last day, when my mother and the other women took him down and washed him and put him away. I have not seen him, have not heard him, though I had a dream once that we were flying together at night over a vast sea, both of us nailed to enormous, fragrant cedar crosses. Fire trailed from the ends of both our crosses and we wrote LOVE, LOVE, LOVE, with flaming letters in the sky, again and again till dawn came and I crashed into the water.

But that was just a dream. Those who have seen him, the ones I know, the ones who have told me all about how he walked with them on some lonely road, or how they saw him by the shore, or wherever, they all saw him while they were waking. His disciples say they see him right and left—he is with them. I don't talk to them much. I wonder if they're exaggerating. Probably they are. Disciples are not entirely to be trusted. They tend, in my opinion, towards cowardice and fair-weather faithfulness. Ask their wives about that.

Today was Friday—not my favorite day. It used to be that I didn't much notice time, that I was only a little aware of its passing. But since my brother died I am always dreading the moment of his death. Three o'clocks are not so bad as Fridays, and Fridays in general not so bad as that particular Friday, the anniversarial Friday. I dread these repetitions, these anniversaries, because they hurt. And not just how you think. They don't just hurt my heart, I get migraines, too. I know, it's all in my head, but still. It feels like marbles in there, rolling around on a raw, painful surface. And more than that, and worse, is just that Friday feeling, which isn't pain but rather this: it's like there's a spider on my head, right on top with her legs wrapped around my ears and temples, sitting tightly, and she's spinning silk into my brain, so I can't think, can't feel, can't quite do anything.

Usually I stay in my room on Fridays, or go to the unfinished room, though not to work. I can't work on Fridays. The clinic is closed, except for emergencies, so I can just sleep, or read, anything to hurry the time by. At midnight everything is better.

I was sitting in my room, on my bed, trying not to think about the spider, trying not to think about my brother, and I was thinking about a nap when Sadie burst in after a hurried knock and said, "Josh! You must come quickly. We've got a Goddamned bloody mess downstairs!"

•

Axes, spikes, hoes and shovels — I have seen all manner of things buried in people's heads. Once a man came in with a narrow bit of apple bough driven straight through one temple and out the other. Lightning had struck in his orchard and splintered his tree in a hundred hurling spears. He claimed to feel no pain, but said he had lost his sense of smell. I fixed him up and sent him back into the dangerous world. He came back two weeks later, kicked in the thigh by his horse. A great moon-shaped hole in his flesh gave blood like a spring. Horses are perilous, I told him. They could kick you anywhere, in the head, in the shin, in the elbow. They'll split your bones like balsa, crack your skull like an eggshell. He came back again three months later, both wrists broken in a fall from his roof. I told him he was growing careless under my care.

Sadie's lady was not bleeding so terribly, all things considered. The ax was stuck in the top and back of her head, as if she had bent at the waist to receive it. The handle thrust forward like a horn. She looked up at me when I pulled the curtain aside. Blood ran down her face and shoulders. I looked into her lovely blue eyes — not so blue as my brother's, but close, not quite so pretty, but quite pretty — and smiled gently. Conscious and frightened, she grabbed my hand.

"Rabbi," she said. "Help me!"

"I'm not a rabbi," I said. "You mustn't call me that." I unwound her fingers from my hand. "But I'll help you. You're going to be all right now. Just relax." The wives were bustling around the room. Sadie rushed up with a basin, and I washed my hands.

"Her husband did this," Sadie said.

"Doesn't that figure!" said Anne, coming up to me with the crown. I took it from its box, tugging a little to get the thorns free from where they caught in the velvet. I set it on my head, and turned back to the woman, still smiling. Julia was cleaning around the ax, and Anne and Sadie were each holding one of the woman's hands, stroking them. When the woman saw me, smiling at her from under the thorns, she cried out again, "Rabbi!" and "Save me!" I didn't correct her this time. It's true that I look just like my brother, except for the eyes, and the hair, which is much shorter than he ever kept his.

Most people assume the crown must be very painful to wear, but it's quite comfortable. I have calluses now that thwart the thorns. After I put it on there's a rush, familiar now, an electric feeling that runs down my head, through my spine, out my arms to my fingers. When my hands were tingling at the right pitch, I nodded at Julia and she wrapped her big hard hands around the ax handle and pulled it, with one heave of her powerful, fat forearms, out of the woman's head. This freed the blood, but I was ready.

While the woman passed out and fell back into Sadie's arms, I raised my hands to catch the blood that was rushing at my face. My hands burned now, like they do, with purple fire, and I pushed. At my pressure the blood moved back into her head. I lay my hands on her hair, on either side of the wound, and looked inside at the wet workings of her brain, suspended now in my brother's purple fire. I saw the red and the blue, and the gray, the messy mix of color, and my will willed it right. It has always been that simple. I closed her up with a single finger. Sutures of fire drew her bone and scalp together, then faded, leaving not a scar and hardly any baldness at all.

Anne and Julia wheeled the lady away to recover in the atrium. I took the crown off and felt a loss — a small one, you'd think it would feel bigger. I put it back in the box and gave it to Sadie. "Thanks," I told her. The Friday feeling, dispelled momentarily by the excitement, was on its way back. "I'll be back in my room," I said, "if you need me." I expected her to smile and touch my hair, or put the box down and rub my shoulders, like she usually did, but she looked at me seriously and said, "Joshua, I've got to talk to you."

•

I met Sadie at a wedding at Cana. It was not the famous Wedding at Cana. This was long after that wedding. My friend Ben was getting married again. I knew him from school, hadn't seen him since his last wedding, when my brother was still alive.

"Josh," he said to me, before the ceremony. This was his third time. He wasn't even nervous. I remembered that Jesus had held his head for him, on the morning of his first marriage, while he vomited up his breakfast. "I'm so glad you could come," he said. And then, "Sorry about your brother."

I said yes, and looked at him solemnly. I used to say thank you when someone told me they were sorry about my brother, but later I realized that yes was a better response. Yes, I know. Yes, I too am sorry. Yes, I am sorrier than you. Yes, you cannot know.

Sadie was the weeping woman in the fifth row. She cried hard all through the ceremony. I found that remarkable because this third-time ceremony was winnowed of all the sentimental, tear-jerking elements that you see at first weddings, that I saw with my brother at Ben's first wedding. Jesus wept at Ben's first wedding, at the lovely, eternal-sounding vows; at the adorable ring boy and flower girl; at our friend whose joy rattled his voice and twisted his stomach. I cried, too.

But Sadie's weeping was rather out of hand. She wailed even

louder towards the end of the streamlined, efficient ceremony. She hid her face in her hands and pulled violently on her hair. Even as the guests filed out, she sat disconsolate in her chair and wept. So I went to her.

"Are you going to be all right?" I asked. She raised her face, a mess of makeup, smeared and dirty with bright and dull colors.

"He's gone," she said. She put her head down. "You see he's gone, and this reminds me."

"Gone . . ." I said. "Has someone died?" My heart rose in sympathy.

"No," she said. "Not dead. Gone. Gone away with that rabbi, that Jesus person. Left me for *him*." She raised her head again and took a long look at me. "With you!"

"Me?" I asked. She stood up and raised her fist to shake it at me, then dropped it.

"No," she said. "I thought you were that rabbi. You look like him."

"That rabbi," I said. "He's dead."

"Some say that," she said. "Others don't. It doesn't matter to me. He took my husband."

"I see," I said. I thought about that circle of men my brother had taken to him. I knew Peter. I knew them all. They never mentioned their wives to me.

"I'm sorry," she said. "It's the wedding. I hate weddings. Why did I come?" I didn't know what to say. I just looked at her.

"I wasn't even invited." she said. "I just came in." She started crying again.

"It'll be all right," I said, not knowing that it would. "Maybe if you had something to drink, you'd feel better." I held out my hand to her. "Come," I said, "we'll go to the reception."

"I can't," she said. "I'm not invited. They'll throw me out."

"No, no," I said. "You'll be with me." She glanced at my hand, still crying. She looked at it some more, studied it. Then she took it. We went to the reception and drank, and she danced with Ben. At one point even I danced with Ben. At one point he asked me to "do that wine trick," and he laughed—it seemed to me cruelly—and I might have done something, cried or spat or hurt him, but Sadie took my arm and put her hand on my shoulder. And I danced with Sadie and we drank more—they weren't really in danger of running out of wine—and later still, still dancing, she talked to me about my brother.

"I often saw him," she said. "I'd like to say I knew him, but I didn't, though Simon talked enough about him for me to feel like I did. It was always the Master this and the Master that, about everything. It grated—you understand? I'm sorry about him. Don't think I'm not."

"Yes," I said. I had my face in her hair, lost in long blackness.

"I talked to him once," she said.

"Really?" I said. I inhaled and brought my face back to look at her.

"Just once," she said. "Towards the end. Simon had been gone with him for weeks, and they came back and expected me to serve them dinner—mind you, dinner for thirteen—but I did it. Afterwards I got him alone. I touched him on the shoulder and he turned around, looked at me with those eyes. I said 'You're taking my husband, Rabbi. He doesn't love me anymore. He loves you, instead.' I told him, 'You're breaking my heart.'" She was silent for a little. We danced. I put my face back in her hair again.

"What did he say to that?" I asked.

"He said, 'Woman, I have not come into this world to break hearts.'"

I stopped dancing and looked at her. People were swirling all around us.

"But he did," I said.

•

"Simon's asked me to come to him in Rome," she said, after Anne and Julia took the lady away. "And I'm going to go."

"I see," I said. In fact I *had* seen. I'd seen this on its way—the letters from Peter, and all that. At first she wouldn't take them, but then she would, and then she'd take them in the next room, elsewhere, where she could have privacy with him, with him thousands of miles away.

"This doesn't mean what you think it means," she said. "It doesn't mean forever."

"No," I said, "of course not." I took her hand, but then she pulled away—gently.

"Got to go pack," she said.

•

I followed him around, too, for a while. I tired of it because he didn't have time to be my brother anymore. This rabbi was not the boy who raced me in the coracles Papa made for us; not the man who sat up with me and a bottle of wine and drank until his heavenly eyes shone like the sky, and my plainer ones shone like dark wet earth. He was different. Mama and Papa thought so too—a further difference from his usual state of otherness. You think—and you're right, people say this, people believe this, I lived with the evidence all my life—that he was God and his Son, all that. Right, but he was my brother, too. But suddenly he wasn't, on those hills, at the weddings, on various shores, in various cities. "Something larger is upon me," he'd say when I tried to get him to sneak out of our tent, away from his ever-present disciples, away from everything but the two of us. "You will forgive me, little brother?" he'd ask. I always said yes.

Eventually I went back home—back here—and stayed, helped Papa with his carpentry. We tracked Jesus through rumor, and sometimes he wrote us a letter. "Can anything good come of all this?" Papa asked. Our mother only cried. It would have been easier for her if another angel could have come to her with some kind of comforting word. You know who she was. Wouldn't you think they would have attended her, those angels? Certainly there are enough of them, too many, it seems. And what do they do? It seems my brother does all his father's work. You'd think they would have brushed her hair out, every evening, a full hundred strokes.

But they didn't. They weren't, like you might think, a common sight around the house. I only saw one once, in the last days. "Do not go to Jerusalem!" it told me. It *intoned* it at me, really, looking quite fierce in its robes of silver, in all its ornament of jade and malachite and turquoise. I went anyway, of course. I've never liked angels.

•

"Moo goo gai pan!" says Mai Lin, as she lays down a plate. She was Matthew's wife, until he left her. She's been happier since he left, I think. She came from so far away to marry him. Her father arranged it all, taking much of Matthew's money and sending his daughter in return. So she didn't see him till the day of the ceremony. It must have been hard for her. Nobody liked Matthew because he was a tax collector, and no one liked her, by association. Did she ever love him? I don't know. I've never asked her.

"Braised duck in oyster sauce!" she cries, laying down another plate, then hurrying back to the kitchen. Dinner is in full swing. After now, I imagine, it will be mostly downhill. We're all here. Sadie sits across from me, at the far end — the place of honor. The other wives have been crying since she broke her news to them. But she'll be back — she says. Didn't my brother say he'd be back? Others have seen him. Not me.

"Moo shu pork!" Mai Lin cries. The plate she puts down is enormous. The others help themselves. I'm not very hungry. I watch them eating. They've cheered up considerably since early evening. I raise my glass to my eyes and look at them through the wine. There are Anne and Julia, who were Andrew's and James's wives, the blond of their hair is burgundy through the glass. And Fat Jemma, John's wife, whose beauty is even larger than Julia's. And Paula, married to Philip. And Betty and Theodora, Bartholomew's and Thomas's wives. All of them are toasting Sadie with great swallows. And on the other side of the table: Jane, who was married to the other James — I was always confusing them because they looked alike, though they were unrelated — and Theresa, married to

Thaddaeus. And Mai Lin, finally sitting down. And Sue and Judy, still married to Simon the Zealot and Judas. Do you think I bear some grudge against Judy? Listen: she had nothing to do with it.

And listen: they're making joyful noises—joy in the face of parting!—glasses clinking, little bits of song in high voices, laughter. But they have not forgotten their losses, their full dozen partings. They cry at night. I hear them despite the thickness of the walls. Our thick, sturdy house trembles at night with a dozen weepings—Sadie's included, even though I hold her against my chest and neck and whisper at her that it's all right, after all—look what we have Sadie, look. And now look what we had.

No one is talking to me, Sadie, but that's fine. I can see you, there across the table, beyond the cashew chicken and the braised bean curd. And with my wine I feel like I've got all night, at least, to remember you.

•

After Ben's wedding she took me sailing on the Gulf of Pigeons. Her family had fished there for generations. Peter the social climber married into an old family with many nets and boats, and sea wisdom. Her empty house was nearby.

We sailed out from her dock and raced over the water. There was a storm coming up. She didn't care.

"I don't think I'll be able to help if we capsize," I called to her over the wind.

"Don't worry!" she called back. "I've been doing this forever!" She worked the sail with one hand, the tiller with the other, and it seemed to me she had a third hand, with which she massaged my heart into ripe fullness. She stopped in the middle of the bay and put out a little sea anchor, then drew me to her there, on top of all that water, with fathoms of mystery coursing below us, and I thought to myself, I've *found* something, something's found me, after I had gotten so terribly used to hideous loss.

•

So I went to Jerusalem. When I got there I asked around after my brother. It was that last night. I found him in the garden. I watched and listened, and went down to him where he was weeping.

"Come home, big brother," I said. He looked up at me and smiled.

"Go home, little brother," he said. "Go home to our mother."

"Our mother is coming here," I said. "Coming to take you back. We've put a new room on. You can have it."

"I think not," he said. He kissed my eyes and I slept. That's something he never did. You might think I had in youth been the butt of divine humor, impossible, mystical, practical jokes. But he didn't do that. Sometimes he'd take me with him on the water, or in the sky, or draw for me with colors in the air. But only now did he reveal his power over me. I was his creature, subject to his will. When I woke he was in prison.

So I went there. I slipped in through his window. It was not difficult. Security was lax. It was as if someone wanted him to get away. He lay on the floor, scourged, exhausted, a crown of thorns upon his head. I knew what to do when I saw him. I switched our clothes, rolled in the filth of his cell. He didn't wake, even when I took the crown off — it was stuck by scabs to his head and scalp. I put it on tight, so I bled, and tucked him away in a dark corner. Then I waited.

They came and led me out. Everything had been arranged while I was sleeping in the garden. They put the log across my back and I started out of the city. A crowd had already gathered along the road.

Understand that I looked just like him, he looked just like me, except for the eyes, and I kept mine averted, looking at the ground while I walked. Back then my hair was long and curly, just like his. No one noticed that I wasn't him.

They spat at me, yelled obscenities. I smiled in my beard. They didn't notice! I fell once, and a little while after that a woman rushed from the crowds to mop my face. But when

YOU CAN HAVE IT

I looked up at her I saw my blue-eyed face, my brother's face. I saw my brother in a woman's robe.

"I wrote you a letter," he said, "explaining." I tried to move, but I couldn't. I looked around and saw that no one else was moving, either. They stood frozen, ugly. He took off the crown and settled it on his head. "This is for you," he said. "Come and get it when it's all over."

He touched my heart and I blinked, and after the blink I was part of the crowd, shouting with sorrow, wiping the blood from my eyes. But I still couldn't move my feet. I could only watch him wander up the hill.

Later, when I could move, I ran up the hill, along his path. At the top I saw him, heard him—"Father, Father, why hast thou forsaken me!" I saw our mother kneeling beneath him, weeping. And I cried out to my father—wasn't he my own foster father?—"Father, Father, do *something!*" There was thunder, and my brother's voice again, but I couldn't watch anymore. I ran away into the city. I ran and hid like a pathetic disciple.

•

I brought Sadie home, eventually, but not to meet my parents. They'd already gone away, moved to Joppa because Mama couldn't stand anymore to live in the house where my brother grew up. I can hardly stand it myself. The memories are sweet—his bed was here; in this chair he taught me how to tie my shoelaces; in this room he sang while I played the guitar—but sometimes they cut.

Of course my parents wouldn't have approved. Sadie is still married. I've never told them about her, never will. It was my plan merely to live with her, to continue finding and not losing things with her—that's all. The clinic was her idea, when I showed her what the crown could do. And when she saw the big empty house she said, "You know Josh, if you're looking for boarders, I've got some friends in need."

•

    This dinner has spawned quite a mess. I promised Mai Lin I'd clean up if she'd cook for us. I smile at her and raise my glass. She's red in the face from the wine. We've all had a little too much, I think. It's late. Sadie is taking the latest caravan out, an early morning caravan—first to Jerusalem, then to other cities, but finally to Rome. In fact it's almost time for her to leave.
    I'm thinking I should say something—a speech?—but I don't want to. I don't trust myself not to cry. I want to say, Sadie, I'll miss you. Sadie, don't go. Sadie, I love you better than Peter does. But I have learned that it is not right to interfere with a loss that's made up its mind.
    In the end it's Sadie who stands. "Everybody!" she calls out, raising her empty glass, "I'll miss you! I'll visit! I'll be back!" She tilts her glass back, notices the emptiness, giggles. She'll be back, she says. I'll be back, he said. And I never even got his letter.
    "Sadie," I say. "It's time for you to go, if you're going. It's late."
    "I'm going," she says, standing up and staggering toward the door. I follow and catch her, support her. The others rise and follow behind us. I hold her close—last moments!—while we walk to the door. But when we open it up there's a man there, all bloody, with a familiar ax in his head.
    "Goddamn!" Sadie says, and sits down on the floor and cries. Mai Lin rushes forward and guides the man in. Julia has already gone for the crown. I follow Mai Lin, and now Jemma, who's taken the man's other arm. They lay him on the table, over the dishes. He's groaning, barely conscious now, when the crown arrives.
    The purple fire clears my head. The rest is easy.
    Mai Lin takes a napkin and water and cleans the man's bald head. Jemma is cleaning the ax with wine and a rag. The man lies on the table, still groaning, then sits up. I help him.
    "Steady there," I say.

"The bitch!" he cries, raising his hands to his head. "Axed me in the head! Axed me!"

"Who axed who first!" says Jemma, shaking the blade at him. Clean, it looks less wicked.

"We ought not to have let her go home," says Anne.

"I knew this would happen," says Julia.

"She insisted!" says Jemma.

"No matter," I say. "Everything's fine now. Would you like some wine?" I ask the man.

"Axed me in the head!" he cries, then sobs without words. Mai Lin brings him wine while Anne holds him to her breast. I go back to Sadie, still sitting by the door. Now she's asleep, drooling a little on her traveling cloak. I take it off without waking her, take her upstairs without waking her, and I take off her clothes and put her in our bed. Then she wakes for a moment.

"Josh?" she says. "Simon?"

"Yes," I say. "You're home. Sleep."

"Yes," she says, smiling through the hair in her face. She stretches and rolls over on her side, snores gently. I go back downstairs. Mai Lin is mopping up the blood in the hall.

"Man's fine," she says.

"I'll clean up," I say. "I said I would."

"Go to sleep, boss," she says. "You had a hard day."

I shake my head.

"I'm not sleepy," I say. "I was thinking of a walk. Want to come?"

She looks into the dining room. There is laughter again — laughing voices and laughing glass, and still that big man crying.

"Okay," she says. "I cooked. They can clean."

"I'll just get my jacket," I say. I get it and she's outside waiting for me. We walk down to the beach. "That was some dinner," I say. "A kingly feast."

She shrugs. "So we've still got Sadie."

"For another day," I say.

"I appreciate that," she says.

"Me too," I say. Suddenly she runs down to the water. Dawn

is breaking — so blatantly that I think I should be able to hear it. Mai Lin stops. Waves are nuzzling her feet. She throws up her arms. "What a glorious day it will be!" she yells. I smile a little, for a moment and try to imagine the coming day, but the effort is somehow too wearying.

I am not a person who cannot appreciate small joys — reprieves, second chances, beautiful breaking days. But even now, with God's own Greatness breaking like joyful glass all around me, I still say take this crystalline creation, this beauty, this water moving like liquid peace to touch the land in hug after hug after hug, this ocean daybreak. Take the gulls from the sky, and the crabs out of the sand. Take that holy creature from her place in the water, take her away, and take the house, and all the creatures in it, and take it all, take it all away. You can have it, I don't care. Just give me back my brother.

Ghosting

John Hodgman

He had not been desperate when he answered her ad in the paper. He had already lost two other sublets — the second because the tenant felt that he had an untrustworthy face, and told him so. Plus, he thought, most people don't warm up to the name Vince. But he had plenty of money now, and if everything fell through in New York, he would fly to Wyoming, a place he always thought he would like. All he wanted, really, was a change of scenery, a place to spend the summer.

So when she first invited him over to see the apartment, Vince was very casual and tried to enjoy himself. It felt something like a first date, with her pouring him wine and sitting him down on the couch, and he allowed himself to get a little drunk and charming. The living room faced the rear court of the building, and the windows were open to the summer air. He complimented her on the bookshelves which lined the room and were clearly custom-built, but though it was all spacious and nicely furnished, he really wasn't that impressed. He worried about taking care of the cat, which was gray and lumpy and blind in one eye. But without him asking, she told him that it was going to stay at her mother's in Nyack. She would spend the summer touring Italy.

She asked him what he did.

"I'm a coauthor," Vince said, and when she didn't seem to understand—she was a poet after all, and a college professor, and she clearly traveled in a literary world far removed from his own—he clarified: "A ghostwriter."

Her eyes lit quickly with recognition. "I see, I see," she said, nodding. But why did he want to live here if he already had an apartment downtown?

He explained that he had been contracted to write an autobiography for a famous wrestler, but the deal fell through. His agent had arranged for him to keep the advance money, however, so now he was a little richer and wanted a change of pace. "Like a vacation," he said, and because of the red wine, he felt a little forward and went on:

"Once I didn't have to write this book, I had this huge, blank stretch of time ahead of me—this empty, liberating hole I had dug in my schedule. I just thought that I should take advantage of it. That I should go away, or sublet an apartment and just be, well, *nowhere* for a while."

He hoped that, because of her poetic background, this would make sense to her. But she was more interested in why the wrestler he had been contracted to write for was called "Mighty Pipes" Cabrera.

"He wasn't just a wrestler," Vince said. "He was also a tenor. In the Louisville City Opera."

"That's fantastic," she said. "Why did the book fall through?"

"He was killed, suddenly," Vince explained. "In the ring."

She bit her lower lip in shock. But she couldn't keep from giggling at this, and Vince joined her.

"Well," she said. "Let's show you around."

They took their wine with them as they left the living room. She made an obligatory wave to the tiny bathroom, let him linger for a moment in the windowless kitchen, and then led him up a spiral staircase that led to a loft-style bedroom which filled with light, he was told, in the morning.

All this time, Vince felt calm and assured, and he swam in his light drunkenness with some abandon. At the very least, he thought, he would have spent a nice afternoon with a very pretty poet, not too much older than himself. While he was politely studying a photo of Trafalgar Square in a cheap plastic frame, she opened a trapdoor in the low ceiling.

"Come up," she said.

It was the roof deck that changed everything. It was modest, and even a little tacky: green indoor-outdoor carpeting, a picnic table with an umbrella and a couple of chairs; a low trellis concealed and surrounded the deck on three sides, and a tall, chain-link fence with barbed wire at the top cut it off from the building next door.

As he climbed the shallow set of stairs and came up into the June light, he was stunned by the silence and the sudden breeze, and he almost dropped his glass of wine. Though they were on West End Avenue in the hundreds, the air smelled bright and salty like the sea. He pictured it all as his own, seeing himself in the blue, canvas-back chair with a glass of water and a book . . . in all the quiet and the sunlight, enjoying *nowhere*. That was when he became desperate, and since desperation was a feeling he knew well, Vince feared that his desire alone would now ruin it for him. That, and his untrustworthy face.

He became less bold, more eager to please as they sat across from each other at the picnic table. "I'll need to ask you a few questions," she said.

"Of course," he said.

She wanted to know if he was married, or if he had a girlfriend.

"No," he said, and he worried his lower lip with his thumb. In fact, he had recently tried to seduce someone and failed, and he felt ashamed.

"Any friends going to drop by?"

"Not really," he said. "Most of my friends have families. They're on vacation."

"Oh, it doesn't bother me if you have friends over," she

said. "I just want to know that you have a social life. A support network."

"Oh," he said. He told her that he did.

What about family, she wanted to know. Where were they? Did he see them often?

He told her Boston, and every holiday, which was the truth.

She wanted to know about his medical history. Had he ever been hospitalized?

"Broke an arm once in tenth grade playing soccer," he said. "Nothing more."

And disappointment. "How do you deal with disappointment, Vince?"

He felt himself blush when she called him by name, and he blinked a little, confused. The question seemed invasive and inappropriate, as—he realized suddenly—most of them had been. But mainly he thought that she was trying to tell him something: to prepare himself. That he wouldn't be staying in her apartment this summer. That, in fact, he had never had a chance.

"Fine," he said, shading his eyes from the sun with his hand and managing to nod. "I deal with it just fine."

"Good," she said. She smiled kindly, nodding also. "That's fine, Vince."

She went on to explain that there would be a lot of mail, most of it junk, and he should just put it aside.

He picked up the spare key from her the following Thursday. The cat was already gone by then, and when he arrived with his old army duffel on Saturday, the apartment was filled with the long shadows of summer's lingering twilight. He had spotted a few books he wanted to read when she showed him the place and, as he inspected the bookshelf by the door, he noticed unexpected incongruities. Among the Audens and the Williamses were a line of thin Ian Flemings. He had never read James Bond. He slipped an old copy of *Moonraker* out from its neighbors and carried it with him as he toured the apartment, the first time alone.

He had taken the mail in when he arrived, and though

there was a lot of junk, as she said, there was also a considerable number of letters that were clearly personal. He stacked them on the large table she probably pulled out when she had dinner parties.

Above the table, on a small shelf, were a few candles of various heights in tall, narrow glass jars. He imagined that she liked them because they were windproof and could be used outdoors. He took two down, placed them on the table, and lit them.

He went into the bathroom and opened the medicine chest. She had a prescription bottle from a British pharmacy—Tylenol with codeine. He took one, and then smelled at an ancient bottle of men's cologne that was on the top shelf.

Next he examined the kitchen. Opening the cabinets, he found a lazy Susan full of various spices. He was surprised to see that she kept the wine—the wine he had drunk the other afternoon—in the cupboard beneath the sink with the Mr. Clean and the Hefty bags. He turned out the kitchen lights, retrieved one of the lit candles from the table and climbed up to the deck.

Dusk was settling in now, and the windows in the taller building across the street were beginning to reflect gentle reds and oranges. He placed the candle on the picnic table and sat with his book. He could hear the radios of other apartments across the court, the sound of an outdoor dinner party filtering up from the terraces below.

The Tylenol had started to work by then. At first he felt a little queasy and wondered why he had taken it. But soon it felt like cool hands stroking his hair. He read until the candle faltered and eventually burned out, and he stared at the darkening sky after that.

Later, when he went to put the book back in the shelf, he realized that he didn't remember where it went. He found the other Flemings and slipped it in somewhere among them, though possibly not in the right place. It's as though I'm haunting the place, he thought. Moving the books. Burning down the candles. Taking a pill. Not quite *here*, but here enough to make a difference.

After a few days, he began to fall into a pattern. He slept late, drank coffee on the roof, listened to the radio. In the afternoons he tried to write a little. The mail continued to pile in. He stacked it each day on the table, as many as thirty letters a day. He found a knot of rubber bands in the kitchen drawer and began to bundle the letters in stacks of twenty.

He didn't leave often. He went to Gristedes to stock up. He put steaks in the freezer, and a whole chicken that he planned to roast. He bought fresh produce daily and made lots of salads. The poet didn't have cable, so he stopped by the local video store and opened an account. He began to rent James Bond movies.

On the fifth day, as he sat on the couch, bundling the daily load of letters, he noticed that one was different. It was addressed simply to YOU. He had never seen that before, and he wondered what it meant. The address was hers, typed out. But YOU was handwritten. When he turned it over, looking for a return address, he saw that on the back there was more: YES: YOU.

He looked over his shoulder. No one was there, of course, and he had to laugh at himself. He thought that it might be from a friend of hers playing a joke. But another part of him wanted to believe that the letter was, in fact, for him, yes him.

He opened the letter with his finger, and immediately he felt something drag along inside the envelope as he broke the seal. It felt fuzzy like the skin of a peach, but dry and brittle as well. He pulled his finger back sharply, and the envelope, now open, flew from his hands. From it, he saw something flat and dark emerge and flutter lifelessly to the floor like a leaf. It was a butterfly.

He watched the butterfly as though it would jump at him and reached slowly for the envelope. Inside, there was a single sheet of paper with a single line of type in the center: *Where do YOU fit in?*

He began to look over the rest of the mail. There were similarities among some of the letters he hadn't noticed before. Aside from the magazines and the other clearly legitimate mail, about seventy percent of the rest had certain things in common. The addresses were typewritten—he could feel the indentation of the letters where the hammers had struck the paper. But the poet's name was always handwritten, and the handwriting was always the same: loose and scratchy. Some of the stamps were from the same set. Though the envelopes were different, they all were postmarked in New York City.

He turned on a lamp and held one up to the light. Through the paper, he could discern the outline of the broken, segmented body, twisted antennae and the delicate wings—their colors, muted and yellowed through the paper, still visible. He removed the lamp shade, holding one letter after another to the bare bulb, and he found that they all contained butterflies, wedged in with scraps of papers—letters of various length—the print folded over upon itself, unreadable. Finally, he could not resist and opened one from the first stack he had bundled. Inside he found a note, handwritten this time.

Why are you leaving me?

It had been in the early spring, on the Number 1 train heading downtown, and entirely by chance: that was when Vince had begun to keep his eye on her. Monica was fifteen years younger, pale-eyed and beautiful. But she had never seemed more beautiful than when he spied her through the window, where he stood in the small open space between the subway cars. She wore a charcoal gray dress—wool or maybe heavy cotton. She had straight dark hair that seemed to shine, reflecting some unseen light, and her shoulders were brown and freckled from the spring-vacation sun.

She was not reading. Just looking out of the opposite window, not intently, but patiently. He was close enough that he could see her brown eyes dart from side to side as she watched the stations pass. She scratched her bare knee absently. She crossed and uncrossed her legs, steadying herself in the shift of the train as it moved. She narrowed her eyes slightly and smiled, and he wondered if she was recalling something he had said or done. If she ever thought of him. The train slowed, and if he had called out her name then, the sound would have been lost in the hiss and whine of the brakes.

He slid open the door and walked through into the car.

"Hi," he said.

She didn't hear him, or pretended not to.

"Monica," he said, more loudly than he had to.

She looked up with a quick inward breath, startled. He was sorry to have scared her, he said. He just saw her and wanted to say hi. "It's Vince," he said, touching his chest.

"You didn't scare me," she said.

"Your mother is my agent," he explained. "We met in the office a couple of times."

Of course she remembered. "How are you?" she asked. She straightened up in her seat, and a calm smile crossed her face as she tilted her head slightly to the left, the way her mother did. She was trying to look adult and professional, but he had seen that particular pose before.

"May I sit down?" he asked. And he rode with her four stops past his own.

That was how it had started. It was pure chance that he had seen her. That private smile, her shoulders, the dress which was a little too tight-fitting for the office, but probably the only dressy one she had. Much later, after it had all fallen apart, and she wouldn't return his phone calls, not even to be polite, what was it he had asked her? Was it, Why are you leaving me?

The police recognized the address as soon as Vince called them. He was put through to a detective named Simms.

"Butterflies, right?" Simms said.

"Yes," Vince said.

"Well, don't worry. We know all about it." Simms explained that this guy was just a mail freak. That the poet had been receiving these letters, in waves, for more than a year. And as disturbing as it was, she had just learned to live with it. "We did all kinds of surveillance," Simms said. "Some postal traces. But with this kind of thing . . ." his voice trailed off.

Vince said that he didn't know how to get in touch with the poet. "She left a fax number at a hotel, but she won't be there for another two weeks."

"Well, you know," Simms said, "with this kind of thing, I wouldn't be alarmed. It comes and it goes."

And it was true that over the next week, Vince received only bills, circulars and credit-card applications.

All the same, he began to feel as though he were being followed. He was confident that the YOU in the letter meant *him*, and that someone was keeping careful track of his movements. Figuring out where I fit in, he thought. Though he was tempted to leave the sublet altogether, he was afraid that he might just lead whoever was out there back to his own place, and then it could go on for months, years even. And as disturbing as it was, he would just have to learn to live with it.

Instead, Vince began to keep watch. When he went down for the mail in the late morning, he would stick his head out the door and peer from one end of the empty street to the other. In the evenings, he turned out the lights in the living room and sat by the window, watching closely as the shades rose and fell in the building across the court. Sometimes, sitting there, he would think of Monica. He wondered if someone could see him through the window as he remembered her, and what he looked like to that person.

He had never actually followed Monica during that spring. He just managed to be wherever she was—at a party held by her mother; at a movie she had mentioned that she wanted to see. And when this happened, he was embarrassed about it. He wasn't trying to scare her. After a while, when he saw her, he would just throw his arms up in the air. "This is so weird, isn't it?" he would say.

Some nights, when he couldn't sleep, he stood by the security intercom with his thumb on the talk button and listened to the airy static, the sound of cars passing, a couple walking by. When he sat on the roof, he still brought up a book, but he kept his eye on the neighboring buildings. One afternoon, he thought he saw the pink smudge of a head quickly disappear in a top-floor window of the building across the street.

But nothing ever happened, and as the week went on, he became bolder. The third Saturday he was there, he walked up Broadway in the evening, scanning the faces of the people he passed, waiting for someone to make eye contact with him. He ducked around corners and waited to see if anyone followed. He turned suddenly at intersections to see who was crossing with him and who was veering off onto a side street. He found that this made the other pedestrians nervous. A few stepped aside and waited until he moved on.

At a discount pet store on 110th Street, he asked a thin boy with a faint mustache where someone would buy butterflies.

"Alive or dead?" the boy asked.

"I don't know," Vince said.

The boy shrugged his shoulders.

As it began to grow dark, Vince headed west to the park and walked down through the wooded paths that led south. He wasn't alone. In the shadows, he saw the burning ends of cigarettes and heard radios blaring salsa music in the distance. But no one approached him, and he found a bench near a small pond and sat. He watched as the last light dropped out of the sky, as the last joggers retreated to the streets, glancing nervously at the bushes and at him.

When he had stood near Monica at a nightclub or saved a seat for her on the Amtrak to Boston, he had wanted her to feel safe, and nothing else. He had wanted her to lean against his body gratefully, and so he made sure that his body was always near. He had wanted her to feel that their chance encounters were part of something larger, a kind of destiny. And he had enjoyed being the agent of that destiny, of weaving that feeling of fate and rightness into her life without her even realizing it.

He recalled that when he found an excuse to drive the thirty-five miles to her college campus, when he looked up her name in the student directory and stood for three hours outside her dorm, he thought at heart that it was still love. But he worried too that it was something that wasn't love at all.

When he returned to the apartment, he found that he had received sixty-three letters that day, all addressed, in the same sloppy handwriting, to Vincent DeRay.

It was past midnight when Vince went up to the roof and sat at the picnic table with the bottle of wine from the kitchen. He had found the switch to the outdoor lamp, but he left it, bringing instead two candles, now lit, and two of the Tylenol tablets, which he swallowed with the wine. The new letters were stacked in front of him, and before opening them, he watched as the corners of the envelopes were caught in the light breeze, rising and falling with a delicate rustle. He had bound them with rubber bands, and he thought how strange and quickly this new habit had come to him.

Then, with the end of a pen he had taken from the kitchen, he tore open an envelope from the middle of the first pile of twenty. He was surprised by his disappointment when he saw that it did not contain a butterfly, but a short note, the same he had received before: *Where do you fit in?*

The following nineteen did carry butterflies, their wings dull and velvety, and he pushed them into a small pile to the side as he dug out the accompanying letters. They were all one line of type each, some statements, but mostly questions.

Why has she left me?
Did she ask you to move in?
Did she give you permission to use the candles?

Many of the notes were repeats, but among the next stack of twenty, he found a few new ones.

What has she said about me?
Are you her lover, or her friend?
What happened to the cat?

By the middle of the last stack, he saw that the type grew fainter, as though the ribbon had been worn through. Finally, the notes were handwritten in blue ink, the cursive letters sloping down to the bottom of the page.

I know your name.

Do you think she loves you?
I know your face.
The table was covered now with butterflies, some half-emerged from their envelopes, some listing gently in the wind. They gave off a light musky smell, and Vince brushed the ends of their legs from his fingertips as he turned to the last three letters.
Will you see me? each of them read.
And folded in with the last, he found something else: a blank postcard, stamped and addressed to a post-office box at Cathedral Station.
Vince felt his blood begin to rush as he passed the card from one hand to the other. The first thing he thought was that he had the solution in his hands. Simms or another detective could simply stake out the P.O. box and they would have their man. In fact, he realized, he had had the answer the moment he saw his name on the first envelope. It was just a question of where he had given it out. The video store? The dry cleaner? Each possibility was the beginning of a trail back — to a worn-out typewriter and however many more butterflies, waiting to be dispatched.
But he calmed down as he looked over the notes again — all those questions that now seemed less menacing than plaintive — and he knew that the card meant something else. It was an invitation to respond — and for an answer to even one of his questions, whoever it was had already given himself up.
Vince took a long drink from the bottle and pushed his chair back. It was deep into the night now, the sky purple with the city's glow and empty of stars. As he sat, feeling the codeine and the wine work on him, warming the tops of his hands, the back of his neck, he recalled his first conversation with the poet.
"How do you deal with disappointment?" she had asked, and he wondered again why. Was it because she had seen what disappointment could do to a person? Was there someone out there whom she had disappointed so greatly that it had led to all this: countless butterflies, each tagged to a question that would never be answered?

Will you see me?

And suddenly he remembered what it was he had said during that spring that felt so remote now, as he spoke again and again into Monica's answering machine. He remembered it clearly: "Why won't you see me?"

Or when he learned from her roommate that she had already left for Paris for the summer, and had been gone for weeks without him knowing: "What did I do?" he had asked himself. He imagined Monica's private smile on the train when she didn't know he was there. He thought of her shoulders, and how he would never see them in the sun on the one clear day in Paris, and how she would never tell him about it. "How do you deal with disappointment?" the poet had asked, and he realized that he still didn't know.

Will you see me? the last letter read and, hardly thinking about it, he picked up the pen from the table and wrote his answer on the card.

Vince took the bottle of wine and held it in his lap. He knew that his time haunting this place would soon be over, and it would be returned to another, not just the poet, but someone who also knew about the blind cat and where the candles went. But first he would mail the card, and he would not call the police, or fax the poet just yet. He would be a ghost here for just a little longer and wait for a reply.

As he fell asleep there on the roof, he saw against the sky an empty space along the top of the chain-link fence where the barbed wire had been removed. Now he could not remember whether the wire had been there the day before or if it had ever been there at all.

NOTES ON CONTRIBUTORS

FICTION

Chris Adrian graduated from the Iowa Writers' Workshop and is currently a medical student at Eastern Virginia Medical School. This is his first published story.

Peter Ho Davies's work has been selected for *The Best American Short Stories 1995* and *1996*. He received a Transatlantic Prize from the Henfield Foundation and teaches at Emory University. His short-story collection *The Ugliest House in the World* is forthcoming this year.

Elizabeth Gilbert's fiction has appeared in *Esquire*, *Story*, *The Mississippi Review* and *Ploughshares*. Her short-story collection, *Pilgrims*, will appear this summer. She is at work on a novel.

Joyce Hackett works as a book editor and teaches creative writing at New York University. This is her first published story.

John Hodgman works as a literary agent in New York City. This is his first published story.

Michael Knight is from Mobile, Alabama. His fiction has appeared in *Playboy*, *Virginia Quarterly Review* and *Shenandoah*. A collection of short stories is forthcoming this year. He teaches at the Gilman School in Baltimore.

Rob Owen was born in Liberty, North Carolina, and now lives in Brooklyn. This is his first published story.

J. David Stevens is a student in the MFA program at Penn State University. His fiction has appeared in *Virginia Quarterly Review*, *Kinesis* and *Crescent Review*.

NOTES ON CONTRIBUTORS

POETRY

Alan Ainsworth's poems have appeared in *The Atlantic, The New England Review, Nimrod* and other magazines. He teaches at Houston Community College.

Anna Akhmatova (1888-1966) wrote *Requiem*, the underground anthem of those who suffered under Stalin. Her translator, **Jo Ann Clark**, is a poet and translator living in Rome. Her poems have appeared recently in *Western Humanities Review* and *The New Republic*.

Agha Shahid Ali directs the creative writing program at the University of Massachusetts at Amherst. Originally from Kashmir, he is the author, most recently, of *The Country Without a Post Office*.

Scott Cairns directs the creative writing program at Old Dominion University. His books are *Figures for the Ghost, The Translation of Babel* and *The Theology of Doubt*.

Kevin Cantwell teaches literature and writing at Macon College in Georgia. His poems have appeared in *The New Republic, Southwest Review* and *Antioch Review*.

James Cummins lives in Cincinnati, Ohio. His second book, *Portrait in a Spoon*, will be published this spring.

Jennifer Franklin received an MFA from Columbia in 1996. Her poems are forthcoming in *Western Humanities Review*. These are her first published poems.

Rick Hilles, a Wallace E. Stegner Fellow at Stanford, has poems forthcoming in *The Nation* and *Salmagundi*.

Richard Lamb writes junk mail. This is his first published poem.

Kate Light, a violinist in New York City, has work forthcoming in *Hellas, Western Humanities Review, Feminist Studies, Wisconsin Review* and *Sparrow*.

Edward Nobles's first book of poems, *Through One Tear*, is forthcoming this year.

Nick Norwood lives in Phoenix. This is his first published poem.

Eric Ormsby is the author of *Bavarian Shrine and Other Poems*, which won the 1991 QSPELL Award for poetry, and *Coastlines*. He lives in Montreal.

Mark Scott's poems have appeared in *Poetry, Western Humanities Review* and *Raritan*. He lives in San Francisco.

Brenda Shaughnessy is completing her MFA at Columbia University. She has poems forthcoming in *Western Humanities Review*. These are her first published poems.

Marc Woodworth is assistant editor at Salmagundi and a lecturer in the Department of English at Skidmore College.

Baron Wormser is the author of three books of poetry, including *Atoms, Soul Music and Other Poems*.

Charles Wright lives in Charlottesville, Virginia. His latest book is *Chickamauga*.

FEATURE

Silvana Paternostro's work has appeared in *The Nation*, *The Miami Herald*, *Spin* and *World Policy Journal*. She grew up on Colombia's Caribbean coast and now lives in New York City. Gabriel García Márquez calls her a *gringa-barranquillosa*.

INTERVIEWS

Henri Cole (Helen Vendler interview) is the author of three collections of poetry, most recently *The Look of Things*. He is the Briggs-Copeland Lecturer in Poetry at Harvard University.
Eliot Weinberger (Gary Snyder interview) is the editor of *American Poetry Since 1950: Innovators and Outsiders*. His books of essays are *Works on Paper*, *Outside Stories* and *Written Reaction*.

ART

Arturo Cuenca was born in Cuba and now lives in New York City.
Rochelle Feinstein's work appears courtesy of Max Protech Gallery in New York City.
Randolfo Rocha was born in Brazil and later moved to the United States. His work appears courtesy of Elga Wimmer Gallery in New York City.

The Paris Review
is pleased to announce
our 1996 prizewinners

Patricia Eakins
has been awarded
The Aga Khan Prize for Fiction
for her story
in issue 140,
"The Garden of Fishes"

Elizabeth Gilbert
has been awarded
The Paris Review Discovery Prize
for her story
in issue 141,
"The Famous Torn and Restored
Lit Cigarette Trick"

Sarah Arvio and John Voiklis
have been awarded
The B.F. Conners Prize for Poetry
for, respectively,
"Visits from the Seventh,"
in issue 140, and
"The Princeling's Apology,"
in issue 139

Petaluma

1ST. AVE. AT 73RD. ST., NEW YORK CITY
772·8800

Available now from the Flushing office
BACK ISSUES OF THE PARIS REVIEW

No.		
18	Ernest Hemingway Interview; Giacometti Portfolio; Philip Roth.	$25.00
25	Robert Lowell Interview; Hughes Rudd, X. J. Kennedy.	9.50
30	S. J. Perelman and Evelyn Waugh Interviews; Niccolo Tucci, 22 poets.	9.50
35	William Burroughs Interview; Irvin Faust, Leonard Gardner, Ron Padgett.	8.00
37	Allen Ginsberg and Cendrars Interviews; Charles Olson, Gary Snyder.	8.00
44	Creeley and I. B. Singer Interviews; James Salter, Diane di Prima.	7.00
45	Updike Interview; Hoagland Journal; Veitch, Brautigan, Padgett, O'Hara.	9.50
46	John Dos Passos Interview; Thomas M. Disch, Ted Berrigan, Kenneth Koch.	7.00
47	Robert Graves Interview; Ed Sanders, Robert Creeley, Tom Clark.	7.00
62	James Wright Interview; Joe Brainard, Christo Portfolio.	9.50
63	J. P. Donleavy and Steinbeck Interviews; Louis Simpson, Robert Bly.	7.00
64	Kingsley Amis and P. G. Wodehouse Interviews; Diane Vreuls, Thomas M. Disch.	10.00
66	Stanley Elkin Interview; Richard Stern, W. S. Merwin.	7.00
67	Cheever and Wheelock Interviews; Maxine Kumin, Aram Saroyan.	7.00
68	William Goyen Interview; John Updike, William Stafford.	7.00
69	Kurt Vonnegut Interview; William Burroughs, Ed Sanders, John Logan.	7.00
70	William Gass Interview; Peter Handke, William S. Wilson, Galway Kinnell.	7.00
72	Richard Wilbur Interview; Joy Williams, Norman Dubie.	7.00
73	James M. Cain and Anthony Powell Interviews; Dallas Wiebe, Bart Midwood.	7.00
74	Didion, Drabble and Oates Interviews; Vincente Aleixandre Portfolio; Max Apple.	7.00
75	Gardner, Shaw Interviews; Handke Journal, Dubus, Salter, Gunn, Heaney.	7.00
76	Ignatow, Levi, Rhys Interviews; Jean Rhys Memoir Louis Simpson.	7.00
77	Stephen Spender Interview; Mark Strand, Joseph Brodsky, Philip Levine.	7.00
78	Andrei Voznesensky Interview; Voznesensky/Ginsberg Conversation; Edie Sedgwick Memoir; T. Coraghessan Boyle, Tom Disch, Odysseus Elytis.	9.50
79	25th ANNIVERSARY: R. West Interview; Paris Review Sketchbook; Hemingway, Faulkner, Southern, Gass, Carver, Dickey, Schuyler, Gellhorn/Spender/Jackson Letters.	12.00
80	Barthelme, Bishop Interviews; Reinaldo Arenas, J. D. Salinger Feature.	7.00
81	T. Williams, P. Bowles Interviews; Wiebe, Atwood, Federman Fiction; Montale Poetry.	18.00
83	J. Brodsky, S. Kunitz Interviews; Gerald Stern/B. F. Conners Prize Poetry.	9.50
84	P. Larkin, J. Merrill Interviews; T. C. Boyle, Edmund White Fiction.	7.00
85	M. Cowley, W. Maxwell Interviews; H. Brodkey, Bill Knott Poetry.	7.00
87	H. Boll, Infante Interviews; Milosz, C. K. Williams Poetry.	7.00
88	Gordimer, Carver Interviews; Hill, Nemerov Poetry; McCourt, Davis Fiction.	7.00
89	James Laughlin, May Sarton Interviews; F. Bidart Poetry, Zelda Fitzgerald Feature.	7.00
90	John Ashbery, James Laughlin Interviews; C. Wright Poetry; E. Garber Fiction.	7.00
91	J. Baldwin, E. Wiesel Interviews; Morand, R. Wilson Fiction; Clampitt Poetry.	7.00
92	M. Kundera, E. O'Brien, A. Koestler Interviews; E. L. Doctorow Fiction.	7.00
93	30th ANNIV: Roth, Ionesco, Cortazar Interviews; Rush, Boyle Fiction; Brodsky, Carver Poetry.	12.00
97	Hollander, McGuane Interviews; Dickey, Kosinski Features; Dixon Fiction, Wright Poetry.	7.00
98	L. Edel, R. Stone Interviews; R. Stone Fiction; L. Edel Feature.	8.00
99	A. Robbe-Grillet, K. Shapiro Interviews; E. Tallent Fiction, D. Hall Poetry.	7.00
100	DOUBLE 100th: Hersey, Irving Interviews; Gordimer, Munro Fiction; Merrill, Milosz Poetry.	12.00
104	Brookner, Taylor Interviews; Kittredge Fiction; Levine, Wright Poetry; Beckett Feature.	7.00
105	Calisher, Gaddis Interviews; B. Okri Fiction; A. Zagajewski Poetry.	12.00
106	35th ANNIV: Lessing, Yourcenar Interviews; C. Smith Fiction; Logue Poetry; Styron Feature.	12.00
108	A. Hecht, E. White Interviews; C. Baxter, J. Kauffman Fiction; S. Olds Poetry.	7.00
109	Mortimer, Stoppard Interviews; Burroughs, Minot Fiction; Mathews, Simic Poetry.	7.00
111	Fowles, Fugard, Spencer Interviews; Tucci, Gurganus Fiction; Proust, Rilke Translations.	7.00
112	Kennedy, Skvorecky Interviews; Malamud, Maspéro Fiction; Perec, Pinsky Poetry.	7.00
114	Sarraute, Settle Interviews; Matthiessen, P. West Fiction; F. Wright Poetry.	7.00
115	Murdoch, Stegner Interviews; Bass Fiction; Laughlin Poetry; Merwin Feature.	7.00
116	Angelou, Vargas Llosa Interviews; Perec Fiction; Ashbery Poetry; Stein Feature.	7.00
117	Atwood, Pritchett Interviews; R. Price, Stern Fiction; Kizer, Logue Poetry.	7.00
118	Bloom, Wolfe Interviews; Tolstaya Fiction; Ashbery Poetry; Carver, Burgess Features.	9.50
119	Grass, Paz Interviews; M. McCarthy Feature; DeMarinis Fiction; Bonnefoy, Hacker Poetry.	9.50
120	Hall, Morris Interviews; Milosz Feature; Brodkey, Mailer Fiction; Corn, Lasdun Poetry.	7.00
121	Brodkey, Price Interviews; D. Hall Feature; Minot, West Fiction; Z. Herbert Poetry.	7.00
122	Amichai, Simon Interviews; J. Merrill Feature; Konrád, Fiction; Montale, Zarin Poetry.	7.00
123	Mahfouz Interview; J. Scott Fiction; Ashbery, Sarton Poetry; Schwartz-Laughlin Letters.	7.00
124	Calvino, Paley Interviews; Grass, Johnson, Moore Fiction; Clampitt, Herbert Poetry.	7.00
125	Guare, Simon Interviews; Bass, Lopez Fiction; Hollander, Mazur Poetry.	7.00
126	Clampitt, Helprin Interviews; J. Williams, Eco Fiction; Goldbarth, Zarin Poetry.	7.00
127	Logue, Salter Interviews; Carroll, Shepard Fiction; Ammons, Swenson Poetry.	7.00
128	40th ANNIV: DeLillo, Morrison Interviews; Canin, García Márquez Fiction; Graham, Merwin Poetry; Cheever, Hemingway, Pound Documents.	12.00
129	Stafford Interview; J. Scott Fiction; Yenser Poetry; Salter, Trilling Features.	7.00
130	Kesey, Snodgrass Interviews; Braverman, Power Fiction, Paz Poetry	10.00
131	Bonnefoy, Munro Interviews; Moody, Pritchard Fiction; Hacker, Merrill Poetry; Bishop-Swenson Letters.	10.00
132	Auchincloss, Gottlieb Interviews; Gass, Thon, West Fiction; Kinnell, Tomlinson Poetry; Kazin Feature.	10.00
133	Achebe, Milosz Interviews; Byatt, D'Ambrosio Fiction; Hirsch, Wagoner Poetry.	10.00
134	Hughes, Levi Interviews; Fischer, Schulman Fiction; Ammons, Kizer Poetry; Welty Feature.	10.00
135	Gunn, P.D. James, O'Brian Interviews; DeMarinis, Mayo, Prose Fiction; Rich, Wright Poetry	10.00
136	Humor: Allen, Keillor, Trillin interviews; Barth, Boyle Fiction; Clifton, Updike Poetry; Bloom Feature.	20.00
137	Sontag, Steiner Interviews; Bass Fiction; Seshadri Poem; Russian Feature.	10.00
138	Screenwriting: Dunne, Price, Wilder Interviews; Díaz Fiction; Hecht Poetry; Southern Feature.	10.00
139	Ammons, Buckley, Cela Interviews; Davenport, Franzen Fiction; Kizer Poetry.	10.00
140	Ford, Oz Interviews; Butler, Eakins Fiction; Bidart, Olds Poetry; Cooper Feature.	10.00

Please add $3.00 for postage and handling for up to 2 issues; $4.75 for 3 to 5. Payment should accompany order. For orders outside the U.S. please double the shipping costs. Payments must be in U.S. currency. Prices and availability subject to change. **Address orders to: 45-39 171 Place, Flushing, N.Y. 11358**
MASTERCARD/VISA # _____ EXP. DATE _____

The Paris Review Booksellers Advisory Board

THE PARIS REVIEW BOOKSELLERS ADVISORY BOARD is a group of owners and managers of independent bookstores from around the world who have agreed to share with us their knowledge and expertise.

ANDREAS BROWN, *Gotham Bookmart, New York, NY*
CHAPMAN, DRESCHER & PETERSON,
  Bloomsbury Bookstore, Ashland, OR
ROBERT CONTANT, *St. Mark's Bookstore, New York, NY*
JOHN EKLUND, *Harry W. Schwartz Bookshop, Milwaukee, WI*
JOSEPH GABLE, *Borders Bookshop, Ann Arbor, MI*
THOMAS GLADYSZ, *The Booksmith, San Francisco, CA*
HELENE GOLAY, *The Corner Bookstore, New York, NY*
GLEN GOLDMAN, *Booksoup, West Hollywood, CA*
JAMES HARRIS, *Prairie Lights Bookstore, Iowa City, IA*
ODILE HELLIER, *Village Voice, Paris, France*
RICHARD HOWORTH, *Square Books, Oxford, MS*
KARL KILIAN, *Brazos Bookstore, Houston, TX*
KRIS KLEINDIENST, *Left Bank Books, St. Louis, MO*
FRANK KRAMER, *Harvard Bookstore, Cambridge, MA*
RUPERT LECRAW, *Oxford Books, Atlanta, GA*
TERRI MERZ AND ROBIN DIENER, *Chapters,*
  Washington, DC
MICHAEL POWELL, *Powell's Bookstore, Portland, OR*
DONALD PRETARI, *Black Oak Books, Berkeley, CA*
JACQUES RIEUX, *Stone Lion Bookstore, Fort Collins, CO*
ANDREW ROSS, *Cody's, Berkeley, CA*
JEANETTE WATSON SANGER, *Books & Co.,*
  New York, NY
HENRY SCHWAB, *Bookhaven, New Haven, CT*
RICK SIMONSON, *Eliot Bay, Seattle, WA*
LOUISA SOLANO, *Grolier Bookshop, Cambridge, MA*
JIM TENNEY, *Olsson's Books, Washington, D.C.*
DAVID UNOWSKY, *Hungry Mind Bookstore, St. Paul, MN*
JOHN VALENTINE, *Regulator Bookshop, Durham, NC*